# T H E
# BORDERLAND

# THE BORDERLAND

## A NOVEL OF TEXAS

EDWIN SHRAKE

HYPERION

NEW YORK

Loren Eiseley quote on p. vii courtesy of Collections of the Archives and Records Center, The University of Pennsylvania.

Library of Congress Cataloging-in-Publication Data

Shrake, Edwin.
    The borderland : a novel of Texas / by Edwin Shrake.
      p.  cm.
    ISBN 0-7868-6579-2
    1. Texas—History—Republic, 1836–1846 Fiction.  2. Indians of
North America—Texas Fiction.  3. Cherokee Indians—Mixed descent
Fiction.  I. Title.
PS3569.H735B65  2000
813'.54—dc21
                                               99–41394
                                               CIP

FIRST EDITION

10  9  8  7  6  5  4  3

To Bill Wittliff

Though I meekly pass
where you plow and fire,
everywhere I leave
fox fur on the wire—
And a fox's face,
masked in human skin,
sometimes wild and sharp
holds its laughter in.

—Loren Eiseley

Here we enter the land of border romance. Hence to the
Rio Grande southwest, and to the Rocky Ridge west and
northwest, every grove, canyon and valley has been the
scene of some romantic and daring incident; but should I
attempt to repeat all that are told here, the world itself, to
borrow a simile from Scripture, would not contain the
books that should be written.

—J. H. Beadle

# THE BORDERLAND

# PROLOGUE

In February of 1839 a monster cyclone formed in the Pacific a thousand miles off the coast of Sinaloa and whirled counterclockwise toward the continent, tearing the ocean into waves eighty feet high that smashed over the beach at the village of Teacapan and flung boats into the mountains. Every human within five miles of Teacapan was drowned.

The storm collided with the Sierras at the ten-thousand-foot peak of Yerba Buena. Wind ripped goats out of the rocks and hurled them down into the jungle. Wooden crosses that had been planted by angels flew away from mountain passes they had guarded longer than memory. Settlements of Indians vanished forever. The storm poured seven feet of rain on the ancient town of Zacatecas, eight thousand feet high at the head of a valley. Barefoot friars huddled and prayed with their human and animal flocks inside the slate-roof buildings of the college as the silver mines flooded and thousands perished in the tunnels.

Hailstones the size of grapefruits crushed the mud and timber breastworks of the rebels at Guanajuato and left them to be slaughtered by the soldiers of one-legged president Santa Anna. The storm turned north and battered Monclova and the old capital city of Saltillo with gale and lightning. Leaving tornadoes drumming through the *campo*, the storm rumbled across the Rio Grande and struck fresh warm clouds blowing in from the Gulf of Mexico. The Pacific storm and the Gulf clouds merged into two hundred miles of blackness above the western mountains and central hills of Texas, where heat rose from limestone cliffs to spark the coming deluge that gathered itself, growing and brooding over the Colorado River valley.

The Fighting Man, the Talking Man, the Thinking Man and the Dark Man, who had become the Magician, sat on their heels around their twig fire in a cave on the west bank of the Colorado River and thoughtfully passed among them a pipe of Mexican tobacco. Beyond the mouth of the cave facing toward the east, they could see three miles away on the other side of the river the shapes of a stockade fence and rooftops, the newest outrage by the invaders.

This valley had been a holy place since the beginning of the families on earth. Now these invaders called Texans—the men with hats—had marched into the valley with threats and insults and had begun building structures that looked to be intended as permanent. The families had become uneasy in their camps a hundred and more miles west in the hills and forests of Comancheria. They had been at war against Mexico for generations and had strewn the land with dead Mexicans and stolen hundreds of thousands of Mexican horses and taken thousands of Mexican captives as slaves or for trade. But these new invaders with hats were becoming a more sinister enemy than the Mexican army. The Fighting Man, the Talking Man, the Thinking Man and the Magician had been asked by the council of families to study the Texans and to come back with suggestions so the council could decide what must be done.

"We must kill them," said the Fighting Man, who was called Turk because he had looked like one to his father, a French fur trapper, twenty-five years ago when Turk was born in a sod roof dugout at a trading post on the high plains of Comancheria in sight of the snowy mountains. Turk wore three copper bracelets on each arm. A necklace of turquoise and silver and bear claws lay among the hairs of his chest. Having a hairy chest made him an oddity among the people, and most were frightened of him. With the stone axe he wore on his hip, Turk had killed many of the people's enemies, though none of the white ones as yet.

"I respect your wisdom and courage, and I agree that to kill every one of them and each new one that arrives, this would be the best of all solutions," the Talking Man said. He wore four necklaces made of beads and quartz crystals and panther claws. Beneath his deerskin leggins on a rawhide thong that touched his genitals hung his medicine pouch. As a youth he had earned the name Osage Killer by his performance in battle. Late in his prime, he became a speech maker who enthralled about half of his listeners at councils with elocutions that might go on until dawn. No speech maker was ever interrupted for any cause, and Talking Man took full use of this courtesy. "But I believe we have waited too late to kill them all. They come in mighty numbers."

"If we would stop killing Mexicans, then the Mexicans would be strong enough to kill all the Texans for us, and then later we could go back to killing Mexicans as we always have," said the Thinking Man, whose fingers were tugging the dozen stringy hairs that grew out of his chin. He was called Young Owl Hatching because as a boy he had been plump, almond-eyed, silent and always looked wet, and he had gone at night to sit alone in the forest or on a hill. It was assumed by the people that because he was silent, Young Owl Hatching must be wise, and he tried to say as little as possible so none would doubt him. He could pass a month without speaking to his three wives, who were sisters, and their children. Having given his opinion on solving the Texans matter, the Thinking Man retreated into the safety of silence.

The Dark Man leaned back on his heels and raised his arms toward the roof of the cave with a ripple of stretching muscles. The smoke of the wood fire with its odor like roasting acorns rose around his face, which was scorched black except for white rings painted around his eyes and three white finger slashes on each cheek. His black hair was greased and brushed straight back and clasped in a gold ring before it dropped between his shoulders.

"What do you see, Magician?" asked Turk, the Fighting Man.

"I see death."

"Whose death?" asked Young Owl Hatching, the Thinking Man.

"The four of us here today. I see us dead."

Osage Killer, the Talking Man, drew in tobacco smoke from the pipe until he felt fire inside his breast. Slowly he exhaled and looked at the Dark Man.

"Yes, yes, it is very easy to see death in a turn of events like this one. Anyone can forecast death. That's all we have talked about," said the Talking Man. "But for us to kill the invaders entirely dead, man, woman and child, and drive them away so that they will never come back, this is only a dream. Just as they will never be able to climb this cliff and enter our country, also we will never be able to drive them out of this valley. This valley is our place. I have spent many happy times in this valley. I hate to see the invaders here. But I say we must not be hasty to go into battle over a mere piece of land. The Sure Enough Father has given our people dominion over more land than we will ever use up. We must meet with the leaders of these men with hats and reason with them. They can settle in our beautiful little valley, but they can come no closer. We will make an agreement with them. Then we will steal their horses and their corn."

Turk had been staring at the Dark Man.

"Are you predicting the four of us will die because it seems reasonable, or do you have a *portento*?" asked Turk.

The Dark Man rolled his eyeballs like marbles beneath his upper lids, which were circled with white paint. The others waited in silence except for the snapping of wood in the fire and the grunts of the horses that were hobbled on top of the cliff twelve feet above the cave. The Talking Man sucked on the pipe with a smacking sound, wishing to draw their attention back to himself, but Turk and Young Owl Hatching were watching the Dark Man.

The Dark Man began talking in a trance.

"I see a great battle at this place where we are. I hear screams of dying. I hear the explosions of many rifles. I smell powder. I smell blood. Turk, I see your spirit standing up from your dead body. I hear horses running and our people shouting, and the enemy shouting. I see Young Owl Hatching has thrown away his body and his spirit is leaving. I see my own dead body, and I know my spirit is taking me to my next station on the path that never ends."

The Dark Man's eyeballs rolled down in their sockets and peered at the Talking Man.

"Well?" said the Talking Man. "What is it?"

"I don't see you here at this battle, Osage Killer."

The Talking Man nodded. He had no intention of throwing away his body at such a battle. He would persuade his family of families to move to the snowy mountains to avoid a battle with these new invaders, the men with hats. Riding into this river valley in the moonlight and stealing the invaders' horses and slipping out again, that made sense. But a full battle, face to face against the invaders' guns? This is foolish, thought Osage Killer, the Talking Man, leader of his own band. He would talk against it and vote against it at council, and if his side lost the vote, he would lead his families away to join another family of families farther out in Comancheria.

"That much of your *portento* is accurate, if nothing else," said the Talking Man.

"I see your dead body beside a wall somewhere that is not so far from this valley. I see you are dead before our battle ever takes place," the Dark Man said.

"It will be raining soon. I am ready to go back to the council of families," said Turk. "I think we should kill these Texans, but the council must decide."

He stood up. Turk was six feet high, tall for one of the people. He reached down with a powerful arm and said, "Up we go, my brother."

The Dark Man grasped Turk's arm and pulled himself upright. The Dark Man's legs were thin and all but useless, like the legs of a newborn foal. Lightning that split from a black cloud had struck the Dark Man when he was a young warrior. The crack of fire crippled his body and darkened his skin but gave him powers. Living with lightning inside caused him to have much to think about and changed the course of his life. His powers obligated him to be a magician with responsibilities to his people.

Turk bent forward and the Dark Man crawled onto Turk's back, arms clamped around Turk's neck, legs dangling.

Young Owl Hatching scraped dirt over the fire. A coal flew into the cave wall behind him and flared out against a drawing of a black panther with a long, curling tail scratched into the rock and outlined with red ochre.

"I don't accept your *portento*. I don't believe in it," Osage Killer said.

"It doesn't matter what you believe," said the Dark Man. "This is coming."

The Fighting Man carried the Magician out of the cave and up the white cliff.

# O N E

## TOWARD THE LITTLE PIGEON

"I am busy and will only say how da do, to you!
You will get your land as it was promised, and you
and all our Red brothers may rest satisfied that I
will always hold you by the hand."

—*letter from Sam Houston to Chief Bowl*

# 1

enry Longfellow was thinking about women, how wicked they are. While he was passing through a rainwater swamp five hours ago, a perfumey odor had infested his dreams as he drowsed in the saddle, and for a dizzy moment he was sniffing the silk drawers of the whore he had taken to his hotel room in New Orleans last month, a redheaded bitch who was about to scorn him before he split her lip with his fist.

The sweet, rotting flower fragrance of swamp gas reminded him of the cosmetics and colognes his wife had kept in crystal bottles on the marble-top table in front of her mirror, and he remembered the sight of her pale, skinny legs kicking in the air, her heels behind her ears, on either side of the hairy buttocks of a teamster in Henry's own four-poster marriage bed on the second floor of their new home in Athens, Georgia.

Riding along the trail toward Austin, growing ever more clear of mind and angry in his heart, Henry thought of his mother, a shrieking Hardshell Baptist whose mean and spiteful tongue and frequent blows with a skillet had driven his father away from their family in Memphis, Tennessee, when Henry was a child of six, an awful thing to do to a boy. On the topic of the wickedness of women, Henry Longfellow would hold forth with gusto to the laughter of men and harlots in Blue's Tavern in San Antonio. Women love the devil, Henry told them. His audience laughed, Henry believed, from nervousness, because he frightened them; they recognized that he was speaking a truth so profound that it could not be faced by their common minds in the cold and serious light that Henry saw.

When Henry was in higher social company, as an adviser to President Lamar, his former colleague in the Georgia legislature, he was polite, tried to be charming to the women he was forced to endure at dances and dinner parties, and he measured his words like speeches an actor might recite on the stage. But he saw through the fabric of their pretty dresses to their wicked souls.

Henry's knees ached. His bones were too long for the stirrups of this silver concho-studded saddle that had been thrust upon him by the President. Henry had thought it presumptuous for Lamar to insist that the ride from San Antonio to Austin would be more significant if seated on the President's ornamented saddle rather than in Henry's two-horse buggy with the padded bench, but Henry accepted as if honored and delighted. He was, after all, partly on a mission for the Republic. He was searching for a choice site on which to build the presidential mansion in Austin. Lamar stipulated the house be on high ground but fed by its own spring, with a grand view but near enough to the city center that its property value would increase as Austin grew.

Once out of sight of Main Plaza at the beginning of the eighty-mile journey on a rutted track the width of an ox cart, Henry had climbed off the bay horse that also was urged upon him as a loan from the President. He tried to let out the stirrups to their full length but discovered they were already at their full length. Henry cursed the stubby-legged bastard Lamar, but he needed the President's continued warm association until the documents were signed for the lands Henry was on his way to select for himself in the new town of Austin, soon to become capital of the Republic. Lamar was creating Austin in the heart of a river valley favored by savages. There was scenic land, praised for its beauty by Lamar writing as a poet, abounding with water and timber, to be owned for bargain rates—often no more than the correct signatures. Lamar asked Henry to consider investing as a partner in commercial lots along the spring-fed creek that was being renamed Congress Avenue and would run from the river to the square reserved for the new capitol building. If Henry acted with reasonable haste and care, his prosperity was assured.

He would build a plantation house on a hill near the capitol, Henry thought. His house would have a long, shaded veranda and white Doric columns like the houses of the cotton growers of LaGrange who had supported his entry into the Georgia legislature in Athens. Henry had solicited their political backing because they were wealthy and ignorant men by his view, most of them outright stupid compared to how he saw himself. With his law degree from Memphis College of Jurisprudence as credential, Henry had won a cotton-fraud case against a Georgia seller in a Georgia court and attracted the attention of the cotton growers of LaGrange. His menacing demeanor in court, his ability to twist the truth and intimidate witnesses, proved to the cotton growers that he would enforce their will in the statehouse without scruple. He rammed their desires through the legislature and appeared to have a bright future in Georgia politics. Perhaps he would become a national figure.

Henry married the daughter of a plantation owner. His bride was a bony, homely girl who had been educated at a fancy finishing school in Philadelphia. She was a debutante who entered the adult world riding in an open carriage filled with peach blossoms on the main street of the small commercial center called Atlanta, where her father and his friends had begun bringing their trade and building their city mansions.

Although the judge and the jury found displeasure in Henry's ungainly appearance and unrepentant attitude in court, they ruled him not guilty of murder in the deaths by gunshots and stabbing of his wife and the teamster. As Henry knew the judge and jury would be, they were guided by the unwritten code that protects a gentleman from the treachery of his wife, especially as it applies to adultery, most especially to fornication with a lover in the husband's own bed.

However, his late wife's father and four brothers lived by still another part of the unwritten code of gentlemen, which required satisfaction be paid in blood for an injury or insult such as Henry murdering their beloved Dorothy. Her father and each of her brothers sent cotton gentry or military men as seconds to challenge Henry to duels with pistols or sabers. He was denounced as a craven to his face in restaurants and saloons by her father and brothers. He was called a consummate coward and a dastardly poltroon. His political financing from the LaGrange cotton growers vanished. There was scandal put about the state that Henry had regularly ripped the clothes off his skinny debutante bride and beaten her naked breasts and thighs with a switch from a peach tree. But the worst blow of all to Henry was the disgrace when he learned she had betrayed him with more than twenty men and boys—including the grocer's son—before he caught her with the teamster, and by now the whole town knew it.

Henry saw himself not as a coward but as intelligent. He was not at all reluctant to shoot and stab Dorothy's father and four brothers, one at a time as the code demanded, but what then? Even if he survived five duels, he was ruined in Georgia. Henry called his two slave boys into the house and told them to start packing. A couple of years earlier, Henry's legislative colleague, Mirabeau Buonaparte Lamar, had suffered the deaths of his wife, sister, father and brother in a short period and had gone off to Texas to leave the pain of their memory behind and look into land investments. Lamar distinguished himself in the revolution against Mexico, and now he had been elected second president of the Republic of Texas. Henry reminded himself that Heraclitus said nothing is permanent except change. In Texas, anyone could invent a new life. Henry decided to move to Texas and renew his friendship with Lamar and become a land speculator. Soon he would be as rich as the plantation owners in LaGrange. He would have his house painted white with white shutters and a gallery above the Doric columns. He would buy twelve more slaves to add to the two boys he already owned, and several would be tender young girls who would heat water for his bath and fill the tub and remove his clothes slowly and stroke his skin with their fingers and crawl into his bed when he tinkled a silver bell on the nightstand. The girls would desire to be with him because he sensed their need to be writhing in lusty embrace with the devil. Eve's daughters came from the seed of the serpent.

He heard a woman's voice.

She was singing in Cherokee. Henry recognized one phrase—*huh-so-suh*—which meant where the sun comes out, or east. Henry had been among many Cherokees in Tennessee and Georgia, and he had read the Cherokee newspaper, *The Phoenix*, which ran columns of English beside columns of the Cherokee printed language. Henry had read *The Phoenix* to see what the savages might be writing about him. In the Georgia legislature, Henry had voted to outlaw the Cherokee Nation and banish the savages from Georgia after gold was discovered in the mountains the Cherokees called their own. Cherokee laws and customs were declared null and void. The mountains where gold was found were sold by lottery to whites only. The newspaper, *The Phoenix*, was seized by the Georgia government to stop the spread of news. The United States Supreme Court ruled Georgia's action against the Cherokees unconstitutional, but President Andrew Jackson—like Henry, a slaveholder and a loather of aborigines—said, "If the Supreme Court wants to make law to help the Cherokees, let Justice Marshall enforce it himself." Henry considered this Jackson's finest moment.

Defeating the Creeks at Horsehoe Bend in Alabama was a commendable act by Jackson, whose policy of promoting new opportunities in business for the common white man had helped Henry rise in the world. The press and the pulpits persistently attacked the President for adultery, but Henry blamed the evil of women. Jackson's legacy, in Henry's mind, was taking the mountains away from the savage Cherokees, a magnificent achievement.

Henry listened to the young woman singing. Other than the musk of their women, the only thing Henry admired about the Cherokees was their melodious speech. Henry understood hardly a word of their language, but sounds like Chatahoochie, Tuckaseegee and Hiwassee struck the part of him that would have become a musician had his choices in life been different.

Henry's saber in its scabbard dangled by a leather thong from the saddle horn. He felt the blade against his left leg and nudged it so that he could cross-draw without hitting the horse's neck. His cap and ball pistol lay in its holster against his right thigh, nestled beside his powder horn and bullet pouch. The woman's voice was coming from the other side of a thicket that was blooming with purple blossoms thirty feet ahead of him, at the edge of the path. It was a girl perhaps not yet twenty years old.

He needed a girl right now. The trilling of her voice aroused him. He heard the deceit in her voice, the lure of seduction, the cry of sexual longing.

He knew it would be remarkable if this young Cherokee female was alone in the Texas wilderness. Her kind of subhumans traveled in bunches, Henry had observed. But if there were only two or three more Cherokees with her, Henry could soon have her. Shooting aborigines was fair sport and regarded in his society as good and necessary. Henry pulled the shotgun out of its saddle sheath. If there were too many Cherokees, he would bid them 'morning and ride on toward the ferry. Henry's groin began to ache. He felt his pecker crawling like a snake against the saddle. He was swelling up. A flash struck him, a burning. He must have relief. He knew this girl was thirsty to swallow his seed.

# 2

Though the sky to the west was black with clouds, Cullasaja Swift was singing an eastern mountain people song about a golden sunrise. She was gathering berries from a thicket and placing them in a straw basket. Already she had built a tiny cooking fire beside the lean-to shelter where she had been camping with her brother. He would be hungry when he returned from a night in Austin, where she imagined there was no cuisine that could please her brother's sophisticated palate, which had been trained in New York and Paris, in Edinburgh and London. Cullasaja could offer only coffee, corn, beans and dried beef, but Rommy ate what his sister prepared on the trail with as much pleasure as he would show in a fine restaurant, and he praised the old Cherokee ways. She loved the feeling that he was trying to please her.

Her brother told her they could not stay in a hotel or boarding house in Austin, so they would camp south of the river not far from the ferry while he did what he needed to do in the town. With his light skin and brown hair and the body of the bare-knuckle boxing champion he had been in the Gentlemen's

Boxing Club of the University of Edinburgh, where he studied medicine, her older brother was known in white society as Dr. Romulus Swift—Doc Swift, medical physician. In the Republic of Texas, no one had suspected that her brother was half Cherokee. Cullasaja Swift inherited the gleaming blue-black hair and bronze skin of their mother, a North Carolina pure-blood named Carrie Lee. Romulus bore the wide shoulders, flat belly and Irish countenance of their father, Fletcher, a sea captain and owner of merchant ships in the harbor of New York. The arrival in Austin of a Cherokee woman, especially one as beautiful and educated as Cullasaja, whose name means "sweet water" in their mother's tongue, would cause too much commotion, her brother said. The political situation for Cherokees in the Republic was uneasy. Tension with the whites was increasing. Doc meant to enter Austin on the evening ferry, find his man and then be out again the next morning, and the brother and sister would continue on their journey.

Cullasaja smiled. Her brother, twenty years her senior, was worried about leaving her alone for a night. He had been away at college or gone exploring the vast oceans or living in his flat in Cheyne Place, London, for much of the time while she was becoming a woman. He still thought of her as a child who needed protecting.

When her brother returned from his errand in town, they would pack their three mules, and she would saddle her thoroughbred stallion, and they would ride northeast through the pine forests and cross the rivers and arrive eventually in the Cherokee town that was being built by Chief Bowl and his family of families. Bowl's Town was said to be on a clear blue lake full of fish and bordered by moss hanging from cypress limbs. The pine forest around the chief's new town was fresh with game, and the black land was prime for farming. Bowl's Town would be protected by the promise of settlement made by Sam Houston acting as president of the Republic of Texas. For Cherokees escaping the troubles in Georgia and Tennessee and the Carolinas, Bowl's Town would be a sanctuary for peace and industry.

Picking berries, Cullasaja remembered the yearning in Chief Bowl's eyes as he had gazed at the bowler hat of the legendary Storyteller, Knows All Charlie. In her childhood, Captain Fletcher Swift and Carrie Lee would send their young daughter every summer away from the wet heat and pestilence of lower Manhattan Island, where they lived in a three-story brick house within sight of the Hudson River and the black smoke of the fires that burned all summer to ward off yellow fever and cholera. Until he began spending summers at sea, her brother, Romulus, was her companion to guide her safely into the mountains of North Carolina. Their grandmother owned a farm in a high meadow in partnership with an ancient, blind uncle and seer named Knows All Charlie. They grew corn, beans, squash, apples, peaches, strawberries, grapes, plums and tobacco for nourishment and for trade and sale. Certain areas of their fields were red and pink and white with poppies. Grandmother Tobacco grew poppies for Knows All Charlie, who used the plants for medicine for the benefit of the Bird clan. She was called Grandmother Tobacco because she smoked a pipe that was always filled with choice tobacco she tended with her own hands. Grandmother Tobacco owned twelve Negro slaves who worked her fields and crops and her flocks of sheep with help from her many Cherokee cousins and two black and white border collie dogs from Scotland. The dogs were a gift from Captain Fletcher Swift, who bought them from a breeder at Fort William in the Highlands of Scotland and carried them across the Atlantic as pups in his own quarters on his queen of the line square-rigged merchant ship. Cullasaja and Romulus brought the dogs with them to North Carolina as six-month-old pups that already knew how to handle sheep.

Cherokees came to Grandmother Tobacco's valley from the blue and green mountains all around and from as far as Georgia and Tennessee in August at the time of the Green Corn ceremony for councils in seven-sided lodge halls near a high, tumbling, shining waterfall among maple and pine trees and mountain laurel. Elders taught the Cherokee way of community to the young. They taught the old way—the Right Way, they called it—which involved a balance of mind, body and spirit. The Right Way was to take from the earth only food and medicine. Religion was the heart of the Right Way, not politics. The Right Way had been shown them in ancient times by a man from the stars who was called *Hasi*. This *Hasi* told them to keep their sacred fires burning in an Ark, and then *Hasi* vanished into the sky, Knows All Charlie said. The elders taught the young the importance of families. The sacred fires were kept burning. Sweat lodges were steaming with stones and water. People danced always counterclockwise and sang, ate meat and fish and drank wine, smoked pipes, prayed and made trances. Knows All Charlie was a fabulous Storyteller with a memory of the Cherokees that linked from one old Storyteller back to the one behind him and so on back to the days before selfishness, when the first people arrived on earth from the stars.

Knows All Charlie said the first people were Cherokees—a man and a woman—who landed on the first new moon of autumn south of the place that was now known as Mexico. First Woman—known as the Woman of the East—gave birth to seven sons and seven daughters who became seven clans that traveled north all the way to the inland seas that crossed the border into the land called Canada. Over the ages—there was no need then for measuring time—the Cherokees roamed. The ancient people survived the greatest of all floods, and they mingled with a tribe called the Hebrews and accepted the Hebrews into their Right Way of living. Knows All Charlie said the Cherokees moved toward the rising sun and at last settled in their beloved green and blue and smoky mountains that were home to deer, bears and elks as well as rushing rivers and a benevolent climate.

Knows All Charlie told the audience that in his own lifetime the Cherokees ruled the east from the blue and the smoky mountains to the ocean, and from the great swamp in the south to the frozen lakes of the north, and the whites were wretched, dirty, ugly creatures hacking down trees to build cabins that were crude and ugly by Cherokee standards, and hiding behind walls, and killing the animals of the forest and pulling the fish from the rivers as often for pleasure or money as for food, a crime against life for which the Master of Breath punished all humans by sending them rheumatism.

Knows All Charlie said for every animal that is killed needlessly, the Master of Breath sends a disease. But the Master of Breath also sends a living plant that will cure the disease if a stricken one is treated in the Right Way.

Standing on a platform outside the heptagon before the hushed crowd in the blue mountain night, Uncle Charlie paused and rubbed the tattoos on each bicep. Silver bells tinkled from his wrists. The tattoos were pictures of fish swallowing fish in a band around his arm. The same symbol carved in ivory— fish swallowing fish swallowing fish—made a band around Knows All Charlie's bowler hat.

Cullasaja remembered that she had been surprised to see envy on the face of such a great person as Chief Bowl as he listened to Knows All Charlie and admired the old uncle's black satin-covered bowler hat. Chief Bowl was in his sixties in those days. The Council of Beloved Men of the Cherokee Nation had selected him as the white chief for the Cherokees of Texas. The Beloved Men charged him with making Cherokees a secure home in Texas. On this pilgrimage to Grandmother Tobacco's farm, Chief Bowl, also known as Duwali, wore a silk peach-colored turban. His mustache was wispy white hairs. In later years he would keep his silk jacket open at the chest to show the medal that was awarded to him for valiant service to the Republic of Texas by his son-in-law, Sam Houston.

Duwali's turban was pinned in front by a brooch of polished diamonds, rubies and emeralds from the North Carolina mountains. Soft French slippers covered his feet. The peace chief of the Texas Cherokees would sit before the standing Knows All Charlie the whole cool night under the clear mountain sky with stars bright as fire, and listen to stories of the long-ago days of the first people as they came at last to where the Master of Breath desired them to be. Cullasaja and her brother, Romulus, would sit all night on blankets beside Chief Bowl and look up at the empty eye sockets and the floor-length white waterfall hair of Knows All Charlie, who hadn't cut his hair in one hundred years.

This morning in Texas as Cullasaja was singing at the berry thicket, United States government soldiers had begun driving the Cherokees out of their green and blue mountains in the east, away from their lakes and rivers and forests, and marching them to the harsh and unknown western frontier. Grandmother Tobacco remained hidden in her high valley, but most of the Cherokees who had come to the storytellings at the Green Corn ceremonies at Grandmother Tobacco's farm were walking toward the forbidding, mysterious west with their belongings in carts, prodded in the ribs by army bayonets.

Captain Fletcher Swift yelled in anger when Cullasaja declared her desire to leave white society in New York and go live in the Right Way with her mother's people. He wanted to keep his precious daughter close by his side. Fletcher Swift's cousin, Jonathan Swift, an Irish writer and clergyman, whose satirical book *Travels into Several Remote Regions of the World* was popularly known as *Gulliver's Travels*, had died when Fletcher was a boy in Dublin. With Jonathan's prestige and influence gone to the grave, religious and political enemies persecuted his relatives in Ireland. Fletcher's father, Edwin, escaped by moving his family and shipping business to Edinburgh on the east coast of Scotland. Life was hard for Fletcher as an Irish boy growing up among the Scots in the streets and on the docks. He had fistfights once or twice a week. A gang of Scots boys gave the Mick bastard a serious beating before the first summer he was to go to sea as cabin boy on a family ship. Living as an outsider at a harbor city where all the races of the world came and went, Fletcher dreamed of feeling secure. When he at last worked his way up to captain of his own vessel, then became master of the family merchant fleet, his five ships with their Scottish flags sailed to America and slipped through the barrier of hatred against Irish immigrants. Captain Fletcher Swift moved his shipping business and his residence to the free, new world across the Atlantic and became a citizen of one of the United States—New York. Middle-aged and never married, he fell in love with a beautiful black-haired woman who was matched to sit beside him at dinner at the East River mansion of one of his shipping clients.

Her hair was braided and wound around on top. She wore a green silk Empire gown, low-cut at the bodice, showing smooth coppery skin, with a high waist, long skirt and long, tapered sleeves. Carrie Lee was a Cherokee who had been born in North Carolina but sent to Miss Finch's Academy for Girls in New York City for her education, followed by two years of the study of classical history at New York University, all of it paid for by Grandmother Tobacco. For the first and only time in his life, Fletcher Swift realized this must be romantic love he was feeling. He courted Carrie Lee at New York restaurants, theaters and social affairs. He went with her to the opera. Carrie Lee had read *Gulliver's Travels* at Miss Finch's, and her respect for the wit and sense of Jonathan Swift led to respect and love for his second cousin Fletcher, who proved to her that he was that rare thing, a good man. He was thirty years older than she, but nervous as a boy when he asked her to marry him. She told him they must go to the Carolina mountains to ask her family for permission. Carrie Lee was from the Chiltoskie family of the Bird clan. The Chiltoskies were pleased to accept Captain Fletcher Swift as a member of their family. Fletcher and Carrie Lee married first in the mountains in the Right Way, presided by Knows All Charlie. Fletcher and Carrie joined their two blankets into one by tying a knot, and they became man and wife. All that would be required for a divorce was to untie the knot and separate the blankets. The only other thing that would dissolve a marriage was adultery.

Then they wed in a Presbyterian church on Fifth Avenue in New York, attended by merchants and politicians and rival shippers and their wives. The son and daughter of Fletcher and Carrie Lee Swift were born twenty years apart, but both were born in New York, citizens of the United States of America. Though a U.S. citizen by marriage, Carrie Lee claimed citizenship of the Cherokee Nation. The Swift name and fortune and associations formed in the shipping business protected her from open prejudice in New York. It was vital in the code of the clans of Fletcher's Cherokee in-laws that a family protect itself. This was also the belief by which Fletcher Swift had been raised on the Edinburgh waterfront. "Your mother's people are being blown away in the storms of history," he told Cullasaja. "You must stay here where you were born and educated and become part of this world here. You are smart and beautiful. You have a glorious future here where your mother and I can be your support and protection. You will get killed for no good reason in that murderous wilderness."

During the argument between her husband and daughter, Mrs. Carrie Lee Swift was expecting a visit from her lawyers. Carrie had been a financial backer of *The Phoenix* newspaper and continued to argue in the courts for freedom of the Cherokee press. When she heard a doorbell jingle, she waved the maid aside and answered the door herself.

Carrie was surprised and delighted to be embraced on the front steps by her son, Dr. Romulus Swift, returning from London and from visiting Knows All Charlie and Grandmother Tobacco in North Carolina. The timing of Romulus's arrival and his announced desire to go to Texas were seen as propitious omens by Carrie Lee.

Together the mother and son persuaded eighty-nine-year-old Fletcher Swift and nineteen-year-old Cullasaja Swift to compromise. Romulus would escort Cullasaja to Texas, where she would live for one year in the utopia being created by Chief Bowl. At the end of that time she promised to come back to New York for another family conference. Then she would make up her mind between living a privileged intellectual life under the protection of Captain Fletcher Swift, or following the Cherokee Right Way of life that was being clung to as sacred and wise by many of her mother's relatives. "You'll be back to stay, you'll see. The old ways are gone," her father told her.

From his travels in exotic lands as a sailor, Romulus expected that the Texas frontier would be a dangerous place, full of the strange and threatening creatures that thrive in unknown corners of the world. He bought the three newest pistols made at the Colt plant in New Jersey. The brother and sister and their two best horses sailed from the port of New York on a merchant ship around the horn of Florida and across the Gulf of Mexico to land in Texas at Galveston Island. They bought supplies and pack animals in Houston City and began their trek to Bowl's Town by first veering northwest toward Austin.

Cullasaja heard the snort of a horse and a stream of urine gushing onto the earth and looked up to see a strange rider approaching. He looked to her like an enormous bird, long legs, round body, long arms, a long neck that slowly turned its beak and its slitted, blinking eyes back and forth, as if seeking a flying insect.

"Hidy, young woman," said Henry Longfellow. "Don't you be alarmed. My water bag is tore. I need to climb down and get me a drink of pure water from that creek over there."

He slithered out of the *concho*-studded saddle and settled like a big bird on the ground, beak swiveling around, the shotgun in one claw and the saber in the other.

# 3

On the previous evening Dr. Romulus Swift had led his white-faced Kentucky horse down the ramp to the shore as the *Waterloo Queen* ferry, a flat-bottom barge, rocked and groaned in the chop at its dock on the north bank of the Colorado River. The smell of rain was in the breeze. A splash of yellow and purple lit up inside the vast black cloud as the sun went down beyond the hills, and the air felt heavy and wet against his face.

"That's the last trip for the *Queen* for a week, is my supposure," Googleye, the boatman, said to his only passenger. Googleye's eyes bulged like ripe fruits: a condition Doc Swift recognized as exophthalmos, caused by a tumor. "Soon as you get off, I'm hitching my mules and dragging the *Queen* as far up on shore as we can pull it."

"I need to cross again at first light," Doc said.

"Mister, you see them clouds yander? How big they are? When they cut loose into rain, this damned old river will grow a mile wide. The *Queen* ain't doing no more crossing until this storm is over and the river goes back down. Probably a week, I'd reckon."

Googleye's powerful arms and shoulders tossed the twenty-foot hardwood steering pole onto the bank easily as bamboo. His bloody hands smelled of the three forty-pound catfish that lay on the deck with their guts ripped out. He glanced again at the black clouds. This was a crazy place for weather, Googleye thought. The Colorado River had twice frozen solid only a few weeks ago. Horses and wagons had crossed the ice while the *Waterloo Queen* lay helpless. Now look at that river coming at them, the water turning brown already from the storm in the hills, little whitecaps forming.

"I want you to wait for me," Doc said.

The assurance in Doc's voice made Googleye turn his plum-sized eyes toward the tall man in the black wide-brimmed hat and black knee-length coat with the reins of the white-faced horse in his gloved fingers.

"Ain't no use in threatening me. I'm too stupid to give any mind to a threat," Googleye said.

"I'll pay you sixty dollars to wait here for me and take me back to the south bank. If the flood hits before I return, you can keep the money."

"If you're talking about red-back Texas money, I wouldn't do it for sixty thousand," Googleye said.

"American gold dollars."

"Shit on my head if I believe that."

Doc unbuckled the strap on a saddlebag and pulled out a leather pouch. He dug three twenty-dollar gold pieces out of the jingling pouch. Doc handed the three gold pieces to Googleye, who studied them against the crusted blood in his palm with his normal expression of bewildered dismay. Googleye had never held so much gold. He liked the weight of it.

"How do you know I won't run away with your gold?" asked Googleye.

"Because I will find you if you do," Doc said.

Googleye tried to tighten his vision on this stranger. The man appeared to be strongly built and graceful. He moved like a fellow who assumed natural authority over others, which made him dangerous. Googleye professed to be stupid, but in his heart he felt he was wiser than most and could sense a person's character; he could feel the heat from the fire that burned in the best and in the worst and made them equally to be feared.

"I reckon I'll likely be here waiting on you, mister, but I ain't going to drown for gold or nobody," said Googleye.

"Agreed."

Doc tightened the cinch and then mounted Donnybrook, his white-faced stallion. Half a mile to the north, at the end of the rutted path through the high grass and oak trees, Doc saw part of the stockade fence that was being built to protect the approaches to Austin from what the citizens feared would be attacks by savages. Looking toward the west, across a bend in the Colorado River, Doc saw a high limestone cliff that ran as far as his eye could follow north and south. The uplift made a natural barrier between the Republic of Texas and the beginning of the plateau and hills and mountains and forests and rivers of Comancheria. The white cliffs that formed the boundary west of the river from Austin were spotted with dark spy holes that Doc guessed to be caves. He supposed there would be Comanches up there, at this moment, watching over this valley. Soon Doc must climb that cliff. He believed he would find what he sought somewhere in Comancheria.

Romulus remembered the summer he had turned nine years old. Knows All

Charlie had been telling a story to a gathering in the North Carolina mountains. Tired from hiking in the forest, the boy was falling asleep when he heard his uncle say, ". . . half man and half beast."

Romulus woke up and listened.

". . . during their great journey from Mexico to Canada, the people of the early time were forced to leave much of their treasure in a cavern in the west that was in the domain of a tribe of creatures, not man or beast but living animals something between the two—human apes. The human apes are guarding our treasure even today."

The image had frightened young Romulus. That night as the boy lay on his pallet under the stars, the man-ape appeared in his dreams. The creature's large brown eyes peered curiously from beneath a protruding ridge of brow. Bending near the boy's face, the creature gave forth a stench like rotten meat. The man-ape's expression was both inquisitive and menacing. His lips trembled as if trying to speak. Romulus woke up with a shout, and was calmed back to sleep by Grandmother Tobacco.

At fourteen, Romulus began shipping out to sea in the summer, first as a cabin boy, as his father had done. In the North Carolina mountains, he was Romulus of the Chiltoskie family of the Bird clan, son of Carrie Lee. To his teachers in New York he was Master Romulus, son of Captain Fletcher Swift. But on board a brig a thousand miles from land in the South Pacific carrying ice to Borneo, he was a deckhand who hauled sail and climbed the rigging and bled with the able-bodied seamen. At sea he realized it was how he met each moment that made him who he was, not a reputation or a title or money in a bank. It was at sea at the age of sixteen that Romulus held one arm of a sailor whose infected leg was being removed below the knee by a surgeon with a handsaw. The shock of crimson blood, the intensity of Romulus's sensations, the immediacy of romancing death but saving life as the leg flopped onto the deck and the cauterizing iron seared the blood vessels shut in a plume of smoke and the reek of burned flesh—the thrill of this started him thinking of studying to be a medical doctor, and a healer.

The summer voyage after Romulus completed his first year as a student in philosophy at King's College, Columbia, he got into a brawl with two Portuguese sailors in a bar in Barcelona and was badly beaten. Romulus interviewed the toughest fighter on each of the ships in the Barcelona harbor. He found a West African named Nigerium who had tribal scars on his cheeks, as well as mounded brows, a crooked nose, crumpled ears, sloping shoulders of a naturally powerful puncher, and a tight waist. Nigerium had fought professional bare-knuckle fights—legal and illegal—in Europe for twelve years until he was poisoned by a gambler who dropped belladonna in his water bucket during the twenty-third round of a match against a Spaniard in Madrid. Nigerium was the heavy favorite among bettors. They accused him of laying down the fight. To escape with his life, Nigerium shipped out in the merchant service. Romulus hired Nigerium to teach him to fight. A year later, early in the summer before he entered medical study at Edinburgh, Romulus issued a challenge to the champions of all the ships in the merchant fleets in Southampton harbor in England. Six men answered his challenge. Romulus and Nigerium went to each of their ships, one per day. Romulus fought six boxing matches using Broughton's Rules—bare knuckles, no hitting while an opponent is down, no gouging, no grabbing the hair. Romulus won each match, and every gambling sailor in the Swift fleet had money for grog and women. Romulus rewarded Nigerium with a pension and a cottage within sight of the sea in the south of France.

On his final summer voyage two weeks before entering medical college in Edinburgh, Romulus filled the post of second officer for a fast run on an opium clipper from London to Algiers. His ship encountered a Mediterranean storm that hurled waves three times higher than the masts. Death appeared certain. During the howling and crashing and pitching of the storm, Romulus confronted the ultimate question of what happens next. Where did I come from, and what am I, and what becomes of me? The philosophers he had studied at Columbia were irrelevant now that death found him lashed to the mast in suffocating rain. As the ship stood on its bow and then on its stern and the waves crashed down from the sky, Romulus had a vision—suddenly emanating from his own body, as if emerging from a home, stepped the part man, part beast that had haunted his dreams as a boy in the mountains. The man-ape smelled of rotten meat, his fur was speckled with blood, but his soft brown eyes looked at Romulus reassuringly. By hand gestures the creature, standing so close that wiry hairs pricked Romulus's arm, seemed to be making a sort of blessing. Then Romulus received a clear, strong thought, almost seeming to be printed in his brain: *You will not die here. You will live to find wisdom.* Romulus fell into a hypnotic, dreamy state, peacefully, thinking he was drowning. But when he awoke, the wind and waves had subsided, the sun had broken through, and the smashed clipper was still afloat. Romulus thought he had entered the realm of death and had hallucinated this strange creature that had been planted in his mind by Knows All Charlie. But there was the puzzling aroma. Despite having been drenched and almost drowned, Romulus could still smell on his flesh the sweet stink of rotten meat.

Romulus studied medicine for two years at the University of Edinburgh, the best medical and surgical college in the world. He received a license that

entitled him to call himself Dr. Swift. He liked the word doctor, as he liked
the word healer. Dr. Swift practiced in New York City, but mostly in London,
where he was known as a top herbalist, often using herbs sent from North
Carolina by Knows All Charlie. At the Explorers Club in Mayfair six months
ago, Dr. Swift had dined with Sir Samuel Pluck, a geographer recently returned
from West Africa. Sir Pluck told of taking a seventeen-bearer safari into the
jungle to look for the source of the Iribi River. Sir Pluck's safari entered an
area of jungle ruled by what he had regarded as a mythical creature—a man-
ape. Half of Pluck's porters recognized the creature's presence by its odor of
rotten meat and threw down their bundles and fled. Sir Pluck pressed forward
with his riflemen. "I nearly got a shot at that blasted whatever-it-is," Sir Pluck
said. "I saw its shape crashing through the brush, and I could smell it—like
the shit of a buzzard, it smelled. Damned bad luck I couldn't catch it or kill it.
But one thing for certain—this creature exists."

One week after dinner with Sir Pluck, Doc sailed from Southampton to
Charleston. He traveled to Grandmother Tobacco's farm and asked Knows All
Charlie to tell him again about the creature that is part man and part beast.

His ancient uncle grinned, sightless eyes seeming illuminated from inside.
He wore his bowler hat with the ivory band around it that depicted a fish
swallowing a fish swallowing a fish. "Sit with me and share a pipe. I have
heard news of the creature."

Several boys were playing stickball. A cousin, a woman in a silk dress,
served Knows All Charlie and Romulus two mugs of a hot, sweet drink made
from honey locust pods.

Two months ago, Romulus and his uncle had sat on a boulder overlooking
a green valley, hearing the water running in the river, and the waterfall crashing
down from the clouds. Romulus smoked only on ceremonial occasions, or at
the request of people he loved, like Knows All Charlie, who handed him a pipe
with a stone bowl and a two-foot stem made of soft wood and decorated with
Bird clan feathers. Grandmother Tobacco's blend tasted like almonds and was
smooth in his bronchial passage and lungs.

Knows All Charlie held in his lap a divining crystal. But this news had
come from the words on the wind.

"A white man has crossed Comancheria. He has seen the man-ape. He has
seen our people's treasure in the cavern."

Romulus bent closer to concentrate on his uncle's words.

"The man is a German. He has a hatchet blade buried in his skull. He
brought forty pounds of gold from the cavern."

"Where is he now?"

"He is in a new white man's town in Texas, far west of Bowl's Town. He is dying. But we must save him. I will make medicine, and you will take it to him and heal him."

"This German has seen a man ape?" asked Romulus.

"Yes. This creature guards our people's treasure."

"You mean gold?" asked Romulus.

"No. Our treasure is the next wisdom."

"I don't understand."

The white-eyed old man touched the right palm of Romulus with spider-veined fingers.

"Our people have been given two great wisdoms. We have learned the Master of Breath is the force of life. *Hasi* taught us the Right Way to live on this earth. Now it is time for the third wisdom to be revealed to you," Knows All Charlie said.

"But why me?"

"You are chosen. It is no accident you have come here. You must find this German and heal him. Then you must find the creature who guards our next wisdom."

"Forgive me, Uncle. But I don't understand," said Romulus.

"You will understand and spread the wisdom," Knows All Charlie said, eyes white as marbles.

Six weeks ago in New York, Doc had looked through the archives of the *New England Journal of Medicine* and found an article by the eminent surgeon Dr. Franz Bebault of Harvard, who had been visiting in Texas when the German staggered into San Antonio. Dr. Bebault had treated the German's wound. The article expressed wonder that the German was alive but mentioned nothing about the gold or a man-ape

A living being that is neither human nor beast figures in the creation myths and oral legends of peoples all over the world, as Doc knew from his reading and his travels. Doc believed the man-ape did exist in the primeval wilderness of Comancheria. He was determined to confront the creature, as a scientist and as the representative of his mother's people—and to satisfy his curiosity about this image he had seen in a dream and had hallucinated during a storm at sea.

Texans called every settlement a city, but to Doc Swift's eyes Austin was a crude town under construction that would never be grand enough to be called a city even if it ever got finished. He thought of New York or Philadelphia as examples of what an American city is. The town of Austin was located in a bowl surrounded by wooded heights through which the Colorado River and broad feeder creeks and streams cut their beds flowing toward the Gulf of

Mexico, two hundred miles to the south. Doc rode in at the Colorado Street gate. The yellow lights of candles and kerosene lanterns began appearing in windows. Branches of oak trees rustled with black birds. Cicadas took up their evening whirring songs. Doc was surprised to see several houses of a quality one might expect in Baltimore. Some were of two stories, built of hardwood and stone, with rock chimneys and shaded verandas.

Donnybrook clopped across a plank bridge over a rushing stream. Bullock's Inn at Pecan Street and Congress Avenue in the center of town reminded Doc of the State House Inn in Annapolis, with its two-story red stone walls, white shuttered windows and wide, covered porch with four columns in front. Near the hotel arose the construction framing of a government building. In the darkness he saw other buildings partly built, and much land on which the trees had been chopped down, but the lots were empty. He passed the land office, a structure being built of granite with slits for windows, made to be defended. Doc rode along, reading signs hanging on poles or painted on the walls of buildings—a hardware store, a barber shop, a surveyor's office, an apothecary, a lawyer's office, a general merchandise store. Standing off a ways on its own corner was Dutch John's Saloon. Doc saw light through the open door and heard the loud voices of drinking men singing and yelling above the pounding on a piano keyboard by someone with an education in music hall tunes.

The sign Doc was looking for was painted on a slab of oak in black block letters: PARADISE FOR SALE, *Fritz Gruber, agent.*

The door was latched. The office was dark. Doc swung down from the saddle and read the paper notices in the window and on the door. The notices announced tracts of land for sale. The German's business was selling land to other Germans. With a partner in Bavaria to distribute their literature and collect half the money in advance, Fritz Gruber was growing wealthy. Once he got the business going, he used his clients' down payments to buy land from the Republic that he then multiplied in price and deeded to his clients, so there was no risk to him at all. The land he sold to German families was in the black earth east of Austin for the farmers or into the hills to the south for goat and sheep raisers. The Germans sailed from Europe to the Gulf of Mexico coast and then came up the rivers—navigable if they cleared the jams of timber and flotsam at the mouths—into central Texas and claimed their holdings at the price demanded by Herr Gruber. The Germans were tough, hardworking and intelligent. Where the Germans settled, there was prosperity. Germans felt a love for the soil and stuck it out in situations when immigrants from the southern states of America would have moved on with their notes unpaid.

Gruber was a Hessian, a mercenary soldier who had fought for the British twenty-seven years ago in the second war of the American revolution. He deserted during a battle in the snow in Pennsylvania and escaped into the western wilderness with an Irishman, an Arab, a Frenchman and a Polish Jew. With them they took four wagons loaded with salt, mirrors, cloth, beads, hammers, hatchets, smooth-bore muskets, gunpowder, rope, coffee, sugar and pepper, and six dozen red tunics, some with chevrons on the arms, all of it stolen from the king of England. At the Great Rocky Mountains they traded their goods to the natives for mounds of fur. The partners drove the wagons piled with furs east to St. Louis and returned the wagons to the west with more goods to trade. After several successful trading expeditions into the wilderness, they opened an agency in Independence, Missouri, and decided to deepen their trade route. They would drop down from the Santa Fe Trail into the high plains of Comancheria. All the partners went on every expedition, as it was well known they did not trust each other. Eleven months after the partners turned off the Santa Fe Trail and drove their wagons into the southwest, Fritz Gruber staggered out of Comancheria with a shard of an axe blade stuck in his skull and forty pounds of gold in his arms, raving that his partners had been murdered, betrayed by a Comanche chief called Osage Killer. The German told a preposterous story about the gold. Nobody believed him. He was clearly out of his mind. The San Antonio magistrate determined that the German had stumbled across ingots lost from an old Spanish expedition. The gold was stored in Gruber's name on Commerce Street in the vault at the Royalty Coin Company, whose president looked after the sale of the gold personally for a thirty percent fee. While struggling for life in a room at the Fincus Hotel beside the San Antonio River's most fashionable bathhouse, bleeding and sweating and dizzy with fever, Fritz Gruber dreamed of an inspiration. In his native Bavaria his family and friends were suffering from civil wars and high taxes and crowding and oppression. They desperately wanted freedom and land. Fritz Gruber would sell them both in the Republic of Texas. This would be their paradise on earth. Gruber knew they were so eager to buy hope that they would pay in advance, without seeing the land.

"Pardon me, sir. Could you please tell me where I might find Mr. Fritz Gruber at this hour?" Doc asked a man who was stomping in a zigzag path toward the lights of Dutch John's Saloon.

"Who wants to know?" the man said. He was flushed and sweating in his gray wool suit, and more drunk than not. His breath sucked in open-mouthed gasps. His stomach had popped the top button on his trousers.

"I am his doctor."

"Is that a fact? Well, I am his lawyer, and I happen to know Fritz Gruber doesn't have a doctor."

"Your client's skull was cleft by a hand axe. I recently studied his case history. I need to see him before it is too late," said Doc.

The lawyer studied Doc for a skeptical moment and then stuck out his hand.

"Ridgewood Bone is my name. Princeton Law, class of '32."

Doc shook his hand. "Dr. Romulus Swift, University of Edinburgh Medical College, class of '26."

"You don't sound like a Scot to me."

"I am also King's College, Columbia, class of '22. We took Princeton twelve times in polo and never lost once."

"You rode for King's College?" Bone said, impressed.

"I was their captain."

"Meaning no offense, Dr. Swift, but you look like a rather, ah, rough character, not at all soft like a physician, not in my opinion, and strangers inquiring about the whereabouts of individuals around Austin is, ah, fraught with impending violence. We attract many frauds claiming to be doctors and lawyers and men of substance, just as we also are a mecca for passionate men with scores to settle. Now that I know you're a King's College man and an authentic physician, I will confess my client's wound is oozing more than usual. Damned unsightly and foul-smelling. Turns my stomach to look at it."

"Then tell me where he is," said Doc.

"Right now he will be in the corner bedroom upstairs over the saloon in the Redbud Hotel. He will have started humping on Mrs. Ruth Hunboldt, a widow. He will hump on her for the next two hours."

Doc looked around. "Two hours?"

"Amazing, isn't it? Two solid hours of humping every evening that he's in town. I've wondered, could the blow from the axe have anything to do with his voracious appetite for sex? Set off some fireworks in his brain, perhaps?"

"I believe it could," Doc said.

"I doubt the pain would be worth it, though," mused the lawyer. "At any rate, two hours and fifteen minutes from now you will find Herr Gruber eating a beefsteak and playing poker at Dutch John's with the land commissioner, the mayor, a surveyor, and some land speculators, all of them my clients in one way or another, sooner or later. What kind of doctor are you? A bleeder or a shatter? A purger? A doper?"

"What sort of doctor do you want?" Doc asked.

"I mean no offense, sir, but there are more kinds of medicine being practiced these days than there are ailments. Quacks abound like locusts in Egypt. Doctors have told me to eat bark. Doctors have twisted my neck until it popped. Doctors have stuck lancets into my arm and drained my blood into a bucket until I fainted from weakness. They have put leeches on me. They have filled me with bilious fluid until I shat myself inside out."

The lawyer paused for a breath.

"There are regulars, irregulars, Broussaisans, Sangradoarians, Morrissonians, Brandrethians, Thompsonians and reformed Thompsonians," he said. "There are botanics, regular botanics, theoretical, practical, experimental, dogmatical, emblematical, magnetical, electrical, diplomatical, homeopathians, rootists, herbists, florists, and Mesmerists. But I do believe the best cure always is opium. I love laudanum. Whoever thought of mixing opium with alcohol is a genius. If you should happen to have some laudanum in your bag I'd be most appreciative. Our lone apothecary is stingy with laudanum—hoards it for himself."

"Why don't you grow it?" Doc asked.

"Grow it?"

"Plant a few of these fields in poppies. Soon you'll have all the opium you need."

"I might try that. Yes sir, I might. I have a little farm a few miles outside the city. I could grow poppies there," the lawyer said. "Perhaps you will join me in drinking a jug of poison at Dutch John's while you're waiting for the German to finish wallowing on that poor woman?"

"If I have two hours to wait, I need to care for my horse first," Doc said.

"Splendid form. Would have expected nothing less from a King's College captain. I'm thinking maybe you played the ruggers for them, too."

"No."

Lawyer Bone observed the white ridge of scar tissue in the doctor's right eyebrow, and the small knot that indicated the nose had been broken.

"Some other rugged sport, surely."

"At Edinburgh I participated in the Gentlemen's Boxing Club."

"Boxing? As in pugilist? I wouldn't have thought of boxing as a gentleman's sport."

"We call it the art of self-defense," Doc said.

Doc looked at the lawyer's red-streaked eyeballs. The sweet odor of corn whiskey drifted from Ridgewood Bone's breath, and the sour smell of sweat clung to his clothes. His crotch showed a dark stain. The gold chain of a watch dipped into his vest pocket. On the frontier a watch was a rare thing. Time was judged from the passing of the sun and the moon.

"Once again, I mean no offense," said Bone.

"Fascinating as this conversation is, lawyer Bone, I must not keep you from your clients and companions at Dutch John's."

"Begging pardon, Doc, but if you have just a minute more, maybe you could give me a bit of advice, eh? I'm feeling a little off my stick."

"From observing you, I would think that you have swellings in your upper colon—lumps on the left side of your stomach—and irritable bowels with much flatulence and red blood in your stool. Distended abdomen. Heartburn, nausea, vomiting."

"Good Lord, Doc, you hit me right on the nose."

"You have dyspepsia. Probably a diseased liver as well. But the liver is remarkable for its power to heal itself of abuse, if you will give it a chance."

"How should I treat it?" asked Bone.

"Orthodox treatment for dyspepsia calls for a heavy purge to blast the corruption out of your body. I suppose that's the best thing for you. Pour a bottle of castor oil down your throat and spend two or three days squatting in the woods. Take sweat baths. Get a lot of sleep. For you to cure your liver, you must stop drinking whiskey and stop stuffing your belly with fat, greasy food. Eat vegetables instead—a little willow tree bark would be good for your intestines, in fact—and start drinking twelve large cups of spring water every day, chopping wood and going on walks or brisk rides for exercise. But you're not going to do those things. Are you?"

Ridgewood Bone grinned and whiffed a pinch of snuff up each nostril. He shook his head at Doc Swift. He wiped sweat out of his eyes. Though it was a cool evening, the humidity was rising. Ridgewood Bone was uncomfortable; he felt the lumps growing in his colon, a pain stabbed his liver, he passed gas. He needed a drink of Kentucky bourbon to put joy back into his heart.

"You're new to Texas, Doc. You'll learn. Everybody drinks whiskey in Texas. Whiskey makes you not bother so much about the fleas and ticks and chiggers and mosquitoes, and the damned clouds of nasty flies, and the weather that is freezing one day and burning the next. In Texas all the bugs are ugly, and they jump high. This will be the capital city of a great republic, and its future as a moneymaker for a skilled lawyer like me is unlimited, but I can't stand the damn place without my jug of poison to rearrange reality. Mind you, I trained to practice in New York City. This is all rather unlike Princeton."

"Why don't you go to New York, then?"

"I told you. The United States economy is in a panic, but there's a lot of money to be made in Texas, although it is damned dangerous and unpleasant."

"You didn't know what you were getting into?"

"Nobody in Texas knows what they're getting into. That's one great thing about it from my point of view. I can pick the plums. But you, a doctor, I must warn you that Texans like doctors, but they hate to pay doctor fees. They have been known to shoot doctors who fail. I hope you practice here in Austin because I like your cut, sir. I believe we're sophisticated enough as a city to treat a doctor fairly who comes from King's College stock."

"I'm not going to practice medicine here. I want to examine Fritz Gruber's wound and try to help him," said Doc. "Then I'll be gone."

"Well, if I'm not going to see you again, I might as well take more advantage of our encounter. I'm having trouble drawing in a good lungful of air. I hear a crackling sound when I breathe. I feel a pain in my side. Do you think it might be the walking pneumonia?"

"In my opinion, it is infection and abuse of your bronchial tubes and upper respiratory tract, maybe caused by pollen from all these juniper trees."

"Would laudanum help it?"

"Laudanum would certainly help you forget it."

"Thank you, Doc. Thank you. I'll go straight to the chemist and demand that scoundrel comes across with a bottle. I wish you'd change your mind and hang out your sign in Austin, but I can't blame you. Between you and me, from the talk I hear at Dutch John's, I think we're in a race against time here. If Lamar doesn't send the army to protect us, the vicious Comanches will burn us to the ground. That is what the Indian Joes who live on Shoal Creek told Ed Waller."

A frown wrinkled Bone's forehead as a new thought struck him.

"Oh, yes, there's the God damn Mexicans," said Bone. "They didn't give a damn about this place till we started building our capital here, but now there are rumors a Mexican army is headed our way. What will we do? Throw whiskey bottles at them?"

Bone wheezed deeply, stirring his resolve.

"But if we triumph here, old chap, this piece of dirt is a bonanza," the lawyer said.

"I hope you live long enough to spend your fortune, lawyer Bone. Now, good evening to you, sir," Doc said, and led Donnybrook down the red dirt road to a livery stable that was within view of the Redbud Hotel. The Redbud was built of pine, not yet painted but already doing enough business to need a second floor added.

Looking through the carriage door of Boone's Livery, Doc could see across the road to the outside wooden stairs that led up to the second-floor bedrooms. The German would have to come down those steps. Doc fed, watered and groomed Donnybrook. He warned the stable hand to stay clear. "This horse kicks and bites, and he might decide to sit on you," Doc said.

Doc opened a saddlebag, removed a book and sat down on a three-legged stool where he had a view through the carriage door. He heard the leaves of the oaks rattling in the breeze and saw a dust devil dancing along the road. Inside the livery stable the horses were snorting and farting and whinnying back and forth to each other. Doc could smell the oats and hay and ripe odor of dung.

With his right forefinger Doc opened the book and began reading from chapter one in Genesis. The Bible was the only book Doc was carrying on this journey. He had read Aristotle and Plato, Milton and Dante, Lord Byron and John Keats and Percy Shelley, was a friend of the new pantheist poet William Wordsworth in London, had read Descartes and Spinoza, as well as the wisdom of Confucius, the Buddha and the Hindus. But the Bible was the book he was drawn back to again and again. Doc admired the teachings of Jesus. He believed Christ had died on the cross in a sacrifice meant to elevate the human psyche from the animal to the spiritual. Doc appreciated the mystery, profoundly dramatic tales and the sternness of the Old Testament. He believed in the uplifting power of love, and at the same time he believed in the righteousness of vengeance. Knows All Charlie had taught him that vengeance must be paid for harm done a clan member, and Fletcher Swift had taught him to protect his family with any violence necessary. The Old Testament told him that God had laid out rules for humans to live by, and disobedience must surely be punished in this life or the next.

Doc yawned and rubbed his eyes and began reading in Genesis:

*"And God said, 'Behold, I have given you every herb bearing seed, which is upon the face of all the earth, and every tree, in which is the fruit of a tree yielding seed; to you it shall be for meat.' "*

Doc thought of the German and smiled. How apt, considering what Doc planned to do.

Then Doc turned to a page he had tagged with a strip of doeskin. The passage had caught his eye as he read beside a campfire the first night he and Cullasaja landed in Texas. Doc read from the seventh chapter of Isaiah:

*"...In that day it shall be that in every place where there were a thousand vines, worth a thousand dollars, there shall be briers and thornbushes. With bow and arrows they shall come there, for the whole land shall be briers and thornbushes..."*

# 4

**M**rs. Ruth Hunboldt lay back in bed exhausted and sweating and bone sore with her eyes shut. She felt the mattress and frame groan and shift as Fritz Gruber rolled off her and heaved his weight upon the floor, feet first. She heard him thumping across the wooden floor and then heard the stream and the splashing as he urinated into a chamber pot.

"One day I will marry you," he said.

She opened her eyes.

"Ruthie, you hear what I say? One day I will marry you."

She looked at his broad, hairy back, which was striped with red welts as if he were wrapped in ribbons.

"Oh, Mr. Gruber, don't you be getting my hopes up," she said.

In the three years since her husband and child died of pneumonia in their broken wagon on the bank of the Sabine River while fleeing Santa Anna's soldiers during the Great Runaway Scrape, she had sunk so low, she told herself, that attaching her future to the German sounded promising. Despite his fierce appearance and his bloody reputation, Herr Gruber was the kindest of her lovers.

"Call me Fritz from now on," he said, turning and looking at her, a purple puckering of flesh standing up an inch and a half the length of his bald skull. She knew the flesh grew around a broken hatchet blade that he was thoughtful to keep away from her face while they were in bed. "I been forking you for nearly a year now, and I like it. I don't like to think of you forking for other fellows."

"I have to make a living, Fritz. You know that."

"One man a day should be enough."

"It would be all I'd want, that's for sure, but one man a day doesn't pay enough to buy me a nice piece of land and build me a house. Life is not as easy here for a woman as it is for a man. Oh, Fritz, if you knew the things I am forced to endure."

She sat up and leaned on an elbow and watched him stretch the cotton shirt around his torso. He stuffed his heavy, muscled legs into trousers but left his genitals hanging free. He walked across to Ruth and waggled his penis in front of her face.

"Pet Big Willy," he said.

Ruth leaned forward and patted her fingertips lightly against the head of Big Willy. Smiling and satisfied, Fritz Gruber pushed his balls and penis inside the trousers and pulled up his suspenders. Then he bent down and kissed Ruth on the forehead, tenderly. He smelled of the ginger tonic he always splashed on himself when he visited her so Ruth wouldn't be repulsed by the dead dog odor from the wound in his skull.

Doc Swift was standing in the shadows beneath the wooden stairs when he heard the door slam shut above and felt the frame shake as the German's boots came clomping down.

"Herr Gruber."

The German turned, squinted into the darkness. He wore a red bandana wrapped around the top of his skull and tied in a knot. Doc stepped out of the shadows.

Gruber looked him over, judging him. Gruber was a brawny man, larger than Doc, and he carried a pistol and wore a Bowie knife on his belt.

"If this is a robbery, you are taking a foolish chance," Gruber said.

"I'm not here to rob you," said Doc.

"Business?"

"Personal. Urgent."

"Then come to my office in the morning. Right now I am going to Dutch John's to eat a steak and play cards. I don't like to talk business while I eat and gamble," Gruber said, "and I don't want your company."

Doc held up a large clay jar with the lid tightly bound by rawhide cord.

"This is for you. I bring it from the Carolina mountains."

"A rare whiskey?" asked the German.

"I have brought these medicines to draw the sickness from the wound in your skull."

"Why?"

"I know your headaches are worse and your wound is growing putrid, and without proper treatment you will die soon. I am a medical doctor and a healer. I'm going to save your life."

The German stepped two paces closer to Doc and peered at him.

"You have no reason to help me," the German said.

"But I do," Doc said. "Had you rather die?"

"How do you know me?"

"A Cherokee storyteller told me about the German who came out of Comancheria with a hatchet in his skull," Doc said. "I looked up your medical history and read it. While I am healing you, I'll take my payment in information. There are a few questions you must answer."

Gruber grunted and a pain twitched his cheek. He felt an itching of sweat on his bare skull beneath the bandana, except he knew it was blood and he felt it leaking down between his shoulder blades.

"Let's go to my office," Gruber said.

They walked past Dutch John's onto Pecan Street. Three pigs, snorting and huffing, trotted across the road in front of them. Hens squawked in the trees. The night air felt close and humid, and the breeze had stopped. Doc smelled the ginger tonic that soaked Gruber's clothes. He saw a drop of blood roll from beneath Gruber's bandana and slide down his massive neck. The moon had risen above the crown of hills on the eastern rim of town. The eastern sky was pale, but beyond the river and the cliffs to the west the sky was ominous black. The German stopped at the PARADISE FOR SALE sign, unlocked his office door and lit a whale oil lamp on the oak table that he used for a desk.

Gruber sat down in a chair and peeled the bandana off his head.

His bald skull looked as if an elf's plow had turned a furrow up the middle of the field, and one inch of the plow blade had broken off. Rotting meat festered along the furrow of iron.

Doc stuck the dipper into a water barrel, half filled a bowl on the sideboard, and shook in a mound of herbs. He poured poppy syrup and crushed ladybugs from the clay jar into the bowl. The smell was like roses mixed with vinegar. Doc had been given the herbs—bear's bed ferns, cinnamon ferns, crow's shin, beaver's paw roots and many others—and ladybugs by Knows All Charlie, who also selected the most potent of his poppy syrup to bind the mixture. There was nothing modern medicine could do for the German. An axe had cleft his skull and sunk into his brain. He should be dead. Dr. Bebault, a prominent Boston surgeon visiting in San Antonio, had probed along the sides of the blade to determine if it might be removed, but the powerful German screamed in pain and threw down the men holding his arms and legs. The examination ended because of the patient's obstinance. Dr. Bebault was of the orthodox school of physicians who believed surgery and pain fit naturally together in God's plan. Dr. Bebault refused on principle to use ether, nitrous oxide, chloroform, opium or anesthesia of any sort, not even whiskey. "Would you want to be full of narcotics, blind drunk, when something as crucial as silver knives are slicing into your skin and your very life is at the threshold? Don't you want to feel every sensation?" Dr. Bebault asked him.

"Yah! I do!" Gruber said. He was persuaded by the reputation of this eminent Boston surgeon, who wore thick eyeglasses and had the forearms of a stevedore.

But when Dr. Bebault began digging a knife point into the furrow in Gruber's skull, the German changed his mind and with a roar hurled his handlers down and grabbed the knife away from the surgeon.

Dr. Bebault parted from Gruber with hearty good wishes, reminding him that every day he lived was truly a gift from God.

"Sometimes my head hurts so bad I want to die," Gruber told Doc Swift. "Will you pull the blade out of me?"

"I'm not keen on surgery. First let us stop your pain," Doc said.

The water and the herbs and the crushed ladybugs and the poppy syrup mixed into a mud that Doc's fingers painted in a thick plaster on the puckered flesh along the edge of the inch-high blade that showed above the German's skull.

With his fingers touching Gruber's wound, Doc spoke the Cherokee healing words: "O Man and Woman, you have caused it. You have put the intruder under him. Ha! Now you have come from the Sun Land. You have brought the small red seats with your feet resting upon them. Ha! Now they have swiftly moved away from you. Relief is accomplished. Let it not be for one night alone. Let the relief come at once."

"I thought you were a medical doctor," the German said.

"I am."

"What's this silly talk, then?"

"I'm a medical doctor and a healer. You need all the powers we can muster. Now be still and listen to me," Doc said.

Laying hands on the German's skull, Doc repeated the healing words four times. The German sat stiffly. Beads of blood rolled down his forehead.

"Will this cure me?" the German asked.

Doc said, "It will if you follow the taboo. For four nights you must apply the poultice to your wound. For seven days you must not touch a squirrel, a dog, a cat, a fish or a woman. You must sit on a seat by yourself for four days. Let no one else sit on the same seat, even if you should leave it for a moment."

"This is nonsense."

"You will have no pain if you do as I say."

"Will I live long enough to get married?"

"I believe you will," Doc said. "Tell me how this wound happened."

"You wouldn't believe it. Nobody believes it. They said the hatchet in my brain made me crazy. Oompossible! Oompossible! That's what they told me. Well, fork all of them and their mothers. I know what I saw. Say, my head is feeling like it's got ice on it."

"The pain? How is it? It's gone, isn't it?"

"There is no pain," the German said. His eyes followed as Doc Swift walked around the front of the desk. Doc wiped his hands on his trousers and sat in a chair facing Gruber. "There is no pain," the German said again, in wonderment. "But I feel sleepy. This is very nice. So sleepy."

"You will sleep for many hours."

"No, first I eat a hunk of meat at Dutch John's," the German said, and sat up.

"Too late, Herr Gruber. The medicine is taking effect. You're not going anywhere except to sleep. When you wake, I've mixed up five more batches of this poultice. You smear it on your head and sleep again. The fourth time you wake, go to Dutch John's and eat all the meat you can put in your stomach, and then apply the poultice once more and sleep again while your body heals itself. Perhaps Mrs. Hunboldt will look in on you while your wound mends. But do not touch her."

"How do you know her? Did you fork her?"

"Your lawyer Ridgewood Bone told me."

"That crooked bastard, I'm going to kill him. He cheats my Germans out of their land with his fees for doing nothing, and now he spreads tales about my Ruth."

The German blinked his eyes and rubbed his big, broken knuckles across his lips. He was terribly sleepy. What was happening here? Had this stranger poisoned him? But, mysteriously, joyfully, there was no pain. Even if he was dying now, it was good because there was no more pain.

"A murdering, betraying savage Comanche buried this blade in my skull," said Gruber. "I tell you, those Comanches are different than real people. They might look much like real people, but under the skin they are savage animals."

"Tell me what you saw out there," Doc said.

"Me and my business partners with ten wagons of trade goods was crossing a good-size stream the Comanches call the Little Pigeon River in the hill country in Comancheria. The Jew was our leader. I was driving the fourth wagon, so I was just following, not paying close mind to where the Little Pigeon River was, or our location on it. The Jew was taking us to the camp of this savage named Osage Killer. The Talking Man, they call him. He came out to meet us, and he smiled. Hell, we had done trade in peace with Osage Killer and his family up on the Arkansas. I thought we were friendly. Suddenly the look on his face changed. He give a shout and they leaped on us, hacking with knives and hatchets, even the women and girls stabbing and slashing us. They was hacking off my partners' arms and hair and ripping their cocks right out from between their legs while Osage Killer was trying to pull his axe out of my skull so he could give me another whack. They shot arrows into the Jew. Osage Killer and his family murdered my business partners and stole our goods. Just look what he did to my head. He would have finished killing me but the—oompossible!—the mountain ape scared him off. There was a roar from the woods, and the ape come tromping into camp beating his chest. Them Comanches took off running. They're scared of ghosts and monsters. Osage Killer was cussing all the way, but he ran as fast as he could. Listen, Mister, Doctor, medicine man, whoever you are, I'm going to sleep now. I'll finish my story tomorrow. Thank you very much. There's no pain. This is very good."

The German's face fell forward onto the desk and he snored.

Doc took a hypodermic syringe from the leather pouch of medical items in a coat pocket. He filled the syringe from a brown pint bottle of cocaine solution. With a grunt Doc heaved Gruber, still snoring, into an upright position in his chair. Doc pinched a thumb and two fingers of flesh from the German's forearm and plunged the needle into the vein.

Gruber felt himself coming back up from a deep black pit, rising through exhaustion, his heart thumping, his eyes opening. He saw the stranger sitting now on the edge of the desk. The stranger was staring into his eyes. The German felt a gentle smack of a hand on his cheek.

"Finish your story," Doc said.

"My heart is going to blow up."

"No, your heart will calm and you will sleep again. But first, you must finish your story. What about the ape?"

"The ape dragged me into his cave. Blood was pouring in my eyes, but I could tell the cave entrance was a small opening partway up a hill, hidden by boulders and brush. Them hills and mountains all through Comancheria are full of limestone caves. When I got inside—oompossible!—I saw it was not just a cave, it was a huge cavern with many ice columns falling from the ceiling way up in the darkness and many passages leading off and a kind of altar in the middle of the main room. Oompossible! I saw rooms filled with gold coins, gold pots, gold shields, gold necklaces, gold statues of strange-looking people with big eyes and big lips. Gold bars stacked up three times as high as my head. And jewels, too. Rubies, emeralds in necklaces and chains and crowns. Oompossible. All that gold. So much wealth. Holy Jesus, I'm breathing so fast I can't catch my breath. I think my heart is going to tear open."

Doc pressed his fingertips against the German's eyelids.

"Shut your eyes. Breathe deeply," Doc said.

The German moaned, and his respiration became more regular and a bit slower. Doc counted the man's pulse. Dangerously fast.

"How did you get out alive?" Doc asked.

His eyes shut, the German said, "There was a peculiar savage with his face burned and painted black. Funny little spaghetti legs. He moved around the cavern by using his hands and arms, dragging his legs behind. I think he took pity on me. I swear he talked back and forth with the ape. To hear them talking and crooning, it was hard to tell which was human and which was beast. It was the ape that was the master. Together they tried to pull the hatchet out of my skull. The ape was the strongest, and he broke the blade off. I saw a white light, and God was with me for I don't know how long. I heard music and soft voices talking about me. I couldn't tell what was going on, so I supposed I was dead. Then everything got black and very silent, and when I came out of the dark place I was walking on the Camino Real north of San Antonio with an armload of gold. Oompossible, huh? Look at me. Didn't I start my land business using money from the gold? Do you see the mark of the hatchet? I'm not crazy."

"What does the ape look like?"

"Long arms, covered with hair, sort of light gray, nearly white. Big, bulgy forehead. If you put a barber to his face he might look almost human. But he wasn't human. He had a horrible odor, a stinking ape."

"Have you ever seen an ape before this one?" Doc asked.

"I've seen drawings. I saw two Java apes in a circus in New York, but they were skinny, pitiful creatures, not like the ape that saved me from Osage Killer. This was a big ape, taller than me, could almost have been a hairy person except for the funny-shaped skull—and that god-awful stink."

"Are apes known to roam the mountains in Comancheria?"

"I never heard of any until this one."

"Why didn't you go back for the gold?" Doc asked.

The German snorted. "Never. Never. I don't want nothing more to do with them savages or anything else in Comancheria, except I pray I could be the death of Osage Killer. But you're looking at a dead man. They've already killed me. What chance would I have to get their gold and escape across Comancheria with it even if I could find the Little Pigeon River and the cave again? None. Oompossible."

"Can you tell me where the cavern is?"

The German opened one eye. His lips tried to turn up in a smirk, but his facial muscles went limp.

"That's what you want, eh? The gold? I don't know where it is. Somewhere in the hills, more north than south—I don't know how many days west of here, maybe weeks, maybe longer. It's in a cavern on the Little Pigeon River, and that's all I know. You'll never get that gold, healer. Them savages will kill you and make a squaw's robe out of your skin."

"It's not the gold I'm after," said Doc.

"Why not? Everyone is after gold."

With his elbows on the desk, Gruber lifted his hands to clasp his face, and in an instant he was asleep despite the injection of cocaine solution. The sedation of the rose-smelling Cherokee poultice with its base of poppy syrup had overwhelmed the energizing quality of the South American coca bush.

Doc timed the pulse in the German's wrist. The man's heart was pounding hard but in a steady rhythm. The German snored at his desk with his face in his hands and his skull smeared with the red mud of herbs and ladybugs and poppy syrup, smelling of roses and vinegar. Doc parted a curtain and saw Gruber's bedroom. It was large and tidy with the sheet stretched tight on the bed. He thought about dragging the German to the bed, but he recalled Knows All Charlie's healing instructions that the patient must remain in a seat. Doc considered the axe blade in the skull of the sleeping body and decided Gruber's story must be true, as Knows All Charlie had foreseen. But the German had said nothing about wisdom—only gold and murder. Doc extinguished the lamp. He left the office and walked toward Boone's Livery Stable, feeling a sprinkling of rain and a freshening wind. From the black western sky above the boundary of Comancheria, Doc saw a tree of lightning and a few seconds later heard the distant drumming of thunder.

# 5

Cullasaja Swift watched the tall man moving toward her campfire, his neck bobbing, his beak probing. He reminded her of a crane wading in shallow water, searching for a fish among the reeds.

"I see you fixing food for more than one," Henry Longfellow said, squinting at the Cherokee girl's form under her soft deerskin dress. He detected swelling breasts, hips that begged to be bitten, a crotch that gave forth heat that he could feel and smell. It was the smell of the devil. She would be pleading for his prick. In his mind he could already hear her moaning, overwhelmed by her thirst for wickedness as he squirted in her mouth.

"Yes, I am," Cullasaja said. "I am not alone."

"You a Cherokee girl?"

"The spring is over there if you want water. If you don't want water, you'd best be on your way."

"You speak English very well. You're a schoolhouse Indian."

Cullasaja began judging the distance to the cooking fire, where her new Colt pistol lay in a fold of her blanket.

"I know a lot of Cherokee girls," Henry said, neck bobbing. "They like me, those young Indian girls do. I know what they want most in this life, you see?"

Longfellow fired a shotgun blast into the tree above his head. With a clatter, birds cried and flew away. Leaves and bits of wood fell onto Henry's hat and shoulders. The boom of the shotgun was followed by an instant of utter stillness, and then they could hear rain starting to tap lightly among the trees.

"Now we'll see who comes running," Henry said, grinning at the Cherokee girl. He saw fascination in her eyes. Rare was the mind that could bear the truth without turning away, and she was a rare one, a strong one. She wanted him, he knew. She pretended to reject him because she was wicked and coy, playing with him, seducing him. She needed for him to take her by force.

Cullasaja moved toward the campfire. Reaching out with one long leg, the tall man hopped into her path.

"I don't hear anyone coming," he said. "We've got plenty of time to do what you want to do."

"I want you to step back and stand away from me," Cullasaja said.

"No, I know what you really want," Henry said.

With his left hand he balled up a mound of his crotch.

"Come closer, girl," he said.

"I'm not alone," Cullasaja repeated.

"It's the devil you seek, and you have found him. I am the devil," Henry said.

With the point of his saber, he ripped down the front of her dress, exposing her naked flesh. He saw her dark nipples and the patch of sweet hair. He felt his penis grow hard as a log.

Cullasaja leaped sideways, toward the blanket by the fire.

Henry swung the dull edge of the saber and cracked Cullasaja on the shin six inches below her right kneecap, and they heard her bone snap. Cullasaja tumbled onto the blanket. A rush of pain soared up and down her leg. She bit her lower lip and began fumbling in the folds of the blanket.

She saw the tall man tear open his britches and let them drop to his ankles. She saw his stiff penis rising above her. Henry looked into her eyes as she looked at his penis. He knew she wanted him to explode in her mouth, to suck him dry. He was in ecstasy already, anticipating the power of his squirting.

"Stop fighting, girl."

Cullasaja felt the pistol grip in her hand. The tall man prodded her forearm with the tip of his saber, and blood appeared. A fresh wave of pain rose up from her leg.

With his left hand Henry was rubbing the head of his penis, and she could see that it was wet. He was intent upon his penis, caressing it, staring into her eyes, poking her with the tip of the saber, in his obsession not noticing that her right hand was hidden in the blanket.

"All right, you want me to put it in for you, don't you, little girl?" he said.

As he bent toward her, she lifted the Colt pistol and stuck it into his face.

Henry's long neck recoiled back. He looked at the strange weapon, and then he laughed.

"That pistol is not even primed, girl. By the time you could prime it and cock it, I'd chop your head off with my saber," he said. "You're wearing out my patience. You drop that pistol and put my prick in your mouth, or I'll kill you right now and squirt all over your corpse."

"I'll shoot you if I must," Cullasaja said.

"I can't wait any longer, girl. You take me now."

They heard the whinny of Lamar's bay horse, rearing up in warning, and then the hooves of Donnybrook pounding the muddy road.

Henry Longfellow turned toward the noise and saw with peculiarly intense clarity a wide-shouldered man leaning from the saddle of a running horse. Henry cursed himself that he'd emptied his shotgun, but he slashed the air in front of him with his saber—and felt suddenly jolted as Doc Swift dived out of his saddle and slammed Henry's body against the trunk of an oak tree.

Doc smashed his left fist into Henry's solar plexus and then his right fist against the hinge of the jaw beneath Henry's left ear. Henry saw bright balls of color and felt tree bark grinding into his back and his skull. Henry's head bounced off the tree, and Doc's left fist hammered his right temple, and Henry saw a dazzling burst of sunlight, as though a bright new day was beginning. This could not be happening, he told himself, this was all wrong, and then Henry slid down the tree trunk on his back and lay unconscious. Independent of his awareness, Henry's penis stood erect on its own.

"Cully, don't move your leg," Doc said.

He knelt beside his sister. He found a compound fracture of her right tibia. The bone protruded about an inch. Doc grabbed his Italian leather medical satchel from beside his bedroll. He took out a brown bottle of tincture of opium that contained sixty percent morphine. Doc grabbed a jar of poppy syrup. Cullasaja choked off a groan of pain.

"I was about to kill him, Rom," she said.

"Swallow from this bottle a couple of times."

"I don't need opium," she said.

"I'm the doctor here, Cully. Take your medicine."

Doc opened his Italian leather suitcase and tore one of his white shirts into strips. He broke off a straight oak limb. He pulled two handfuls of grass and packed it mixed with poppy syrup into the wound in his sister's leg. With his strong hands he rejoined the tibia bone and bandaged the wound with another of his shirts and continued working quickly to pad the limb and tie the splint into place with strips of fine cotton that had been tailored in London.

"Are you feeling cold?" Doc asked.

"No, I'm not going into shock," said Cullasaja. "I'll tell you if I start feeling like fainting. This opium compound is already working. I feel marvelous . . . Rommy! He's sitting up!"

Doc took two steps, kicked Henry Longfellow in the kidney and returned to finish splinting her leg.

"The fool thought my pistol needs priming, but he's never seen one of these new revolvers. I was about to kill him," she said.

Cullasaja stared at the length of the fallen tall man, whose muscles were jerking in pain. In another moment, she thought, she would have pulled the trigger. She would have taken a life. She dug her fingers into her brother's shoulder as he gently shifted her broken shin bone back into one piece. Staring at the ridiculous figure of the tall man, crumpled at the base of the tree, his trousers around his ankles, his penis drooping at last, she felt her brother's hands and his chest as he leaned against her and bound two sticks to her leg in a splint. She lay naked before her brother, her dress opened all the way down the front by the saber. She realized her brother hadn't seen her naked since she was three years old. She began to settle into a deeply relaxed daydream exceptional for its vivid colors.

"I didn't want to kill that man, Rommy," she said. "Please, don't you kill him."

Doc opened another of their suitcases that had been borne by the mules and removed a cotton dress. His sister helped him take off her torn doeskin. She felt carefree, nude in the wilderness, and started humming a Cherokee song. Doc wrapped the cotton dress around his sister's body.

"We've got to get you out of here and back across the river before the flood comes," Doc said.

"What about him?" she said.

Doc looked around at Henry Longfellow, who was struggling to sit up. Blood seeped from his nose and lips and ears. His breath had a whistle in it.

"Yes. We must deal with him," Doc said.

He rose and walked over to Henry, whose eyes fell to the stranger's black leather boots. They looked like foreign boots to Henry.

"Pull up your britches," Doc said.

Henry looked up at this angry stranger and wiggled into the trousers, each move a dozen agonies. He said, "Wooo."

He spread his long fingers on his chest to test his heaving heart, and wheezed a fleck of spittle.

"Let me explain," Henry said. "My name is Henry Longfellow. I am a personal adviser to President Lamar and representative of the Republic of Texas."

"How did he break your leg, Cully?" asked Doc.

"With his saber."

"Stand up," Doc said to the tall man.

Clutching the trunk of the tree, Henry clawed to his feet, hauling up his trousers.

"I am on my way to Austin on an important errand for the President, a very official matter, but this Indian girl stopped me," Henry said. "I am in a hurry, but she tempted me with her sex. These Cherokees are like animals, the way they do it when they're in heat."

Doc grabbed Henry by the throat and dragged him over to the stump of a tree that had long ago been chopped down for firewood.

"Feel that rain?" Henry said. "It's coming down harder. I need to be off to catch the ferry on President's business before the river comes out of its banks. You'll get in a great deal of trouble if you interfere with me."

Henry knew himself to be a strong man, but he felt helpless as the stranger's fingers dug into his biceps and threw him onto the ground.

"You're hurting me," Henry said. "I'll report you to the Texas Rangers. They'll hunt you down and hang you from a tree. You and the Indian bitch both."

"Lift your right leg onto that stump," Doc said.

Doc picked up Henry's saber.

"Whatever for?" Henry said.

"Do it," Doc said.

"I tell you, I am very close to President Lamar. You are already in serious difficulty, but I can still save you."

"Lift your leg up there."

Henry laid his ankle on the stump, his trouser leg sliding down almost to the knee to reveal a long, thin white bone covered with hairless, translucent skin.

"Certainly you don't intend to break my leg," Henry said. "This is barbaric. White men do not do such things to each other. We have a system of laws."

"Rommy, let him go," Cullasaja said.

"This must be done," he said.

Doc raised the saber above his right shoulder.

"No!" screamed Henry Longfellow. "Please, no! Have mercy!"

Swinging the saber like an axe, Doc brought the dull edge down on Henry's shin and cracked the bone in half.

# 6

**B**rown water swirled around the hooves of their horses and mules as Doc urged them aboard the *Waterloo Queen*. He had paid Googleye sixty dollars in gold—much more than the boat had cost to build—to borrow the *Queen* for his crossing. Googleye, wisely fearing the flood, had stayed on the north shore. Cullasaja sat straight in the saddle on Donnybrook, the pain of her splinted leg removed by opium-morphine compound and by poppy syrup. As Doc jumped aboard and untied the ferry from a tree, he felt the deck rise beneath his feet. Rainwater from the monster storm that had broken over the western hills was pouring into the Colorado upstream and lifting the river fast.

Rain beat upon them as Doc poled the *Waterloo Queen* out into the current. Their three mules carrying all their luggage stood forlornly, ears down, sensing doom. The two thoroughbred Kentucky horses clattered nervously on the planks. Doc's plan was to pole into the current and to fight crosswise until they were carried against the far diagonal bank downriver. Because of Cullasaja's broken leg, he was determined to find shelter for her in Austin. There was no thought of waiting out the storm on the south shore. No telling how long the rain would last and the river would stay at flood. Cullasaja needed to be warm and dry and cared for at once, lest her leg wound become infected or the bone heal crooked.

A fat sow and three smaller pigs struggled past the *Waterloo Queen*, keeping their noses above water. A swimming possum bumped against the boat and tried to crawl aboard. Through the gray rain Doc could see Googleye standing at his landing on the north bank as the ferry picked up speed and left Googleye and the landing behind. Doc threw all his muscle into ramming the pole into the river bottom and got one more strong heave before the pole no longer touched bottom.

The *Queen* rushed on an oblique course toward a neck of land a hundred feet downriver. Doc calculated the *Queen* would strike the bar, which was still four feet above the surface, and he was starting to tie Cullasaja's arms around the neck of Donnybrook, the strongest swimmer on the *Waterloo Queen*, when his sister shouted, "Rommy! Look out!"

Roaring at them faster than racing horses, sounding like a mountain falling down, rose an ocean-like wave of brown water twenty five feet high that carried boulders the size of houses, and trees, animals, boards and blood and pieces of west Austin—a hand stuck up from the water, fingers imploring as it swirled toward them.

Doc grabbed his sister in his arms and pulled her against his body, as if he could protect her from the power of the giant rolling wave that crashed over the *Waterloo Queen* and flipped the boat upside down, sucking Doc and Cullasaja under the water along with the horses, the mules and the baggage.

She was aware of the boat tearing apart above her head, the planks splintering and flying, and she rolled over and over under the water, tight in the arms of her brother. Cullasaja's mind flickered with pictures of events she recognized, and she felt calm and at peace, with her brother clutching her against his body. They spun in the current, whirled and tumbled, clinging together.

Then her head popped above the water. She felt a slam as her brother's back struck the spit of land, which was all but covered by the river, and she knew she was being pulled upward, and that Romulus was lifting a heavier weight than he would have ever dreamed he could lift, and so she roused from her intensely secure state that was made of opium and of having peeked through the gate into the other side of death, and she grabbed a root and fought to clear herself from the river as Romulus heaved backward and they both fell onto land.

Doc and Cullasaja inched along the vanishing neck of earth, him with forearms under her armpits, helping her move as the pain in her leg wrenched forth a scream that was lost in the booming of the torrent.

He glanced downriver and saw Donnybrook and Cully's thoroughbred and the three mules tumbling and turning and thrashing and being swept away amid twirling baggage.

Doc and Cullasaja crawled onto solid earth and then kept crawling another fifty yards to be safe for now from the flooding river. She sat up in the mud and leaned forward over her twisted leg. The wooden splints had been torn off by the current. The bone had parted again and poked through her flesh. The matted grass and poppy syrup were washed away. Her wound was bleeding. Cullasaja touched her forehead to her knee. Doc knew her spirit was trying to make peace with her pain. He had no more opium to give her, and only wet grass and mud to stop her bleeding. His Italian leather physician's satchel containing all medicines and tools was in the river on its way to Mexico, along with their money, horses, three new revolvers from the Colt factory in New Jersey, his rifle, their citizenship documents, Cully's books and clothes, gifts for Chief Bowl—everything was gone, including his Bible.

Three miles south of the flooding Colorado, President Lamar's bay horse plodded through the rain on the road that led southwest to San Antonio.

Henry Longfellow draped across the *concho*-studded saddle on his belly, his long neck and arms hanging down one side of the horse, his long pale legs hanging down the other. Henry's right leg flopped awkwardly with each stride of the horse, each movement sending a streak of pain from his toes to his scalp.

Fearing he might fall off the horse and drown ignominiously in some shallow rut or gully that would now be full of rainwater, Henry fought to stay conscious, and the pain kept his mind sharp and cold.

In his mind it was clear what had befallen him. A wicked Cherokee girl had seduced him into an ambush by a thug. Henry swore he would endure and see both of them dead.

# 7

At the height of a yellow noon, a Spanish mustang carrying Captain Matthew Caldwell pounded chunks out of the earth at a dead run toward the line of trees that marked the Guadalupe River sixty miles southeast of San Antonio.

Caldwell glanced back over his left shoulder at the Mexican cavalry patrol that was a mile behind him but coming on in a gallop led by a scout riding a mule. The mustang's ears flicked toward Caldwell as the animal listened for instructions, and then the ears flopped forward to pick up information of what lay ahead. The horse's eyeballs were wild and wide, his chest heaved with strain, his breathing came in great groans. Caldwell knew the mustang—rangy and long-legged, a dun with black mane and tail—was pouring his life into this run.

Clods and dust flew. The horse and rider crashed through the brush and arrived at the bluff that fell to the river ten feet below. Without hesitating the Spanish mustang and the Texas Ranger leaped off the bluff. In midair Caldwell looked down at the water and heard the mustang give forth a rasping sigh, as if this moment of lightness was an almost unbearable joy.

Minutes later a dark little Indian heeled his mule at the lip of the west bank of the Guadalupe.

The sleeves of his cotton shirt hung heavy with sweat as he lifted his straw hat and wiped his forehead and looked down at deep hoofprints in the water's edge ten feet below. His right knee nudged a bugle that clung by a leather thong to the wooden horn of his saddle. The Indian removed the nub of a cornhusk cigarette from his hat band. Tobacco crumbled in his fingers. With a sad little shrug the Indian tossed the cigarette down into the water and watched red shiner minnows tug at bits of tobacco that twirled off in the current.

The Guadalupe River twisted down from its source in the mountains of Comancheria. During the recent flood the Guadalupe was a mile wide as it dropped off the escarpment and chose its course across the coastal plain, and ten miles wide where it emptied into San Antonio Bay on the Gulf of Mexico.

In periods of drought—which came about every fifteen years and were so harsh that it seemed human life might no longer endure here—the river would become little more than an interesting creek; gray boulders would rise from puddles in the riverbed and reach toward debris that floodwater had left seventy feet high in tree branches.

Now the river was up, but the water was clear in the shallows and moved with a pleasing, peaceful gurgle past yellow violets and red strawberries that bloomed in the shade of pecan trees that did not begin to make branches until the trunks had climbed fifty feet into the air. Hackberries and white elms formed an understory beneath the canopy of pecans and red oaks. Grapevines as thick as a man's leg dropped like cables from the roof of the forest more than one hundred feet above the river.

The little Indian's eyes looked up from the flowing water and swept the opposite bank. His thighs moved with the labored breathing of his mule. He listened to the music of the river. He heard squirrels fussing among their nests far above, and blue jays screeched; the squirrels and the jays were always at war over the pecans. The Indian's saddle creaked as he put his hat back on. He was careful to keep his hand away from the bugle, for he knew to be wary of every gesture when his instincts warned of danger.

The Indian sensed he was confronting death across fifty yards of water.

On the other side of the river, concealed by flowers and chinquapins, and by the trunk of a pecan tree big around as a wagon, Matthew Caldwell lay with the carved walnut stock of his double-barreled ten-gauge shotgun that he called Sweet Lips pressed against his right cheek, aiming at the dark little Indian.

A deerfly buzzed at Caldwell's nose. A lizard crept along a pecan root to arrive at the strangeness of metal of Sweet Lips and freeze into gray, scaly ridges of bark.

"He's gone, Captain," the little Indian called from the far bank.

Caldwell peered along the Damascus steel barrels of Sweet Lips and saw a young officer on a thoroughbred horse appear beside the Indian scout.

The officer's black and silver hussar's helmet caught a spark from the sun as he studied the bank where Caldwell lay hidden. Despite the warmth of midday, the officer wore a black cloak over his red tunic. His hair was braided into loops around each ear.

"It's too bad, but he's got away by now," said the Indian.

The officer looked down at the hoofprints in the mud.

"He must have made a big jump for his hind hoofs to dig so deeply when he landed," the officer said. "That means he's frightened. He's running for his life. Look, there is silt floating in the tracks. He must have passed here only moments ago. Why is it I have to explain how to read signs to you over and over again? You're supposed to be a scout."

The young officer was speaking Spanish, but Caldwell recognized the accent as European. From the look of the cloak and the helmet and the braided loops of hair, he was French or Hungarian. Military academies in France and Hungary trained mercenary officers for service in Mexico, and professors from Prussia taught them to speak Spanish in an angry tone, as if defying foreigners not to understand them.

"Go across and look on the other side of the river," the officer said.

"There's no use," said the Indian.

"You damn fool, I'm giving you an order," the officer said.

Entering through the trees and underbrush behind the officer came a white Arabian stallion ridden by a man whose face was shaded by a sombrero covered with green oilcloth that was strapped to the crown by a chain of silver *conchos*. The chaps that protected his legs from thorns were made of mountain goat skins. A bullwhip was tied coiled against his heavy Spanish saddle alongside a drinking shell that had been a clam when the ocean had covered this land.

"Why have you stopped here?" the man said.

Caldwell felt a rush of joy and excitement. Fortune was delivering to him his old enemy, the murderer Cristolphe Rublo. The aim of Sweet Lips shifted toward the chest of Rublo. Fortune would soon provide a fine white Arabian stallion as well, Caldwell thought. Caldwell's Spanish mustang lay in an elm mott twenty yards away, dead from an exploded heart following the final mad run that had ended five days and nights of hard use as Caldwell rode his ranging patrol.

Caldwell had covered his sixty miles of territory back and forth from Goliad to the vicinity of San Antonio, looking for Indians or Mexicans, or trouble of any sort, always ready for sudden violence. He had found his area of the frontier peaceful other than a water-rights dispute between two neighbors that would wind up in shooting without doubt. There was nothing worth reporting to the ranging station at Boca Chica Crossing, where the Guadalupe River narrowed like the neck of an hour glass between two deep, wide pools. Caldwell had been on his way to a marriage agent in Houston City, ninety miles east of the river, to pick up the letter that awaited him from the bride in Germany he had asked to join him in Texas for arranged matrimony, sight unseen. It was common for mail to get lost in the Republic. But land speculators and marriage agents tended to hire the most expensive messengers and usually got their letters through. Caldwell had encountered the Mexican army expedition three miles west of the Guadalupe. He counted half a dozen mounted soldiers in the advance patrol and four mule-drawn wagons that transported maybe sixty infantry and their gear. He suspected they would be the lead party for a larger force. The peace treaty to end the revolution had been signed by Santa Anna at the demand of Sam Houston three years ago beneath a tree at San Jacinto, with Matthew Caldwell standing so close he could have broken the little emperor's neck with a blow from the butt of Sweet Lips. But the war had never ended. The Mexican Congress had torn up the treaty a month after it was signed. Santa Anna was back in command. The Mexican army kept making probes into the Republic of Texas. Both governments were desperate for money, but they continued to grapple in a homicidal embrace like two wounded foes who were determined to die together. Caldwell intended to circle this advance party and explore behind them, looking for the size of a main force, but a shout told him he had been seen, and he gigged his mustang into a run toward the river the Texans called the Warloop.

"He's gotten away by now," the Indian scout said.

"Are you sure that's Caldwell we're chasing?" asked Rublo, the aristocrat on the white stallion.

"Yes, that is Captain Caldwell," the officer said, annoyed. "That is the famous Old Paint."

"How do you know?" said Rublo. "There's no point keeping up the chase if this is just some surveyor."

"I saw him through my glass, clear as could be," the officer said.

"You recognized Caldwell?" Rublo said, doubting.

"How could I fail to recognize him? I saw him in the Fincus Hotel lobby in San Antonio before I reported to my army post. My God, what a show. He was like some theatrical star the way people stared at him and moved aside to give him space. How could I forget that black and white spotted beard, colored like the coat of a paint horse, and the black hair full as any woman's hanging down to his shoulders and the white deerskin tunic with the beads and fringes? Those big gray cat eyes? Now, you tell me, have I ever seen Old Paint?"

Rublo spoke to the scout. "Go across and have a look."

"There's no use," the scout said.

The scout's home was south of the Rio Grande, far from the Warloop, but he had heard of this Old Paint. He had heard Old Paint took the scalps and the ears of Mexicans and cut their bellies open.

"I'll shoot you if you don't," the officer said.

"I'll die either way," said the scout.

"Ten pesos for you to go across and have a look," Rublo said.

The Indian accepted a ten-peso note from Rublo, placed it inside his hat, climbed off his mule and led the beast down the sandy bank to the edge of the river. The Indian had not decided what to do, but he was ten pesos richer.

Caldwell felt a pinch as the deerfly bit his nose. With a short, sudden move of his left hand, Caldwell snatched the deerfly and crushed it in his fingers. He saw the Indian's dark eyes note the movement. The Indian looked straight across the river at the place Caldwell lay hidden. Turning up his palms in a gesture of futility, the Indian dropped his trousers and squatted. The mule waded a step into the river and thrust his mouth into the water and drank noisily. The other animals began crowding toward the smell of water, their riders trying to hold them back.

"What the devil are you doing?" the officer shouted at the scout.

"Your honorable sir, I am making a little mountain," said the scout.

"Why must you do that at this very moment?" the officer said.

"No man can rule over his own gut," said the Indian.

The officer turned toward the other soldiers. "Listen to me, men. This is a very famous Texas Ranger we are chasing. He is not only a Ranger captain and the sworn blood enemy of all Mexican patriots, he is also a congressman in the Assembly of the Republic of Texas. If we can capture or kill this man they call Old Paint, you'll be heroes. There will be medals for all of you."

The two soldiers in dirty blue cavalry uniforms scowled at the officer. Caldwell had seen Mexican conscripts forced from their villages or rousted from prisons fight with insane bravery at the command of foreign officers. He had seen Mexican soldiers who were barefoot, hungry and unpaid, many of whom had never fired a musket, howl and charge into certain death on orders from pimply boys from the military academies of Europe. But these two soldiers in cavalry uniforms stared at the officer as if he were urging them to embrace a leper.

"Aren't you finished?" the officer shouted down at the scout. "How much of that can you do?"

"I feel a big load more on the way," the Indian said, still squatting.

"This is the Texan they call Old Paint?" one of the soldiers asked the man on the white horse.

"Yes, because of his spotted beard. There's nothing magical about him," Rublo said. "He's just another gringo land robber and murderer. When we catch him, we'll hang him. Get out of my way, I'm crossing this river."

The young officer thrust out an arm to prevent Rublo from passing him.

"This is my command," the officer said.

The officer spurred his horse. The horse balked at the lip of the bluff. Unable to see what was directly ahead or below because of his double vision, which presented separate pictures of trees and vines in shades of gray, the frightened horse fought against the bit, waving his head up and down and from side to side, trying to judge what would be required. The officer whacked the horse's shoulder with his right hand and slammed his silver rowels into the horse's flanks. The horse reared and was surprised to find his forelegs coming down several feet below where anticipated. In terror and confusion the horse plunged down the sandy bank. The officer rode lightly and gracefully, but the horse broke both forelegs with sharp pops like sticks snapping.

The officer flew over the neck of the horse and sprawled face first into the river. Rising to his knees in the water, the officer gazed at his palms, bloodied by gravel. He emptied water out of his helmet. The officer waded out of the river. The horse struggled to stand up on broken legs. The horse snorted and screamed. Thinking the situation had resolved itself, the little Indian scout pulled up his trousers and knotted his rope belt.

"What a pity," said the officer, putting on his helmet. "That is a fine, courageous horse."

Up on the bluff, the two soldiers nodded. Rublo dismounted and led his white Arabian stallion down the sandy descent to the edge of the river. Rublo looked at the officer and said, "It's a pity to lose a good horse. If something had to get broken here, it should have been your neck."

"Shoot my horse," the officer said to the scout.

"Me?"

"I'd rather not do it myself," the officer said. "This horse has been dearer to me than any human friend."

"You want me to kill your horse for you?" asked the Indian.

The officer turned his head away. He was distressed by the animal's cries.

"I can't bear it," the officer said.

"In the name of God, let's get moving while we still have a chance to catch Old Paint—if this is Old Paint," said Rublo. "Shoot the fool's horse, please, little friend."

The Indian shrugged. He stuck his flintlock pistol against the horse's eyeball. The officer gazed toward the south bend of the river, where a browntail hawk cruised beneath the cathedral of arching trees. The cap snapped with a flash and an explosion and the smell of powder. Blood spurted onto the Indian's forearm. The horse squealed and flopped sideways with his muzzle in the sand. Smoke rose from the red hole where the eyeball had been. The dark little Indian began reloading his pistol. With tears on his cheeks, the officer looked at the dead thoroughbred, steamy mist drifting from the horse's head.

"I will ride your mule now," the officer said to the Indian.

"This skinny old mule of mine?" said the Indian, surprised.

"It's not much of a mule, true, but it will have to do," the officer said.

"This fine gentleman"—the Indian pointed toward Rublo—"is riding a horse far superior to my old mule. A noble officer like yourself shouldn't ride a mule."

Rublo waded into the river, leading his white stallion.

"What am I to ride if you take my mule?" the Indian said.

"I don't care what you ride," said the officer. He slapped water off the braids and buttons of his tunic and wrung water out of the hem of his cloak. "Esteban! Peña! Come down here and put my saddle and gear on this mule, and hurry up about it!"

The dark little Indian bit his lip and pondered his predicament.

"Peña! Esteban! Damn your eyes! I'll have both of you shot if you disobey me one more time!" shouted the officer.

The Indian glanced at the pecan tree that concealed Caldwell on the other side of the river. The Indian slowly lifted his reloaded pistol as if to tuck it inside his trousers. But he was considering the situation from his own best interest, his thin lips drawn tight, his dark eyes squinting.

He turned and raised his pistol and shot the officer in the chest.

The middle button of the tunic blew apart in a spray of blood and bone and tiny pieces of cloth. The officer flew backward, snagged a boot heel against a rock, twisted and fell facedown in the shallows of the Guadalupe River.

"Now they'll hang us all," wailed the trooper Esteban.

"The famous Texas Ranger killed the officer in an ambush," the Indian said. "You saw the Texan kill him, didn't you, noble gentleman?"

They heard the loud click of Peña cocking his scattergun.

"I don't give a damn about this foreign officer son of a bitch," said Rublo. "I spit on his stupid body. Who cares who killed him?"

"I don't trust this noble gentleman," Peña said. "I think he will report us to the general, and they will stretch our necks."

Rublo yanked a long-barreled percussion-cap pistol out of a saddle holster and pointed it back and forth from the Indian to Peña.

"Indio, get on your mule," Rublo said. "You two troopers, come down here at once. I am in command now, as an agent of President Santa Anna and the government of Mexico. We are going to catch that Texas Ranger. The three of you will ride in front of me, so you don't shoot me in the back."

"We can shoot you in the back and the front right here without riding across the river," Peña said.

"If you harm me, Santa Anna himself will scourge your villages and destroy your families," Rublo said. "I am no stupid young foreigner. This very land we are on, my family has owned it for centuries. My family domain stretches many leagues to the north and to the east. Threatening me is like threatening your own nation. You will be harshly dealt with unless we catch this Texas Ranger!"

The little Indian peered across the river and yelled:

"Hey, Old Paint! You have seen what happened here. I did my best. Now you must kill this rich man for us. I promise to go home to the mountains and never chase you again."

Rublo suddenly understood the little Indian's behavior.

"Caldwell!" Rublo shouted. "Is it you?"

What the little Indian and the troopers next saw was to them an enchanted moment that struck them with awe.

Caldwell revealed himself from the vines and flowers on the opposite bank of the river. He took off his floppy hat to show his face. His gray cat eyes seemed to glow against sun-weathered skin above the dappled beard and mustache. Black and white chest hair thrust around the suspenders Caldwell wore on an otherwise bare and muscular torso. Twin Paterson Navy five-shooter pistols in holsters swung from each suspender. A bone-handled knife in a sheath stuck out from his right hip. He could feel the derringer concealed inside his right moccasin boot. Sweet Lips lay in the cradle of Caldwell's arms.

"You see?" the little Indian said to his army comrades. "That foreign officer led us into an ambush, like I said."

"Ambush?" cried Rublo. "He is one against our four! At last I have captured you, Caldwell! Throw down your guns!"

Caldwell laughed. He cocked one of the two hammers on Sweet Lips.

"Surrender or die in your tracks, Caldwell!" shouted Rublo.

Caldwell squeezed one trigger of Sweet Lips. The hammer struck the cap in the percussion lock, and the roar of Sweet Lips echoed along the river like the boom of a cannon. The shot tore off a tree limb the size of a human arm on the bluff above Rublo. The branch crashed to the ground between Esteban and Peña. Splinters and dust of bark drifted down on them. Squirrels and jays ceased their shrill disputes in the canopy of leaves. A turtle slid off a log and *plomped* into the Warloop.

"I am no friend of this rich gentleman who owns so much land, Old Paint," the little Indian said. "I am not mad at you. I want to go home to my wife and family in the mountains."

"I don't fight for this rich bastard, either," called Esteban. "He don't speak for me, Texas Ranger."

"You disgrace the uniform of Mexico," Rublo said.

"Hey, a uniform means nothing to me," yelled Peña. He plucked off his shako and hurled it into the river. He ripped open his tunic and began struggling out of it, holding his scattergun aimed at Rublo. "I was a clerk in a bank until they dragged me into the army. I am no soldier. Look—here's what this uniform means to me!"

Peña wadded his tunic and threw it toward the water. The tunic fluttered as far as the sandy slope, where it fell with sleeves spread wide.

"It appears it's just you and me, Rublo," said Caldwell, his baritone voice in clear frontier Mexican carrying across the river.

"So be it," Rublo said.

"You can't hit me from there with that pistol," said Caldwell. "But Sweet Lips can blow you to hell. Either you swim your horse over to me, or Sweet Lips will knock you down in the Warloop and one of these former soldiers will swim your horse over to me. Take your choice."

"You will kill me if I come over there," Rublo said.

"Maybe not," said Caldwell. "I'll damn sure kill you if you keep standing where you are."

"Kill him now, Old Paint," said the little Indian.

"No. Wait. I will bring you my horse," Rublo said.

"Dump your weapons in the river," Caldwell said.

The little Indian, Peña and Esteban all lifted their weapons relucantly.

"I mean the noble gentleman, not you boys," Caldwell said. "You boys can keep your guns and go home if you swear never to come back to Texas."

"On my word of honor," said Esteban, who was removing his tunic. "I entered the army in handcuffs with a whip laid to my back. Not because I had a burning desire to see Texas."

Rublo dropped his pistol into the river and waded deeper, leading the Arabian stallion.

"What is the name of your battalion?" Caldwell said.

"It is not my battalion," said Peña. "I renounce it! Because a few pesos were missing from my bank, they stuck this filthy uniform on me. I didn't steal the money. I am innocent. I don't even know how to shoot a gun."

"What battalion is it you are renouncing?" Caldwell asked.

"It's called the Volunteers of Monclova," said Peña. "Ha! Some volunteers! Rich gentlemen like this one here and foreign officers are the only volunteers in the battalion. The rest of us are from the prisons."

"What are you doing this far into Texas?" asked Caldwell.

"I didn't know this is Texas," Peña said. He had stripped to the waist, and his ribs showed that he was much underweight. "The general said we are chasing Comanches who have been stealing horses and cattle and murdering Mexican ranchers. But I swear I didn't know this is Texas. It looks like Coahuilla to me."

"This is Mexico, not Texas," shouted Rublo, who was now swimming with the stallion. "There is no such thing as Texas!"

"Who is your general?" Caldwell asked.

"His name is Savariego," said gaunt Peña, who began retching in a small way and blinking his eyes, feeling dizzy. He needed food. He had to be gone from this place. If this was Texas, he hated it. "The battalion is hunting Comanches, but Savariego is willing to strike at Austin if it can be done by surprise. What is Austin? I don't even know. That rich bastard swimming the river with his white horse, he is a friend of Savariego. He wants plunder."

"That's a lie!" shouted Rublo, arms around the stallion's neck as the horse swam smartly, leaving a wake across midstream.

"Little Indio, you and the others, you kick fire to your mounts and get out of Texas for good," Caldwell said.

The little Indian was looking at the dead officer's horse and saddle. A thick yellow alpaca pad showed beneath the saddle. Silver *conchos* patterned the flanks and stirrups. The saddle horn was ivory. The powder horn was gold-plated.

"Hey, Old Paint, can the three of us divide up this dead bastard's stuff?" asked the Indian. "I can live in the mountains for the rest of my life with the silver on that saddle."

"Take it," said Caldwell.

Esteban and Peña clawed sand scrambling down the bank.

"The bastard's got a good musket and pistol and sword," Peña said. "Good boots, too."

"Foreigners hide money in their boots," said Esteban.

"My feet are bare. I deserve the boots," the little Indian said, lifting one of the dead officer's legs and planting a foot in the corpse's crotch to brace himself as he hauled at the boot heel.

Slipping and grasping at brush, soaked to the chin, Rublo crawled up the east bank of the river. He heaved himself to his feet, slapped water out of his green-covered hat and led the Arabian stallion up the bank behind him. Rublo's goatskin chaps bulged and poured water.

"I hope my horse throws you off a cliff," Rublo said in Spanish.

"Tie the reins to that tree," Caldwell replied in frontier Mexican.

They eyed each other in silence, broken by Rublo's heavy breathing and the snorting and shaking of the stallion. Rublo was thick-chested, with beefy arms, not as tall as Caldwell. Before the revolution the two men had been social friends.

Inspired by speeches from Sam Houston that were printed in St. Louis newspapers, Matthew Caldwell had come to Mexico two years before the revolution to get his own tract of land for his family and to live as a free man, intending to be friendly to Mexican authorities without accepting interference from them. Rublo was a Mexican aristocrat, Creole son of Spanish parents who held title to a million-acre grant from the king of Spain. Rublo's main ranch house had been set back from the San Antonio River near La Bahia, also known as Goliad. Thousands of peons had worked Rublo's fields and tended his farm animals. Three hundred armed vaqueros had herded Rublo's cattle and defended his property against Indians and rustlers. Rublo and Caldwell had met in San Antonio at a poker game in the Fincus Hotel, a mingling place for leaders of Anglo and Latin cultures.

Caldwell was clean-shaven the night of that poker game, a patrician profile on a rugged face. He was the biggest man at the table, clearly the strongest, a natural leader. Such a man bred tales and gossip. Rublo had heard Caldwell was married to an Italian aristocrat. When this proved to be more or less true,

Rublo struck up a friendship with the Anglo immigrant. As a gesture, Matthew invited Rublo to drop in sometime for supper at Gonzalez, where the Caldwell family farmed cotton. Rublo called on the Caldwells within a month. The aristocrat was charmed by his wife's mother, the Countess Rossini. Rublo admired the two young Caldwell sons and wished aloud for heirs of his own. A few weeks later, Matthew took his family for a pleasant visit at Rublo's palatial hacienda near Goliad. The Mexican aristocrat and the Anglo immigrant became as close to being friends as their situations in life would permit.

Then the revolution had broken out, and the two men were on opposing sides.

"I'll grant you one virtue, Rublo. You're a masterful judge of horseflesh," Caldwell said, looking at the powerful, graceful form of the Arabian stallion.

"This stallion is a pacer. He can pace day and night, night and day, until other horses fall dead with exhaustion. Well, now he is yours. Go ahead and shoot me and steal my horse and be done with it. *Madre de Dios*, but you are a treacherous bastard."

Even now, facing death, Rublo sneered at Caldwell like an aristocrat being inconvenienced by a creature of a lower class.

Matthew had been involved in the revolution from the first scrap with Mexican officials over ownership of a cannon in Gonzalez. This was the sort of government interference Matthew had sworn to himself and his family that he would never accept. Caldwell rode a hundred miles in a day and night raising one hundred and sixty volunteers to join the new Texan army. The *Galveston Times* called him "the Paul Revere of Texas." Though born in Kentucky, Matthew had grown up on the Missouri frontier among brutal battles against the Indians and the wilderness. He had been a warrior long before he came to Mexico. He fought beside Old Ben Milam when the rebels captured San Antonio and left behind a small contingent that would soon gather at the Alamo. Caldwell was at the first meeting of the Texas Congress at Washington-on-Brazos, where the representatives were writing their Declaration of Independence when the Alamo became besieged by Santa Anna. Matthew had heard Rublo was riding at the head of his personal cavalry troop and had passed around the Alamo heading east, but the next time Caldwell heard Rublo's name was as the source of a nightmare.

"I want to be sure you know my wife Nancy's body was never found," Caldwell said. "Neither was the body of her mother, the countess. My two little boys were brought back to Gonzalez and I buried them, but my wife and her mother were swept away."

"I heard your family was drowned crossing the Navidad. I am sorry. But I am not to blame for what happened to them." Rublo shrugged. "They are victims of the war you started against my country, after the kindness and generosity we showed you."

"You were leading the murderers that chased my family into the river."

"I am not a man who would chase your family, Matthew. I wouldn't harm your wife and sons or the old countess. You must know me better than that. We weren't chasing anybody in particular, just Anglos who were fleeing from Santa Anna. You can't blame me for the rain that flooded the Navidad and drowned so many poor souls. If I had known your wife and sons and the old countess were up ahead in that disorganized rout, I would have risked my life to save them."

"You burned my house."

"Some of my men did that. I didn't know."

"The hard fact is, you were born on the wrong side, Rublo. But you didn't have to stay there. You could have come in with us."

"I was born on my own family's land, and I am defending my family land and honor, as it is my duty to do."

"You knew the law we passed at the first congress. Anybody who claimed a home and habitation in Texas must fight for it as a Texan. To oppose the revolution means exile or death."

Though his throat was dry, Rublo mustered a string of cotton, which he spat onto the ground. He untied his goatskin chaps and let them fall with a splat.

"Revolution? You stole my family land. Savage Anglo swine who carried an Alabama flag attacked my home. They killed my people, stole my livestock, left my hacienda in ruins. I didn't choose to be on Santa Anna's side. You foreign invaders forced me to do it. I could not be a traitor to my family tradition or to Mexico."

"There's no being neutral, Rublo. You've taken arms against us, so you are my blood enemy. Forcing my wife and boys and mother-in-law to drown, that makes your fate beyond appeal," Caldwell said.

When he had found his house burned and his family dead, he joined the Rangers and devoted himself to service. Something happens to a group of men, like the Texas Rangers, who volunteer to band together for a common purpose against common foes. They develop a love that is as profound as that of brothers. Leaders arise because of ability, not wealth or class. There were only two ranks among the Rangers—private or captain. In his first week Caldwell was elected captain by his peers. If Caldwell had a religion that he would sacrifice his life for, it was his belief in the Republic of Texas.

On the far side of the Guadalupe River, the little Indian and the two soldiers finished stripping the officer and his horse and dragged their booty to the top of the bluff.

"Thank you, Old Paint," shouted the little Indian. "May good luck always follow you."

"God be with you," yelled Caldwell.

"Hey, Old Paint!" Esteban shouted. "That rich son of a bitch you've caught with the white horse—I heard that bastard tell General Savariego to kill all the Texas Rangers and cut off their balls."

The Indian and the two soldiers disappeared into the trees, their horses and mule loaded with items that had belonged to the dead officer.

"He's lying. I never said that," Rublo said.

"Savariego would think of that on his own. He dreams about killing Rangers, but it's only a dream. We'll get him," said Caldwell.

Rublo allowed himself a small sigh of resignation.

"I have wondered what angel Death would send for me," Rublo said. "Do you not consider it an irony that my own angel of Death would be a man I respect, a friend who has shared my table and me his, a man who is dangerous at the poker table but an easy mark at rummy? How odd that I would die at the hands of a friend."

"Don't look so gloomy, Rublo. I am going to give you a chance to live."

Rublo brightened. "A chance? Not a pardon but a chance?"

"A fighting chance."

"Then I propose knives, inside a ten-foot circle we shall draw in the dirt."

"I didn't say I'm giving you a chance to kill me. I said a chance to live."

"What do you have in mind?" Rublo said.

"See that knothole that goes all the way through that pecan tree?" said Caldwell.

"Yes."

"Stick your left arm through it."

"What for?"

"This is your chance to live. Do you want it or not?"

Rublo rolled up his sleeve and thrust his thick forearm into the knothole.

"All the way through," Caldwell said.

"It's too tight, my arm won't go through."

"Make it go through."

Shoving mightily, huffing, scraping flesh from his arm, Rublo at last forced his left hand and wrist to emerge, scratched and bleeding, on the other side of the pecan trunk.

Caldwell placed Rublo's pouch full of bullets into Rublo's palm. "Make a fist around this bag. That's right." Rublo's fist tightened around the bullet pouch. Caldwell fetched the drinking shell from Rublo's saddle, drank from it and then cut off the rawhide strap by which it was carried. Using a length of Rublo's bullwhip, he began binding Rublo's fist shut around the bullet pouch. He poured water on the rawhide to make it shrink as it dried. Rublo's left fist became a large knob.

"Reach around with your right hand and see if you can touch your left fist," Caldwell said.

"Plainly I cannot touch my fist. You can see the trunk is too thick."

"Yeah, it is for a fact." Caldwell nodded. "Well, I am going to enjoy your horse, Rublo."

"You're going to leave me here like this?" said Rublo.

"I do this in memory of my wife, Nancy, and my little boys," Caldwell said. "And the Countess Rossini would be very happy to see you this way. She never liked you a bit, Rublo."

"No, you only want to steal my land," said Rublo.

"You don't own land in Texas. Not anymore."

"What if the Comanches find me?" Rublo asked. Caldwell could hear fear in his enemy's voice at last. Being bound to a tree on the bank of the Warloop and abandoned to predators was more terrifying to Rublo than facing the barrels of Sweet Lips.

"Maybe your friend General Savariego will find you first, if he's coming this way," said Caldwell.

"Please, Matthew. Shoot me now. Don't leave me like this."

Caldwell tossed a bag of corn and a buffalo stomach water pouch at Rublo's feet.

"There's something for you to eat until something eats you," Caldwell said.

"Please, Matthew, this is inhuman. Bears and panthers and wolves come to this crossing every night."

Caldwell squinted and rubbed his mottled beard as he looked at the trembling Rublo.

"Hellish murderer that you are, you're still a human and you do make a stirring appeal to my conscience," Caldwell said. "I can't leave you helpless."

From a scabbard tucked in his waist, Caldwell removed the bone-handled knife that he used for anything from dressing game to scraping the mud off his moccasin boots.

He tossed the knife into the grass at Rublo's feet.

"Defend yourself," Caldwell said.

He mounted the stallion. The horse skittered sideways, but Caldwell controlled him with the pressure of his thighs and an easy touch on the reins.

"I'll leave your saddle and gear in an elm mott nearby. The buzzards will show you where it is when my horse starts to stink," Caldwell said.

"Please, Matthew, I am begging you. Don't abandon me here!"

"Adios, Rublo," said Caldwell.

Riding away to retrieve his saddle, Caldwell heard Rublo's voice whining and crying and raging behind him.

"You son of a whore, I'll kill you! I'll kill you!"

Caldwell rode on. He wanted to report to the Ranger station at Boca Chica Crossing tonight. He believed Savariego was truly searching for Comanches. Frontier gossip abounded with Comanche raids that desolated towns and ranches in Savariego's military district west of the line of settlement of the Republic of Texas. But Matthew knew Austin was unprepared to repel a Mexican battalion if Savariego should turn in that direction. Caldwell would explain the situation to the Rangers at Boca Chica Crossing and then be off on his ninety-mile ride to Houston City. About Rublo, he felt a twinge of sorrow and remorse, for he once had taken pleasure in the man's company, but most of all he had the cold satisfaction of revenge. This could not bring back Nancy and their two little boys, or dull the pain of losing them, but it did do them honor as he saw it.

Caldwell's heart lurched with apprehension and excitement at the thought of the letter that awaited him at the marriage agency. Rublo's pitiful cries became fainter as Caldwell nudged the white Arabian stallion into a steady pace that ate up the miles away from the tree where Matthew expected Rublo would die an ugly death.

Matthew Caldwell's desire for land and his grim view of the struggle for a place on earth were set firmly in his mind as a child.

As the baby with four brothers and one sister, little Matthew had slept in a crib near the fireplace in the Caldwells' log house on the Kentucky frontier. On the wall above Matthew's crib hung a metal shield decorated with the Caldwell coat of arms and the family's Latin motto.

Once each year—in Kentucky and later in Missouri—Andrew Caldwell would gather his wife, Joyce, and five sons and one daughter beneath a tree upon which the father would fasten the shield with the Caldwell coat of arms: three ships, twenty horsemen, a cold well with a man drawing water, a castle on a hill, all this painted in red, blue, black, green and purple enamel.

"Six grandfathers back from young Matthew," their father would begin, "there was grandfather Andrew of Toulon, France. Grandfather Andrew and his two brothers became captains of their own three ships and fought beside the pirate Barbarosa to capture or sink French ships. Why would they attack their own country? Because Andrew and his brothers were driven off their land in France by religious persecution from the pope."

Andrew would pause and study their faces, making sure they were memorizing their family history.

"Grandfather Andrew—six removed from you boys—and his brothers settled in Scotland on estates they bought from King James I. Anne Caldwell of Solway Firth gave birth, alas, to the despised Oliver Cromwell. Young Cromwell grew up to challenge the very Crown that had sold us our estates. Cromwell's Puritans fought to overthrow the Royals, and Caldwells fought and died on both sides. Cromwell won. He robbed Grandfather Andrew and his brothers and sons of their estates. Cromwell stole our land, Caldwell land. He stole land from his own kin."

Andrew would glare at them.

"Do you know what the importance of today is?"

They all knew, but none spoke.

"This," said Andrew, "is to commemorate the day King Charles Second dug up Oliver Cromwell's rotten body and impaled his head on a pole in London."

Andrew gave them a moment to imagine Cromwell's head, ghastly, leering hollow-eyed from a pole.

"My own father, your grandfather, was raised on his estate in Kent that was bestowed on him by King Charles Second as a reward for killing Puritans, including our own kin. I was born in our great manor house. Alas, my father's enemies conspired and caused the Crown to turn against him.

"The tax collectors came to seize our land. They killed my father. But I killed two of the king's men with my sword, and so went into exile in this new world. I am charged with murder at my birthplace in England. If I ever return home, they will hang me."

Andrew pointed to the Latin motto on the Caldwell shield. "Thus I say to you—HOMO HOMINI LUPUS—Man is a wolf to man."

# 8

February 8, 1839
Kingdom of Hannover, German States

Dear Matthew Caldwell:

If this is too bold and presumptuous an opening, please forgive me. I hardly know how to begin such a peculiar letter. I fear I may express myself awkwardly in the English language, which I do not speak or write nearly so well as my native German or the tongue of my neighbors, the French.

But I will become proficient in English through hard work and study. Please forgive crudities of grammar in my writing—and forgive this awful penmanship, if you will. It is near midnight and is very cold in my room, and my page is lit by only the nub of a precious candle. It is difficult to see the marks my pen is making.

This letter is to introduce myself to you in time that you may stop our marriage arrangement if you are made unhappy or disappointed by the information contained on these pages of paper that are sent from so many thousands of miles away and are written in an uncertain and frightened mind.

Herr Growald, an official marriage broker representing the Republic of Texas, has recently arrived in Hannover with requests for wives and with descriptions of men who need women in that far-off land of yours.

I confess that I am both anguished and excited at the thought of entirely pulling up the roots of my life, leaving my home and family and friends and being transported across the ocean to a wild country to marry a stranger. This is a frightening fantasy for me. I would not consider making such a marriage bargain except that the conditions here in Hannover are very bad for us.

My father is a brilliant and famous scholar at Gottingen University, but he has spoken out against the king of Hannover, Ernest Augustus, and has put himself in grave political difficulty and perhaps in danger for his life.

It was my suggestion that I make my father's burden lighter both politically and financially by finding a husband who is far from Germany.

For me to marry a countryman, I would be forced in public to adopt my new husband's political position. But I could not marry a man who opposes my father.

In the unlikely event I could find a husband of substance who supports my father, I fear I would lose such a husband to death or prison soon in what appears to be a civil war about to befall us. My father begs me to leave Hannover while I have the opportunity. He and my mother do not have the means to escape—for that I shall send them money from Texas—and my two brothers appear determined to stay and fight against the king. I pray I may be of good use to you in the Texas wilderness, where the names of Ernest Augustus and Professor Bernard Dahlman mean nothing.

My name is Hannah Dahlman. I am twenty years of age and in robust health. I am strong enough that I can carry a silver candelabrum in each hand the length of a great dining hall without dipping a flame. I am quite a good dancer (do people dance in Texas?) and possess a pleasant singing voice and a modest talent at the harpsichord.

I will not attempt to describe my physical appearance, as it seems a coarse and stupid thing for me to do. If I were to brag that I am beautiful, you would have every reason to think of me as vain and silly or even a liar. Were I to say I am ugly, you would believe me and wouldn't want me, even in the wilderness.

No doubt the marriage broker, Herr Growald, has described me to you and has laid out the virtues of my appearance without mentioning any flaws that your eyes may discover. I am sure that is accepted practice among marriage brokers, but it does leave one with the uncomfortable sensation of being judged like a side of lamb in the butcher shop.

Herr Growald has told my family that you are a stalwart man, a hero of the Texas revolution. He said you are something like an officer of the Cossacks. As a thoroughly political person, my father was quite impressed to learn that you signed your name to both the Declaration of Independence of the new Republic of Texas, and to the Constitution of the Republic; and to hear that you are an elected delegate to the Congress brings tears of emotion to the eyes of my father, who believes every person should have the vote.

Herr Growald said your courage in battle won you a grant of ten thousand acres of wilderness across a river from the new capital city that is being built. Herr Growald does admit that your ten thousand acres of wilderness are totally occupied by savage red Indians at this time, but he said if any man can wrest ten thousand acres away from savage red Indians, you are that man.

I find it curious that you would fight the native peoples and the Mexican armies to grasp ten thousand acres of wilderness from nature and call it your own, but I do understand that is how kingdoms are made.

Struggling against the calamities of nature in the wilderness is itself a challenge of noble proportions, even if there were no human foes to combat. I believe I am strong and resourceful enough to aid in your quest, although I admit I am frightened and know only the sophisticated city life of Hannover and nothing of the perils of the great western wilderness.

Whether I can bear you children remains to be seen, but I am confident that I can.

You must appreciate the turmoil that is enwrapping me as I write this letter. My father may be driven to ruin and exile, perhaps even to death, for his belief in human freedom and democracy and for land reform, as you may be slain for your own beliefs before you receive my letter. The forces that you are opposing are very different from those that oppose my father, I feel sure. But I know what life offers here in Hannover, and I do not know what awaits in Texas; I fly to those ills that I know not of, as Hamlet more or less said it. But I fly with a thrill in my heart.

I will sail for Texas in three weeks' time aboard the *Sea Swallow*, a British ship I will board at the port of Bremerhaven. Herr Growald says I am to land on the Texas coast at a place called Matagorda. The name has a romantic sound, like an exotic jungle outpost. Is Texas a jungle? One hears conflicting reports: that Texas is a jungle, a swamp, a desert, a magnificent forest, a mountain range, a prairie covered with grass taller than a man. One hears Texas is unbearably hot, beastly cold, that it rains fit for Noah but is as dry as the heart of Arabia. One hears Texas has wonderful farmland, but one also hears the Texas earth is hard as stone. One hears the savage red Indians are eight feet tall, that Mexican armies plunder the settlements, that brigands and outlaws roam free, that the people of Texas are friendly and generous, mean and selfish, of high degree and of the very lowest.

Herr Growald says you have a beard that is spotted black and white, and a perpetually sunburnt face and eyes that are gray or green, depending on the light. I must admit that such a portrait of you does quicken my pulse. But I am curious why a man like yourself, a hero and adventurer with much to gain in an exciting new republic, would entrust so dear a matter as marriage to a commercial agent rather than selecting a wife from women close at hand who would be eager to share in your career in politics and estate building and enforcing the code of laws without which we would have no society. Herr Growald says you are kept so busy fighting savages and Mexicans that you have no time to pay court to the ladies, and he says there is some tragedy in your past that I shall not hear from his lips. This information does not calm my doubts and fears, but it does indeed arouse my desire to test my character on the frontier, where there are possibilities for great achievements. The future holds no prospect for me in my country. My hope lies with you, if you will have me, and with Texas.

Unless a messenger arrives telling me you have changed your mind, I will soon become your wife. Please do not expect perfection.

Most respectfully yours,
Hannah Dahlman

# 9

Caldwell folded the letter and replaced it in an oilcloth packet that he had bought for the purpose.

"You say this woman is beautiful?" he asked.

Herr Growald, the marriage agent, leaned his elbows on the table he was using as a desk and pinched his plump cheeks with thumbs and forefingers, making a kissing hiss, his black mustache wiggling like a caterpillar. The toes of Growald's brogans dug into the mud and straw that made up the floor of his office, which was roofed by a tent, its canvas speckled with mildew. A sign above the door said: WEDDED BLISS GUARANTEED. The side panels of the tent were rolled up and tied in the hope of a breath of wet breeze in the suffocating heat of Houston City.

"She is so beautiful that it tore my heart just to gaze upon her," said Growald.

"When did you see her?"

"A few months ago while I was traveling through the German states, seeking clients. Her father approached me. I went to their home and observed her in the kitchen and listened to her play the piano. What a marvelous young woman. Delightful in conversation. And she can cook."

"Is her father in real danger?"

"I should think so, yes. Oh, but his daughter, Hannah Dahlman, such radiance glows from her like a charge of electrical sparks. She will furnish you fifteen years of delightful appearance before her beauty fades. She is diligent and industrious, rare qualities in any person. There may never come along another for you so perfect as she is."

Matthew still owned the 640 acres that had once been a cotton farm near Gonzalez, but he had let the land go wild. When he and Nancy and their sons had moved into what was still the Mexican state of Coahuilla, the government had given him the cotton land, plus a headright of 4,400 acres and one labor of 170 acres southeast of Gonzalez. After the revolution, Caldwell could have chosen as a reward from the Congress of the Republic of Texas another headright of 4,400 acres of rich soil, timbered, with flowing springs south of Gonzalez. Instead, he asked the Congress for a double headright and two labors of land in the hills and valleys west of the Colorado, in Comancheria, where no other veterans of the revolution were clamoring to settle. He sold his original headright for $2,400 in gold notes, deposited in New Orleans. That was plenty enough to live on while he was ranging. Caldwell wasn't interested in making money or in dying rich. But he did desire a large spread of land to be the lord of and to bequeath to his children. It was in his blood to resume the tradition of the Caldwells.

Since Cristolphe Rublo and Mexican cavalry had burned the cotton farm, Caldwell had lived at Ranger stations or under the stars or in a room at the Fincus Hotel in San Antonio. The farmhouse near Gonzalez stood as a few silent black timbers. The cotton fields were overgrown with grass and wildflowers.

He had no home. But a young bride was on her way.

"Do you accept her?" asked Herr Growald.

"Yes. I think she will do fine," Caldwell said.

"You don't mind that she is Jewish?"

"What?"

"Professor Dahlman is a prominent Jewish intellectual in Hannover. His daughter, Hannah, is a Jew. Do you object?"

Matthew's father had hated Catholics and Puritans but had never mentioned Jews. The Ranger held no bias about Jews. Matthew hardly knew what they were.

"Will she require special treatment? There are no Jewish temples in Austin. There are no churches of any kind."

"No, no ceremonies or rituals, I assure you," Growald chuckled. "The young woman is a strong-minded freethinker, like her father. She will flourish in a frontier like this. But I want to be sure you know she is a Jew before you sign the contract of acceptance. I have had clients object and force me to send the Jews away. It is very unpleasant."

Growald unrolled a paper document, unstopped an inkwell and dipped his pen, fashioned from a turkey feather, into the ink. He held out the dripping pen toward Caldwell.

"I guess I can marry a Jew, all right, but why would a Jew want to marry me?" Caldwell said.

"My dear captain, you are quite a catch," said Growald.

"Besides which, she is desperate," Caldwell said.

"Well, yes, but what she really wants is to make you happy."

"Good. It's going to take a desperate woman to make me happy. Give me that pen," Caldwell said.

After he signed the agreement, he ducked through the door of Growald's tent and stepped into the smothering steam of Houston City. The air was alive with heat and the tiny insects that swam in it. Caldwell had paid $250 of Growald's $1,000 fee—the remainder due upon the bride arriving in good health in San Antonio. Professor Dahlman had refused to accept money from Caldwell for Hannah's passage to America. The professor sent apologies that he was not able to pay a dowry, a notion that had never occurred to Caldwell. Matthew was too proud to marry a woman he was paid to take.

With Hannah Dahlman's letter secure inside his belt, his fringed doeskin jacket hung across his back from a thumb, Sweet Lips cradled in an elbow and his two Paterson pistols swinging from the scabbards on his suspenders, Matthew Caldwell sloshed along the muddy main street in his moccasin boots, heading toward the saloon at the Palace Hotel, where General Sam Houston was holed up on a long drunk that Caldwell had heard about from Rangers at the station at Boca Chica Crossing.

The moisture in the air caused tricks with Caldwell's vision. The tents and shacks that made up the greater part of Houston City around the bayous rippled before his eyes. On a cold winter day in Houston City, the chill soaked straight to the skin. Caldwell preferred Missouri blizzards to a clammy winter in Houston City. But when it was hot, which was most of the year, the city lying on the same latitude as Calcutta, mosquitoes and flies rose out of the bayous in black curtains, and dogs rolled over, their tongues hanging out, and died in the sun.

Three years ago this place along Buffalo Bayou had been called Harrisburg, but Santa Anna's army had burned it to the ground. Two land speculators bought the ruins of Harrisburg the moment news came that Santa Anna had been defeated nearby at the Battle of San Jacinto. The Allen brothers named their new enterprise Houston City in honor of the victorious General Sam Houston.

Houston City boasted the capitol building of the Republic of Texas, built of pine logs and needing paint, three hotels, a theater for musical performances and stage plays and a racetrack. On either side of the main street Caldwell could see saloons in tents, saloons in shacks, saloons in buildings of some presumption. There were thirty-six saloons in Houston City—Caldwell and the Old Chief, General Sam Houston, had hoisted a whiskey in every one of them, so people later reported, during an epic drunk six months ago, during which Caldwell had decided to hire Herr Growald to find him a German bride. There was not one bank or church in the town.

The Palace Hotel was a two-story structure of whitewashed pine with touches of New Orleans style in tall green shutters on either side of each window, and on the second floor French doors opened onto a wrought iron balcony. Caldwell walked past the lobby entrance and went around the corner to the saloon door, which stood open to let out tobacco smoke and entice whispers of fetid air.

"By God, it's Matthew Caldwell! Come and give me a hug, my darling boy!"

The Old Chief, General Sam Houston, the first elected president of the Republic of Texas, slammed a crooked, ivory-knobbed mahogany cane onto the plank floor of the Palace saloon and rose as close to full height as he could manage, with arthritis clutching his lower spine and a load of whiskey affecting his balance. At six feet six, General Sam Houston was nearly half a head taller than Caldwell, and when they embraced, Matthew felt against his chin the wet purple indentation of the general's old broken collarbone wound. Caldwell's arms went beneath the Old Chief's armpits in a Mexican *abrazzo* and clasped the backs of his shoulders, feeling the muscles in the wide, powerful torso that had absorbed so many stabs, slashes and lead balls that the scars were thought of as Sam Houston's medals of valor, a true copy of his deeds compared to the ribbons and medallions he was authorized to wear on his tunic. Now forty-eight years old and no longer with official powers, General Sam Houston was regarded by Caldwell and many other fighters in the revolution as the Old Chief, their leader.

"It's wonderful to see you, Matthew, my good friend," said the Old Chief, stepping back and gazing into Caldwell's face as if admiring a painting. "Let me gaze at you for a moment. So colorful you are."

"Compared to you, I'm a dullard, Chief," Caldwell said, thinking the general looked older than he remembered from their recent drinking bout. Wrinkles creased the Old Chief's eyes and forehead. Tangled gray hair curled around his ears. Of course, Matthew thought, he had to consider that probably the Old Chief had not slept last night, possibly had not eaten, and the perspiration on his skin tasted like brandy. The Old Chief winked elaborately and held a finger up to his lips.

"Quiet, Matthew. We must speak softly. I am in hiding. Please sit with me a spell." The Old Chief waved a long arm at the fat man behind the bar, whose apron was dark with sweat. "A jug of rare French brandy for Captain Caldwell!" Sam Houston shouted. "By God, it is a good thing to have friends!"

Leaning on the cane, the Old Chief lowered himself into the hardwood and rawhide chair, allowing a grunt of pain to escape. Caldwell pulled up another chair and sat down. He laid Sweet Lips in a third chair at the table.

"Is this an old wound that's bothering you, or have you been in another scrape?" Caldwell asked.

"This is not a wound. It's a mere injury. You might say it is because of this injury that I am in hiding."

"If somebody is pestering you, Chief, all you need to do is give me their name," Caldwell said.

The Old Chief laughed and began to wheeze. His face turned red and his eyes bulged. His big right hand with the sharp knuckles scooped up his crystal snifter, and his Adam's apple bobbed as he swigged brandy. Caldwell accepted his own clay jug from the fat man, bit into the cork and pulled out the stopper.

The first rush of brandy down his throat burned his stomach and chased a shudder up his spine.

"General Savariego is in the field a few miles west of the Warloop," Matthew said.

"Not so loud," said the Old Chief.

"What?"

"Lower your voice, please."

Caldwell leaned both elbows on the table and bent forward and spoke barely above a whisper.

"General Savariego is in the field east of San Antonio. I caught some of his scouts. They say Savariego is hunting Comanches, but he may raid Austin. What do you think?"

"I wouldn't be surprised, or especially disappointed, if Savariego plunders Austin," said the Old Chief. "Austin is a troublemaking place that should not exist."

Caldwell whispered, "Why are we being so quiet?"

"I am hiding from my future mother-in-law," the Old Chief said. "She is a ferocious old bitch. A dragon."

"With all respect, Chief, how can you be getting married again?"

"Oh, I've so much news for you, my brave Captain Caldwell. First, the sad news, the very sad news. Diana Gentry, my wonderful Cherokee wife, who saved my life more than once when rum and the devil threatened to do me in, well, poor Diana has died of a fever as she was being removed from Tennessee to the western territories. Ah, if only she had let me know she was being moved, I could have saved her. I would have grabbed Andy Jackson's throat if that's what it took. But Diana was too proud to ask me for help, and, damn me, I was too vain and self-involved to inquire after the well-being of this noble woman. May she rest in peace in heaven, for she was ill treated as an angel on this earth."

"I'm sorry, Chief. I know you loved her," said Caldwell, waving to the fat man to bring him a cheroot. Caldwell had swiftly examined the saloon for indications of danger to the Old Chief but had found none. Two drunks lay asleep and snoring at a table in the corner, their heads on maps of plats of land in Houston City. Caldwell guessed these were land speculators who had tried to drink with the Old Chief in hope of winning a favor from him but had overloaded themselves, and now would be forever weaklings in his eyes. One sad-looking drummer, his suit sweated through, his satchel of samples on the floor beside his muddy shoes, stood and drank at the bar. Usually wherever Sam Houston was, a crowd gathered. This was a mid-morning lull.

"But now two pieces of excellent news," said the Old Chief. "The first is that my divorce decree from the once precious but no longer desired Eliza Allen, the belle of Gallatin, has at last been granted in the state of Tennessee, and I walk this earth today a free man, without any wife to criticize me."

"Then why are you in hiding?" Caldwell asked.

"The second piece of excellent news is I am about to become engaged to be married. A wee tiny wifey. Every man needs a wee tiny wifey if he is to find peace and happiness and fulfillment on this earth. You must find yourself one, Matthew. You have grieved long and devoutly over the loss of your family, but now you must move toward the rest of your life."

Sam Houston swirled his brandy and smiled at Matthew's expression of curiosity.

"I arrived in Mobile on a commercial venture, looking for investors in a land speculation," the Old Chief said, tapping his game leg with his cane. "This was only two months ago, mind you. I was still a married man, though I had no wife at hand. In fact, I was still married to two different women at once, but had not a hint of the comfort a woman's touch brings to my oh so human skin."

The Old Chief hunched foward at the table, leaning on his elbows. His cotton shirt was open at the neck. A red scar ran up his breastbone, the testimony, Caldwell knew, of the Old Chief's fight at Horseshoe Bend, Alabama, against the Creek Indians twenty-five years ago while he was serving in the United States army as a lieutenant under General Andrew Jackson. The Old Chief's right forearm and shoulder had been shattered by musket balls in that fight, and an arrow had pierced his groin, leaving a wound that Caldwell heard had never ceased to ooze. The Old Chief accepted a cheroot from the bartender but declined to have it lit. He chewed on the cigar, rolling it in his lips as if it were nourishment. The Old Chief said he had arrived in Mobile two months ago to cast his net for investors in Texas land. As he was walking off the ship on the gangplank, his right heel caught in a piece of rope and he twisted his right knee and fell heavily, rendered unconscious by the sudden pain. His enemies, the Old Chief said, spread the slander that he had toppled over in a drunken swoon, but he swore to Caldwell that he was sober as a Puritan, and was eagerly looking forward to checking in at La Grande Hotel and hurrying to the hotel bar to remedy his condition.

"At the very center of my soul as I lay unconscious, a poem sprang forth: 'Oh, love, thou hast returned to me, whose heart homeless toward the grave did veer. I behold thy face that God hath sent to keep me here.' "

The Old Chief's upper lip twitched as he peered at Caldwell, and he peeled a strip of tobacco off his teeth.

"I opened my eyes—and there she was! The creature sent to me from heaven. Seventeen years old but wiser than any of my political or military advisers ever were, excepting you, Caldwell, if you did ever give me advice, I can't remember now."

"Just once, Chief," said Caldwell. "I suggested you let me execute Santa Anna."

"You did? Well, there were a lot of opinions being tossed back and forth at that moment. But how could I shoot a fellow Mason who claims to get ten erections every day? Don't be upset with me, Matthew, it was just damned politics that saved Santa Anna. But I am in love and had rather not talk politics right now. Let me continue to speak of Mobile. I am lying there, looking up at this darling spirit, yearning to have her for my own, devastated to remember that I am already married to two women. I don't know if I am deliriously happy or utterly miserable—and then I pass out again, from the pain and the strain on my nerves."

He had been revived and carried to the hotel, where a physician diagnosed his knee as having a stressed but not torn ligament and prescribed one hundred drops of laudanum to be swallowed instantly and followed by a bottle of white wine from France. When the general awoke the next morning, he placed fifty drops of laudanum on his tongue while humming a polka tune, had a vigorous scrub in a tub of hot water, with his black slave Andre handling the brush and the lye soap, massaged honeycomb and lard into his swollen knee, wrapped the knee in cotton, shaved and dressed in a blue velvet tunic with a white shirt of fine Georgia cotton and white linen trousers freshly pressed by the hotel valet, and ordered a walking stick of noble quality to be brought to his room. All of that accomplished, the Old Chief drank the rest of the bottle of laudanum and went to eat breakfast in the hotel restaurant, where the customers openly stared at him, this hugely tall and notorious former president of Texas, former governor of Tennessee.

The hotel owner had rushed to have coffee at the invitation of the illustrious Sam Houston, who made inquiries. The girl on the dock was named Margaret Lea, and her mother was a rich widow, known all over southern Mississippi for her fierce rejections of every one of her daughter's suitors as being unworthy. Through the hotel owner the Old Chief arranged a meeting with Mrs. Victoria Lea at her lawyer's office, where he invited Mrs. Lea, who was thirty-eight and quite attractive in a mean-eyed way, to come to Texas to see for herself the prospects for vast wealth in land and cattle and cotton. He was delighted when Victoria and her lawyer accepted, but he was disappointed that they refused to bring Margaret Lea, who was attending school and learning to speak French and play the harp.

The Old Chief twirled a finger above his gray head in the Palace saloon and said:

"What winning graces, what majestic mien! She moves a goddess and she looks a queen! I am going back to Mobile today and marry my Margaret Lea, Matthew, I swear it. Victoria opposes me, but she shall not defeat me."

Caldwell heard the clack of hardware upon a door frame and saw the ruddy, bearded face of Big Foot Wallace ducking to peer into the dimness of the saloon from the yellow heat of the muddy path outside, the Bowie knife on his belt scraping against wood as he craned his body sideways. Big Foot was six feet two, weighed two hundred and forty pounds with hardly an ounce of fat, and he entered the saloon moving softly as a breath. For the past year Big Foot had been scouting from the Ranger station in Boca Chica Crossing, where he shared his one-room house with his dogs, but he had been on a confidential assignment from President Lamar two days ago when Caldwell stopped to report the Mexican battalion that might be marching toward Austin.

"The stout Wallace!" cried the Old Chief. "How da do, man? How da do?"

"I feel almost as good all over as I do any other place," Big Foot said.

Caldwell laughed. He felt affection and respect for his comrade. Big Foot was born William Alexander Anderson Wallace in Virginia to Scots Highlander parents descended from William Wallace and Robert Bruce. Wallace came to Texas three years ago after his brother and cousin were shot by the Mexican army in the massacre at Goliad. He sought revenge against the Mexican army and took payment in blood. On his first patrol after joining the Rangers, Wallace found the track of a cow thief and told his mates, "Boys, that is one hell of a big-footed son of a bitch." Wallace trailed the cow thief and shot the man through the chest from fifty yards. Upon inspection of the corpse, he discovered the thief to be a Kiowa Indian wearing a new pair of handsomely beaded moccasins. Wallace tried them on, and the moccasins fit as if made for him. Henceforth the Rangers called him Big Foot.

The Old Chief thrust himself up to his feet in a sudden burst of energy that surprised Caldwell and waved his heavy, ivory-knobbed cane in the air like the baton of an orchestra conductor.

"You brave hearts join me," the Old Chief shouted. "We are going to sing once again the song that won the day at Peggy McCormick's farm!"

The Old Chief began singing in a roar: "Come, all you reckless and rambling boys who have listened to my song." Caldwell stood and made it a duet with his rough baritone. "If it's done no good, sir, I'm sure it's done no wrong. But when you court a pretty girl, just marry her when you can. For if you ever cross those plains, she'll marry another man. , , ."

The Chief stopped and glared at Big Foot. The Old Chief seemed to grow even taller, rising above Big Foot. Caldwell heard dangerous drunken anger in the Old Chief's voice.

"Damn it, sir, I demand that you sing with us," the Old Chief said to Big Foot.

"I mean no disrespect, Chief, sir, but over where I was we didn't sing 'The Girl I Left Behind Me,' " Big Foot said. "We sang 'Come to the Bower.' Soon as I wet my goozle out of that jug, I'll sing so loud it'll deefen ye."

Big Foot turned up Caldwell's clay jug and swallowed heartily, wiped his mouth and then sang in a clear, thin voice that had a southern mountain accent:

> "Will you come to the bower I have shaded for you?
> Our bed shall be roses all spangled with dew.
> There under the bower on roses you'll lie
> With a blush on your cheek but a smile in your eye."

Hearing Big Foot's song made Caldwell remember the black drummer boy beating the rhythm and the German fifer playing on the right flank as seven hundred men, many of them singing, had trotted across Peggy McCormick's farm at San Jacinto at four o'clock in the afternoon of April 21, three years ago. Motts of live oaks and magnolias rose from the high grass. Caldwell remembered the sounds of pounding feet and heavy breathing and the voices rising in song. He felt exhilarated and free. The Texan line was fifteen hundred yards wide. The Old Chief had ridden thirty yards in front of the rest, mounted on his stallion, Saracen. Caldwell saw the Mexicans become aware of the charge and scramble to their weapons, and he saw smoke from cannons and rifles and heard explosions and snapping zings popping past his ears.

A volley had killed Saracen, and the Old Chief had grabbed a riderless horse and swung into the saddle. The stirrups were short for him, so he rode with his long legs flailing. Mexican *escopeta* balls smashed the Old Chief's right ankle and killed the second horse. The general hauled himself onto the back of a third horse and galloped through the smoke and flames and bayonets into the Mexican ranks. Dead Mexicans were piling in heaps on the breastworks of dirt and field packs. Caldwell killed five men with Sweet Lips and stabbed another. The fight was over in minutes, but the slaughter continued. Caldwell had seen the Old Chief, with blood flowing from the hole in his boot, still mounted, shouting, "Parade, gentlemen! Parade!" But nothing could stop the lust for killing. Hundreds of Mexicans tried to escape across a marshy bayou to their rear, but they drowned or were shot. Many who tried to surrender were clubbed or slashed or strangled in the Texans' blood rage.

Caldwell had walked among the dead and wounded, searching for the body of Santa Anna. All around in sulfur clouds Caldwell heard weeping and praying and moaning, and the war whoops of the Texans. He saw the clothing of dead Mexicans being searched for loot. Two dentists knelt among the bodies, filling their bullet bags with teeth they pulled out of skulls. As darkness came, the Texans built fires to dry their clothing and threatened to burn their prisoners. Santa Anna was found in the morning wearing baggy pantaloons of a slave and hiding in a thicket. Sam Houston was lying with his back against an oak tree, weaving a garland of vines to send to Diana Gentry as a surgeon cleaned and bandaged his ankle. The Old Chief had looked up and seen the emperor of Mexico being prodded before him. Caldwell had carefully reloaded Sweet Lips in the hope that the Old Chief would order a prompt execution. Caldwell wanted to pull the trigger. But after allowing the emperor the comfort of chewing a ball of gum opium to make his humiliation bearable, the Old Chief had spared Santa Anna's life on his written word that Mexican armies would retreat to the Rio Grande, and Mexico would never invade the free Texas Republic again.

Out of loyalty to the Old Chief, Matthew had refused to join the rebels who dragged Santa Anna and his officers off a ship in Galveston Bay with the intention of lynching the president of Mexico. The Old Chief, with Caldwell at his side, intervened, faced down the mob and then escorted the Mexicans to Orizombo, the plantation of Dr. James Phelps, twelve miles north of Columbus. For the next ten months Santa Anna and his officers were kept in leg irons, abused, starved. Caldwell had become a Texas Ranger by then, and he heard how poorly the Mexicans were treated, but he had no sympathy for Santa Anna. The Old Chief had finally sent Santa Anna to President Andrew Jackson, who returned the Mexican president to Veracruz. A year ago in Veracruz the French navy had blown off Santa Anna's left leg with a cannonball. Matthew had heard Santa Anna's valets carried the emperor's spare legs in cases like musical instruments.

After Big Foot finished singing in the Palace Hotel Saloon, the Old Chief and Caldwell applauded and the three men sat together at the table and drank crystal snifters of French brandy poured from clay jugs.

"The boys at Boca Chica tell me you're doing a confidential duty for Lamar," Caldwell said.

"Aw, hell, nothing is confidential where you and the Chief are concerned," said Big Foot. "Lamar sent me down here to buy twenty barrels of gunpowder and two oxcarts full of lead for shot and then guard the shipment until it gets to San Antonio. That's one part of my assignment. The other part is, the President told me to find you and tell you he needs to see you on an urgent personal matter, Matthew. Maybe you could give me a hand watching over this cargo on the road, since San Antonio is where our president is holed up at the old governor's palace doing government business and waiting for you."

"The scoundrel won't come to his president's office in Houston City when he knows I am in town," the Old Chief said. "It's to spite me and kill Indians that he's moving the capitol to Austin this summer. Two years from now I'll be elected president again, and I'll see that damned Austin deserted with grass growing in its streets."

Caldwell nodded and scratched his beard, wanting a bath. He believed the Old Chief would let Austin rot if he had the chance. The Congress named the new capital for Stephen F. Austin, a Missouri politician who had founded a settlement of immigrants from the United States on a tract between the Colorado and Brazos rivers three years before the revolution. The Old Chief beat Stephen Austin in the first election for president but named the former Missouri territorial legislator as secretary of state in the first cabinet as a gesture to Houston's many enemies. Caldwell, as elected representative from Gonzalez, voted in favor of moving the capital to Austin. Matthew listened to the Old Chief's diatribe and smiled inwardly. How many towns in Texas could be named Houston?

When the Old Chief paused for a drink, Matthew looked at Big Foot.

"What does Lamar want with me?" Caldwell asked.

"I don't know. All he told me is it's very important."

"Beware of Lamar," said the Old Chief. "Our Republic is worse off today than it was when we fought at Peggy McCormick's farm. We are destitute where before we were only moneyless. The whole United States is in a financial panic and can't help us. Rabble are pouring across the Sabine. Every fool and thug and confidence man in the South is coming here to find his fortune. The land contagion has us in its clutches—even you, Matthew, with your blasted ten thousand acres in Comancheria. Lamar wants to start wars with the Indians to clear out more land to sell, and it's men like you two who will die in the doing of it. You won't find real estate bankers riding headlong into Comanche lances. There is treachery all around. Tens of thousands of greedy second-raters are flooding into our Republic to get fat off the fruits of our struggles. We are surrounded by angry Indians, Mexican armies plunder our out-country and menace our cities, our government is bankrupt, the French and English and Dutch are looking for a justification to move in on us, and our president, Mirabeau Buonaparte Lamar, is a liar, schemer and dangerous man, and besides, he is a damn terrible poet. Have you read any of that sappy nonsense he writes?"

"No, sir," said Big Foot.

"Not me," Caldwell said.

"Consider this place, Austin, that Lamar has chosen for our new capital," said Sam Houston.

"I was at the site with Waller's surveying crew last fall," Caldwell said. "It's a frontier Eden up there. Enclosed by hills in a crook of the Colorado River. Plenty of flowing water, springs, timber, fish and game. The elevation makes a healthier climate than here in Houston City. Lamar says it is a natural hub for roads that will run from the Red River to Matamoros and from the Gulf of Mexico to Santa Fe."

"How many miles is it from Austin to what Lamar claims as our Republic of Texas westernmost outpost, the city of Santa Fe?" asked the general.

"About eight hundred miles," Caldwell said.

"And how many forts or even settlements do we have between Austin and Santa Fe?"

"Well, none, as you know," Caldwell said.

"Now let's tell the truth about Austin, with its abundant water and game and magical scenery, the favorite resort and spa for the whole Comanche Nation for thousands of years. Do you not agree that establishing our capitol building in Austin will provoke an all-out war with the Comanches?"

"Chief, I fall in with Lamar on that one. We're going to have to fight those Comanches to the death. I ain't against all of the Indians, not by any means. Your Cherokee friend Chief Bowl is doing fine in East Texas. But we're going to have to whip those Comanches. They've killed or captured three hundred immigrants along our southwestern border in two years. I found another family hacked to pieces a week ago. If building Austin will make the Comanches come out and fight, I am in favor of it."

The Old Chief laughed. "Come out and fight? If the Comanches would all join together and come out and fight, it would be like twenty thousand of Genghis Khan's Mongol cavalry howling down on helpless villages. How big is San Antonio? Maybe two thousand residents, less than half of them Anglos? And what do we have in Austin to face the Comanches—a thousand lawyers and land speculators. What can you put in the field against the Comanches, Matthew? Two hundred Rangers?"

"About a hundred and sixty right now," Caldwell said. "We've had some people hurt."

"Then there is the Texas army," said the Old Chief. "Maybe six hundred are left, but there's no money to pay them. I furloughed the rest so they wouldn't form a mob behind Felix Huston and try to invade Mexico. Don't count on the Texas army to help you Rangers defeat those Comanche warriors. Two or three years ago you could have gathered a militia of civilians to help you. But now our civilians are rabble from the east who want to buy and sell land, not fight for it."

"Well, then, I'm glad the Comanches aren't organized, because we are going to have to fight them," Caldwell said.

"Tell me, Matthew, if the Indians could send feathered chiefs to our Congress to vote as landholders just like the white man, what do you think would happen at our next assembly?"

"Which Indians?" asked Caldwell.

"The Indians that live in our Republic—the Cherokees, Comanches, Apaches, Kiowas, Alabamas, Shawnees, Karankawas, Tonks, Delawares, Kickapoos, Patawonatres, Caddos, Creeks, Wacos, Pawnees and all the rest. What if they had the vote, like we do? What would happen?"

"They'd vote our ass right out of Texas," Caldwell said.

"Lucky thing most of these tribes hate each other worse than they hate us. Otherwise, they could destroy our republic in a week," said the Old Chief. "The only way Texas can maintain itself against its enemies is to join the union of the United States and call upon the U.S. Army to do the bloody work."

"I fought to become a citizen of the Republic of Texas, and I will fight to remain so," Caldwell said. "But I will not fight for the United States. My place is here."

"Ah, but you will fight for your ten thousand acres, will you not?" the Old Chief said.

"Unless you can sweet talk the Comanches into turning it over to me, I will," said Caldwell.

"Matthew, you're an imperialist at heart. You want your own kingdom," the Old Chief said.

"I stand for a free and independent Texas," Caldwell said.

"I'll drink with ye on that," said Big Foot.

"I daresay you would drink with Matthew on anything," the Old Chief said.

"You know me well, Chief," said Big Foot.

"That's what we're all doing here, ain't it, Chief?" said Caldwell. "Building a republic?"

"Drink to Texas," the Old Chief said.

The three men drained their snifters.

"Sam Houston, you swore to me you would go to bed and get a full night's sleep, but I can plainly see you chose to stay up all night and get even drunker with your fellow sots," said Victoria Lea.

A tall woman, wearing white, with a broad-brimmed hat to protect her face from the sun and a net hanging from the brim to fend off insects, Victoria Lea stood in the lobby entrance to the saloon. Behind her was a soft, plump little man with side-whiskers, wiping his face constantly with a handkerchief, looking as if the slightest relaxation of inner tension would cause him to wilt into a puddle.

The Old Chief shot up abruptly from the table, knocking over their brandy jugs and breaking their crystal snifters, standing up straight and tall as if he were reviewing troops, huge in his blue tunic and his white cotton shirt, now torn open to the waist, revealing a chest crisscrossed with scars.

"The beautiful Mrs. Victoria Lea, may I present two heroes of the Texas Republic? Captain Matthew Caldwell, a congressman and our senior Ranger, and the famous Ranger scout and warrior Big Foot Wallace."

Caldwell and Big Foot scrambled to their feet. Mrs. Victoria Lea studied Caldwell with interest, then glanced at Big Foot and back at Caldwell. Though he could hardly see her eyes through the mosquito netting, Caldwell felt them exploring his body.

"And the puny gentleman is her esteemed attorney, Mr. Ned Boodle, Esquire," the Old Chief said.

"Victoria, please, we're going to miss the steamboat and have to spend another day in hell," said Ned Boodle.

"General Houston, I have decided to invest a large sum in Texas. I shall require you to accompany Mr. Boodle and me back to Mobile to sign the necessary documents," Victoria Lea said.

"He'll make us late. We can do it without him," said Boodle.

"Why, Mr. Boodle, you think too short of me," the Old Chief said. "My man Andre is sitting behind the hotel at this minute with my bags packed and a pony cart to take me to the dock. I was returning to Mobile today in any case, dear Victoria, to propose marriage to your darling daughter, Margaret Lea."

"I don't want you for a son-in-law," said Victoria. "You're old. You're crippled. You're no longer a president or a general or a governor. You have no power. You are not rich. You stink of whiskey and tobacco. I do want to buy the land you are representing and will appoint you as my agent for buying a cattle herd. But you will never marry my daughter, you stinking old drunk."

Victoria Lea whirled on her heel in a flutter of white and marched into the lobby, closely tailed by the miserable Boodle.

The Old Chief looked back and forth from Caldwell to Big Foot. He straightened his shoulders, sucked in air and stuck out his chest. He made a formidable figure, as fierce a sight as any Comanche warrior.

"Do either of you see my hat?" the Old Chief asked.

"You don't have no hat, General Houston," said the bartender. "You give it away yesterday as a souvenir to some little child."

"So I did. Quite right. Andre will have me another hat," the Old Chief said. He shook hands with Caldwell, then with Big Foot. He clutched each man on the shoulder in a powerful grip. He looked them in the eye.

"Texas can be heaven on earth if we love her well," the Old Chief said. "I'm leaving Texas in your care, my noble friends, while I go woo the sweetheart of my life. You brave Rangers remember what I tell you—beware of Lamar. He will sacrifice your lives to serve his greed and ambition. I'll find you a different piece of land, Matthew, a better piece, bigger, your own empire. Stay alive until I am elected president of Texas again, and we'll do things right next time. The streets of Austin shall once more become the feeding place for buffaloes and the hunting ground for red men. Don't risk your scalps for that damned hole called Austin! Adios, my comrades."

# 10

They had painted themselves to look like devils masked in human skin. Black stripes crossed their faces. Seashells hung from their earlobes. Their hair was braided with bear grease, and their scalp locks were tied up with ribbons and fur. Some had birds or beasts painted on their chests. Others wore tattoos in circles around old wounds as badges of honor. Several wore buffalo horns on their heads, and all carried near their loins their personal magic—bits of hair, feathers, shiny stones. Turk, the Fighting Man, carried a butcher knife, a stone axe and a Mexican *escopeta*. The rest had bows and arrows, lances, shields, hatchets and clubs with heads of iron or stone. All wore deerskin leggins. Their horses were painted with stripes and circles, manes braided and tails wrapped into bobs. The masked devils were gazing across the fount of the spring that fed the running stream they had long known as Cold Water. What they saw was a stockade fence, a large barn and a stone house that had not been at the spring when Turk had led his raiding party down the Colorado River valley on their way to Mexico two full moons ago.

Turk was trying to decide on this early morning whether to accede to the wishes of the majority of his twenty raiders and destroy this intruder, or return with their Mexican plunder, which included a monkey and a green and yellow parrot and six captives and hundreds of Mexican horses, to the hills of Comancheria and present the problem of the intruder at the spring of Cold Water to the council of families.

"I smell women in there," said a warrior called Fat Jack.

"I want a woman," said Isimanica, a lithe and muscular young warrior, entering his prime, preparing to lead his own parties. Isimanica was the closest to being Turk's competition as leader among those present, all of whom had come on the raid of their own volition. But the decision at this moment was being made not by Turk or Isimanica but by a vote of the painted men discussing as a group whether to ride through the gate and loot the place, or let the intruder stay for now and continue toward their families bearing prizes from Mexico.

"They have pigs and horses inside that fence, too," said another warrior.

"They have sugar," said another.

"That is women we are smelling," Isimanica said.

Turk grunted. It was clear to all that the decision had been made. A raiding party must be led, not driven. Turk was pleased with the decision and ready to lead. He was Fighting Man.

Inside the house on this Sunday morning, the lawyer Ridgewood Bone was snoring with slobbering blats in the bed. He sprawled red and naked beside the half-wit daughter of the caretaker couple he had moved into this fine new farm, five miles southwest of Austin on Barton Creek at the head of what the lawyer had named Bone Spring.

The lawyer Bone had foreclosed on the farm from the unfortunate original settler, Castorp, in lieu of the legal bill for handling Castorp's immigration. Bone felt no guilt over taking this idyllic place away from his client; Bone had left Castorp a free citizen with access to many other plots of land, just not any longer to this glen with the gushing spring that made a sound which induced him to relax.

Two years ago Billy Barton had built a house about two miles nearer the city on creek-side land that had three flowing springs that Barton named for his daughters—Parenthia, Zenobia and Eliza. Barton was starting work on a sawmill that would be powered by water moving in the creek. Castorp went exploring farther up Barton Creek until he found his own building site. The

Indian Joes had told lawyer Bone that there was an unspoken agreement with the Comanches that the settlement line for Texans was at the Treaty Oak, a giant tree west of Shoal Creek on what was planned to be the extension of Pecan Street. About fifteen years ago, Stephen Austin—at that time a Mexican land impresario with a colony forty miles to the east—made a treaty with the Wichitas and Tonkawas in the shade of the hundred-foot-tall live oak tree. Bone knew his new property was several miles too far west of the Treaty Oak. Bone knew the danger. But the flowing spring water was beautiful and calming, and the little immigrant girl was so sweet that Bone felt reasonably safe here.

In the other room of the house, divided by a dog run, the caretaker couple and their younger daughter got up and rolled their blankets that served as beds when the lawyer Bone was occupying the only true bed. The caretakers were Jake and Wanda Mecom, mountain people from Tennessee, penniless wanderers who had met the lawyer Bone in Austin on their vague path west. Bone was entranced by their half-wit daughter, Pearl, who was fifteen and full of love for everything, even the lawyer Bone.

"Listen to the drunk idiot snoring like a pig," said Jake Mecom, a tall, blond, slack-jawed man with darting fox eyes. "First he's squealing like he's being whipped while he lays the sausage to Pearl, and now listen to him snort, the damn fool."

"You're the one that told him he could fornicate on Pearl. Don't come complaining about it now," Wanda Mecom said. She was short and dark, like their ten-year-old daughter, Rose, who was picking up the water bucket to go to the spring.

"Well, he give us this place to live and pays us a wage besides, don't he, woman? All he wants in return is to plug Pearl on Saturday nights. That don't amount to nothing. Pearl had just as soon do the dirty as eat."

"I ain't going to be this son of a bitch's nigger," Wanda said.

"We're just taking care of a few goats and pigs and a cow. It ain't like being a slave."

"And we take care of his damn horses."

"We can ride them horses when we decide to move on," said Jake.

"Are you crazy? They hang horse thieves in Texas."

Pearl appeared in the doorway. They heard the lawyer snoring behind her. She wore her blue cotton shift and was barefoot. Her blonde hair was tangled. She smiled at her family. "Water," she said.

"I'm going to the spring, Pearl. Come with me," said Rose.

The two sisters stepped into the yard, each with fingers on the bucket handle. The sand was warm on their feet, and their tough skin shed the burrs.

"Did you have a good time last night?" asked Rose.

"Yes."

"It sounded awful. I'm never gonna let a man do that to me."

They walked toward the stockade gate which led to the spring. Four goats nibbled the sparse grass inside the fence. Three horses nuzzled their feed trough. The milk cow bellowed from the barn.

"Mama's gonna have to milk that damn cow. I'm not gonna do it," Rose said.

"Milk cow," said Pearl.

The lawyer Bone woke up. Pain stabbed his gut. For a moment Bone couldn't remember where he was. Ah yes, this was his fine new country place, not his quarters at Bullock's Inn. Pain hit his gut again. The new physician in Austin, that strange pugilist chap from New York City who was living with a Cherokee woman he claimed was his sister—no one believed it, of course, she must be his concubine, but Austin needed a good herbal doctor—had given him several draughts of a botancial brown liquid that had soothed his irritable bowels. Bone resolved to see Dr. Swift tomorrow morning and buy another jug of the stuff that the Cherokee woman helped to gather from the bushes and streambanks, even though her right leg was in a clay cast.

Bone planted his feet on the wooden floor—Castorp had been an artist as a carpenter, how neatly these boards fit—and with whiskey-trembling hands pulled himself up off the bed, which was a buffalo skin tied to four posts.

Naked, he walked to the window he had left unshuttered the night before. That had been a dangerous slip, he told himself. A panther might have entered in the night through the open window. Bone could hardly remember leaving Dutch John's Saloon, much less how he had managed to ride five miles without falling off—or had he fallen a time or two?—but he did remember the delicious Pearl lifting her cotton dress above her head and wiggling her tongue at him. Between her legs was a pot of warm honey.

He heard that little hillbilly woman complaining in the next room, her accent almost as peculiar to his Princetonian ear as Chinese. He wondered if he should devise a way to get rid of her and her husband and have Pearl appointed as his ward by the court. Maybe the other girl, Rose, should be under his care, too. The thought of Rose sharing the bed with Pearl and himself made the lawyer Bone begin feeling sexed again, and he wondered where Pearl had gone. He needed Pearl again now.

Bone looked out the window and saw the two girls walking toward the gate, carrying the water bucket between them. He began pulling his cock with his fingers as he watched the girls moving their bare legs, and then he saw at the gate a sight that jolted him like an ancestral nightmare remembered in his blood.

Barking and crowing and tooting eagle-bone whistles, the Comanches burst through the gate into the compound. Isimanica tossed a rawhide loop around Rose and Pearl and dragged them in the dirt behind his shaggy pony. Jake Mecom rushed out of the house with his musket but was pierced through the lungs by Fat Jack's fourteen-foot lance and pinned to the ground, where he wriggled like a minnow on a hook.

Three warriors ran inside and emerged with a shrieking Wanda Mecom. She saw Fat Jack kneeling and sawing her husband's head with a butcher knife and heard the pop like a gunshot as Jake's scalp came loose. Isimanica leaped to the ground and ripped open Wanda Mecom's dress, then tore off her cotton slip and her drawers. Turk glanced at the two young girls, one of them screaming, the other seeming stunned, and back at Isimanica, who pushed the mother down and prepared to mount her. As the leader, Turk could have stopped this rape, claimed the woman as his slave, but why should he? He looked at the woman and decided she was not worth the trouble. To humiliate and rape and murder the enemy was desirable within the code of the families. It was Isimanica's right to treat them as he pleased.

"I'll pay you a ransom! I'll make you rich! My family is worth millions!" shouted the lawyer Ridgewood Bone as he was wrestled, red and naked, out of the other half of the house by two warriors who were grinning at the sight of excrement oozing down the lawyer's thighs. "I will ship boatloads of gold to your people!"

With a stroke of his already bloody butcher knife, Fat Jack hacked Bone's penis. Fat Jack reached over and grabbed the almost severed member and tore it out of Bone's body and flung it to the ground.

The lawyer screamed and looked down at blood spouting between his legs and at the piece of red gristle lying in the dirt.

"Put it in his mouth," one warrior said.

"Make him get down on his knees and eat it," said another.

Turk slid off his horse and walked over to the lawyer and smashed his skull with a stone axe.

Isimanica was grunting on top of Wanda Mecom. He howled in orgasm. Another warrior took his place.

Pulling up his leather breechclout to cover his genitals, Isimanica looked down at the dead lawyer. Isimanica was wishing Turk hadn't killed the man so quickly.

"I got his pecker. I want his hair, too," said Fat Jack.

"Take it," Turk said.

"I want the two girls," said Isimanica.

"They belong to you," Turk said.

Warriors were coming out of the house carrying pots and pans, a mirror, shirts and dresses, a stuffed cushion, a doll. One held up a brown bottle half filled with liquid.

"Whiskey!" cried Fat Jack. He jerked off lawyer Bone's scalp and stuffed it in his belt with the scalp of Jake Mecom and reached up and grabbed the brown bottle. "I love whiskey, and whiskey loves me!" he cried. Fat Jack turned up the bottle and drank it dry.

"Do you want the woman?" asked Turk.

"No," said Isimanica.

"Does anybody want the woman?" asked Turk.

"I'll take her," said a squat, broad-chested warrior called The Ram. His oriental features were painted like butterflies. "She will make a worker."

"Burn the buildings," said Turk.

While painted figures set fire to the house and the barn, Fat Jack began to stagger.

"Look at him! He's drunk!" laughed a warrior.

Fat Jack dropped to his knees, his hands clutching his stomach. The roof of the house and the loft of the barn began to blaze. The black and gray smoke would be seen in Austin, Turk knew. It was essential that they leave Cold Water at once and ride for the protection of Comancheria.

"Get up, Fat Jack," Turk said. "All of you—be quick. Hey, Fat Jack, get up! You can act foolish when we return to tell our families about this raid. Now, get up!"

Fat Jack made a strangled gasp and flopped onto his belly, his legs kicking.

Turk rolled him over and saw the glaze come across Fat Jack's eyes and his mouth fall open and his tongue flop, and Turk felt the tingle of Fat Jack's spirit leaving his body.

Lying nearby, fully conscious, trying to gather thoughts that refused to come together, Wanda Mecom did realize one thing. The liquid in the brown bottle that Fat Jack had drunk was arsenic that Jake had used to poison baits he set in wolf traps.

# 11

The two-hundred-mile journey from Houston City to San Antonio required the crossing of seven rivers and fifteen creeks with two freight wagons, each drawn by three yokes of oxen, and it took them the better part of seventeen days.

East of San Antonio late in the afternoon they saw in the distance rising from the prairie the cupola above the stone walls of the Cathedral of San Fernando, and they began to make out the shapes of more buildings. Unencumbered by the freight wagons, Caldwell felt he could ride to town in a matter of minutes. But Comanches had stripped three travelers, chopped off their hands and feet, scalped and disembowled them, within sight of San Antonio only weeks ago. Caldwell's responsibility toward his friend and brother Ranger, Big Foot, and the freighters was absolute; the summons from President Lamar could wait.

They arrived at the governor's palace on Military Plaza in the moonlight. To the east across the San Antonio River they saw the white ruins of the Alamo. In the plaza candles flickered on the tables of the chili queens, and iron pots of chili con carne simmered on mesquite fires. Vendors were selling eggs, chickens, goats, melons, straw hats, blankets and peppers. Caldwell could hear water running in San Pedro Creek and in Military Ditch, and the sounds of guitars and voices in the warm darkness down Soledad Street. On Dolorosa Street they heard pianos playing in the saloons and whorehouses. While Big Foot saw to the teamsters checking the powder and lead in at the quartermaster, Caldwell splashed water on his face from a trough, combed his beard and hair with his fingers and from a saddlebag on the white stallion dug out his white doeskin jacket with the fringes on the sleeves and the blue and red stars garnished in beadwork on each breast. The windows of the governor's palace were alight, and the doors were open, and Caldwell saw people dancing and heard the fiddle music. Caldwell enjoyed a fandango.

Above the carved walnut doors of the governor's palace was the date 1749 and the double-headed eagle of the Hapsburg coat of arms of King Phillip V of Spain. The hardwood doors and thick stone walls were scarred by shot and shell. The governor's palace was now being used as a restaurant, saloon, ballroom and offices.

People broke off conversations and made way for Caldwell as he nodded to acknowledge greetings. He saw Anglos, Tejanos and Creoles dressed in their best. Miss Arceneiga wore a maroon cashmere gown and black pheasant plumes in her hair as she spun past dancing with a young Anglo wearing a white linen jacket and trousers. Mrs. Yturri, in a new silk gown, was so tightly corseted that she smiled gamely as she struggled for breath. Three fiddlers, a guitarist and a cornet player played a Mexican waltz. Roque Catahdie, a Greek shopkeeper, wore a black frock coat and danced with Mrs. Mary Maverick. Caldwell saw the Navarros, the Sotos, Garcias, Zambranos, Seguins and Veramendis dancing and talking with the Trasks, the Higgenbothams and Dancys. He stopped at the punch bowl, where he looked up from a cup and saw a lovely redheaded woman, in her early thirties he would guess, as she waltzed past in the grasp of a banker. Caldwell was not a graceful dancer, but he was a powerful one and easy for a good partner to follow. He saw that this woman danced so lightly she would feel like a spirit in his arms.

"Captain Caldwell, may I introduce myself? My name is Lawrence Kerr," said a man who had come to the punch bowl. He was as tall as Caldwell but thin and ropy, and his clothes were fine wool expertly tailored and expensive. "The woman you are staring at is my Dora, my wife."

"Sorry, Kerr. I didn't realize I was staring."

"Oh, I'm quite accustomed to it by now. If I took umbrage at every man who stared at my wife, I'd have time for nothing but duels. I first saw her singing in *The Marriage of Figaro* at Niblo's Garden Theater in New York City twelve years ago, and I still stare at Dora myself, almost every waking moment. I have a friend who every time he sees an astonishingly beautiful woman he says, 'Remember, somewhere, somebody is tired of her.' But that will never be the case with Dora and me."

"My compliments," said Caldwell. He nodded courteously at Kerr and started moving away from the punch bowl. But Kerr tugged Matthew's sleeve and offered a business card.

"Please, Captain. We may have transactions to discuss."

Matthew looked at the card: KERR LAND & CATTLE COMPANY, *Lawrence Kerr, President*

"You own a piece of land in Gonzalez that I am interested in," said Kerr.

"You're new to Texas, I take it," Caldwell said.

Kerr laughed. "I'm a Wall Street man, sir, in Texas less than a week, here to invest a fortune in land, but I'm not so new that I haven't heard of the famous Captain Caldwell."

"I'm not selling my Gonzalez land," Caldwell said.

"Pity. I like that black soil around Gonzalez for cotton farming. Cotton will be a booming business in Texas. But maybe you will change your mind as we get to know each other. Looking through the documents at the land office, I saw you have laid claim to a ten-thousand-acre tract that nearly bumps up against the spread the Kerr Land and Cattle Company owns. We are practically neighbors, in a vast sense."

"What piece of land did you buy?" asked Caldwell.

"West of yours, sir, by some day or two's ride. I haven't seen it, of course, myself—just the plat and the map that shows the two hundred fifty thousand acres that are deeded to the Kerr Land and Cattle Company. Dora and I haven't been here long enough yet to organize a visit or even put together a surveying party."

Caldwell looked at the well-bred features of the face before him, the prominent cheekbones, the proud brown eyes of an apparently sincere, if somewhat drunk, middle-aged New York upper-class gentleman who had bought a quarter of a million acres in the middle of the Comanche Nation.

"Who did you buy it from?"

"I'm curious, why would you ask?"

"I wonder who thinks he has the authority to sell that land."

"The Kerr Group, sir, is on the New York Stock Exchange. We deal with the top people, always. I myself, with the approval of our board and our investors, purchased the land certificates from official representatives of the Republic of Texas who came to New York to transact the business."

"Don't get your bile up, Kerr. I was only curious."

"Ah, here's Dora at last," said Kerr as the tune ended and the sweating banker delivered her to the punch bowl. Kerr and the banker bowed their respects, and Kerr said, "Darling, this is Captain Caldwell . . . my wife, Dora Kerr."

The nearness of the beautiful redhead aroused Matthew's loins. Caldwell brushed his lips against the back of Dora's hand. She was thrilled at the gentle touch of this rough-looking frontier man. Dora had never seen his equal in overwhelming physicality in New York society, not even on the stage.

"My pleasure, Mrs. Kerr."

"I'm honored, Captain. May I have a glass of punch, please? I'm a bit winded. Still tired from the travel, I'm sure," she said.

Lawrence poured the punch in the light of candelabra on the table.

"Thirty-seven days on the sailing ship *St. George* from New York to New Orleans, uncomfortable as hell, then days and nights on the ghastly coach ride, crossing all those rivers and bayous from Louisiana through those giant thickets and forests of east Texas, it's not a trip many would enjoy," Kerr said.

"There are easier ways to get here," Caldwell said. "You could come overland. People do it every day."

"Oh, Lawrence planned this one on his own." Dora smiled and licked a smudge of punch off her upper lip.

"There certainly will be easier ways to get to Texas in the near future," Kerr said. "I picture steamboat lines on all the rivers, overland roads packed with wagon trains. Why, this place is one of the glories of earth, as I heard Sam Houston say years ago in a speech at the Metropolitan Club in Manhattan. Of course, he was representing a New York investment syndicate, but I, for one, believe in his vision. We must open this republic up to commerce. Nature has been bountiful here, and we must share her generosity with the right people."

Mary Maverick, in hand with her husband, Sam, approached and said, "Dora, would you please do us the great honor of a song?"

"Oh, Mary, you embarrass me," said Dora.

Caldwell saw Lawrence nod and smile at his wife. Sam Maverick, who lived with Mary in their stone house on the Soldedad-Main Street corner of Main Plaza nearby, was a Yale man, a politician and debater who had immigrated to Texas from his family estate, Montpelier, in South Carolina. Sam Maverick was an important citizen of the Republic, a proper person for the Kerrs to know.

The crowd applauded. Mary Maverick sat down at the piano and looked at Dora with bright expectancy.

"Do you know 'The Banks of the Blue Moselle'?" Dora asked.

Mary's fingers struck the opening chords.

As Dora sang, Matthew folded his arms and parted his lips in pleasure. Caldwell admired singers. He had no talent for it himself, but he could listen to good singing, all night, especially if it was a beautiful woman who was singing. He looked at the smooth curve of Dora's throat, the pink of her tongue as she sang an angelic soprano, and her eyes met his for a moment.

During the applause after Dora's song, as she modestly declined to do another, the musicians struck up a polka, and Caldwell started forward to ask Dora Kerr to dance. A hand touched his shoulder. Caldwell turned and saw General Albert Sidney Johnston grinning at him. Johnston was a couple of years younger than Caldwell and had recently been named secretary of war by Lamar. A West Pointer and graduate of Transylvania College, Johnston had resigned his commission as a major in the United States Army in Mississippi four years ago, come to Texas a year later and joined Sam Houston's army as a private.

By the finish of the fighting, Johnston had been promoted to brigadier general and head of the Texan army. With most other men Caldwell would have ignored the shoulder touch and continued to lead Dora Kerr into dancing, but he respected Johnston, who had been shot in the hip during a duel with General Felix Huston to establish authority as chief of the army. Caldwell was sorry Huston survived the fight. Huston's loud mouth and bullying manner were correctly seen by the Old Chief as a danger to the Republic, Caldwell believed.

"Matthew."

"Hello, Albert."

"Lamar wants to see you in the fountain room."

"In a few minutes, Albert."

"Now, please, Matthew. I'm asking. The President is very upset. He needs you for an urgent assignment."

Caldwell looked at Dora's swaying hips as she walked with her back toward him and joined her husband. Dora and Lawrence danced well and looked good together, almost professional, Matthew thought. She glanced his way. Caldwell looked into her eyes for an instant. Her husband spun her away to the sound of fiddles and guitars and trumpets, and Matthew turned to follow the general.

Fronds of banana trees hung over the spring-fed fountain that bubbled in the private patio where Lamar was waiting. Two bottles of mustang wine from local vineyards sat on the table. A mestizo maid was laying out plates of cabrito, beans, corn tortillas, onions and figs. Lanterns glowed in the window and door of a whitewashed room where the President was staying.

"Captain Caldwell! It's good to see you again, sir. Thank you for coming so promptly," Lamar said.

"Mr. President," Matthew said.

Lamar's hand felt small and moist to Caldwell, but it was heartily offered. Caldwell looked down at the thin patch on the crown of the President's skull and was pleased that his own hair was still thick though the two men were the same age. Lamar had been in command of the cavalry three years ago on the day they whipped Santa Anna at Peggy McCormick's farm. Until four years ago, Lamar had been a newspaper publisher and state senator in his home state of Georgia. He owned a cotton plantation in Georgia, was a lawyer, former private secretary to the governor of Georgia, and had twice been defeated for a seat in the United States Congress from Georgia. During his two-year term as the first vice president of the Republic of Texas under Sam Houston, Lamar had spent eight months on personal business back home in Athens. Last year Lamar had stood for election to the presidency of Texas, because the Constitution that Matthew had helped draw up and sign at the assembly at

Washington-on-Brazos denied Sam Houston the right to succeed himself as president. Of the two men who opposed Lamar as candidates for office, one flung himself off a steamboat and drowned at Galveston, and the other shot himself to death a few days before the election.

Caldwell rolled a cornmeal tortilla around beans and a strip of cabrito. He drank a glass of the tart wine.

"That Wall Street fellow out at the dance. Kerr with the beautiful wife. Who sold him two hundred fifty thousand acres of public land?" Caldwell asked.

"The land was public domain, and Kerr's money went into the public treasury," Lamar said. "He paid sixty cents an acre. The Republic needs income."

"Did you tell him his land is in Comancheria?" said Caldwell.

"Matthew, my mind is not so fogged with affairs of the Republic that I have forgotten I was in the Senate chambers the day we passed a bill granting you a double headright and double labor in recognition of your original citizenship and your valor in fighting for our cause. You chose your own land in Comancheria, did you not?"

"I did. But I knew the Comanches are living there."

"No doubt Mr. Kerr has heard of Comanches," said Lamar. "If not, he soon will."

Johnston was finishing his second glass of wine. He rubbed his finger around the rim of the glass, uncomfortable and pondering.

"Matthew, did you actually see a Mexican army battalion east of San Antonio, or has this report been exaggerated as it was passed along to me?" Johnston asked.

"I had a scrape with their scouts. General Savariego is putting on a show of force against the Comanches and might be threatening Austin. It kind of bothered me that Cristolphe Rublo was with the Mexicans."

Caldwell did not mention that he had left Rublo to die in a trap made of a pecan tree.

"What is specially bothersome about Rublo?" asked Lamar.

"Rublo wants his million acres back."

"Perhaps I should send troops to the former Rublo estate," said Johnston. "You agree, Caldwell?"

"No, I don't. The Rangers can handle this."

Johnston said, "And the menace to Austin? How many troops are needed?"

"How many do you have?" asked Caldwell.

"Almost none within a hundred miles," Johnston said.

"I will deal with it," said Caldwell.

"You will keep me informed of the situation? I mean, just in case the twenty or thirty Rangers between Austin and the Rublo land in Goliad get in over their heads against a Mexican battalion?" Johnston said.

Caldwell smiled "It's not Rublo's land, Albert. This is Texas now."

Johnston rose from the table.

"If you will excuse me, then, gentlemen," he said. "I must be off to a dinner at the Fincus with the few remaining members of my staff who are loyal and noble and willing and able to work without pay. Good night to you. And I'm glad to see you made it out there among the savages and the Mexicans and back once again, Matthew. You're a clever old rascal and damned lucky."

Standing with military bearing in his black frock coat, frilly collar and cuffs and red vest, Johnston bowed abruptly to the President, then to Caldwell, turned on his heel and hurried out. Matthew wondered what had become of Rublo. That had been two weeks ago. Most likely, Rublo was bones by now.

"Matthew, could you leave for Austin tonight on a special commission?" asked Lamar, refilling their glasses. He offered Caldwell a cheroot and lit it for him, and the two exhaled smoke.

"My horse and I require a good night's rest," Caldwell said.

"Tomorrow, then?"

"If it's the Mexican army you're worried about, I'll find them if they're anywhere close to Austin," said Caldwell. "But not tonight."

"It's more than just the Mexicans," the President said.

"What is your problem in Austin?"

Lamar called, "Would you step out here, Henry?"

The birdlike face on its long neck bobbed into view from Lamar's room, and then the gawky frame of Henry Longfellow stooped to pass through the door, a crutch scraping against the tile floor. Gradually the entire body emerged, crutch under his right armpit, his right leg in a cast.

"Captain Caldwell, this is Henry Longfellow, my former colleague in the Georgia legislature, a great friend to the cotton growers and now one of my advisers in land development and other matters," said the President.

"How do?" Caldwell said.

"I am in agony, damn it," Longfellow said, lowering himself onto a wooden bench. "They had to break my leg bone and reset it again last week. That's three times broken, not counting the whack that thug gave me in the ambush. So I am not doing well at all, sir, thank you very much for asking."

Lamar poured Caldwell's wineglass full again.

"Henry went to Austin recently at my bidding, official Republic business, riding my own favorite horse," the President said. "Tell him what happened, Henry."

Longfellow squinted in pain as he shifted his weight on the bench so he could bring his beak to bear on Caldwell.

"A young Cherokee whore enticed me off the road just short of the ferry, pleading for my help at repairing her broken wagon," Longfellow said. "Once I was dismounted, she displayed her breasts to me and offered sex for two gold dollars. Well, I'm only human, Captain Caldwell. The wicked bitch lured me into a glen, and when I produced my purse, her accomplice leaped upon me from concealment, beat me, robbed me, broke my leg and left me to drown in the great overflow from the river. Somehow I managed to climb onto Mirabeau's horse, and the beast followed his nose back here. The doctor tells me I might have to use this damn crutch for the rest of my life. I will be in pain every day. I want that thug and his whore arrested and brought to justice."

Caldwell looked at Lamar, who was twisting a finger in his sideburn as he listened.

"Why me?" Matthew asked.

"You're my number one Ranger, my top law enforcer."

"Mr. Longfellow is sitting here still alive. An incident like this is not my job. I have a ranging area to patrol and a station to be in charge of. I'm going to take a loop through Austin—but not to punish a man for whipping your friend," Matthew said.

"What if I told you the man who broke Henry's leg is a foreign spy who is trying to stir up a Cherokee rebellion? said Lamar.

"Is that the truth?"

"Do you have any idea how many foreign nations wish to wrest our Republic away from us?" the President said. "The Dutch, the Spanish, the British, the French, just to name a few. Our Republic is crawling with foreign agents. My informants in Austin tell me this foreign agent has been crossing the Colorado River and walking on the white cliffs up there. That is your land he is exploring, Matthew. He must be conspiring with the Comanches against us, as well as with the Cherokees, and he is doing it on Caldwell land. Is this a good enough reason for you, Captain?"

"If this man is trespassing on my land and conspiring with the Comanches, I will take him in hand," Matthew said.

The President entwined his fingers angrily and popped his knuckles.

Lamar said, "Captain Caldwell, I want you to bring that spy and his Cherokee whore to me with chains around their necks."

## T W O

---

## AUSTIN

While gazing on the splendid scene,
I sometimes think I see
My long-lost friends with smile serene,
Waving their hands for me—
As if they fain, from earthly woes,
Would call me to their own repose.

*—poem by Mirabeau B. Lamar*

---

# 1 2

**R**omulus Swift rapped on the door of the room next to his on the ground floor in the rear of Bullock's Inn. "Cully, are you ready?" he said.

"Just a minute," his sister called from inside.

The sun was low in the eastern sky. It was about ten o'clock in the morning—time for their walk around town to get exercise for Cullasaja. Doc never let his sister wander the streets without him. After their walk Doc would massage her thigh and foot above and below the cast of clay and moss that he had fashioned for her broken tibia. Three weeks ago they had crawled barely alive from the flood, all their possessions swept away and Cullasaja's broken leg bleeding and dirty. Doc had carried his sister in his arms through the rain to the only place in Austin where he knew they would find shelter—Fritz Gruber's Paradise for Sale office and living quarters. Doc had not locked the door behind him when he left the German asleep before the rain came. They had discovered Gruber still snoring with his face on his desk, the thick red poultice covering his skull.

Rain fell for four days and nights. The sky was black and thunder shook the building. Lightning ripped and crackled. Rain tore holes in the German's roof as the fury of the storm hovered over the city. Doc cleaned his sister's wound with coal oil, splinted it and kept her in the German's bed. He dosed her from a bottle of laudanum he found on a shelf in the bedroom. At the same time Doc applied the herb and poppy poultice to Gruber's skull at the intervals prescribed by Knows All Charlie. Doc made sure the taboos were observed. Gruber was drowsy and delirious. He raved about the treacherous Comanches, the man-ape, the cavern of gold. Mrs. Ruth Hunboldt waded knee deep through the mud the second morning of the big rain with the idea in her mind that she would try to make Fritz Gruber be more specific about marriage. Mrs. Hunboldt took in the strange scene—the snoring Gruber with his pink plastered skull, the Indian girl with the broken leg, the handsome man who claimed to be a doctor—with the equanimity of a woman whose years on the frontier had dulled her capacity for surprise. Mrs. Hunboldt prepared a caldron of venison and vegetable stew that fed the refugees in Gruber's office for four days, while she stayed away from Gruber so as not to touch him accidentally.

On the fifth morning, Fritz Gruber suddenly sat up straight at his desk and said, "What the hell?"

Doc had been drowsing on a blanket in the corner, listening to the steady hammering of the rain.

"How do you feel?" Doc asked.

The German squinted at him.

"I remember you. You're the healer," the German said.

Doc rose and walked over to Gruber. The poultice had caked around the axe blade. Doc peeled back a strip of poultice and was pleased to see the flesh beneath it was pink and healthy. Cullasaja parted the curtain and came in from the bedroom, leaning on her crutch. If Gruber was surprised to see a beautiful young Indian woman wrapped in a sheet, he didn't show it. He was absorbed in his own situation. The German was watching in a hand mirror as Doc slowly scraped and washed away the remainder of the herb and poppy syrup and revealed a skull that had healed. There was no more seepage. The only odor was roses and vinegar. Except for the axe blade rising like a one-inch-high fin along the crown of his head, Gruber looked as normal as a person with his characteristics possibly could.

"Thank you, Doctor. Thank you," Gruber said. "I am your friend for life. Anything I have is yours. Not Ruthie, but anything else."

"You could lend me two hundred dollars until I can get some funds sent to me somehow from New York," Doc said.

"My friend, I will not lend you two hundred dollars," the German shouted. "I will pay you five hundred dollars right now, in Mexican silver, not in redbacks, and more as you need it. Call it your fee. You have made a miracle! You have given me back my head!"

With the silver, and backed by the force of Gruber's personality, Doc rented two rooms that opened onto a dirt road called Pecan Street. Richard Bullock, owner of the inn, was enchanted by Cullasaja's looks and charm and touched by her predicament with the broken leg. He shrugged when Doc told him they were brother and sister. Who cares? thought Bullock. She's a sexy-looking woman, and we need a doctor in town, and they've paid in silver, and only a foolhardy person would turn down a request from Fritz Gruber.

The news of Gruber's astounding recovery instantly swept the two hundred or so Anglo citizens of Austin. Patients began to line up outside Doc's room at Bullocks. He treated them with herbs he and Cullasaja gathered along the creek banks, with his knowledge of physiology and folklore, and with patent medicines from the chemist that contained alcohol, coca and opium. Lawyer Ridgewood Bone was one of his first patients. Doc's rate of cures was high. In three weeks he became one of the most popular people in a city that in the same time had grown from two hundred residents to more than six hundred. He and his so-called sister did not socialize as a couple, but they were welcome in the restaurant at Bullock's, where the daily fare was bread, beef, wild honey and game. No one failed to treat Cullasaja with respect, no matter how much they might gossip about the doctor and his Indian lover. Doc spent some of his evenings at Dutch John's, watching the poker games. Even though Doc drank only water or ginger ale, the regulars found his company refreshing. The first two doctors who had come to Austin were drunks. One drowned in Shoal Creek, and the other was shot dead in a card game.

Though it was founded on the nearly miraculous healing of Fritz Gruber, Doc Swift's reputation as a healer grew even greater on the morning two wood-choppers in their wagon brought in the mutilated but still living body of Ridge-wood Bone. He had crawled three miles from Bone Creek toward town when the woodchoppers found him. They brought the ghastly naked figure—red and blue and white and fat, flesh and hair ripped from his head, his penis missing— to Doc at Bullock's Inn. Citizens who gathered around had never seen a human hacked up this way. They expected lawyer Bone to die very soon. But Doc had seen much worse in the surgery arena at Edinburgh. He and Cullasaja bathed the lawyer and treated his wounds with poultices and fed him herbs to put him to sleep and stop his pain. Bone was carried to his own room at Bullock's and placed in his own bed, where many citizens who owed him money hoped Bone would breathe his last. But the lawyer persisted in staying alive. This was attributed by the citizens to the almost magical skills of Doc Swift and his Indian nurse.

Because of the peculiarity of one of the lawyer's wounds, the citizens nick-named him "Lawyer Boneless."

"Did you go across the river last night?" Cullasaja asked her brother. She was making good time on her two crutches, swinging her broken leg, as they set out on their exercise stroll around Austin on a warm morning.

"No, I stopped at Shoal Creek and talked to some of the Wacos camped over there. I'm not going to climb the cliff again until we get you on both feet and in the care of Chief Bowl."

"Do you honestly believe there's some half-human ape across the river and a cave of treasure and gold?" she said. "You're sure you didn't read this in a story by Daniel Defoe? It has a Robinson Crusoe ring to it, I think. Or Uncle Jonathan might have dreamed up such a tale."

"Uncle Knows All Charlie believes the creature exists."

"Rommy, you're a sophisticated, highly educated modern man. Do you believe it?"

"You've heard Gruber raving about it in his delirium as well as speaking of it when he's sober. You see the evidence of the blade in his skull, and you know he had gold ingots. Is he telling the truth?"

"You're not answering me."

"Yes. I believe it. Knows All Charlie has ordered me to go there."

"For what?"

"To find wisdom."

"Have you been eating opium?"

"Knows All Charlie says I am fated to do this. This is a new wisdom for our Cherokee people."

"What do you mean—new wisdom?" Cullasaja said. "The Old Way is the true wisdom."

"I don't know why, Cully. But I know what I'm looking for is on the other side of the river."

They stopped to let a dozen pigs trot across Pecan Street, followed by two large white hogs. Cows roamed the streets, and chickens were clucking everywhere. At least three dogs were barking at any given moment, day or night. Pole pens were being erected on Congress Avenue to restrict the passage of domestic animals. There was a constant clamor of saws and axes. Buildings · of pine and cedar were going up fast as the craftsmen could manage. Many newcomers lived in tents, most of them waiting for a house to be built. Because of the crowds and the difficulty of supply—shipments of hardware and staples and condiments came by ox wagon from Houston City or San Antonio—flour was a hundred redback dollars a barrel. But there was no shortage of food. As well as holding many domestic animals, the fields and woods of the valley were crawling with deer and birds and other game. The creeks were full of fish. Tonk and Lipan Indians—enemies of the Comanches—loitered around the edges of the city with stacks of buffalo hides and beaver and raccoon pelts for trade. It was unthinkable for Comanches to fight each other, but they fought everybody else. The Tonks and Lipans moved closer to the men with hats.

The city was laid out from south to north, beginning at the Colorado River. At what became Congress Avenue and the river had been a settlement named

Waterloo—five families at a confluence with Shoal Creek that always disappeared in the regular floods. Waterloo was swallowed by the growth of Austin. Congress Avenue was being beaten out of the ground, its springs buried under rocks, its ravine filled with earth, to run north from the river's edge, called Water Street, to Capitol Square, the site that had been selected for the first capitol building. Because of a dispute between contractors a temporary capitol building was in fact being constructed several blocks to the south and west.

Doc and Cullasaja enjoyed walking in Austin. Twenty streams flowed through the town. The north and south streets were named for the biggest Texas rivers—Rio Grande, Nueces, San Antonio, Guadalupe, La Baca, Colorado, Brazos, San Jacinto, Trinity, Neches, Red River and Sabine. Congress Avenue ran up the middle. The southern boundary was marked by the river and Water Street, and the northern by North Avenue, two blocks north of Capitol Square. The west to east streets were named for native trees—Live Oak, Cypress, Cedar, Pine, Pecan, Bois d'Arc, Hickory, Ash, Mulberry, Mesquite, Peach and Walnut. West Avenue was the western boundary of the city and East Avenue was the eastern edge. College Avenue—on which land was set aside for the building of a university—went east and west from either side of Capitol Square. Waller Creek defined the eastern boundary, and Shoal Creek ran along the western. Both creeks flowed steadily year after year, even during times of no rain. Doc and Cullasaja could see the framework of the new French legation under construction on a hill east of East Avenue.

Cullasaja knew the names of the wildflowers abloom in the fields in their spring colors—bluebonnets, winecups, redbuds, Indian blankets, honeysuckle, wild verbena, Indian paintbrush, sunflowers, goldenrod, agarita berries and purple sage. The twenty streams that flowed through the city were lined with cypress, cottonwood and sycamore trees. Oaks, hackberries, chinaberries, elm and willows grew in abundance. Evergreen cedars were being chopped down to make fence posts and rails. In and around the city were rabbits, possums, squirrels, raccoons, foxes, armadillos, roadrunners, pigeons, pheasants, wild turkeys, coyotes, wolves, panthers, otters, beavers, hawks, and often a bear or an eagle would be seen.

Yesterday they buried the immigrant from Tennessee—no one knew his name—in the new cemetery on the eastern side of East Avenue. Lawyer Bone, sweating and moaning in his bed at Bullock's, whispered that he was not acquainted with the immigrants and bore no responsbility for the woman and two daughters, who had been kidnapped by the Comanches. The citizens who attended the funeral, about twenty in all, most of whom were saddened and frightened by the plight of these strangers, asked Doc to say a few words over the grave, since there was not a preacher in the city. Doc said, "Lord God, we ask you to bless and welcome this soul in his eternal life while his body returns to dust here in Texas." Then Fritz Gruber stepped forward. "It was a big mistake for this man to bring his family to Texas, but please forgive him. It rains on the just and on the unjust. Amen," the German said.

Doc and Cullasaja passed the Loafer's Log in front of Bullock's and nodded greetings to two land agents who sat with maps and plats unfolded across their knees. They heard a commotion from the direction of Dutch John's and saw Fritz Gruber run out the front door.

"Doc! Doc! Come quick! The judge is dying!" the German yelled.

Doc and Cullasaja followed Gruber into Dutch John's, where Judge Loftin, the magistrate for the city which had no law officers, was writhing on the floor, moaning and clutching his belly.

Doc helped Gruber and Dutch John and others lay the judge atop the billiard table. Doc tore open the judge's shirt and saw a swollen belly. The probe of a finger to the abdomen brought forth a cry of pain.

"He has a temperature," Cullasaja said, her hand on the judge's forehead. "His pulse is very fast."

Doc decided the judge's appendix was infected. If it should burst, the judge would surely die. It must be removed at once. Doc asked Cullasaja to organize the bringing of hot water and rags. He told the barber to run fetch the straight razors from the shop. He sent a lawyer to fetch sewing needles from the cobbler, and another to bring a ball of twine from the general store. Doc helped the German and Dutch John and others lay a tarpaulin under the judge. "This is going to get bloody," Doc said. "No point ruining the billiard table."

"Very thoughtful of you, Doc," said Dutch John.

The chemist came in with a tiny bottle of opium tincture that was almost empty.

"This is all we have in my shop. The shipment hasn't come through," the chemist said.

"Liar," said the German.

"I would not lie!" the chemist said, flushed.

"Bring a quart of rum," said Doc.

"Oh, the judge is a Puritan teetooler. When he's sober, he is very much against drinking," the land commissioner said, draining his mug of hot beer. "I guess we'll see how strongly he holds to his Puritan beliefs when you slice him with that razor."

"I'll make willow bark tea to help his pain," Cullasaja said.

"Get somebody to round up six small flat smooth stones from the creek, and bring a bucket of moss and mud. Get the swamper to pull down those cobwebs from the corner to stuff in the wound. Find a bowl of sugar. Bleeding is going to be the main problem."

"Coffee grounds are good for stopping blood. I'll find a bowl of them," she said. She stumped off on her crutch, giving orders to heat water and tear rags. The daytime drinking crowd in Dutch John's was mixed in its willingness to take orders from a Cherokee woman, but some men did run to do her bidding. Most stood fascinated by the judge's agony.

"I am dying!" screamed the judge.

"All right, then," Doc said, "you men grab his arms and legs. Fritz, you stand at his head and don't let him break his neck. Put a piece of wood in his mouth."

Doc selected a straight-edge razor from the barber, dipped it in a pan of hot water and looked at the pink flesh of the judge's abdomen. He touched the edge of the blade to the judge's skin and, as in cleaving meat, he drew down a line of blood.

# 1 3

O n his first day at the medical college in Edinburgh, Doc had been invited by a professor to accompany him into the surgery arena to watch a double amputation. "Both legs just above the knee, poor chap. Silver lining, though. A few inches higher and the cartwheel would have crushed his knocker and his balls," the professor said.

A wild-eyed man wearing nothing but an undershirt crashed between them and ran toward the road, screaming unintelligibly of horrors. Two hospital attendants appeared. Their work required them to be built like blacksmiths.

"That's Kendrick running there. See? He just fell down. With that tumor on his brain, he's too dizzy to go far," the professor said.

The attendants approached Kendrick. He scrambled up and tried to run.

They tackled him and threw him to the ground. He wrestled and fought furiously, screaming all the while. They twisted his arms behind him and dragged him back toward the surgery building.

"Kendrick is scheduled for surgery later today. He has been trying to escape since last night. He was pitiful. First he got down on his knees and prayed to God to save him or send a lightning bolt to kill him. He begged us to stab him in the heart. Then he tried to jump out the window, and we had to restrain him with leather straps all night long," the professor said.

"Why didn't you put him at ease with opium?" Doc asked.

"The Chinaman's drug? You jest. We use no drugs at Edinburgh."

"No need to go to China. I can send for opium from North Carolina," Doc said. "These people don't have to suffer."

The professor laid a finger against a nostril and blasted out a gob of mucus.

"Suppose your house is on fire," the professor said. "The warning bell rings in the tower. People rush to the bell and stop it from ringing. Does that put out the fire?"

"I don't understand why we don't do both," Romulus said.

"My dear Swift," said the professor, "you come highly recommended as a student, so I would advise you to shut up and listen and learn. Paracelsus discovered ether three hundred years ago. By the name of sweet vitriol, ether was known even three hundred years earlier than Paracelsus. We have known the effects of nitrous oxide for more than fifty years. We know of codeine and morphine. We know of this new substance—chloric ether, or chloroform—that will defeat pain. There is even this so-called Mesmerism. No, if we wanted to defeat these people's pain, we would do it. But that is not our purpose. We are surgeons. We are devoted not to defeating pain but to curing malfunctions and traumas of the physiological system. Pain is part of the process by which our patients are purified, cleansed of their afflictions. Pain is the way God designed life and wants it to be."

"On board ship, we got them drunk before we cut off their legs," Romulus said.

"You are not at sea now, Swift. You are at the greatest medical college in the world, and I suggest you behave as if you are grateful for your good fortune. Now follow me. I have an attendant holding a place for us near the table so we may observe closely."

In the front hall, a haggard woman wearing a cotton gown was on her knees, pleading for mercy. Romulus understood that she was another of the day's surgery cases. People did not resort to surgery unless they had given up hope of living without it, but most patients tried to back out or kill themselves when they heard screams from the operating arena and saw the surgeons in their jackets that were stiff with pus and blood.

Romulus and the professor pushed through the crowd in the operating arena. Friends and relatives of the patient, as well as students and the merely curious or some who were obsessed with blood and torture, filled the room except for the fiery brazier heating the cauterizing irons, the blood-smeared surgeon and his two beefy assistants, and the operating table itself, with its leather straps to hold arms and legs. The patient was a handsome young man who lay naked on the table. His legs were crushed from the knees down. It had been necessary to raise the leather straps so they held him at the thighs. He was sobbing and saying, "Mama . . . Mama . . . Mama . . ."

Romulus still saw in his mind the speed with which the surgeon's powerful forearms had flown into action and sliced both legs off the young man in minutes with a handsaw, ripping bone as blood and flesh splashed and squirted onto the spectators.

Remembering this, Doc used sudden force and cut through the fat and laid open the judge's abdomen. The judge screeched like a cat. The barber, holding the judge's left arm, took a whiff of the foul odor that rushed up from the exposed bowels—and fell over in a faint.

With his hands and the razor, Doc opened the judge's abdomen wider, and intestines bulged out. Cullasaja was beside him, packing round stones into the cavity, soaking up the blood with rags. Doc's fingers dug among the judge's intestines until he found the red, weepy knob protruding from the bowel. He pried the appendix away from the bowel with the fingers of his left hand. With his right hand Doc took the length of twine he was holding between his lips and reached into the judge's abdomen and tied off the appendix with the twine.

His eyes caught his sister's eyes, and he nodded. She began mixing cobwebs, sugar, coffee grounds, moss and mud in a bowl with her fingers as though she were working cornmeal for bread.

Using the straight razor, Doc cut off the wet, red appendix and tossed it onto the floor. It looked like a severed thumb. Dutch John's cat darted between legs, snatched up the appendix and leaped out the window.

Cullasaja removed the smooth stones and then applied her mixture inside the judge's belly, slathering the judge's bowels with her hands. Then she spat into the cavity. Doc heard angry rumbling in the crowd.

"Spit makes the blood coagulate," Doc assured them.

With the cobbler's needle and twine, Doc sewed the judge's belly shut, as his sister soaked up the blood.

Cullasaja smeared the wound with bear grease and covered the judge's belly with linen.

Judge Loftin was conscious throughout. He had been very brave, Doc thought. The judge reached up to shake Doc's hand in gratitude, but when he saw Doc's fingers covered in blood and bowels, the judge passed out.

"Hurray for the doc!" shouted Fritz Gruber.

"Hurray! Hurray!" yelled the crowd.

"Hurray for his sister!" Fritz Gruber shouted.

"Hurray! Hurray!"

"First round of drinks is on the house," yelled Dutch John. "The rest I'll put on the judge's tab."

The crowd rushed to the bar. Cullasaja was still mopping blood from the judge's belly. Doc washed his face and hands and arms in a bowl of warm water. His shirt and pants were splattered with blood.

"You're a great man, Doc," the German said.

"Drink to the doc!" cried the barber, who was sitting recovering from his swoon. Odors had always been his weakness. He didn't mind looking at gore, or even baby shit, just so long as he didn't smell it.

"To the doc!" Dutch John shouted.

The crowd repeated the cry and turned up their bottles and mugs. Dutch John was searching behind the bar. He found the bottle of champagne he had been saving for a special event. What could be more special than this? Judge Loftin's life is actually saved by surgery on top of Dutch John's billiard table? Time to pop the cork to our city's great new doctor and his Indian lover, who makes a very fair nurse.

Dutch John pried the cork with his thumbs, and it exploded against the ceiling. Champagne flowed down the bottle as Dutch John thrust it into the hands of Doc Swift and said, "We salute you, Doc. Have a drink with us."

Doc lifted the bottle high so all could see it. The crowd cheered. "Told you he'd take a drink!" somone shouted, and they laughed. Doc lowered the bottle to his mouth. The champagne was pungent and hot against his lips. Doc had not had a drink of wine or alcohol of any sort in eight years. The taste of champagne made him remember his last night of drinking. He had been in an Irish saloon on the waterfront in New York City with several sailors from the Swift shipping line. They were all very drunk. A sailor from a rival company insulted the Swift name. Doc forestalled a general brawl by challenging the offending sailor to fight man on man, although Doc knew it was not a fair match. Doc was usually a convivial companion on a saloon crawl, and he avoided trouble, but this night he was drunk enough to become dark and violent. They cleared out the center of the room. The rival sailor pulled a knife, but Doc waved off help from the Swift crew. Now Doc was coldly angry. He hit the rival sailor six quick blows and killed him with a left hook to the temple. Because it was clearly self-defense, and nobody much liked the dead man but everyone knew it was good to be a friend of the Swifts, the death was not reported. The dead sailor was thrown into the Hudson River. As a karmic gesture, Doc had never taken another drink. But this champagne was beginning to tempt him.

Googleye, the boatman, burst through the saloon door. He was gasping for breath. He was trying to tell them something. Doc lowered the bottle.

"I run, run," Googleye panted.

"Run for what?" said Dutch John.

"Here. He here," Googleye said.

"What the hell are you talking about?" said Dutch John.

A large figure appeared behind Googleye, who felt the presence at his rear and stepped aside.

Wearing his twin pistols and with Sweet Lips cradled in his right arm, Matthew Caldwell stepped into Dutch John's Saloon. The crowd hushed, awed by the sight of this famous big Ranger in the white doeskin jacket with the stars beaded on it. Caldwell's spotted beard moved back and forth, framed by his long black hair, reading the scene with the judge sprawled bleeding on the billiard table being tended by the Indian girl. The Ranger's gaze settled on the well-built fellow holding the bottle of champagne.

"You call yourself Doctor Swift?" Caldwell said.

"That's right."

"You are under arrest," Caldwell said.

# 1 4

Fritz Gruber thrust himself in front of Doc Swift and confronted Caldwell. Matthew's eyes flicked to the inch-high iron fin in the German's skull; the Ranger was surprised to see Gruber still alive.

"You ain't arresting our doctor," the German said.

"I am arresting Doctor Swift and that Indian woman and anybody who gives me any trouble," Caldwell said.

An angry rumble went through the crowd. Mayor Edwin Waller pushed aside two scowling surveyors who had been treated by Doc Swift last week after they stumbled into a cactus. The mayor's spectacles slid to the tip of his nose.

"What is Dr. Swift accused of, Captain Caldwell?" asked the mayor.

"He and the woman are accused of conspiring against Texas with the Comanches and the Cherokees on behalf of a foreign power. They are accused of being spies and troublemakers. I am told they also assaulted an official of the Republic."

"That is preposterous," the mayor said. "Who makes these accusations?"

"President Lamar," said Caldwell.

Caldwell looked past Gruber and the mayor at Doc Swift, who was now drying the bloody water off his hands and arms. Cullasaja had paused for a moment to look at Matthew, but now she continued to be occupied with stopping the blood oozing from the sutures in the judge's belly.

"Doctor Swift, have you climbed the white cliff across the river and walked on the land over there?" Caldwell asked.

The crowd gasped. To cross Shoal Creek was an appreciable achievement and quite risky. To go farther west and cross the wide Colorado River and climb the white cliffs into Comancheria was unthinkable.

Doc folded his wet, red smeared towel and laid it across a chair. He turned at last to look squarely at the speckle-bearded Ranger with the ten-gauge shotgun and the determined but not yet truly hostile attitude. Caldwell was surprised to see no fear in this Easterner's face. This is an interesting face, Matthew thought, a complicated fellow, certainly with the air of easy confidence that a spy would require. If this fellow is a foreign agent, he must be a good one.

"I have climbed the cliff," Doc said.

Murmurs of amazement rustled through the room. When had Doc climbed the white cliff? Why would he do that? Why did no one know?

"I'll give you a few minutes to finish cleaning up the judge," said Caldwell.

"I'm not going with you," Doc said.

Matthew turned his gray cat eyes squarely into the darkening eyes of the doctor, and neither man looked away.

"Say that again?" Caldwell said.

"What I mean to say is we are not going with you. The woman is not going anywhere with you, and I am not going anywhere with you," Doc said.

Caldwell cocked one hammer of Sweet Lips with a loud snap.

"I am not armed," Doc said.

"Well, it wouldn't matter if you were. You're going with me."

"If you try to shoot our doctor, you'll have to shoot me first," said Fritz Gruber, a gnarled wrist resting on the grip of the pistol in his belt.

"And me," Mayor Waller said. He was carrying a small caliber varmint rifle.

"Ranger, you got a lot of gall to threaten to shoot our doctor," the barber said. He had retrieved his straight razors and was wiping his strop with them in what could be taken as a menacing manner.

"Our doctor is a valuable citizen," said Billy Bonnell, owner and editor of *The Sentinel*, a weekly newspaper. A mountain northwest of the city had been named for Bonnell. Caldwell considered him a substantial man.

Caldwell moved his eyes among their faces and saw that this roomful of men, many of them notoriously violent, was outraged at the notion their un- armed doctor might be arrested for some nebulous accusations. Every man in the room felt he had been unfairly accused of at least one wrong deed sometime in the past.

Moving quickly as a hunting cat, Matthew leaped forward lightly in his moccasins, grabbed Doc Swift by a handful of hair at the scruff of his neck and by a powerful grip on his belt in the back. Doc was unprepared for the swiftness of the move and for the strength he felt in the Ranger's hands. Doc felt helpless for the seconds it took Caldwell to carry the doctor to the saloon door and throw him into the dirt road that was called Pecan Street.

"I don't need guns to handle a New York son of a bitch," Matthew said, stripping off his doeskin jacket and handing his two Paterson pistols to Gruber. Passing Sweet Lips and his butcher knife to Mayor Waller, Caldwell stepped into the street as Doc was rolling over and starting to rise. Matthew whacked him in the chest with a mighty kick from a stout leg, and Doc tumbled over backward. Caldwell followed and kicked Doc in the head when he tried to get to his feet.

"Hey, Ranger, I'll kill you if you kick him again," Gruber said, holding Caldwell's pistols.

"All right, get on your feet, you New York spy," Caldwell said. "You and me and the woman have got a long ride to San Antonio."

"We are not going with you," Doc said. He licked the blood from his lower lip and dusted his knuckles against his trousers.

"Doctor Swift, don't make me whip you like a dog." Matthew said.

Suddenly the Ranger found himself sitting on the ground sucking wind, bent over clutching his hairy belly where a pain stabbed from his kidney. Matthew hadn't seen the blow coming. How could it be? This so-called doctor could not have hit him as fast and hard as it seemed. It was some kind of freak event.

As Caldwell came onto a knee, prepared for the doctor to dive at him or try a kick to the head, he saw that his quarry instead had backed off and was circling slowly, raising his hands doubled into fists, lifting his left shoulder a bit, tucking in his chin—the man was honestly crazy enough to fight with his fists. Caldwell thought of the derringer he had stowed inside his boot, but he shrugged it off. The sun hadn't come up yet on the day he couldn't whip a New York son of a bitch.

Matthew raised himself slowly and carefully into a crouch, his arms spread wide, and circled to his right, away from the right fist of the doctor. He felt it was the right fist that had somehow shot through to drill him in the kidney with such a blow that he knew he would piss blood. Caldwell didn't intend to get into a stand-up, fist-swinging fight, like two drunks in a saloon. He believed a fight should be ended promptly, and the best way to do it was to put his opponent on the ground, where Matthew's strength and quickness and experience could break an arm or if necessary a neck.

"You're going to regret this day, Doctor Swift," said Matthew. "If you think you can affront a Texas Ranger with a show of arrogance and not pay for it, you must be very new to Texas."

Doc felt a freezing within him. The source of his deep anger, which rarely came to the surface, was primal, he felt; anger was his greatest fear, for when it took possession of him, he lost his healing compassion and became without mercy. He became the animal that had viciously beaten a human being to death eight years ago over a mere exchange of words. He had been thrilled by the awful violence of it. Now he looked at this great hairy Ranger crouching before him, threatening to drag his sister and himself to San Antonio. The Ranger was formidable. He had grace and power, and from the look in his gray eyes he intended to do Doc serious harm during this encounter. Doc felt his blood flowing and his nerves singing, and he moved a step closer to give the Ranger a chance to spring.

Matthew was faster than Doc thought and nearly took the surgeon to the ground with his leaping grasp.

Instead Doc ducked to his right, and Caldwell's hand tore the left sleeve off Doc's shirt. Caldwell recovered instantly and in balance and drove at Doc's chest with the idea of bear-hugging him to the ground and using his skull to smash Doc's face by butting him.

Doc met him with a left hook to the heart, a right cross to the jaw and a left uppercut that split Caldwell's nose up the middle and spewed blood over both of them. The blows landed in sequence in two and a half seconds. Caldwell saw lightning. He lost his balance and grabbed at the physician. Doc saw the curiosity and pain in Matthew's eyes, and the blood pouring into his mouth and beard, and Doc knew this fight was finished as far as the Ranger was concerned.

But Doc wasn't quite through with this man yet. Doc shoved Caldwell upright with his left hand. When the Ranger wobbled before him, Doc hammered his most powerful punch, a right cross, into the hinge below the Ranger's left ear. Doc felt the bone break. Caldwell was still looking at him, as if any moment the Ranger would recover and take charge of the situation. Astonishment crossed Caldwell's eyes, and the Ranger fell facedown in the dirt of Pecan Street, blood puddling around his head.

The crowd was each and every one amazed, except for Cullasaja, who watched from the saloon door, knowing what her brother could do.

"My Lord," said Mayor Waller.

"Shit on my head," said Googleye.

"Who would have believed it?" said Dutch John.

"Doc, you are the champion. You are my best friend for life. This Ranger had better get up and get out of town before I jump on his spine and really hurt him," said Fritz Gruber.

"He is seriously hurt already," Cullasaja said, swinging toward them on her crutches. "Turn him over before he suffocates."

Doc watched the barber and Gruber turn the Ranger onto his back. Caldwell's nose was split like a sausage. It would need at least twenty stitches. Anyone could see by the way it hung that the left mandible was broken. Doc felt himself becoming a healer again. His anger had been exorcised.

"Mr. Bullock, we will need another room at the inn for the Ranger while he recuperates," Doc said.

"Sorry, Doc. I've got no rooms. If Bone would go ahead and die—"

"Put the Ranger in my room," said Cullasaja.

"But what about you?" Gruber asked.

"Cully, you take my room. I'll stay with Mr. Gruber," said Doc.

"You can stay with me, Doc," said the barber, who lived in a tent.

"We can put you a cot in our barn," Mayor Waller said.

"No. The doctor stays with me," said Gruber.

"What the hell, let's put the Ranger in the same room with lawyer Bone," Richard Bullock said. "That way, Doc, you and Cullasaja can stay in your own rooms and be there to nurse Bone and the Ranger without turning my whole damn hotel into a hospital."

"Don't forget about the judge," said Dutch John. "He can't stay on my billiard table."

"He's got a house and a wife," the land commissioner said. "Come to think of it, where is his wife? Looks like she'd show up to watch him get cut open."

"Just before he had his fit, the judge was telling me his wife is sick with malaria," said Gruber. "That's four sick people that would probably die if we didn't have Doc Swift in our town. I say, God bless Doc Swift."

The crowd gave Doc a series of hurrahs from the street and the saloon windows.

Mrs. Ruthie Hunboldt was slowly climbing the stairs at the Redbud Hotel. She stopped and applauded Doc. By saving Gruber's life, the doctor had saved her hope for the future.

# 1 5

**M**atthew Caldwell woke up in a gauzy state, hearing a young woman's voice, refined and soothing, murmuring, "You poor man, you poor man."

Caldwell thought she was talking to him, but he couldn't remember where he was or how he got there, or why she should be calling him a "poor man." He forced his right eye to open, an act which required concentration. He saw the young woman's hips from behind. She looked familiar. Appeared to be an Indian from the hang of her long black hair with coral combs in it. She was bent over a figure covered by a sheet in a bed against the opposite wall of the small room. Matthew tried to raise his head, but his neck muscles refused to respond. He framed a question in his mind—where am I?—but when he tried to say the words, he found his mouth would not open. Something was very wrong here.

His left hand crept up to his face, and his fingers touched his jaw. His jaw was swollen, and beneath the skin he felt a stiff binding of cords or wires. His tongue went up to the left inside of his mouth and rubbed along the binding. He reckoned that his jaw was broken, and he tried to remember how it had happened.

Cullasaja finished changing the bandages on Ridgewood Bone's head, covered the lawyer's sweating face with linen to keep flies and mosquitoes off him, then turned and saw the Ranger caressing his cheek with thick fingers.

"How are you feeling, Captain Caldwell?"

Matthew tried so say: where am I? Instead he said, "Eeeee ee e?"

Cullasaja read his rhythms and thoughts and said, "You are in a room at Bullock's Inn. The room belongs to the poor man you see there. The Comanches fractured his skull, scalped him and cut off his penis."

"God damn it, you don't have to blab to every son of a bitch who wanders past," said Bone from beneath his wrappings.

"Mr. Bone, everybody saw you unloaded from the wagon. It's no secret," she said.

"Eeee ee? Aaaaa?" said Caldwell.

"Yes, his penis is gone," she said. "My brother calls it 'urethral meatus in perineum.' But his scrotum and testicles are saved, so now the poor man will be cursed with sexual desire but unable to do anything about it except suffer. Maybe learning to overcome desire will make a saint out of him."

"Shut your mouth," said Bone.

"You'll be asleep in a moment, Mr. Bone. You should be thankful to Mr. Gruber for finding where the chemist had hidden his hoarded supplies. Otherwise, you would be in horrible pain. You, too, Captain. You have lost two jaw teeth, and your mandible is cracked. My brother used twenty-three stitches to close the split in your nose."

Nose? Matthew reached up and touched the ends of waxed thread that ran up his nose from the tip almost to the brow. Now he began to remember.

"My brother coated your gums and teeth and skin with tincture of opium. I poured you full of hot willow tea and laudanum, or else you wouldn't be looking at me in that curiously happy way."

Matthew said, "Ah awn ee oeeeum. Eee ahhh eeee eeee."

"Too late to turn down opium, you're already full of it, and I'm not bringing you a bottle of whiskey. My brother will be here in a few minutes to look you over. This town is keeping him quite busy."

"Errrr?" said Matthew.

"My brother is Doctor Swift. He sewed your nose and wired your jaw. Of course, he's the one who caused your damage in the first place."

"Errr? Iiiiin?"

"Nobody believes he's my brother. The people here think we're lovers," she laughed. "We let it pass. My brother says we should ignore what they say."

"Errr eeee?"

"Yes, our mother is Cherokee. Quit trying to talk. You'll loosen your wires. You just lie there."

"Aaaaahhh awww?"

"I don't know how long. My brother will tell you."

Matthew remembered it now. He had been stomping this New York son of a bitch in the street, and then those fists smashed him, those hammer blows, faster than he could believe, and he was looking into the doctor's dark, furious eyes and then into the dirt, where a scorpion backed away from his gaze as he went dark.

"Don't feel embarrassed. My brother is a sort of Black Knight figure in Austin, if you're familiar with *Ivanhoe*. He emerged from nowhere to astonish everyone with his powers. Let me assure you, Captain, that you should not feel unmanly. My brother has knocked out professional heavyweight pugilists. Taking off your guns was a noble act. I admire you for it. But once your guns were off, the joust was not a true contest. You bravely turned the odds from totally in your favor to completely against you. I like that. The act appeals to me."

As Matthew listened to her tone and her choice of words, it occurred to him that this lovely half-breed was a sophisticated woman. She was no ordinary woods Indian, not by a far cry. And her brother, the doctor, the boxing man, was a half-breed? What would they be doing in Austin? Were they spying for a foreign power? What did the doctor want on Caldwell's land?

Doc Swift entered through the street door in his shirtsleeves, with a soft deerskin bag of tools that had replaced his black Italian leather physician's satchel that vanished in the flood.

"How is the judge?" asked Cullasaja.

"He's going to live, but I left him a trophy of a scar. His wife might die, though. Her malaria is bad, and there's really nothing I can do but burn candles. What about our patients here?"

Doc glanced at the mounds of linen and gauze that hid lawyer Bone from head to foot. Then he looked at the Ranger, who stared back with warm curiosity, influenced, Doc knew, by a heavy dose of opiates. Caldwell's nose made Doc think of a red carrot with hairs sticking out. Wiring Caldwell's jaw had been more difficult than cutting out the judge's appendix. Most physicians did dentistry, but Romulus had stayed away from it. Prying out the Ranger's broken teeth with pliers and a screwdriver had been tedious work. With chicken wire from the hardware store, Doc devised a binding of the upper and lower jaws. Only the lower was broken, but the upper was puffed up around the missing teeth.

"You'll be drinking soup for a week," Doc said. "You have a bruised kidney and blood in your urine, and I believe a short rib is cracked. You'd better stay in bed for a few days. Cullasaja will nurse you, and I'll look in on you and the lawyer every so often. We'll get you back on your feet. After that, we'll see what happens."

"Aaaar ah ah—" Matthew said.

Doc held up a hand to stop him.

"I understand that you have a solemn duty as a Texas Ranger to arrest me and my sister and take us to San Antonio to stand trial for some trumped-up charge," Doc said. "Well, you can forget about that, Captain Caldwell. Soon as her leg heals, I am delivering my sister to Chief Bowl's town. Then I am going exploring in Comancheria. I fear if I turn myself over to Texas justice, I will be murdered."

"Eeeeee uuuuhhhh?" said Matthew.

"Your guns are laid against the wall beside your bed," Doc said.

Matthew tried to say: I'll be damned. Instead he said, "Eeeee aaai."

Doc turned his attention to the lawyer, who was sleeping.

"Now, here's a fellow with real problems," Doc said.

# 1 6

On the Hickory Street hill, two blocks north of Pecan Street and two blocks east of Congress Avenue, a dozen carpenters hauled and hewed and notched boards of Bastrop pine and north Austin oak and hammered them together to frame fourteen rooms that would become the presidential mansion. The loblolly planks had been planed at the Austin City Steam Saw Mill in Bastrop and carted thirty miles to the capital. Lower down on the Hickory Street hill, four carpenters were building six small cabins that would become slave quarters. Hickory Creek was fed by a constant spring that bubbled from rocks near the crest. A grove of oaks ran from Hickory Hill all the way south to the river. The supply of wood and water appeared inexhaustible.

When Henry Longfellow had failed to reach Austin and find a site, President Lamar wrote to Mayor Edwin Waller, a Virginian who had fought at San Jacinto. Lamar presented his requirements and asked for guidance. Waller knew the perfect spot. It was the Hickory Street hill. He went to the land office and looked up the title. In the first auction of six hundred and forty acres of public land in the City of Austin, conducted three months ago by Mayor Waller, he thought he remembered selling the Hickory Street block to the incredible-looking German, Fritz Gruber. The mayor found the title in a steamer trunk that held Republic documents. He was right. Gruber bought the entire Hickory Street block between Brazos and San Jacinto Streets east and west and Bois d'Arc Street on the north for $6,000 paid in silver to the Republic of Texas.

Gruber was not impressed by Mayor Waller's first offer to buy the Hickory Street hill for $6,200 in gold or $55,000 in Texas redback currency. Thinking it would be persuasive information, Waller broke down and revealed the true buyer was President Lamar. Gruber remained unimpressed. Politicians come and go. He had served under the emperor of Austria. What did he care of Mirabeau Lamar? Appeals to Gruber's patriotism to the Republic were laughed off. He was a Hessian deserter, not a Texas revolutionary. Gruber thought it was a stupid error in salesmanship for Waller to tell him the President wanted to buy his hill. Gruber had traded with the Sioux and Cheyenne and many other tribes in the wild for years before the Comanche called Osage Killer had wiped out his business. Gruber knew not to give away an important secret during negotiations. Hickory Hill was a beautiful place, where he and Mrs. Ruth Hunboldt had picnics under the trees and made love in the soft grass on the bank of Hickory Creek. Yes, the hill on Hickory Street was lovely and romantic and dear to his heart, but it was, after all, real estate, and he was a dealer in land. He sold the block to the mayor for $9,000 in gold bullion to be banked in Gruber's account in St. Louis.

Waller sold the block to Lamar for $10,000 in Mexican Treasury gold bonds that were negotiable in New Orleans at the bank where the Republic kept accounts. The mayor was hired by Lamar to supervise construction of the mansion with the proviso it must be completed before the temporary capitol building, which was being built three blocks to the west, on Colorado between Hickory and Ash on land that had been set aside by the Republic. Waller was given $115,000 in Texas money and a working crew of twenty that would grow to two hundred by July. Lamar's schedule called for the temporary capitol building of two large meeting rooms, five committee rooms and a dog run for breeze, to be finished in the middle of the coming September, five months from now. The Republic of Texas government would be moved from Houston City to Austin in the month of October. Long before moving to the new capitol the crates of archives and government records that would fill eighty wagons, the presidential mansion had to be ready, according to Lamar's plan. He had begun calling the mansion The White House and was dreaming of the wonderful galas he would hold on Hickory Hill, as it was described to him by letter from Waller: "It presents a scene of grandeur and magnificence rarely if ever witnessed, I imagine, in any other part of the American continent. Rome itself with all its famous hills could not have surpassed the natural scenery here."

Both days the Ranger and the lawyer had lain in bed as patients, Doc Swift and Gruber had climbed on top of the hill to watch Mexican stone masons erecting a chimney from rocks they had found at the site. These men, Doc thought, were artisans who could hold their own in the Vatican. If I were to build a house, he thought, I would want the skill and care put into it that I see from these Mexican stone masons.

"How does it affect you to see your lovely hill become a mansion for a politician?" Doc asked.

"Me and Ruthie forked right over there under that hickory tree, and under that hickory tree over past it, and still one more beyond. We took off our clothes and swam naked in the creek to cool off. Yah, it was great days," said the German. "There was many great days like that with Ruthie on this hill. Yah, it makes me sad. But I can't stop Lamar from building a house in Austin. Oompossible! If he's coming anyway, if he's bringing the government, it's better he buys his land from me. You know what I do? I keep selling farms to Germans, but I am buying more land in Austin. I find another hill where Ruthie and me can fork and eat sausage and swim naked. There's plenty of beautiful hills and valleys and creeks around Austin. I'm buying land north of Capitol Square and west toward Shoal Creek. Land is worth more than gold. I make you my pardner. Stick with me, and you will be rich."

"Thank you, Fritz. Make Ruthie your pardner instead. I'm not staying in Austin much longer."

"Don't let that damn Ranger run you off. I can make him disappear," said Gruber.

"I need to climb the cliff."

They looked to the west and saw three miles away the white cliffs that marked the entrance to Comancheria.

"You have climbed the cliff already," Gruber said. "In the Waco camp they told me you paddled a canoe across the river and climbed the cliff. You walked inland two or three miles. Very bad idea. Very dangerous. Forget the gold. The gold will get you killed. If you want gold, we are standing on it. Austin land is gold. Water is gold. Trees are gold. Buy land, the way I do. Buy land as fast as you can. Next year you will be rich. In following generations your children will be richer."

It was the middle of the afternoon, time for Gruber's nap. He liked to sleep for two hours before he bathed himself in a hip-deep tub of water. It was an extravagance for Gruber to contract with Richard Bullock to see the water was provided, warm if asked, but business was good and the German felt expansive. Fate had deservedly turned in his favor. His skull no longer oozed or stank, but Ruthie had always liked the way he smelled, so he doused his head and body with ginger tonic before he got dressed to keep his regular rendezvous with her at the Rosebud Hotel. He was in love with Ruthie. Gruber led Doc down from Hickory Hill on the path that workers climbing the hill under heavy loads of construction material and tools had trampled in the grass.

"I want to meet the man-ape that you saw."

"Doc, for a brilliant, scientific person, you are a dumb head. A putrid, stinking ape that stands upright and whistles like a bird? This is worth your life? Take my word for it, Doc. The ape is out there in a cavern on the Little Pigeon River. Believe what I tell you. Comanches are out there by the thousands. If you want to write a paper on the ape for your medical society, use what I'm telling you and invent the rest. *Mein Gott*, I hate to think what the Comanches will do when they catch you. You will make lawyer Boneless look hung like the Duke of Wellington."

In all Texas settlements the first people to arrive left the area littered with tree stumps the height of a man's kneecap, and they became the cause of many falls and curses and gashed shins. In Austin most of the early stumps were being removed by mules in harness to make room for buildings. When he and the German reached the bottom of the hill on Hickory Street, Doc sat down on a knee-high stump to shake a pebble out of his boot.

"Here comes trouble, Doc. I am standing in front of you," Gruber said, pulling his pistol. "I'm not afraid of a Texas Ranger."

Approaching them from Brazos Street was Matthew Caldwell. He wore his brace of pistols on his suspenders and the shotgun Sweet Lips was under his left arm. His hat was pulled low on his forehead. Caldwell paused to let fifty or sixty of Richard Bullock's hogs trot across his path. The left side of his face was swollen and discolored where it was not covered by his mustache, beard and shoulder-length hair. Doc was amazed to see him up and walking well. It had been only two days since his beating. Doc knew from his sister that the Ranger had eaten nothing but pea soup and had spilled as much as he swallowed. Caldwell should have been down for another week.

Matthew Caldwell saw the German yank his pistol. He would have snarled a warning except for the wires that bound his jaws. It hurt to snarl. With his fingers he had pried the wires apart somewhat so that he could speak and take nourishment, and he had stopped in at Dutch John's to buy a bottle of whiskey, which he carried in his right hand. Nobody inside Dutch John's looked at Matthew's stitched-up nose or said a word about anything except the weather while he was there. He had fooled Cullasaja into thinking he had drunk laudanum and would be lazing in the room at Bullock's, listening to Bone complain, but when she went to gather herbs on the streambanks, Matthew hid his laudanum bottle under his corn-shuck mattress, put on his clothes and picked up his weapons and went looking for the cure he really trusted—whiskey. Nothing killed pain like corn whiskey, Caldwell believed. He drank half the bottle, scalding his throat while he walked the three blocks from Dutch John's to Hickory Hill. His jaw and teeth and nose and ribs hurt worse than ever, and now walking was becoming difficult as well.

"You should be in bed, Captain. You're not in condition to be up yet," said Doc.

"Doctor Swift, I am here on business," Matthew said. His words were distinct, but he felt like keeping them to a minimum because of the pain.

Doc tensed. He studied the Ranger's eyes but could see nothing through their grayness. The black and white spotted beard was decorated with the remains of pea soup. Matthew swallowed again from the corn whiskey bottle. His pain was still sharp, except now it didn't matter as much.

The brutish Fritz Gruber, hair growing out of the back of his shirt collar, the blade in his skull catching the afternoon sun, raised his pistol and pointed it at Caldwell's chest and said, "What do you want?"

"Don't be aiming your pistol at me, Gruber."

"Put it down, Fritz," said Doc. Gruber slowly lowered the weapon. Doc kept looking at Caldwell. "My sister and I are not going anywhere with you, Captain."

"Don't get your bile up, Doctor Swift. I've had enough of that for now. I'm here to consult with Mr. Gruber," Matthew said.

"You don't want our doctor?" said Gruber. "What you want with me?"

"I hear you're the top man in town when it comes to finding choice land. I want to purchase a lot to build a house on for my new German bride."

•   •   •

The three men walked north for a block on Brazos beside the hill on Hickory Street and stopped to let pass a teamster prodding his four yoke of oxen that pulled a wagon hauling limestone and hunks of granite. There was a quarry north of the city. Indians and robbers posing as Indians had killed several drivers and diggers in the last three months. But the land office was getting walls of granite.

The city was one mile square, fourteen blocks by fourteen. The three men turned west on Ash Street and crossed Congress Avenue, which flowed with business people, developers, carpenters, horses, wagons, the cook from Bullock's chasing a hen. Bullock's hog herd, which furnished bacon and pork chops for the hotel dining table, saw the menacing figure of the cook and snorted rapidly off toward the east up Pecan Street toward the hill where the structure of the French Legation was nearing completion. It was a lower bayou Louisiana–style house with French doors and a wide porch with columns. From its porch the French Legation overlooked all of the city and the sunset, just as from the west the white cliffs of Comancheria overlooked all of the city and the dawn.

The three men walked along Ash Street under arching oaks and waded across a stream of clear, cold water, heading west. They could see the forest at the bottom of the hill they were beginning to descend. Beyond the forest was Shoal Creek, then another forest to cross and finally their eyes came to the river and to the cliffs on the other side.

They stood at the corner of Ash Street and West Avenue. Three oak trees as big as any Matthew had ever seen grew on the uncleared lot. West Avenue was the western boundary of the city. Across the road lay the lumber for a fifty-foot-long section of a fence being built to protect Austin from the Comanches. The fence was less than one-twentieth finished, but the zeal for it had faded. The fence was a foolish idea, anyhow, the Ranger knew. Bullock's hogs roamed across the city boundaries as they pleased. This fence couldn't keep the hogs in or the Comanches out, but someone in government at the capitol in Houston City had authorized a fence-building contract.

They heard water flowing in Shoal Creek and felt a warm breeze that tickled the leaves of the oaks.

"This is a smart location. You build your house on this corner. I sell you the lot," said Gruber.

With his moccasins planted in the grass, the the odor of honkeysuckle threatening to make him sneeze and tear the stitches in his nose, leaves of the great oaks rustling above the sound of water rushing in the creek, Matthew felt this was truly the right place for him to build the house where he and Hannah would begin their lives together.

The corner had timber and water and was a short walk from the center of the city. From the front porch of a house that would be built facing West Avenue, the Ranger could sit in a swing and look to the horizon where his ten-thousand-acre empire waited on top of the white cliffs three miles away.

"What were you doing climbing that cliff and poking around over there?" Caldwell said to the doctor.

"Meaning no offense, Captain, but that is a personal matter."

"Yes, well, it's a personal matter to me, too, Doctor Swift. I own that land you were walking on. You were trespassing."

"Hey, you want to buy this land or not?" said Gruber. "I've got a busy afternoon ahead of me. I can't fool around and listen to a lot of bull."

"I have no designs on your land, Captain. I want nothing that belongs to you."

"What are you doing crossing the river? Meeting up with the Comanches?"

"I have never seen a Comanche, thank heaven."

"Doctor Swift, I believe you to be an honorable man. I am going to ask you on your word of honor—are you an agent for a foreign power? Have you been sent here to cause trouble for our Republic?"

"If a foreign power sent me, do you think I would tell you?" asked Doc.

"Yes. I do," Caldwell said.

"I am no spy. I am not here to disturb your Republic."

"What are you doing walking around on my land?"

The German stepped between them. He had lit a cheroot while leaning against a giant oak and dreaming of Ruthie's pink flesh. He would bring Ruthie down here and fork her again under this same oak tree before the title passed to the Texas Ranger, maybe later this night. But first he had to know if he was wasting his time. With a hatchet blade in his skull, he felt hours were precious.

"Yah, let's get to business, Captain," said Gruber. "Do you want to buy a little piece of paradise?"

"Excuse us, Doctor Swift. This is a private matter," Matthew said.

Doc went over and sat down with his back against an oak and looked toward the jagged dark green of the trees against the sky on the roof of the white cliffs. He smelled the fresh wet grass and felt the touch of an afternoon breeze on his cheek. He shut his eyes and tried to empty his mind except for the thought of his own breathing coming in and going out. A Buddhist monk had taught him this method of refreshing himself. He could barely hear the voices of the German and the Ranger, but he was not heeding them.

"How much?" Caldwell asked.

"For you, Captain Caldwell, a special price. Eighteen hundred dollars total for two lots, half a block. I do not accept Texas money."

Of the $2,400 he had received for his headright three years ago, Matthew still had about half of it banked in gold in New Orleans, even after paying the fee to the marriage agent. In his heart he was not ready to give up the burned cotton farm in Gonzalez. It was his birthplace as a Texan. But with Hannah coming, Caldwell needed money to keep her up, and from his savings must come the funds to build a house. As commander of one of the Rangers' three battalions, his pay was $1.25 per day, and Matthew had not been paid in seven months. It was occurring to Matthew for the first time since he had hired the marriage agent that the reality of having a wife meant the responsibility of taking care of her, of facing financial facts. He had been on his own for three years, sleeping wherever night found him, and had forgotten that women needed things. Matthew was going to have to confront the necessity of earning money.

"God help me, Captain, I believe I've put you into a trance. I only ask— no or yah?"

"Four hundred gold dollars is all I can afford."

Gruber yawned. Very close to nap time. He thought of Ruthie. He would bring her down here under this giant oak tree before supper. Four hundred gold dollars? He looked at Caldwell, a big, strange character from the German's point of view. That gaudy beard. The Comanches could make a shirt out of it. Caldwell had a reputation as being brave, a dangerous man, a killer. That was good. Austin needed dangerous men who were brave and truly killers in the event the big fight comes against the Comanches. And the Ranger said he is expecting a German bride. That was very good. A stout German wife running a proper German home was what the people in this city needed to see.

Matthew thought the German appeared to be losing interest. What else could he offer? Matthew remembered the labor of land near Gonzalez, 177 acres, set apart from the destroyed cotton farm. He had no emotional connection to that piece of land. He and Nancy had never worked it.

"Make it four hundred dollars gold for two lots, and I'll throw in 177 acres of prime pines near Gonzales."

"For you, a Texas Ranger, I make a special deal."

"Be careful, Gruber. I don't want no special deal. Four hundred in gold and 177 acres of pines. That's more than fair price for two city lots."

"No. I don't want to rob you. Keep your pine woods. Four hundred in gold for two city lots is my price to you."

The German and the Ranger shook hands. Doc glanced around at them.

Their two battered hands clasped together into a mass as big as a coconut. Doc stood up and dusted off his britches. He had been accustomed to the finest wool and linen, but since the flood he was now happy to have these sturdy britches woven from cotton and hemp. At first Doc had been surprised at how little comment the flood had caused. He learned the river flooded at least once every year, often more, and floods were accepted as a routine of life. Citizens of Austin brought clothing and food to Doc and his sister in barter to pay what they felt they owed him for medical service. Doc let them set their own price. By word of mouth the citizens established that for an ordinary visit the normal price to the doctor was a hen or its equivalent. Doc traded the hens and most other barter to Richard Bullock to help pay for two rooms and board in the inn.

"All right, then, it's done," Matthew said. "Now I'm going to leave you gentlemen to your own affairs. I believe Doctor Swift is right. I need to lie down."

The fact was, Caldwell felt as if his mouth were full of hot nails. His jawbone throbbed like a drum. His broken rib was a dagger in his chest. He remembered the bottle of laudanum he had hidden beneath his mattress at Bullock's.

The Ranger took three strides up Ash Street and then stopped and looked back at the doctor and the German. Caldwell swigged from the corn whiskey and wiped his mouth with his hand. He shifted Sweet Lips into the crook of his right elbow.

"Doctor Swift, don't think I've forgotten," Matthew said. "You and me will settle up, by-and-by."

# 1 7

Cullasaja saw the big Ranger walking down Congress Avenue, coming from the direction of Ash Street. She was squatting barefoot on the bank of the spring-fed creek at Congress and Hickory. A mule-drawn wagon rumbled past, scattering hens. The wagon carried casks of rock salt. Bullock's hog herd snorted and snuffled and rooted in a parade back down Pecan Street from the French Legation. The herd today had grown to ninety and more. People stood aside, carpenters pulled their planks out of the way, horses danced sideways, when the hog herd approached.

The Ranger lurched and clutched his chest. He dropped his whiskey bottle. The big battered hat bent over and the beard flattened against his neck as for a moment he hugged the pain in his broken rib. Then Matthew straightened up. He squared his shoulders and picked up the bottle and resumed his march down the road as though he had an important mission. Cullasaja thought Caldwell was a powerfully attractive man. He was dangerous and mysterious, and he seemed to her somehow tragic and appealing. As her patient he had been good-humored and pleasant in conversation. He had never complained. When she told him of her brother's accomplishments as a pugilist, he laughed—and the wires in his jaw brought tears to his eyes. Cullasaja liked Matthew for being able to see humor in the false confidence with which he had walked into those hammer punches.

Caldwell saw her kneeling at the creek. She was the best-looking girl he had ever seen in Texas. The shining black hair, the tan skin, the white teeth, the body and bearing of a confident, athletic person. He had enjoyed listening to her while she kept up intelligently cheerful chatter to him and to the suffering lawyer Bone. Despite the wires in his jaw, Matthew had managed to ask her questions about her life and was astounded at her answers: born and educated in New York City. Daughter of a Cherokee woman and a ship line owner from Scotland. She had given up a life that Matthew pictured as one of incredible luxury to travel into the perilous wilderness of Texas. She was nothing like the Cherokee whore Henry Longfellow had called her. She was an intelligent, re-fined person with a good heart. Cullasaja was the first reason he had ever found to like a Cherokee

"Good afternoon," he said, touching his hat brim. She saw the stitches sticking like hairs out of his nose. She saw pain squinting in his gray eyes.

"I suppose it is quite manly for you to get out of bed and buy a bottle of whiskey and swagger around the city with your shotgun, but it is rather stupid," she said. "You are likely to have made your injuries much worse."

"You could be right," he said. "What are you looking for?"

"I have crushed three dirt dauber nests. Now I am digging some fine mud from the crawdad holes in this creek, which I will mix with the nests for a healing potion."

"Who is this medicine for?" he asked.

"Mr. Bone. The poor man has been stung by bees."

"Stung by bees?"

"The poppy odor of the poultice must have attracted them. How are you speaking so well? What have you done with your wiring?"

"I loosened it a little."

She shook her head. "Captain, I fear your face may never heal if you behave this way."

Matthew took her hand and helped her to her feet. She held a ceramic bowl of mud and dirt dauber nests. She caught a toe on a rock and stumbled against him. His body felt hard and massive and comforting. To her, his fantastical appearance, with his black hair and spotted beard and gray eyes, was magic. She imagined when his jaw healed, his voice would be deep and melodious.

"I want to thank you for taking good care of me while I was laid up," he said. "You are a fine girl."

"Woman," she said.

"Looking at you from my age, you're a girl."

"You're not so old," she said, carefully clutching the bowl of mud and nests as they picked their steps up from the creek and emerged onto Congress Avenue.

"I'm old enough to be your father," he said. He enjoyed walking beside her. She made him feel good, and she was wonderful to look at. Citizens stopped discreetly and peeked around at the Ranger walking with the Indian.

"My father is eighty-nine," she said. "He's old enough to be your father."

"How old is your mother?"

"She would say she is Prime. In the Old Ways there are four ages—Infant, Young, Prime and Old. You are prime as long as you feel you are prime, no matter what the number of years."

"I know most Indians believe that, but I'm asking as a white man who keeps count of his years."

"Mother is sixty." She walked around a building block that had fallen off a wagon. "I'll spare you figuring it out. She was forty-one, he was seventy when I came to this life. Mother was twenty-one, Father was fifty when my brother was born. So you see, you're not so old."

A block to the south they saw a crowd gathered around the Loafer's Log at Bullock's. There had been much for the citizens to talk about of late.

"Hey, Captain Caldwell," called the barber, who was taking time off to smoke his pipe. "How about them Comanches? Are they coming to take our scalps?"

"Hell, I'd rather lose my scalp than my dick," said a young developer who was passing almost beside Caldwell with horse manure prominently on one boot. The young developer wore a white woven straw planter's hat from the South. Caldwell noted the hat. He liked it. His own hat was torn and dirty and shapeless. And this fellow had annoyed Matthew by saying "dick" in front of Cullasaja.

"What's your name?" Matthew said to the man in the straw hat. Matthew's jaw was hurting crazily, and he hoped he would not lose control of his temper while taking this fellow's hat. He was trying to show Cullasaja how reasonable he could be.

"Winston."

"From where?"

"Athens, Georgia. I've been in Austin for a month, putting together deals. Look, Captain, I'm not a citizen of the Republic, but I will be as soon as I can sign the correct documents," said Winston.

Winston looked up and saw the shiny thread stitches sticking out of Matthew's nose. The sight unnerved the developer. As a reflex and a means of breaking contact, Winston removed his woven straw hat and wiped his golden hair with his fingers, as if the afternoon had just turned hot.

"May I?" Caldwell said.

Matthew took the hat from Winston and studied it and nodded in admiration. "Good quality," he said. He ran a finger around the inside brim. "Very nice." Matthew looked down at Winston. "You know a Georgia man called Henry Longfellow?"

"I've heard of him," Winston said.

"President Lamar, he's a Georgia man. You know him?"

"We have mutual friends back in Athens."

Matthew took off his old, floppy hat and replaced it on his head with the woven straw from Georgia. The fit was comfortable, tight but easy. The hat felt like it belonged on him. He thought of the fierce summer sun that was only weeks away. He needed this wide brim for shade. He thought of the heat. He needed this woven straw for coolness.

"Did you happen to write a report to Lamar on affairs here in Austin regarding this woman by my side and Doctor Swift?" Matthew asked.

"No, no, certainly not. Never," said Winston.

"Do you know what can happen if you lie to a Texas Ranger?"

"Why, Captain, surely you wouldn't doubt . . . ah . . . I am a gentleman, sir."

"Don't get your bile up, Winston. What will you take for this hat?"

"Please, Captain, do me the great honor of accepting the hat as a gift from me, Harry Winston, the Winston Land and Cattle Company. I'm a great admirer of what you Ranger fellows do. It's a pleasure for me to present you with my hat. Perhaps you will save my head someday."

"Like as not," Matthew said. He tossed his old hat to a small boy who was staring in awe at the Ranger. "I once slapped Santa Anna with that hat, son. Show it to your grandchildren." He glanced at Winston. "Appreciate the new hat, Winston. Next message you send to the President, tell him the Ranger has got it under control in Austin."

Matthew took Cullasaja by the elbow, and they walked toward the rear of Bullock's Inn. She was hoping the bees had not returned to sting the unfortunate lawyer Bone again while the Ranger dallied with the man about the hat. She wondered if Caldwell was drunk. He had left the whiskey bottle on the creek bank, but he had the aroma of whiskey about him. The white straw hat with its wide brim fit his figure well, she thought. He was a person who gave off magnetic waves, as her brother did.

"I wish I could talk you into going back to New York," Matthew said. "There's nothing ahead for you in Texas but trouble."

"At Chief Bowl's town we will live in peace with the earth and with each other. All we ask is to be allowed to live in the Old Ways."

"What's so good about the old ways?"

"The earth is created each moment by the Master of Breath, and we are here to take care of the earth, to cherish and preserve it. White people insult the spirit of the earth. Everywhere the white culture touches, there is a sore and bleeding wound. You put a price of money on everything. Your God is money. The true God is the Master of Breath that loves us into being, so that all things are holy and all things are alike. For every ill, earth has a cure. I want to live in peace among my mother's people and observe the Right Way. They are my people, more than the whites. The Master of Breath is in everything in nature. It offends the Master when we buy and sell nature. That is sacrilege and doom."

Caldwell looked at her strong brown legs as she neared the door to the room where the lawyer Bone could be heard groaning.

"They're not going to let you live in peace," he said. "There's too many settlers crowding into east Texas. They'll never leave old Bowl alone."

"Sam Houston promised Chief Bowl he can keep his town forever."

"General Houston got outvoted by the Congress. I'm asking you, girl. Go back to New York."

Cullasaja paused at the doorway and dipped one hand into the bowl of mud and nests. They heard Bone muttering, "Why me? Why me?" and then letting out little squeaks like a mouse.

A wasp that was drunk on fermented fruit had just now stung lawyer Bone's upper lip, leaving a throbbing, purple boil.

"Thank you for being concerned, Captain," she said. "I admire you very much. I hope your Rangers will protect Chief Bowl's people with the zeal you expend on these people who are destroying the earth."

"To be honest, that's not going to happen, either," he said. "Go back to your family in New York. Take your brother with you."

"Nobody takes Rommy anywhere he doesn't want to go, as you have noticed."

She entered the room from the road. Matthew stayed outside and leaned one hand against the wall, pain rocking his jaws, the wires burning in his mouth. His voice became a croak.

"I understand what you are doing here, Cullasaja, even though I pity you for it. What is Doctor Swift doing in Texas? He's not an old-ways sort of person. What the hell does he want on my land?"

Cullasaja stuck one hand out the door and gave him the bottle of laudanum he had hidden beneath the mattress. She smiled at his look of relief when he took it from her.

"Come in and lie down," she said. "You need to sleep."

# 18

Mirabeau Buonaparte Lamar stood at the corner window of his second-floor office in the Capitol Building in Houston City and watched gray rain drenching the intersection of Texas Avenue and Main Street. It had been raining almost steadily for two nights and three days, and if the rain paused, black masses of mosquitoes rose up from the bayous riding the steam. What a wretched pesthole of a place this was, Lamar thought. He was sliding into melancholia. Staring at the dismal rain, at the figures struggling through the mud, the President could imagine the murkiness of mind that had led his dear older brother, Lucius Quintus Cincinnatus Lamar, to blow his brains out the back of his skull five years ago in Georgia, at the family plantation, Cherry

Hill. Lucius was melancholy about life. Lucius saw no purpose for living, a younger brother's love notwithstanding. On a day like this, in a mood like this, Mirabeau felt he could almost understand the despair that had driven Lucius to pull the trigger.

Lamar was aware that General Albert Sidney Johnston was pacing the floor, his voice droning on and on. To show respect to the general, Lamar pretended to listen. Johnston was asking him to reconsider moving the capital to Austin. The general, not usually verbose, was today impassioned by the need for security. "I believe the foundation of this town of Austin has no precedent in the history of the world. The government is placing itself on a frontier open to its foes, and we base in Austin the center of our hope for future dominion!" Johnston had clasped his hands behind his back, as had the President. Both men wore frock coats and high collars. Lamar's trousers were tailored to be very baggy, because he liked the space to move his limbs in, and sometimes in his poetic moods he imagined himself an Oriental potentate in pantaloons. Lamar nodded solemnly and pretended to consider Johnston's arguments. The President believed the general to be in the pay of the Allen brothers, who wanted the capital to remain in Houston City, where they owned much of the land. Lamar was willing to let Johnston earn his fee by presenting the Allens' pleas to keep the capital on these stinking bayous. He knew Johnston was loyal to him and would accompany him to Austin as a member of the cabinet, the secretary of war, when he was asked to do so.

The general presented his case, and Henry Longfellow, crutches in his lap, a sour downturn to his lips, draped himself the length of the couch, appearing to listen to Johnston but instead waiting for this harangue to end. Henry Longfellow was pursuing revenge. His broken right leg was hurting fiercely in this wet climate.

President Lamar didn't feel the strength to summon a reaction to Johnston. He kept looking out the window at the rain. A horse was stuck in the mud on Main Street. Lamar fell deeper into gloom remembering the time shortly before the suicide of Lucius five years ago, that horrible period when Mirabeau's young wife, the pearl of his heart, died of tuberculosis. Soon his sister Evalina died of the vapors. Immediately after, their father, Zachariah, fell ill with heart disease. Zachariah had named his children for his favorite people out of the books he was reading when they were born. Mirabeau Buonaparte was named for two heroes of the French Revolution, an inspiration for the boy to carry forward into life. Zachariah quickly followed Evalina to the grave. Then the dear sad Lucius chose to go behind the eternal curtain. On dreadful, dreary days like this, Mirabeau wanted to believe the romance that he could avoid his destiny of being president of a republic that stretched to the Pacific; he could vanish from the world stage of history and hide himself in a monastery like an inspired genius of a hermit and write the great poems that the future would know him for.

Henry Longfellow was pondering on how after Eve had seduced Adam and caused the fall of man, Satan laid with Eve and squirted his sperm into her, and how ever after women have loved the devil. Henry had a whore to his room at the Palace Hotel last night. She had been a fat Cajun with hairy legs, and her evil hole smelled like a carp. A nauseating woman. He peed in her face and she licked her lips. He smacked her with his belt, and she cried for more. Throwing aside his crutches, he mounted her from the rear on all fours like dogs do it, and she grunted and called him honey. She was thoroughly debased and wicked. She had come in to the Houston port yesterday by steamboat from Galveston, where she had a customer at the Tremont Hotel who had sent a message to Henry Longfellow suggesting she be met at the dock. "She is the vilest of whores, without any virtue save that of her willing submission to the desires of man," his friend had written. After hours of violent and perverted sex that exhausted Henry's imagination, the Cajun came up with new ideas. She wore Henry out. She was a proud lover of the devil, a flower of the seed of wickedess. Henry established the Cajun in a room above Bisbee's Hardware. Rooming was difficult to find in Houston City. Only high officials of the Republic, like Henry, were allowed to have single rooms at the Palace Hotel; the other rooms in the hotel had two, three, even four or more men bedded together. At the Palace Hotel women were never admitted unless accompanied by father or husband. Good rule, Henry thought. Devil bitches. Henry would never again bully the Palace manager into letting him take the Cajun to his room. She made it nasty. She shat on his sheets. From now on, he would visit her in her room above Bisbee's. When she became too evil for him to confront any longer, he would lure her into the bayous and shoot her dead and leave her body to feed the creatures and the bugs, as he had done with two other bitches in the last six weeks. Nobody had missed them.

With his hands still gripping his wrists behind his back, Johnston limped back and forth in a nine-foot pattern, three steps forward, a spin, three steps in return. Henry listened for a minute. Johnston was raving that establishing the capital in Austin was too dangerous because of the shortage of soldiers to defend it against the savages and the Mexicans, and furthermore the city was doomed because Sam Houston had vowed to move the capital out again and leave Austin in ruins if Houston was reelected president next year.

"Sam Houston is a fraud, a vainglorious jackass," Lamar said, turning away from the rain at the window. "Henry, did you hear what he did to me at my inauguration?"

Henry Longfellow was mentally wallowing with the filthy Cajun, and his groin was tingling. "What? Sir? You were speaking to me?"

"I am sorry, Henry. I forget what pain you are in," Lamar said.

"Pay no attention to my pain, Mr. President. What were you saying? Something about Sam Houston?"

"At my inaugural ceremony, the jackass was supposed to come and present me to the assembled guests and government and congratulate me and then get the hell out of the way. Instead he arrived drunk, looking like a great fool, dressed like George Washington with a powdered wig and knee stockings, and he talked for three hours about the glory of his administration, all of it lies! He took credit for every good thing that happened in the Republic, and he blamed others—notably me—for every failure and mistake. Do you think I would sit and be insulted so? Tell Henry what I did, General."

"You left, sir," said General Johnston.

"I left and had my secretary read my acceptance speech. Is that right, General Johnston?"

"I don't know, sir, I had gone by then."

Henry Longfellow made a clucking noise meant to sound like sympathy. He was impatient for Johnston to have his say and be done. Henry needed a word in private with Lamar, and then Henry had to be off to a meeting of cotton brokers. His two slave boys were waiting downstairs under the canopy above the driver's seat of Henry's carriage in the rain. With his law degree— a genuine one, not imaginary like so many of the lawyers he encountered in Texas—and his experience in cotton law, as well as his business knowledge gained while representing plantation owners in the Georgia legislature, Henry was prospering. Texas law was a mix of old Spanish law, English common law, and what passed for common reason. Most personal disputes were settled in person, often with violence. But in the makeshift courts Henry was an imposing figure, adept and forceful at argument, quoting impressive passages gleaned from his twenty-three-volume law library, the largest in the Republic. As a friend of the President, doors opened for him. Once Henry had put his mind to the arithmetic and honestly studied the agreements and clauses, he discovered cotton was the Republic's only export that was making big money. Henry bought two thousand acres of cotton land a few miles west of Houston City, and added to the Mexican and white laborers of his farm six new slaves, picked up in New Orleans for six hundred dollars each for the five men and four hundred for the woman, and appointed a Caribbean Negro slave as overseer to be sure Henry got a fair day's work from his people. The two slave boys Henry brought with him from Georgia were house slaves. They drove his carriage and carried him in a sedan chair when his leg hurt severely. They bathed him and massaged him and dressed him and cared for his wound. They cooked and cleaned and were pleasant company. They cared for him more devotedly than girls would do. Henry wanted to buy several young girls to play devil games with, but not yet. Not until he built his big house in the new capital of Austin.

Henry Longfellow looked at his watch. He was one of the few men in the Republic who carried a timepiece on his person. It was a pocket watch inside a gold case on a gold chain. Turning the key wound up the watch for twelve hours. His late wife had given him the watch as a wedding present. Her likeness had been inside the lid of the case for a while, but Henry replaced it with a drawing of his mother, whom he hated. The hag was still rolling and shrieking in the aisles at Hardshell Baptist tent meetings in Tennessee. She was fighting it out with the devil. What a waste of a woman's time. So Henry had a pocket watch, but in the Republic there were hardly any clocks. When Henry ordered a meeting of cotton brokers at his law office at two o'clock in the afternoon, the gentlemen drifted in over a period of hours.

On and on went General Johnston. He said Houston City had rich land, access to deep-water shipping, regular communications via ship with the merchant cities of the world. He said Texas needed to make wary but necessary understandings with the Dutch and British. He said the pending five-million-dollar loan from the government of France—money that would mean fresh blood and breath for the struggling Republic—would be easier to obtain if the capital was in thriving Houston City rather than in a wild valley at the mercy of the savages.

"The Congress has voted on this, Albert," the President said at last. "It's not all up to me."

"With respect, sir, you can demand this move be stopped."

"You are secretary of defense. Defending Austin is your job," the President said. He didn't like Johnston's tone.

"Sir, I do not have the troops necessary. We are under constant threat by the Mexican army. It is all I can do to present a defense against the Mexicans. A war against the Comanches is beyond our resources at this time."

The general tried to strike a match to light his pipe, but the humidity was too thick. President Lamar eyed him wearily, allowing Johnston to continue. The general was embarrassed to keep speaking of weakness. He knew he was beginning to annoy the President. Johnston diverted his speech from the dangers of moving to Austin to the advantages of maintaining the capital in Houston City. He believed in being positive. "Houston City is a flourishing glory of a capital, home to enterprising businessmen, the queen city of the arts in the Republic. We're already building a second Masonic temple, we have citizens with mastery of foreign languages. We are much more secure against Mexican and Indian attack than are San Antonio and this bumptious new settlement of Austin."

"Very well, Albert, I will consider your arguments," said the President.

"Thank you, sir."

"Meanwhile, I pray that you see to training three battalions of regular troops and raising a militia for the defense of Austin," said the President. Looking out the window, he saw the gray rain falling and people slopping ankle deep in mud on the plank sidewalks. Lamar hated this place. His own official dwelling in Houston City was a two-room wooden house with a shake roof. The jackass Sam Houston had moved into that humble structure three years ago and declared it the presidential residence. Lamar was stuck with it until the capital shifted to Austin and he arrived at his White House on Hickory Hill. "General Johnston, may God place His hand on your shoulder in this next year. We are embarked upon a daring episode that will lead to the Republic of Texas taking its rightful standing among the powerful nations of the earth. We need your help, Albert. I personally need you very much. All of Texas needs you."

"I will do my best, sir," said Johnston, caught off guard by this appeal to God and patriotism.

"Now, if you will be good enough to leave me," the President said to General Johnston. "I have pressing affairs, and I'm sure you are terribly busy. Perhaps you will dine with me tonight. The Palace Hotel at dark. If General Burleson is disposed, bring him with you. We'll share a few flagons of wine and thresh out the future of the Republic, hey?"

Lamar had his palm in the small of Johnston's back, urging the general gently toward the door.

"I will bring General Burleson, sir. You may count on it."

The President closed the door behind the general and said, "Sometimes, Henry, I want to shuck this whole empire and go live on a desert island with palm trees and Polynesian women."

"I know you better than to believe you would do that, Mr. President," said Henry Longfellow. "You are meant to be the president of a great republic. It is your fate. Texas will be the trade center of the world, beginning with the strides you are making in the affairs of nations."

"Thank you, Henry. I appreciate your reassurance."

"Have you had word from your little girl?"

"Yes, yes, a letter from her yesterday. She is doing well."

The thought of Rebecca Ann deepened Lamar's melancholy. He missed his eleven-year-old daughter, who had stayed in Georgia with her dead mother's family because Texas had no proper schools for her.

"Please tell her I think of her fondly," Henry said.

The President nodded. "You are so kind." But he wouldn't mention Henry Longfellow to his daughter. The little girl said Henry gave her nightmares. "Now, if you don't mind, I am feeling rather bilious and feverish today, my juices sucked away by gloom, you might say. I need to lie on the couch with a wet cloth on my head for an hour or so and quieten my thoughts."

"Of course. Of course." Henry Longfellow was an expert by now in the use of crutches, and his leg was much stronger. He swung himself upright with dexterity and ease, his bird's head bobbing. "I'll stop by in a while to have a word with you about this question of cotton tariffs."

Lamar waved the puffy cuffs that encircled his hands.

"Consider that we've already had that conversation, Henry. I know what you will say, word for word."

"Very well, then. Another subject dear to my heart. Where are that Cherokee whore and her thug? Why are they not here in chains as you ordered? I swear to you, Mr. President, the Cherokees are as much danger to us here as they were in Georgia."

The President dipped a washcloth in a pan of tepid water. How he would love a chunk of ice. He'd seen no ice since his journey to New Orleans a month ago for a private meeting with the French ambassador, who was assigning a chargé d'affaires called Count Dubois de Saligny to represent the legation in Austin. Lamar removed his collar button and opened his shirt. He wiped his face, then wrung the cloth so that the water trickled down his chest.

"As for the Cherokees, they are, obviously, doomed," the President said.

"Even though old Chief Bowl is Sam Houston's father-in-law?"

"Even more so," the President said. His lips slackened in pleasure as he rubbed his forehead with the wet cloth. "Henry, I've had a message from one of my people in Austin. Captain Caldwell says to tell me he is in control of the situation. You may be assured punishment of the criminals who attacked you will be swift and harsh."

# 19

Judge Theodore Loftin was the magistrate for Austin and served as the district judge for the still undefined district around the capital. He had been approved by the Congress to serve on the first Supreme Court of the Republic of Texas, but the court had yet to sit. Judge Loftin was being helped into a chair at a table in Dutch John's Saloon. Everyone was there—Billy Bonnell, Richard Bullock, Judge Waller, Gruber and Mrs. Hunboldt, everyone the judge recognized and more, packing the room. He waved them back a few feet from his table so he could take a breath without hurting his stomach. People stuck their heads in at the doors and windows and gathered in the street, trying to hear the show.

The Ranger had come to the judge's house that morning and rousted him out of bed. Judge Loftin was feeling fairly navigable again after the appendectomy. Doc Swift had stopped by two days earlier and removed the stitches from the big purple wound. Judge Loftin was thankful for the scar, because it meant he was alive. In her room, his wife cried and shook with malaria. She alternated between freezing with cold and blazing with fever. Negro slaves sat with her night and day. The judge had dressed and let the Ranger assist him in walking to Dutch John's. It was to be an official procedure of some sort, the judge understood. His presence was putting the seal of the Republic on the proceedings, as it were. Since this somehow involved Doc Swift, who had saved the judge's life, Judge Loftin was happy to oblige. The judge hated emetics, which made him vomit, and cathartics, which made his bowels operate on their own schedule, and he despised being bled into a heated glass cup. This doctor had demanded none of those distasteful remedies. Judge Loftin was grateful to him. Probably they are giving our doctor a medal, the judge thought.

Doc was was standing in the front rank of the crowd inside the saloon, looking at the Ranger from a distance of ten feet. Doc was admiring his own handiwork. He had plucked the stitches out of Caldwell's nose last night, clipping them with scissors. Doc was pleased at how well Caldwell's nose had healed with the stitching and the poultices—a red scar ran upward two inches from the tip, but it gave little hint of how ugly the wound had been—and he was surprised about the wiring in the Ranger's jaw. Caldwell had configured it himself with pliers and a knife so that he could speak louder. The swelling in his face was diminished from the use of poultices. Cullasaja had wrapped his torso tightly in linen strips to ease the thrust of his cracked rib. The two men had scarcely spoken last night at Bullock's as Doc unstitched the Ranger's nose. The wretched lawyer Bone, who had begun drinking twenty pints of spring water each day, was sleeping under the influence of herbal tea. The only sounds were the scissors and the two men breathing and the yelling from a fistfight in the street a block away. There had been many fistfights lately, as if Doc's pugilistic exhibition had aroused the desire for individual combat among these pioneers. Finally the Ranger spoke. Caldwell asked Doc to bring Cullasaja to a meeting at Dutch John's tomorrow morning an hour after breakfast. Doc didn't ask why. He knew Caldwell was deciding how he must conduct his duty. Whatever the Ranger decided, Doc was not going to allow his sister and himself to be arrested.

The next morning in Dutch John's, looking at the Ranger, Doc nudged Cullasaja.

"Maybe we've done too well fixing up that one," he said.

"He's quite a specimen," she said.

"I have noticed you are rather fond of him."

"He has appealing qualities."

"Caldwell is a Texas Ranger. He is your enemy, Cully. Be ready to duck at any moment," Doc said.

"What do you mean?"

"If Caldwell tries to arrest us, Gruber is going to shoot him."

"Rommy!"

Matthew's gray eyes scanned the crowd. He was not fazed by their hostility and unrest. He saw a large number of rifles and shotguns. He saw Dr. Swift whispering with Cullasaja. The crowd was gathering behind the two of them. Matthew searched out the big German with the inch-high ridge of blade in his skull. Gruber stood slightly behind the Ranger, armed with pistol, butcher knife and double-barreled shotgun. Gruber wore a red bandana on his head like a pirate. Sweat rolled down his jaws. He didn't look like the real estate dealer Matthew had bought two building lots from. He looked like a Hessian deserter who had become a Comanchero. Wet heat was rising and causing the crowd in Dutch John's to sweat and sneeze and develop a mighty thirst. Horace Wapner, the poet, rapped on a beer keg with his own mug. Horace was covering this meeting for *The Sentinel*. He was inspired to write his report in verse. He needed beer.

"How about I open the bar?" Dutch John said.

"Not yet," said Caldwell.

"Who gave you the right to tell me I can't open my bar?" Dutch John said.

"Please, gentlemen," said Judge Loftin.

"Call the court to order, Your Honor," Matthew said.

Judge Loftin slapped the table with his palm.

"I'm calling the citizens of the Republic to order, and this applies to you newcomers," said Judge Loftin. In a moment the rustling and voices settled. "This is Ranger Captain Matthew Caldwell. Most of you know him already. Those who don't know him, let me tell you this is a genuine hero of the revolution, a hero of the Texas Republic, and he is one tough son of a whirlwind, I can tell you that. Whatever you do, do not cross Captain Caldwell."

The judge turned to the Ranger.

"Speak your piece, Captain," the judge said.

"Everybody knows what I came here to do," Matthew said. "I came here to arrest Doctor Swift and the young woman Cullasaja on accusations of spying and assault."

Judge Loftin's eyes grew wide. He had been laid out on the billiard table when the Ranger arrived in town, and in his sick bed ever since. The judge had no idea what Caldwell was talking about. Matthew heard Gruber cocking both hammers of his shotgun. There were angry murmurs in the crowd. People moved forward to protect each shoulder of Doc and Cullasaja.

"Don't get your bile up until you hear me out," Matthew said.

"Hear him out, boys," said Judge Loftin, who did not want to jeopardize his seat on the Supreme Court by participating in an illegality. But certainly the judge had to resist the arrest of the doctor who had saved his life and the woman who had nursed him and his wife. Loftin wished he had stayed in bed today.

"I am enforcing the Rangers' Prerogative," said Matthew.

"The Rangers' Prerogative?" Judge Loftin asked.

"A Ranger is free to do what he thinks is right even when it is not what some person in authority happens to request. In the weeks I have been in Austin, I have been cared for by this young woman and have come to admire and respect her. Using the Rangers' Prerogative, I hereby declare she is innocent of the accusations that brought me here."

"Innocent, by God!" said Judge Loftin. He slapped his palm on the table.

"Legally innocent, Judge," Matthew said.

"Hell yes, legally innocent," the judge said, and spanked the tabletop.

"But Doctor Swift, he's a different problem," said Matthew. He noted the crowd's hostility suddenly growing again. "Doctor Swift is guilty of breaking the leg of a Republic official with a saber. He did it in cold blood. Am I right, Doctor Swift?"

"I did," Doc said.

"But we all know there is a difference between murder and killing," Matthew said. "Some people should be killed. Some people should get their legs broke, and this Republic official fits that description in my opinion."

"The doctor is innocent?" asked Judge Loftin, hoping this would end happily.

"No, he did it. That is the inescapable fact," Matthew said. Threatening cries arose from the crowd. Gruber stepped forward, flourishing his shotgun. Matthew stayed calm in appearance, as if they dared not interfere with him. Inside he felt his blood pumping and his senses sharpening. "Stand back, Mr. Gruber," Matthew said. "I'm not finished talking yet."

The Ranger's eyes found those of the doctor. Standing beside her brother, Cullasaja could feel the disturbed air that flowed between the two men, like two spirits opposing and probing. She noted the physical contrast between the weather-burned, broad-chested, bearded, flamboyant Ranger and her fair skinned, blue-eyed, wide-shouldered brother.

"Doctor Swift, I am asking for your word of honor that before you leave Texas, you will confront Henry Longfellow about these charges in my presence, and we will see that justice is done. Do you swear?"

"I swear," said Doc.

"Then using the Rangers' Prerogative, I declare Doctor Swift is free until justice is done at some future date," Matthew said.

"The doctor is free! Hurrah!" shouted Judge Loftin, banging on the table.

"Hurrah for Doc! Hurrah for Doc!" the crowd yelled. Dutch John ran to open the bar, and the crowd rushed behind him. Wapner, the poet from *The Sentinel*, was writing notes on the cuff of his shirt as he thrust his beer mug toward the keg.

"You are a strong man, Captain," said Gruber, uncocking his shotgun.

"Who do I see about building me a house?" Matthew asked.

"I'm the one, Captain Caldwell," said a young, slender man with an Alabama Gulf Coast accent. "I'll put you at the top of my list and build your house for what it costs me, plus a little tiny profit to feed my wife and babies."

"I don't want any gifts," Matthew said.

"Yah, this fellow here is Newfield, a good builder, Captain. He has thirty houses under construction right now, so his wife and babies ain't starving," said Gruber. "But he's an honest fellow, as builders go."

"A bedroom and a living room separated by a dog run to catch the breeze? And of course another structure for the kitchen, which I will build especially fireproof for you, Captain. Is that what you want?"

"That sounds about right, I guess," said Matthew.

"Post oak or pine?"

"Pine," said Matthew.

"Consider it done. God bless Texas," Newfield said, and went to the bar with Gruber.

Caldwell came around the table and stuck out his hand. Doc Swift shook hands with him. "Thank you for repairing the damage you did me," Matthew said. "You taught me a lesson about underestimating an opponent. I hope whatever you want in Texas, you find it. But you be careful about poking around on my land or I might have to shoot you."

"I won't harm your land," said Doc.

Matthew took both of Cullasaja's hands in his own. His hands were rough and his fingers were thick. She was thrilled by his touch. His gray eyes drilled into her mind.

"I am very grateful to you, Cullasaja. You are as kind and smart as you are beautiful. I promise I will try to do what I can to protect Bowl's Town, but I have to warn you that my help may not be enough. You are in danger anywhere in Texas. Please go back to New York and read your books and marry some educated fellow and have babies," he said.

She rose on her toes and kissed him on the unfractured side of his chin, feeling bristly hairs against her lips.

"Come visit us, Captain. I would like to see you again," she said.

"I'll think on it," Matthew said. He looked down at the gentle Cherokee girl and smiled. The smile hurt and twisted his lips, but he knew she understood that it was with affectionate intention. "Well, I've got to get back to my job of riding fifty miles a day looking for a fight. I'd just as soon not have found this most recent one."

Matthew straightened the brim on his new woven straw hat and squared his shoulders and settled Sweet Lips under his right elbow. He looked every bit as confident and unbeatable as he had the day he walked into Dutch John's to arrest them weeks ago. The only visible difference was the thin red scar that ran up from the tip of his nose.

"Doctor Swift, after you and me meet face to face with Henry Longfellow, maybe later you can tell me why you want to travel on my land." Matthew said.

"Someday I will tell you," said Doc.

"I want you to know, Doctor Swift, that I learn from a whipping and I don't forget what I learned," Matthew said. "There comes a day of reckoning."

"I will remember," said Doc.

Matthew turned and stepped through the saloon door onto Pecan Street. They watched him walking toward the livery stable, moving lightly in his moccasin boots, the fringes jiggling on his doeskin jacket, the straw hat riding on his dark mane. They saw his white Arabian stallion had been saddled and was waiting for him, the reins in the hands of Googleye, who was going to pole and sail the Ranger across the river in the new *Waterloo Queen*. Cullasaja kept watching as Matthew lightly mounted the Arabian and rode away without looking back.

"Rommy, I have strong feelings for that man. Could I be falling in love with him?" Cullasaja said.

Doc put an arm around his sister and hugged her close.

"Besides all the other reasons against it, Cully, the man is contracted to be married. You must forget about him. The world is full of better men for you than Captain Caldwell. Please believe me."

"I always believe you," she said, but this time she wasn't sure.

# 20

In his teepee in a village in the hills west of Austin, Isimanica rolled off the girl Pearl, sated. Though Isimanica did not understand the concepts of sentimentality or of romance, he did now and then feel in his gut a sensation of bliss. Sometimes it came out of nowhere when he was watching the flames in the clouds of sundown, but most often lately it came when he lay with Pearl or gazed upon her blonde hair and baby face and pleasingly shaped body. This bliss was different from the joy of hacking an enemy to death, and not as instantly satisfying. But looking at Pearl, he felt the yearning that he felt when he watched the sun going away; it left him feeling he would never have enough.

The morning sun cast a path through the front flap. Isimanica lay with Pearl on the smooth side of a buffalo robe. Opposite the cooking hole, Pearl's sister, Rose, lay on another buffalo hide beside Little Bush, who was Isimanica's girlish wife. Rose's face showed bruises, and there were burn sores on her arms and legs. Little Bush had beaten her with a hickory limb and had poked her with hot coals as an amusement—it was the accepted way to treat a new slave—until Pearl entreated Isimanica to order Little Bush to stop the torment. On the day and night of the ride from Ridgewood Bone's farm to this camp of the families in the hills beyond which the earth fell into an ocean of grass, Rose had become exhausted and fallen off the pony on which she was mounted behind Pearl. Annoyed at the delay, Isimanica leaped off his paint horse and ran to the prone Rose with his knife raised. But a cry from Pearl had stopped him from killing her. Already the strange blonde girl touched Isimanica in some way he didn't understand. He had tied Rose with a Mexican riata onto the back of the pony behind Pearl, and they had ridden for hours until they heard the cries of glee of the women and children and elders as they made Turk's raiding party welcome back to their home. Osage Killer and Young Owl Hatching, among men who had chosen not to join the raiding party, smiled upon Turk and Isimanica and the returning hunters. A successful raid was good for all the families. As the leader, Turk would give away most of his share among the lodges. Isimanica would contribute generously to the communal wealth of the families, building respect and goodwill he would need in order to lead his own raiding party one day, but he made it a point to let the whole camp know that the two little girls belonged to him and were not to be tormented by the women.

To celebrate the return of Turk's party, oak logs were piled into a fire, and flutes and drums began playing in insistent monotones. The dancing started. Women and children at first, then Osage Killer joined, followed by several other men who had declined the raid. The returning hunters slowly began to join the dancing. They sang about the raid, the monkeys they had captured, the Mexican horses they had taken, the new Mexican scalps that joined the older ones on scalp poles outside the lodges. They sang about the hacking of the white fool at Cold Water. Isimanica danced barefoot, stripped to a breechclout which swung to reveal his genitals and his medicine pouch. Pearl admired his muscles and his grace and the tattoo of a bull buffalo on his back. Little Bush began beating Rose during the dancing. Pearl saw their mother, Wanda, being dragged by the wrists by the warrior called Ram; they were entering the teepee that had been erected for Ram by the sisters of his dead wife. After sex with

Wanda, Ram would turn her over to the sisters as their servant. If she survived their abuse and proved to be resourceful and hardworking, Ram might take this white woman as a wife. But all Pearl knew was that the brown man was dragging her mother away, and she knew what they were going to do first.

In the morning, Isimanica sat up cross-legged on the buffalo robe and turned his back to Pearl. She scrambled to her knees. This was the sign for her to care for his hair. Like all the warriors and most of the other men of the people, Isimanica devoted much time to his hair. It had never been cut in twenty years, and it touched the small of his back when it was washed and combed out straight. But his hair was seldom washed. He lubricated it with a mixture of bear grease and buffalo grease—two good spirits to pay homage to—and his hair became thicker and blacker. He adorned his hair with combs made of bone and shiny stones and bits of fur. Isimanica's hair was vital to his personal life. His hair carried power. He had been surprised and frightened the first time Pearl tried to help him comb his hair. He grew angry and slapped her for touching his hair. But she was smiling and unafraid. By the end of their first morning, Pearl was caring for Isimanica's hair by herself. It became her daily duty that she performed with pride and pleasure.

# 21

The Texas Ranger station at Boca Chica Crossing sat on the best ford across the Warloop in fifty miles. For as long as anyone reckoned, traveling bands of Indians of many tribes had used the crossing to go east into the pine woods and big thickets and swamps, or south onto the plain that led to the Gulf of Mexico. Two years ago, Captain Matthew Caldwell and Big Foot Wallace had led a dozen Rangers and six carpenters and masons to the burnt rubble on the old site. They built the new Ranger station not only to bar the path of raiding Indians now mostly Comanches—but also to ease the entrance into central Texas for the immigrants coming from the east.

The Ranger station was a large one-room stone structure with a hardwood roof, a stone chimney and a dirt floor. The hardwood roof would not burn.

Rather than windows, there were rifle slits in the two-foot-thick stone walls. The door was a solid mahogany slab that opened inward. An iron bolting bar leaned against the frame. Inside the room were a Louis XIV table that had belonged to some forgotten immigrant, two wooden chairs with brown and white cowhide seats, a stone fireplace with firewood stacked nearby, twenty bullet molds, supplies of lead and powder, six full water bags made of buffalo stomachs, a wall decoration of ten dry Comanche scalps glued to a battered Comanche war shield, a case with a violin in it, and a small bookshelf on which reposed *The Iliad*, *The Three Musketeers,* a volume of poems by Byron and a medical text by Cotton Mather, next to an unopened brown paper envelope.

Big Foot Wallace sat leaning against the outside wall beside the door of the station, dozing in the warm sun, his legs stretched out. His four dogs— Ring, Spec, Brutus and Spot—slept at his feet. Fifty feet away was the kitchen, a separate building that held cookware, a fireplace, a dining table and chairs. The kitchen was well clear of the Ranger station and the half a dozen one- and two-room houses. Big Foot and his four dogs lived in their own house, but when he felt like socializing, he came to the station or to the kitchen at meal-time. Their cook, a Creole called Sabado, was in the kitchen now, building a pot of stew. The odors of onions and potatoes and venison drifted into Big Foot's mind and awoke him. He opened his eyes and saw the boys were playing a game of skull in the clearing between the kitchen and the horse pen near the heart of the compound.

Big Foot listened to their accents as they bantered about the game. The Rangers were English, Scots, Irish, Germans, French, Creoles, Tejano Mexicans who had fought for the Republic in the revolution and had been tough and lucky enough that they stayed alive even after San Jacinto when new Texans viewed all Mexicans as enemies. They wore buckskins, plug hats, sombreros, leggins, bracelets, necklaces, earrings, moccasins, boots. Several were bare to the waist. On their persons or nearby were pistols, derringers, rifles, shotguns, Bowie knives, butcher knives, daggers and hatchets. Some Rangers had been educated but, like the rest, were fleeing into a new, exciting life. The Rangers were young men, nearly all of them adventurers in their twenties. Only a few were over thirty. Big Foot was the only veteran of San Jacinto at the station on this day.

Big Foot heard the voice of Saginaw Boswell.

"I am betting ten coffee beans. Any of you lads have the courage to test me?"

Saginaw Boswell was a young drifter from the far northwest, the Oregon area. Big Foot had seen him ride a horse standing up in the saddle with the balance and ease an ordinary man used in sitting a saddle on a tamer horse. Saginaw had appeared at Boca Chica Crossing six months ago and asked to join the ranging company. He owned his horse and weapons, had no family in Texas, had no desire for money, dreamed of someday owning land, and he loved violence. He did not hesitate to provoke a fight and strike the first blow. He swore to the Rangers that he would never surrender himself or his weapons to an enemy, never abandon a comrade, never quit a battle and if called upon would give his life for the Republic of Texas. Saginaw Boswell was the sort of man the Rangers were looking for.

"Make it twenty beans," said Cyrus from Kentucky.

"Let's see your twenty beans," Saginaw said.

Cyrus opened his fiddle case and pulled out a pouch and counted twenty large brown Mexican coffee beans, which he placed on a rock. The Rangers called him Fiddle Man. He played at the station for their dances—men dancing with men, or men dancing alone—and their funerals. Sometimes in the evening he played lonely mountain love songs that made these rough men want to cry. Fiddle Man wore a Bowie knife that weighed four pounds.

Saginaw Boswell added another ten beans to the mound on the rock and picked up three pistol balls that had his mark scratched on them.

"The challenger should go first, but I'm feeling the spirit right now, Fiddle Man."

"Go ahead," said Fiddle Man, fetching his own three marked pistol balls.

A human skull with its crown removed sat on a stump twenty-five feet from a line scratched in the dirt.

"I bet five beans on the Fiddle Man," called Herman the German, a big, hairy, bare-chested man who was currying his gray horse. He had brought his horse out of the corral so he could participate in the skull game but stay close to his horse, which he liked better than he liked people.

"I'll take your bet, Herman," said Snake, a Cajun who wore nothing but moccasins, a loincloth and a plug hat. A necklace of teeth lay against his chest. The air was sultry with humidity. Thunderstorms were building from the south. They heard a faraway rumble.

Big Foot rose and stretched and yawned. His four dogs looked up at him.

"I got twenty-five beans says I beat you both," Big Foot said.

"Aw hell, Big Foot, this is between me and Fiddle Man," said Saginaw.

"But now things has changed," Big Foot said. He dug his three marked pistol balls out of his his greasy buckskins and tossed them up and down in his palm. "You go first if you feel the spirit, Saginaw. I know how it is. I feel the spirit myself."

The three Rangers took turns lobbing one pistol ball from the line with the intention of landing the ball inside the hole in the crown of the skull. Saginaw and Fiddle Man both made good on their first tosses. Big Foot spat on his ball, rubbed it, let loose a long fart, sighed with pleasure and relief—and tossed his first ball squarely into the hole.

"I bet five more beans on Big Foot," said Herman the German.

"You mean you bet ten he beats them both?" Snake said.

"Yah."

"I take it."

"Good," said Herman the German.

Each Ranger sank his second toss.

"My eyesight ain't been clear since I had the red measles as a child. I can hardly see that skull. Where is it again?" Big Foot said.

"I guess you want to up the bet to thirty beans?" said Saginaw.

"Why, that's a good idea," Big Foot said.

"Somebody lend me five beans?" asked Fiddle Man.

"I'll lend you five for seven back," Snake said.

"The hell with that," said Fiddle Man.

"I'll go you five beans on credit," Big Foot said. "It's your toss, Saginaw."

"I know whose damn toss it is," said Saginaw, controlling his temper. Violence was encouraged, but not against another Ranger.

Saginaw's ball landed in the skull with a clink.

Fiddle Man made a toss that missed the hole by a fraction of an inch, bounced off the skull and fell into the dirt.

Big Foot lobbed his ball into the skull with ease.

"I guess we win," said Saginaw.

"Not yet," Big Foot said.

"The bet was you would beat us both. You and me tied, so you didn't beat us both."

"Not yet," Big Foot said. "But I will. It's your throw."

"Yah! There's no winner yet!" agreed the German.

Fiddle Man was silent. Snake did not contest. Saginaw decided not to argue it further. He retrieved the five balls from the skull and handed theirs to Big Foot and Fiddle Man. Saginaw edged his boot to the line. He swung his arm twice, testing for distance, and then he lobbed and his ball glanced off the rear of the hole in the skull and flopped onto the stump, where it rolled a moment and held still.

Above the sloshing of the river as it flowed past the station, they heard a shrill eagle-bone whistle. Two long toots. Their Lipan scout, who was watching the upriver approach, was telling them a friend was riding toward the station. Nevertheless, each Ranger reached for a heavier weapon than the one he already wore. Comanches used eagle-bone whistles as well as Lipans.

Six Rangers ran to the corral to guard the horses. The others spread into the brush around the clearing or went into the stone station house. They waited.

"Can a man get a drink of whiskey around here?" shouted Matthew Caldwell.

The Rangers stepped out of concealment and watched Old Paint ride into the clearing on a white Arabian stallion.

"Good to see you, Matthew. I was afraid you'd decided to run for mayor up in Austin," said Big Foot.

"Business took a little longer than I'd figured."

Matthew swung down out of the saddle and patted the Arabian's neck.

"Beautiful horse, Captain," Saginaw said.

"I traded a fellow. You boys playing a game of skull?"

"Yah! One more throw!" said Herman the German.

Big Foot edged to the line, nervously tapping the earth with his toes. He squinted in the wrong direction. "Where's that skull at? Over yonder?"

"This other way!" shouted Herman the German.

Big Foot turned. "Oh, there it is," he said.

He lobbed his pistol ball squarely into the skull.

"I'm gonna take care of Pacer here," Matthew said as Big Foot raked the pile of coffee beans into his hat. "Then I'll catch a little sleep and see you boys at dinner. What's old Sabado cooking tonight? Venison or venison?"

"It's venison, Captain," said Herman the German.

Big Foot walked with Caldwell toward the corral. Spec, Ring, Brutus and Spot trotted behind them.

"I've got something to show you, Matthew," Big Foot said.

"Can I catch a sleep first? I've got a toothache," said Matthew.

"Remember you reported here at the station a while back that you saw Savariego and a battalion of Mexicans in the field?"

"The Volunteers of Monclova."

"Saginaw and Fiddle Man went to check on the Mexicans."

"How many did they find?"

"They didn't find the Mexicans. Let me show you what they did find."

Big Foot led Matthew and the walking stallion and the four dogs around a corner of Big Foot's one-room house. In the rear, beside the covered crapper hole, was a lean-to with straw on the dirt floor. A thin man, his ribs clearly etched, sat on the straw. His eyes were glaring with insanity. His front teeth were missing except for the fangs. His hair was long and tangled. A dog collar strapped around his neck was attached to a stake by a chain. The man's left sleeve hung empty.

The man's mad eyes lit for a moment on the white stallion, almost as if behind the eyes a brain was fashioning a thought, and then the eyes moved on, flicking from right to left, looking for danger.

"That lunatic looks an awful lot like old Cristolphe Rublo, don't he?" said Big Foot.

"There is kind of a resemblance, now you point it out," Matthew said.

Big Foot nodded as the men exchanged glances.

"Saginaw and Fiddle Man found him down the river hiding in the trees. His left arm was sawed off, and he was near dead as well as insane. Looks like he should have bled to death, but he went crazy instead. The boys saw lots of sign of crossing. They found the bones of a Mexican officer on the far bank and a horse skeleton by him. They found the bones of another horse that had a black mane and tail in an elm mott. They even found the bones of this fellow's left arm lying next to a tree that had a big knothole through it."

"But no Mexican battalion?"

"Not yet. We ranged toward Austin and down to Goliad and can't find them. I send boys to keep looking in case the Comanches chase Savariego in our direction," said Big Foot.

The madman cowered against the wall of the lean-to at the sight of Matthew Caldwell.

"Saginaw and Fiddle Man and none of the other boys at this station have been in Texas long enough to know who Cristolphe Rublo is," said Big Foot. "I'm kind of surprised they brought him back here. They treat him like a circus bear. They poke him and throw him food. I moved him over to my house to watch after him a little more kindly. What do you want me to do with him?"

Matthew looked at the madman. Rublo shrank back and whimpered and pissed down his leg.

"I don't know. Let's you and me decide after supper."

"Good enough, Matthew."

Matthew took the reins of the white Arabian stallion, now known as Pacer, and walked with the horse toward the corral.

"Oh, Matthew!" called Big Foot.

Caldwell stopped and looked back.

"A courier brought a letter for you. It's in the bookcase in the station house."

Matthew felt a jerk of apprehension. It was sort of fear and sort of joy. He led the horse at a trot toward the stone walls of the station house.

Inside, Matthew found the letter in the bookcase. He recognized the handwriting, as he had known he would. He tore open the thick paper envelope that was addressed to Captain Matthew Caldwell.

Dear Captain Caldwell,

I have arrived in San Antonio. I am living at the Fincus Hotel. I have made friends with Mr. and Mrs. Kerr from New York, who say they are friends of yours. I gather that anyone here who is not a friend of yours would not say so in public. I look forward eagerly to meeting you. It frightens me to know you are about to become a reality, and yet it thrills me also.

Sincerely, Hannah Dahlman.

## HANNAH

Life is the flash of a firefly
in the night. It is the little
shadow which runs across the
grass and loses itself in the
sunset.

*—Cherokee teaching passed
along by Knows All Charlie*

# 22

Hannah Dahlman opened her steamer trunk, straining with the snaps that had rusted on the long voyage, and began pulling out pieces of clothing, looking for something that might pass as a bathing costume. She had promised to meet Dora Kerr at four in the afternoon—the Fincus Hotel had a clock in the lobby—for a cup of coffee following siesta and then for a bath in the Pataki Bath House attached to the hotel where the San Antonio River ran past under cypress trees.

Hannah sat on the bed, and it crunched and gave off an aroma like wet weeds. Lupe, the Mexican girl who cleaned the room, had explained it to her last night. "The mattress is stuffed with moss. In winter we stuff wool in there with the moss. People sleeps real nice here at the Fincus."

Except for her underwear—and a satin and lace nightgown to be saved for her wedding night—nearly every piece of clothing she removed from the trunk was wool or fur. No one had warned her of the Texas heat. She had brought clothes she would wear in a more temperate climate than north Germany, but not for weather such as this in San Antonio. The sun had been blazing the noon last week when Herr Growald, the marriage agent, fetched her in a buggy from the port at Matagorda, a barren plain of stones and mud. In the three days it took them to follow the rutted road to San Antonio, they stopped each night at a farmhouse known to Herr Growald as relatively safe from Indians and bandits. At one two-room log house, five men and four women, including six travelers, slept in one room, and the other was occupied by five Negro slaves and the cooking stove. The sun seemed to blaze hotter with every mile Hannah advanced into Texas. Herr Growald told her that in January of this very same year, only months ago, two feet of snow fell on San Antonio and drifts piled up eight feet high and hundreds of cows and horses froze to death. But as their buggy passed along the trail past the old Spanish missions south of town, Hannah could feel the growing humidity of the river valley. She was immersed in sweat. It was hard to believe snow had ever fallen at such a place. It was like imagining snow in equatorial Africa.

In the hotel room, she withdrew her riding costume, which had seemed the right thing when she packed it in Hannover. The costume was a skirt and jacket of excellent gray wool, a black silk blouse, a gray broadcloth riding cap with a plume of long black ostrich feathers and a white satin rosette. What had seemed right in Germany was wrong in Texas. Nobody at Matagorda, none of the travelers they saw along the way, no woman she had seen during her arrival in San Antonio—nobody wore such a riding costume. The women wore large bonnets that protected their faces from the sun, and calico gowns with long sleeves and gloves, and several women, Hannah observed, were wearing pistols.

Yesterday, Herr Growald had delivered his charge to the Fincus Hotel, seen to it that she had a room accounted for on Captain Caldwell's bill and then had retired to his own room, shared with two traveling salesmen, and slept around the clock. Hannah was inspecting a stuffed bear in the lobby when Dora Kerr introduced herself. Dora was dressed in velvet, perspiring but looking sophisticated as she dabbed her perfect features with a perfumed handkerchief and spoke of the theater in London and New York City. Soon Hannah found herself having dinner of rice, beans, tortillas, beef and honey-filled soapapillas with Dora and her husband, Lawrence, at the Café Sanchez on Main Plaza. There was a merciful breeze that dried Hannah's sweat, and Ingrid Sanchez served strong Mexican beer. In relief at having arrived in good health in Texas after seven weeks of travel, most of it uncomfortable and difficult, Hannah drank several mugs of beer and later remembered talking more than she should, elaborating on answers, revealing more about her life in Europe than perhaps was circumspect. The Kerrs spoke of Captain Caldwell with admiration and clearly wanted to direct the conversation to Hannah's relationship with him. But Hannah felt uncertain in speaking of this man, who was, after all, a stranger to her. Hannah would swallow a hearty draught of beer and guide the talk back to the theater, which she loved. Discussing theater was always near to uppermost with Dora. Hannah and Dora were especially fond of Molière—*The School for Wives* and *Tartuffe* in particular—and Shakespeare, to be sure. Hannah remembered that at dinner Dora had invited her to the bath house the next day after siesta—a Spanish custom that Hannah had not dreamed would be observed in San Antonio. At ten in the morning, Herr Growald came to her door and asked her to write a note he would send by courier to Captain Caldwell at the Boca Chica Station. Herr Growald repeated his promise of wedded bliss, fetched his buggy and trotted off toward Houston City.

Hannah was alone.

What, she wondered, did they call a bathing costume in Texas? Hannah selected a camisole tunic of fine cotton worn over cotton bloomers. To cover herself as she went from her room across the lobby to the entrance of the Pataki Bath House, Hannah chose a linen sheet—meant for her marriage bed—that she draped to resemble a robe. A tall man with a crane neck and a beaky face lounged in the lobby on a calfskin chair with a walking stick in one hand and watched with bright, blinking, curious eyes as she passed. Dora had pointed out the man last night: "That is Henry Longfellow, a cotton grower and land speculator and Republic official of some sort. I find him perverse and disgusting. Avoid him."

The bamboo door of the bath house swung open at Hannah's tug, and she said good morning in Spanish to Doña Maria de Bethencourt, a society woman from one of the original familes in San Antonio, Canary Islanders who had settled and built the town one hundred and eight years ago, as the old string of missions were crumbling from raids by Apaches and neglect by Spain. Many Canary Island descendants now lived on the east side of the river on a hill that overlooked the ruins of the Alamo Church and Plaza. They lived in *jacales* built of mud, straw and boards. But Doña Maria's family owned a hacienda on the west side of San Antonio and a cattle ranch that had remained in the de Bethencourt name throughout the revolution. Doña Maria stood out from the ordinary by her bearing and the aristocratic profile of her face and body. Hannah noticed there seemed to be nothing underneath Doña Maria's silk robe tied at the waist. Behind Doña Maria at the dressing bench stood Dora Kerr and Mary Maverick, undoing the buttons on their dresses.

"Where did you learn to speak Spanish, Hannah?" asked Dora, surprised. Dora knew from last night's dinner that the German girl spoke French as well as English and German—but Spanish? Hannah had spoken only German to Ingrid Sanchez, who had immigrated from Germany a decade ago and married a Tejano who was killed at Goliad during the revolution. Dora envied these European minds that could soak up languages as Dora soaked up written lines on the pages of a play. "Oh, I so wish I spoke Spanish. Perhaps you shall teach me."

"I will be honored to do so. Once I learned Latin, the Romance languages came easily—French, Italian, Spanish," Hannah said in English. She waited as Doña Maria closed the door. Dora and Mary continued to undress. The water was terraced from two to four feet deep against the bank in the bath house, where canvas walls shielded the bathers from view and a tent roof kept out the rain. Bathers could lift a flap and swim into the river if they wished

A pot of coffee warmed in a porcelain holder lit by a candle. Doña Maria poured a cup of the dark liquid for Hannah. The rich chocolate taste of it flooded through her body. This was coffee from the mountains of southern Mexico. Doña Maria's grandmother in Mexico City shipped it to her by the fifty-pound cask.

"What do you have on under that sheet, Hannah?" asked Mary Maverick, stepping out of her skirt.

"My bathing costume," Hannah said. "I didn't know exactly what to wear."

"Let us see it," said Dora.

"I'm embarrassed," Hannah said.

"Be a good sport. We won't laugh at you," said Mary.

Hannah realized she and Mary Maverick were about the same age, about twenty years old. Doña Maria stirred the water with her toes. Dora Kerr shrugged off her velvet blouse and carefully draped it on the bench. All the women were watching Hannah. With a sigh Hannah opened her sheet and stood before them in camisole and bloomers.

"That's what you're wearing into the water?" asked Mary.

"Hannah, darling, you have confused us with a spa in Austria," Dora said.

Doña Maria de Bethencourt peeled off her silk robe and slung it on a hook. She was naked, with high brown breasts with berry-sized nipples, a proud belly and a thatch of black hair at her crotch.

"This is our bathing costume here," said Doña Maria, thrusting out her breasts and smiling as she picked up a handful of soap powder and lowered herself into the river.

"Modesty has gone by the boards on the frontier," Dora said. By now she was naked. Her abdomen had sagged from the pull of her undergarments as well as from age and gravity, but her breasts were full and firm, her pubic hair red as the hair on her head. "It has been the custom for ladies to bathe naked in this river for ages. Tell her, Doña Maria."

"True. For centuries," said Doña Maria.

Mary Maverick, slender and black-haired and very pale, dropped her drawers and leaped nude into the water, showering the others.

"Mary, you have drowned our coffee candle," Dora said.

"One more cup of that coffee, and I would jump clear out of the tent," said Mary.

Again all their eyes turned toward Hannah.

Hannah pulled her camisole over her head and wriggled her bloomers down to her ankles. She understood that the other women were inspecting her. They were looking at the flesh Captain Caldwell had contracted for. They were judging her. Hannah could feel their eyes appraising her breasts, her flat belly and small waist, her curving buttocks and lean limbs. She stood above the top step, folding her bloomers and camisole, long enough that the others finally turned their eyes away and began bathing. Then Hannah walked down the steps into the water. Cold enveloped her legs, gave her a rush of breath, woke her from the siesta heat. She crouched so the water reached her chin, and her feet rested on the flat limestone floor.

"Do you and the captain plan to make a home in Austin?" Dora asked.

Hannah knew she could not continue to avoid talking about Captain Caldwell and herself, and the intimacy of this bathing pool with the women was the best possible place to begin. But what could she say?

"I am not entirely certain."

"Well, you're lucky if Austin it is," Dora said. Hannah heard Dora slip in and out of an Irish accent, as if exercising her craft. "I was warned that to make a home in Texas, one must bring everything—cooking wares, furniture, clothing, pillows, feather beds. None of this mattress stuffed with moss for me. Do you imagine how it would sound making love—goonch, goonch, goonch. Oh, Walter, you're such a man!"

"Walter?" said Mary.

"I mean Lawrence."

Dora laughed. Hannah caught a whiff of wine on Dora's breath.

"My dear, I have brought at least two of nearly everything from New York City," Dora said, touching Hannah's bare shoulder with a finger. "We have so many trunks, it will take a dozen wagons to carry our possessions to Austin. Whatever you need, you just tell me."

"Thank you," Hannah said.

"Judge Waller is having our house built. I tried to make my husband go up to Austin and look at the site and prod the workers, but he had rather lay about the Fincus Bar and the Bull's Head Tavern swilling wine and playing cards. But our architect, Mr. Newfield, has sent us a copy of the plans, which I approved with a number of changes. Who is building your house?"

"I don't know," said Hannah.

"Doesn't Captain Caldwell receive your opinion on such a matter?" Mary asked, her black hair dripping water on her girlish chest.

"I have never met Captain Caldwell," Hannah said.

"He has written to you about your house, surely," said Mary.

"He has never written me a letter about anything whatsoever," Hannah said.

"Last night you told me you are engaged to marry Captain Caldwell," said Dora.

"The marriage is arranged," Hannah said.

"When is he coming to see you?" asked Dora.

"I don't know."

"He's a dramatic-looking man," Dora said. "Big and graceful. I suspect he would be a good lover."

"Always give me a small handsome delicate man as a lover," Doña Maria said in English as she glided on her back across the pool. "The big fellows are usually inept."

"Look! The Peeper!" cried Mary Maverick, pointing at the top of the canvas wall, where a rip had appeared.

Hannah turned and saw an eye, wide and blinking, peering through the torn canvas at the women in the water.

"My husband will blow your brains out!" Mary shouted.

The eye disappeared. They heard footsteps sloshing on the riverbank and a body heaving onto the ground. Hannah and Dora rushed to the rip to look through. Doña Maria raised a wall flap entirely and stepped into view. Downriver a wagon stopped on the Commerce Street Bridge, and the driver dropped his pipe out of his mouth as he beheld the magnificent naked aristocrat, Doña Maria, standing knee deep in the river in the sunshine outside the tent.

Hannah saw the long legs, one of them oddly bent below the knee, scrabbling up the bank and the tall man hobbling swiftly away with the use of his walking stick. She recognized the peeper. He was the man who had watched her hurry across the lobby wrapped in her linen sheet.

"That is the third time we have caught him peeping. Sometimes I wish Lawrence was a violent person," said Dora.

"I told Sam he should challenge that man and give him a whipping," Mary said. "But Sam said he's a harmless friend of the President's, just a little touched in the head."

"I daresay Captain Caldwell will not have such a Christian attitude," said Dora. "What do you think, Hannah?"

"I don't know."

"Oh, but of course, I said Christian attitude—and you're Jewish!" Dora said, laughing. "How could you know, poor thing?"

# 23

On the sundown side of the giant Singing Rock, in a green valley tall in grass and wildflowers, thick with live oak and hackberry trees, a spout of cold, clear water erupts near a boulder covered by moss and pours onto the stones and becomes a river the families call the Little Pigeon.

The Little Pigeon flows for three miles down the valley, creating a garden of life along its path. Then the river disappears into the limestone and is seen no more.

At the mouth of the Little Pigeon is a pool below a five-foot drop where water falls like liquid lace over a ridge of granite. Above the pool is a flat stone ledge forty feet long and ten feet wide. At the midpoint of the ledge a tall red rock backs against the wall but bulges out in front. Around one edge of the red rock is darkness that could be a shadow or could indicate a space inside the wall, perhaps a cavern.

The Dark Man and the Fighting Man rode bareback on their paint ponies along a trail by the river. Plodding behind them came a mule drawing a travois upon which lay the skinned and cleaned carcass of a buffalo that was fat from eating summer grass. The Fighting Man, Turk, carried a buckskin pouch slung over a naked shoulder. From the pouch protruded a hand mirror, a rattle and a silver picture frame. Turk held the pouch under his right armpit, his biceps adorned with copper bracelets, so that its contents would not be damaged.

"Are you certain he is angry?" asked Turk.

The Dark Man steered his pony with pressure from his knees. Since the lightning had changed his body, the Dark Man could not use his legs properly, but he remained a superior rider among people famous for their mastery of horses.

"Yes," the Dark Man said.

Turk feared nothing, and yet he feared everything. Facing enemy lances and hatchets was nothing. But magic was everything.

"I didn't mean to be late in bringing his tribute. I got drunk and I slept a long time and my wives demanded me to mate with them. Will you explain it to him?"

"That won't matter. It all depends on if he likes the gifts."

Turk glanced down at the necklace of turquoise and silver and bear claws that lay against his hairy chest, and he felt the touch of his medicine bag beside his testicles under his breechclout. Turk was stunned with anticipation, in the grip of magic.

The two men stopped their horses a respectful distance from the stone ledge beside the waterfall. They waited in silence for a while. Then the Dark Man pursed his lips and tapped his throat with his fingers and let out a loud whistling cry. They waited and listened to water gushing onto the rocks.

"Why don't we just leave the gifts here?" asked Turk.

"Wait," the Dark Man said.

He sucked in a great chestful of air and twisted his black-painted face and shut his white ringed eyes and produced a whistling scream, like a heron.

The scream echoed off the wall. Then silence. Turk's hand was sweating on the buckskin pouch.

They heard a rumble, low. Then silence again. The splashing of the waterfall grew loud. The two men waited. Their ponies stood nervously, as if expecting a noise.

After a while, the Dark Man said, "We must leave our tribute here on the ground and go away."

"He told you this?"

"Yes. In my head."

They left the buffalo on the travois and the other gifts. As they finished, a roar blasted forth from the wall behind the ledge. Turk's pony danced sideways. The Fighting Man held himself erect, as if unafraid, but he understood the communication: *tribute must be paid.*

# 24

The front page headline of the weekly *Sentinel* that was published every Friday, said:

DOC SWIFT TO DEPART,
CAPITAL CITY MOURNS

Horace Wapner, the newspaper's top writer and only poet, started his byline story with a verse:

This man who is from God sent forth,
Doth yet again to God return?—
Such ebb and flow must ever be,
Then wherefore should we mourn?

Reading an ink-smudged copy of the newspaper, which Wapner had rushed out of his office to give her, Cullasaja weaved through traffic of wagons and horses and construction gangs and made her way up Congress Avenue toward Bullock's Inn. She was limping on her right leg, but she no longer used a crutch or a stick. Around her rose the hubbub of the new city: wheels creaking, whips popping, men cursing, mules protesting. Bullock's herd of hogs snuffled and snorted and shoved through the crowds. The rich odor of manure rose from the road in the heat of May. There had been some cool, sunny days that reminded her of springtime in New York, but now it seemed summer was already here. She saw Mr. Newfield, the builder, bossing a crew that was framing a large new house on Bois d'Arc, a block west of Congress Avenue. She wondered what progress had been made on building Captain Caldwell's house. Thinking about the Ranger gave her a strange twinge in the chest and a lightness in her heart. She could feel the touch of his rough hands and picture his gray eyes. She was moved by the memory of how his mouth twisted when he tried to smile at her with his jaw cinched by chicken wire. She wondered what sort of woman would arrive from Germany to marry Captain Caldwell. Cullasaja wouldn't mind if the bride was fat and had a mustache and bad disposition and would be promptly shoved off on some desperate immigrant widower with a large family. Cullasaja felt in her bones that her connection with Captain Caldwell was far from broken.

Several men she passed called out greetings to her. She was wearing a calico gown that had been sewn for her in barter for nursing, and her black hair was rolled into a knot on top of her head. Her throat was long, patrician, her skin copper. "Like a queen of Egypt," Richard Bullock had said that morning. Everyone who called to her urged Doc to reconsider leaving town. They needed him here, and they would hate to see Cullasaja go, too.

She walked past the closed door of the room at Bullock's which had once housed Captain Caldwell and Ridgewood Bone. The unfortunate lawyer again had his room to himself, and he kept the door shut and locked. He had bought a Negro slave woman named Chloe, about thirty years old, and ordered her to bring food from Bullock's chef to his room and clean his room when required and do his laundry. He had paid five hundred gold dollars for her from the catalogue of a flesh merchant in New Orleans. Chloe slept in a tent in a wooded lot owned by Bone a block from Bullock's. She came to Ridgewood Bone every morning at dawn and helped him to the wooden crapper under the oak tree. She had been seen helping the lawyer walk a few blocks for exercise during the night.

Hobbled in the road outside Doc's room at Bullock's were two unsaddled Morgan horses, their necks set high on their sturdy shoulders, their long, braided tails swishing at flies. One was a dappled brown mare and the other a chestnut gelding with white patches on nose and lower legs. The chestnut reminded her of Donnybrook, Doc's Kentucky Thoroughbred that had been swept away in the flood. An angry black mule was tied by a hemp rope to a hitching pole. The Morgans were hobbled far enough away that the mule could not kick or bite them.

Doc's door and window stood open, searching for a breeze. Cullasaja walked in and saw her brother trying on a new black cotton jacket that reached his mid-thigh. He was attempting to see himself in a hand mirror.

"That's a beautiful coat, Rommy. Let me model it for you," she said, tossing the *Sentinel* onto his bed

Though she was half a foot shorter than her brother, and he was unusually wide in the shoulders, she put on his new jacket and posed in it. The jacket had style and was made of sturdy but lightweight material. She approved of it.

"Mrs. Barker sewed it for me. It's for the time we cut out her son's tonsils and diagnosed her husband as having malingering fever," Doc said.

"That old drunk was never sick," said Cullasaja, taking off the black jacket and draping it on her brother's shoulders. He did look good in it, rather dangerous, which she liked.

"I think Mrs. Barker figured out what malingering fever means and cured him with a poker," Doc said.

"Are those our horses outside?"

"I bought them from Gruber. Rather, I took them off the bill he insists he owes us. We've built up a fat account at Bullock's. Richard is trading us saddles and supplies for the chickens and cows and pigs we are due."

"So we're really ready to set out for Bowl's Town at last?"

"Cully, are you sure your leg is strong enough?"

"You're the doctor."

"But you know your own body."

"I'm strong, Rommy."

"All right. We'll leave at daylight for east Texas. One of the Wacos down on Shoal Creek told me we go near to the town of Jefferson on a fair road and then cut off for Caddo Lake and Bowl's Town. Several rivers to cross."

"And what then?" she said.

"What do you mean?"

"What will you do?"

"After you are settled in with Chief Bowl, I'll go to Pope the gunsmith in San Antonio—your Captain Caldwell recommended him—and have him put together a rifle for me, and poke around and find someone who will sell me a Colts revolver and a good spyglass, and I will trade that beautiful chestnut Morgan outside for one of those tough mustangs the Comanches ride. Then I will go into Comancheria."

"It's insane for you to go into that wilderness, chasing an imaginary creature."

Doc placed a finger to her lips.

"Let's don't talk about my trip here in town, even when we think we're alone. That pest Wapner listens at doors and windows. He was hiding in a tree outside a window at Gruber's office a couple of nights ago and overheard me telling the German we were ready to go. That's how that big story got into the *Sentinel* today. Now the town is giving us a farewell party at Dutch John's tonight. Mayor Waller asked me to be sure you know you are to be honored as well." He sighed. "I was hoping we could just say good-bye to Gruber and Bullock and slip away."

Cullasaja looked at the newspaper lying on the cotton pad that Doc spread over a platform of pine planks that he used as a bed. His room was spare and clean as a monk's cell, except for the area by the window, where an oil lamp stood on a table beside the rocking chair in which Doc sat to read at night from random books that passed into Austin and into his hands.

"Wapner is a pest, but he's a good poet," she said. "His verse does sound a little labored. But I suppose Wapner didn't have much time."

"Wordsworth wrote that verse," Doc said.

"Your friend?" asked Cullasaja.

"He read it to me in a pub in London three or four years ago, before it was published. I don't think it sounds labored. I think it is profound. I have an unexpected admiration for Wapner in having the good taste to find it and to steal it."

"Did you read the story Wapner wrote about you?"

"No. Is any of it true?"

"That's like asking if what Sir Walter Scott wrote is true."

Richard Bullock arrived in a wagon carrying two saddles and gear for the Morgans and saddle packs for the mule. The two men took the animals to the stable. Cullasaja decided to walk to Hickory Hill and swim in the creek. On top of the hill the President's mansion, an imposing structure set among trees, was already framed and partly sided, and carpenters were hammering on the roof. Debris had washed down Hickory Creek into the deep pool where Cullasaja loved to swim. Bottles and boards and hunks of mortar lay on the bank of the blue water, and a green shroud floated in the middle. Cullasaja realized she could swim there no more. In the months since she and her brother had come to Austin, Cullasaja had seen dramatic changes in the city. The stream that flowed directly down the heart of town had now been filled in with stones and dirt to become Congress Avenue.There had been about two hundred residents three months ago. Now the number was more than twelve hundred. Before buildings could be completed, land speculators, lawyers, surveyors, mercantile and hardware salesmen were moving in. Residents occupied their new homes while carpenters were still sawing logs for the walls. Tents and shacks had sprung up around the edges of the city as the tents in the center were replaced by buildings. Many tent dwellers were waiting for homes to be built, and the rest were waiting to see what experience life would bring them next. Tent towns moved west into the area that had been the province of the Indian Joes. Wacos, Tonks and Lipans lived off fish and game that came from Shoal Creek and the Colorado River, and off curious stones and handmade artifacts they traded to white people for food and clothing. The increasing closeness of natives to newcomers caused a lack of elbow room. Newcomers accused Indians of stealing their cook pots and chickens; they demanded Mayor Waller call upon the army for protection. The Indian Joes became sullen, and there were rumors of threats. As Cullasaja passed through the crowds on her way back to the hotel, she could feel scorn and resentment in the eyes of some of the newcomers, to whom any Indian was an enemy. Cullasaja was eager to leave Austin and go to Chief Bowl's town. She found herself hoping Captain Caldwell would visit her there on his white Arabian stallion. She would like for him to meet Chief Bowl and observe a society that operated in harmony.

An hour after sundown, Doc and Cullasaja walked down Pecan Street toward Dutch John's. A cooling breeze had brought the smell of rain. It had hardly rained a drop in Austin since the flood. From doorways and windows lit by candles and oil lamps, voices called out: hey, Doc, don't leave us, and thank you for curing my arthritis, and I'll pay you soon as you get back, or tell me where to send it.

The banner draped on the inside rear wall of Dutch John's said:

BON VOYAGE

All the original Austin residents who mattered, as well as many recent arrivals, had gathered inside Dutch John's to take part in the farewell. A musician from Mobile had struggled for six hundred miles with his crated piano to stagger into Austin, where he now played regularly at Dutch John's for tips. When Doc and Cullasaja reached the door, Mayor Waller gave a shout and the piano player began hammering "For he's a jolly good fellow" on the keys. The crowd sang and roared and howled. Doc and Cullasaja pushed through the room in the wake of Mayor Waller. Hands touched and clutched at them. Cullasaja felt several brushes against her buttocks and breasts. A platform had been built a foot off the ground at the end of the bar. Stepping up onto the platform, Doc and Cullasaja and Mayor Waller looked down at faces made rosy by alcohol.

"Give me your attention, please! Please! Damn it, we've got a ceremony to do here!" yelled Mayor Waller.

The noise in the room lowered to a hum and a clinking of glasses.

"Doc, this city owes you a debt of gratitude," Mayor Waller said.

The crowd cheered until the mayor raised his arms and shouted them into relative silence again. Waller leaned down to Dutch John, who handed him a gunny sack. The mayor opened the sack and reached inside.

"Doc, we are presenting you the eternal key to our city," Waller said. "Come back and see us as soon as you can."

From the sack Mayor Waller produced a polished buffalo horn, which he gave to Doc. Doc lifted the horn for all to see. The crowd resumed cheering. Waller joined them for a moment in shouting, and then he waved his arms for attention.

"And, Doc, we took up a collection to buy you a gift," the mayor said.

Dutch John handed up an object wrapped in tissue paper. Mayor Waller carefully peeled off the layers of paper to reveal a black wide-brimmed hat much like the one Doc had lost in the flood.

"It's genuine beaver, made in Memphis, Tennessee. Try it on," the mayor said.

Doc put on the hat. It fit well. He creased the brim a bit with his fingers and tilted the hat on his brow and smiled broadly. The crowd screamed in approval.

"Don't think we're forgetting you, girl. Without your nursing, about half the people in this room would be dead today," Mayor Waller said, turning to Cullasaja.

From his coat pocket the mayor extracted a necklace made of shiny bits of glass that supported a pendant of clear blue quartz. He draped the necklace around Cullasaja's throat, and the pendant fell between her breasts.

There was applause and a few yips.

"Speech! Speech!"

The crowd gazed with adoration at the broad-shouldered man whose blue eyes looked back at them from under the wide brim of a fine beaver hat. This physician had not only cured many of them, he had knocked out a Texas Ranger with his fists. What greater glory was there? When Doc opened his mouth, the crowd fell into silence so total that they could hear the wheezing rattle in the breath of the barber, who was dying of consumption and had left his bed for this occasion.

"Thank you for this hat and for this key to the city," Doc said. "My sister and I are fortunate that you took us in when we were stranded by the flood."

The crowd grinned and chuckled. They felt close enough to Doc that they could share his joke about this Indian girl being his sister. Doc studied the crowd. He realized Gruber was missing. Of everyone in the city, Doc was fondest of the brawny German.

As if conjured by Doc's imagining, Fritz Gruber appeared in the doorway. He wore a clean white cotton shirt that strained to cover his chest, and there was a new purple silk scarf wrapped around his skull and tied in a knot. On his right arm, her small hand nervously clinging to his melon-sized bicep, was Mrs. Ruth Hunboldt. Her dress was white silk with lace at the neck. On her head, on hair that had been washed and groomed by a servant, the first such experience of her life, she wore a tiara made of gold and precious stones, several of them diamonds.

"Hey, my friend Doc!" roared Fritz Gruber.

The crowd turned and gasped loudly at the couple.

"My friend Fritz!" said Doc.

A path was cleared for Gruber as he entered the room, Ruth close to his side and moving uncertainly in the long dress. She was frightened that she might fall and ruin everything.

"I want you to do me the honor, Doc. I want you to marry me and Ruthie," Gruber said.

"A wedding is more in my line, or Judge Loftin's," said Mayor Waller.

"Fork you," Gruber said. "Will you do it, Doc?"

"The honor is mine, Fritz," said Doc.

"Cullasaja, would you be my maid of honor?" Ruth asked.

"Thank you," said Cullasaja.

"But this man is a doctor, not a preacher," Mayor Waller said.

"This man is who I believe in," Gruber said. "You and the judge can sign the certificate for the law, but Doc performing the wedding is what will make it a true thing."

Romulus had performed weddings as a ship's officer. He knew a simple, nondenominational way to go about it.

Doc asked Fritz Gruber and Ruth Hunboldt for declarations of their love for each other, in the sight of God, and for their promise to continue to love and care for each other. He told them her gold wedding ring was a circle of eternal love. He pronounced them man and wife. Ruth squealed with delight and kissed her husband. Fritz was eager for the honeymoon to begin. He hugged Doc, and he hugged and kissed Cullasaja with a gentleness that amazed her. "Yah, you keep your hair on your head and forget what's across the river, my friend," the German said to Doc. "But anything you need from me, it is yours."

When finally they could escape from their farewell party, which was now combined with a wedding party and would go on all night, Doc and Cullasaja hurried along Pecan Street in the shadows. Fritz and Ruthie Gruber had left the saloon hours earlier. Doc and Cullasaja were laughing softly and talking about events of the night. "Ruthie looked so beautiful. I never saw a happier bride," Cullasaja said.

They saw two figures waiting ahead in the shadow of a pecan tree. Doc's instincts made him concentrate on the moment. He was wary, ready for trouble.

Doc took Cullasaja's elbow as they walked closer and then relaxed when they saw that the waiting figures were lawyer Ridgewood Bone and his slave girl, Chloe. They were out for their evening exercise. The lawyer had stopped to rest. It still hurt to move his arms and legs, and headaches struck like thunder in his skull, and then there was his ultimate humiliation, which was shared with Chloe now.

"Good evening, lawyer Bone," said Doc.

Lawyer Bone replied, "Damn your souls for letting me live."

"I've never seen anyone fight for life as hard as you have," said Cullasaja.

"I don't have secrets from you, do I, nursey girl? Well, I'll tell the two of you something. I am going to get well and healthy. No booze ever again. I'm going to be the meanest son of a bitch of a lawyer in this Republic. See what you have caused? Why didn't you fools let me die? I can never go back to Princeton looking like this. Austin is going to pay for what has been done to me."

# 25

Fronds of banana trees rustled shadows across the patio at the Fincus Hotel, where Hannah sat at a table with Dora and Lawrence Kerr, drinking a mid-morning glass of iced tea, a rare treat. The ice had arrived an hour ago from Galveston in barrels packed with salt. The hotel manager, Mr. Maurice, sent each of the three favored guests one dagger-sized shard of ice, which protruded from a glass of tea topped by a leaf of mint.

"Thank God for this ice and this tiny breeze," Lawrence said. He wiped his face with his neckerchief. His months in Texas had transformed his appearance from that of a Wall Street beau ideal into what Lawrence hoped was that of a man of the frontier. A sombrero protected his face from further sunburn. He wore a cotton tunic and trousers and had cowhide sandals on his feet. Dora smiled. She thought her husband looked comical. Dora's own wardrobe had changed, but stylishly. She had hired a seamstress to sew new dresses of cotton and linen that retained the puffed shoulders and low bodices that she preferred. Her velvets and woolens and furs were packed in trunks, protected from weather and bugs.

Hannah rubbed her knife blade of ice against her forehead. After the bitter winters of Hannover, when snow piled up to the eaves and they shivered around a coal stove, she would never have believed she could yearn for the cold pleasure of ice. Her body was clean from bathing daily in the river, but she could smell sweat in the wool of her dress; there was nothing she could do about it, because all her dresses now smelled of sweat. She was swimming in sweat inside her dress and knew she must smell like a wet sheep.

"Poor dear Hannah, you must let me send my seamstress to you," said Dora.

"Thank you, no. I will start sewing for myself, when I can find any material," Hannah said.

"Then at least let me give you cotton and linen fabric. I have tons. Please, dear, it would make me happy."

"Do her the honor, Hannah. Please," said Lawrence. "It would make us both happy."

Lawrence was entranced by Hannah's large dark moist eyes and her sensual lips and perfect skin—a classic Jewish beauty, he told himself. Lawrence felt his wife looking at him, so he averted his eyes to gaze at a red and green parrot that was chained to a perch. "Funny little bird. Yesterday it said, 'Sin' something. Some Mexican phrase." Dora was amused that he was trying to make her think he did not feel a twitch in his groin when he looked at Hannah. Lawrence had become more interesting in conversation and ardent in bed since they had left New York, but he had not lost his compulsion to fall in love with every pretty girl he met. During their marriage of eight years she had four times caught him in trysts with actresses, and she was sure there had been others if she had cared to snoop further, but these were sufficient to excuse Dora for any dalliances of her own. Two months before they left for Texas, Lawrence had a silly and dangerous affair with the wife of a business partner that almost forced a duel. Lawrence paid $50,000 to soothe affronted dignities in that instance and decided he should go in person to act upon his plan to establish a cattle ranch in Texas. Dora surprised him by coming along. He had expected her to remain behind in their three-story brick mansion on Fifth Avenue and spend the summer at their farm on Long Island. But he hadn't reckoned on her powerful curiosity and imagination—the traits that had made her a star in the theater. She had read wild tales about the Texas revolution and its heroes, and she wanted to see the place for herself. When she grew tired of

Texas, she would return to New York with stories that would dominate any dinner table. And—who knows?—there might be a theatrical piece based on her experience of the frontier. Texas was much on the tongues at New York social gatherings. If Texas became a play, or a musical, who else could star in it but Dora?

"Hannah, dear, you know how I do love to be up on the news of the continent," Dora said. "You have remarked that your people at home are persecuted. Exactly what do you mean?"

Hannah sipped her tea and chewed the mint leaf. "You must understand," she said, "that Hannover is very crowded. The rich live in castles. The poor live several to a room in wretched conditions. Those are the two main classes in Hannover—the few very rich and the many very poor. Somewhere in the middle are people like my father, a university professor, a distinguished man. He believes in a democracy in which every citizen should have the vote, including women. For this he is arrested and threatened. He may be executed for his belief. There was an uprising of students and democrats that he is held much to blame for."

"Women voting? I'm afraid that notion is too bizarre to be popular in any country," said Lawrence.

"There is an idea gaining favor in the king's court that to clean out the poor and the criminals and get rid of the liberals and intellectuals of Hannover, the government should load them onto ships and sail them off to Texas," Hannah said.

"Texas? Why Texas?" said Dora.

"There is a popular book in Germany that says Texas is the garden spot of the world, and there is plenty of cheap land for working-class Germans in Texas. There's no room for the workers and their families in Hannover. No jobs. No homes."

"So you are talking about political and economic persecution? Not religious?" Dora said.

"Being a Jew is a disadvantage, unless you are a very rich Jew, which my father is not," said Hannah. "But the Catholics and Protestants are always at war with each other in different ways, and we endure."

"Why must we talk about poor people?" asked Lawrence.

"We are talking about politics and economics on the European continent," Dora said.

"Then let's talk about castles and banks and stately homes," said Lawrence. "That's where the money comes from to support your precious theater. Poor people don't buy tickets to *Tartuffe*."

"My precious theater? You no longer have an interest in the theater, or in actresses?" Dora said.

"Now, darling, you are the most beautiful woman I have ever seen, and I love you madly, and I am insane with passion about the theater—though among actresses my eyes are only for you—but we are on the frontier of the Republic of Texas now, not in some theatrical drawing room. Let's not spoil a lovely morning by talking about poor people. When in Texas, let's do as the Texans do. Let's talk of the future. Let's make grand plans."

"Have you made a grand plan?" Hannah smiled, rubbing the nub of ice on the back of her neck.

"Indeed, I have," Lawrence said. He waved at the Mexican woman who looked after the customers in the patio. She wore a white blouse and a full skirt. "*Tres mas* of these iced teas, *con* yellow, *por favor*, sweetie. And tell Mr. Maurice *muy muchachas gracias* from the *tres* of us."

"Settle on one language, dear," said Dora.

Lawrence adjusted his sombrero to cut off the morning light, as the sun had moved while they sat. The German girl lifted her glass to finish her drink, and he admired the smooth tightness of her throat; Dora had been blessed with such a throat when he first saw her on the stage.

"We will be neighbors," Lawrence said. "The Kerr Land and Cattle Company is just a short ride—well, a day or two, out here that's short—from Captain Caldwell's estate."

"Which will soon be half yours, dear," said Dora. "Texas has a law that says the wife owns half of the property, and should the marriage fail, for some queer reason or other, the wife is entitled to keep her half."

"I didn't know that. Who told you that?" Lawrence said.

"Mary Maverick."

"Not that it will ever be an issue with us, Dora, darling, but such a law is grossly unfair to the poor husband. He works to build up wealth, and then if divorced he must split it with a hag of a wife? I don't think that will ever be law in the United States."

"Hag of a wife? Have you been sneaking drinks of tequila?"

"Certainly not."

"You did! You've bribed the barman to put tequila in your iced tea."

"Only a wife would make an accusation like that," Lawrence said, looking at Hannah.

"Well, I am catching up with you," said Dora. She shouted at the woman, "*Señorita, mucha tequila en mi copa, por favor*. How do I sound in *español*, Hannah?"

"She understood you."

"How about a touch of the cactus for you, Hannah? Tequila is only a plant, like your German beer is only wheat and hops," Lawrence said.

"No, thank you. At this time of day I drink tea and coffee and water," said Hannah.

"That's not much to face the frontier with," Lawrence said.

The wrought iron gate swung open, and Mr. Maurice hurried onto the patio in his splay-footed gait. The hotel manager was tall and bald and wore spectacles and a small mustache dyed black. A pink scarf tucked around his throat concealed the wrinkles in his neck. He had been manager of the Hotel Madeleine in Paris before his friend the baron got far into debt at the gaming houses, whose operators were unimpressed by his title once his money was gone, and threatened the baron's life. The silliest, maddest thing Mr. Maurice had ever done for love was to accompany the baron to Texas. The baron met an ugly death through dehydration from cholera in Houston City. The baron's mind remained clear until his final hour. He kissed Mr. Maurice on the lips and thanked him for his devotion and swore to love him beyond the grave. So the whole experience was worth it for Mr. Maurice. The baron's family in France refused to accept his body. The funeral at a cemetery near Buffalo Bayou took the last of Mr. Maurice's money. He was reduced to washing dishes at the Palace Hotel in Houston City. There he encountered Theodore Fincus, a favorite guest from the Hotel Madeleine. Fincus was in Texas to invest money for his London real estate firm. Fincus wanted to open a hotel in San Antonio because he was moved by reading the story of the Alamo. He offered the job as manager to Mr. Maurice. And now here came Mr. Maurice through the iron gate onto the Fincus patio, breathing rapidly, his hands fluttering toward his cheeks.

In his excitement Mr. Maurice spoke in French to Hannah. "Captain Caldwell is coming, Miss Dahlman. What a figure of a man he is! I must go be sure his room is ready."

"What's that?" Lawrence asked.

Mr. Maurice dodged around the woman serving a tray of three iced teas—with one last shard of ice for each—and rushed into the hotel.

Hannah felt her heart thumping against wet wool. "He says Captain Caldwell is coming."

Lawrence grabbed his tea glass off the tray, pulled out the shard and drank half of the tea and tequila mixture before he shoved the ice back in. "Well, let's go out and greet him," he said.

Dora sipped her drink and smiled at Hannah. The poor girl looks as though she has fallen on her head, Dora thought. Dumbstruck. Dizzy. Dora knew the anticipation of uniting with a long-sought lover—a divine aspect of life—but that was not what Hannah was facing; her emotion that Dora could most deeply understand was the fear of being judged not good enough, a continual test for an actress.

"Don't be afraid, Hannah, dear. If you don't like this Caldwell fellow, I will take him for myself, and you can have Lawrence."

"You have embarrassed the poor girl," said Lawrence.

"No. I am quite well," Hannah said. So he is actually here, she thought. So the rest of my life begins. She pushed back her chair and stood up. "Please, you will be sure to point out to me which one is Captain Caldwell?"

"Darling, you will know the moment you set eyes upon him," Dora said.

Lawrence held open the gate—which had been installed to keep chickens out of the patio—for the two women. He made sure to shut the gate after he was through it. Mr. Maurice had thrown such a fit the last time Lawrence left the gate open, because chickens shat on the tile floor of the lobby. Lawrence was eager to see this meeting—the big, shaggy Texas Ranger and the young German beauty who looked so Mediterranean. Lawrence loved the life here on the frontier. One never knew what to expect.

The three of them walked around to the front of the hotel on Soledad Street. Groups of people were gathering on either side of the street to watch what was happening. They called to others to come and look. Hannah walked faster, finding an opening in the crowd. She stepped out into the street and looked.

Coming toward her was unmistakably Captain Caldwell. It could have been no one else. The erect way he sat the white Arabian stallion, the dappled beard, the wide-brimmed planter's hat, pistols hanging from his hairy body and the big shotgun slung on the saddle.

She was so intent upon Captain Caldwell that it was a moment before she realized he had a rope wrapped around his saddle horn. The rope was slack, dragging in the dust, but it led at the other end to a loop around the neck of a wildly staring and gesticulating one-armed man who was riding bareback on a donkey and appeared to be insane.

# 26

**M**atthew Caldwell swung down from his white horse and took off his hat. He slapped red road dust off his shirt with his left hand. Leading the horse, the Ranger walked a half dozen paces toward the young woman who stood in front of the Fincus Hotel, looking at him with large eyes bright from curiosity. He saw Dora and Lawrence Kerr edging up behind her. All around him rose a gabble of voices in Spanish, commenting noisily on the arrival of the Ranger and the madman with the rope around his neck. Matthew smelled goat meat smoking over hot coals in an open barbecue pit.

"Hello. I'm Matthew Caldwell," he said, shifting his hat into his left hand and offering his right hand to the young woman.

Hannah put her hand in his, feeling the rough texture of his fingers. She wasn't sure if he intended to kiss her hand or shake it.

"You must be Miss Dahlman," he said.

"I am."

Matthew shook her hand gently, cautious not to crush her fingers.

"I thought you'd be taller," he said.

He was not displeased by her looks. Her black hair gleamed, her skin was pure, her teeth white, her body appeared to be well formed beneath its woolen wrapper. But he remembered the sentence in her letter in which she said she could carry a candelabra the length of a dining hall without dipping a flame. Matthew couldn't conceive of this girl in front of him having the strength for such a thing. He had expected a tall, broad-shouldered girl. This Hannah was not what he would call little, but she was on the small side.

"Would you wait right here, please?" Matthew asked. "I've got to take care of a matter."

Hannah was shaken, though she smiled and nodded. The marriage agent had said Captain Caldwell was like a Cossack. The agent had described to her the dappled beard. But still she was unprepared for the presence of the real person—big, hairy, gray-eyed, spectacular-looking, reeking of leather and sour sweat. She knew he was old, forty-three, but she hadn't pictured him as this old. To her he looked older than her father, who was forty-five. Her father was dramatic in looks, too, in a more civilized way, with his hawkish profile and dark beard and the slender hands and fingers of a pianist, but this Ranger was the kind of man you would wait and look back at after he had passed on the street.

"Yes, of course," she said, but he had already turned and his moccasin boots made fluffs of dust as he walked toward the madman with a rope around his neck who sat on a mule, his left sleeve hanging empty, his eyes rolling from sky to faces to earth, strings of cotton froth dangling from his lips.

"Hey, Batista," Matthew said to a dusky old man, a descendant of the Canary Islanders. Batista lived on the east side of the San Antonio River in a Canary Islander settlement overlooking the ruined, deserted Alamo and its smashed plaza. Batista's face and shoulders were covered in shadow of a straw sombrero. Most of his toenails were missing on his bare feet. Speaking in border Mexican, the Ranger said, "I've got a job for somebody. It's a paying proposition."

"How much?" asked Batista.

"One gold dollar a day."

"For what?"

"I want somebody to feed and shelter this lunatic until I decide what to do with him," Matthew said.

Everybody looked at Rublo, who glared back at them and sputtered and wagged his head from side to side, quarreling with creatures unseen by others.

"He's harmless," Matthew said. "He's just lost his mind. Probably run into some Comanches. Tie him under a lean-to shed out of the sun and give him water and throw him some food every day. If he tries to break loose and terrorize our citizens, you have my authority to shoot him dead."

"I think I know this crazy man," said Batista.

"No, you don't know him," Matthew said.

"Two dollars a day," said Batista.

"Keep him out of sight. I don't want crowds gathering around him."

"My wife won't like it," Batista said.

"One gold dollar a day is a fair price."

"Because I admire you, Captain, I will take him," said Batista. "For one week."

"Or maybe longer," Matthew said.

"That's what I meant to say—or maybe longer."

The Ranger unwrapped the rope from his saddle horn and flipped the end of it to Batista. The Canary Islander tugged on the rope, and dragged the mad-man's head about a foot before a strangling cry made him realize the mule wasn't following. Batista spoke to the mule. "You damn fool, if you come with me I'll give you water and corn. If you want to stand out here thirsty in the sun, I'll take that madman off your back and leave you for the vendors to make tamales out of your scrawny ass." The mule farted and started walking.

Several children followed as Batista led the mule and the madman away toward the Commerce Street bridge that crossed to the Alamo and the Canary Islander settlement. The children began to chant: *loco, loco, loco* . . .

Matthew turned and saw the German girl still waiting in front of the hotel with the Kerrs on either side. Dora was three or four inches taller than Miss Dahlman. Red curls hung out from beneath Dora's straw sun hat. She was fair-complexioned, lightly freckled on the arms, wary of the sun. Miss Dahlman, on the other hand, was bare-headed. It occurred to Matthew that he should buy her a bonnet. The girl was from north Germany. She would have to learn the power of the sun in Texas.

"Welcome back, Captain," Lawrence Kerr said.

"I'm delighted to see you again. But I knew you would turn up very soon after this lovely girl arrived for you," said Dora.

Matthew smiled at them. He felt his lips screwing sideways, and a spear-head of pain struck his jaw. By the look on their faces, he could tell his ex-pression had startled them. They couldn't know his jaw was held together by chicken wire.

Hannah had spoken only five words so far. Despite her education and her eloquence in philosophical and literary discussions in the salons around the university in Hannover, she could not think of even two more words in English at this moment.

"Is that man on the mule your prisoner?" Lawrence asked, made bold by the tequila iced tea.

"Not exactly," said Matthew.

"What's wrong with him?" Dora asked.

"He's scared and confused. It appears the Comanches may have taken hold of him and tortured him out of his senses," said Matthew.

"Good heavens," said Dora.

"We're going to have to kill every one of those aborigine bastards," Lawrence said, draining the last of his tea and chewing on the mint.

Matthew looked at Hannah. The German girl's eyes had never left his face. He could feel the heat of her gaze, and it made him uncomfortable. This girl was soon to be his wife. He wasn't sure if he attracted her or repulsed her.

Why was she staring? If a man dared to stare at Matthew in this fascinated but critical way, there would be violence, or at least a challenge. You don't stare a wild dog in the eye unless you are ready to fight, Matthew thought, but maybe it was different with a German woman.

"I need to take care of my horse and then wash up a little," Matthew said to Hannah. He also needed a swig of laudanum and a siesta. He and the madman had ridden all night, and Matthew's jaw and teeth were hurting savagely. He noticed the girl's eyes shifting to his nose. He wondered how his red and swollen nose must look to her, if she found his scar hideous. Might she be thinking of spurning him? Hannah could not stop herself from staring at his face. What would he say to her? Could he reject her for not being as tall as he had hoped?

"Miss Dahlman, would you have supper with me in the Fincus Hotel dining room at sunset?" Matthew asked.

"Yes, of course," repeated Hannah. She felt dull. Her words refused to flow. She found herself thinking in German instead of English, reverting in the strangeness of this new country.

"But first we'll have our afternoon bath as usual, Hannah. It's my favorite part of the day," Dora said. "And Mr. Maurice has seen to it that Mr. Long-fellow's peeper hole is sewn up."

"Henry Longfellow?" said Matthew.

"Yes, a friend of the President. We call him the Peeper," Dora said.

"Dora, you shouldn't say things like that," Lawrence said, realizing the tequila in the tea had hit his wife, too.

"Why not?" asked Dora. "We have caught him peeping at us through slits he cuts in the canvas while we are bathing."

"Do you know where Longfellow is right now?" Matthew said.

"He left San Antonio days ago and went back, I think, to Houston City," Lawrence said. "Henry didn't do any harm, Captain. It wasn't like he assaulted or raped anyone. He was only curious to get an eyeful of these beautiful women. Is that a crime?"

"I'll speak to Longfellow about it," Matthew said. "Miss Dahlman, I almost forgot the hotel has a clock in the lobby. Let's sit down at the table at six P.M., if that fits into your plans."

"Yes, of course," she said for the third time.

# 27

A fter he stabled Pacer, Matthew went to Rupert's Barber Shop & Tub Bath in an adobe brick building across Main Plaza from the San Fernando Cathedral. Rupert was a good man for cleaning teeth. The Ranger had taken two swigs of laudanum, but since he could not open his mouth wide enough for a thorough cleaning, he told Rupert to scrub only the front ones. Then Rupert trimmed and brushed Matthew's beard and hair and washed his face and neck with a rough cloth. Matthew next went into the bathing room, where an old Mexican woman had filled a tub with hot water. The old woman waited solemnly as Matthew stripped off his clothes. He looked at the purple bruise that still remained on his ribs, a memory of Dr. Swift. The image and spirit of Cullasaja crossed his mind. He was fond of Cullasaja and admired her. He hoped Miss Dahlman would have Cullasaja's qualities. Matthew climbed into the tub. The hot water helped the laudanum to soothe the pain that screamed through his nerves. The old woman hung his clothes on a peg. The water in the tub was turning dark. The old woman grinned, showing her bare gums. She poured a bucket of warm water over his head and washed his hair and beard. She used a long-handled brush to scrub his chest and back. While she was washing his feet, Matthew leaned his neck against the rim of the tub and shut his eyes. The old woman went to Rupert and asked if she should wake him up. "Do not ever disturb him," Rupert said. Rupert removed the OCCUPADO sign off the door of the tub room and replaced it with a sign that said CERRADO.

After their bath in the river, Dora took Hannah to the cedar wardrobe closet which held Dora's linen and cotton dresses. They selected a white linen dress with the low bodice that Dora favored. The seamstress came in and tucked up the waist and raised the hem. Hannah looked at herself in the full-length mirror Dora had brought to Texas. "You're gorgeous, darling. It's the perfect dress for you," Dora said. Hannah told herself not to look in the mirror again, but to trust Dora's praise, overblown though it might be. Hannah's heart was pounding with apprehension.

Though they protested, Mr. Maurice ejected a rock salt salesman, a land speculator and a lawyer from the ground-floor corner room that they shared at the Fincus Hotel. This was Captain Caldwell's favorite room, and Mr. Maurice had to give it to him. The room overlooked cypress trees and flowing water. Mr. Maurice had Captain Caldwell's other jacket and his extra trousers and shirts hung in a cedar closet that was carried into the room by Mr. Maurice's young assistant and protégé, Arias, an immigrant from Spain. The bed linen was changed for the captain. Matthew awoke with a start, still in Rupert's tub. He rushed to the hotel and was relieved to see by the clock that he had thirty minutes before meeting the German girl—his new wife. He dressed in a blue cotton shirt and his cleanest doeskin jacket. Matthew put on a pair of soft suede trousers to go with the blue cotton shirt that had been pressed with a hot iron by Arias. Matthew decided to wear the beaded moccasins he had bought from a vendor in Military Plaza. A jab of pain in his jaw made him think about another nip of laudanum, but he tucked the bottle into his bag. He wanted to be clear-minded.

Matthew entered the dining room at 6:25 P.M. Mr. Maurice guided him to a table that faced west. During the heat of the afternoon, an awning was always pulled down to keep the sun out of the western windows, but now the awning was raised and they could see the slashes of red and yellow and purple on the horizon. Dust in the air blended the colors into a big-sky sunset.

"With my compliments, Captain," Mr. Maurice said. He snapped his fingers, and a waiter hurried over carrying a bucket in which a bottle of champagne sat in cool water with two precious shards of ice. The waiter started to uncork the champagne, but Mr. Maurice rebuked him. "Wait for the lady," he hissed in Spanish.

Five of the ten tables in the dining room were filled already, and more customers kept appearing. Sam and Mary Maverick came in with Lawrence and Dora Kerr. They nodded greetings to Matthew. It became clear to him as other familiar faces entered the dining room that many of these people had come to supper to watch the Ranger with his bride-to-be.

The clock in the lobby chimed, and Hannah Dahlman stepped through the doorway.

Matthew felt his heart move—a curious, breathless, missing of a beat—when he saw her. A pain in his jaw let him know his mouth had dropped open. This young beauty in her white dress, cut low at the breast, her black hair curling on her shoulders, her dark eyes shining: this did not look like the sweaty girl who had met him in front of the hotel. He felt the strange flip again in his heart and in his stomach. He knew what it was, but he could hardly believe it.

This was how he had felt when he first saw Nancy in her father's hardware store in St. Louis, and how he had felt every time he saw her in a ball gown, a feeling that had deepened through the years as the children entered their lives and Nancy slept and worked beside him. Matthew remembered the feeling of falling in love, and of being in love, but he had thought there was no longer a place in his life for romantic love. How could this be happening? He had contracted for a partner and a helper, not a lover and companion. With the realization that he was falling in love with her came the reality that she was twenty-three years younger. His oldest child would have been close to her age. No, love had to be kept out of this. He was meeting this young woman to see if she could become his mate, not his romantic fancy.

Matthew stood up as Hannah was escorted across the room by Mr. Maurice, a happy sentimentalist, judging by the way he was beaming. All eyes followed her, and when she reached the table, every diner and waiter was staring at the two of them, and there was a hush as if a curtain were about to go up in a theater.

"You look lovely, Miss Dahlman," Matthew said.

"Thank you, Captain Caldwell. You look splendid yourself," she replied.

Matthew had bent forward a bit to speak more closely to her, but now he straightened up and looked around the dining room, his eyes taking in each face for a cold instant.

"Haven't you people got something better to do than spy on us?" Matthew said to the room.

"Captain Caldwell, this is the most exciting thing in town," said Dora Kerr from the table where she and Lawrence were drinking French wine with the Mavericks.

"Come on, Miss Dahlman," Matthew said. He grabbed up the champagne bucket with his left hand and put his right hand on her elbow. "Thank you, Mr. Maurice, for your kindness, but me and Miss Dahlman are going for a walk."

They walked across the tiles of the lobby and out the front door and across the patio and out the wrought iron gate into the plaza, where there were benches under a cluster of oak trees in the center. They stopped a moment and looked at the sunset, which had spread across the entire horizon and rose like mountain peaks of purple.

"God's beauty," Hannah said.

"You want supper?"

"I'm not hungry," she said.

"Good. Let's walk by the river and talk."

Matthew plucked the champagne bottle out of the bucket. He pulled a bone-handled knife out of his belt and started to saw at the cork.

"Please. Let me," Hannah said.

Swiftly she unwrapped the wire and placed both thumbs under the cork, and with a sharp pop the cork flew away and champagne bubbled down the neck onto her hands.

Across the plaza two men dived headfirst into the dirt at the sound of the cork popping.

"Take a swallow," Matthew said.

She drank from the bottle, and he watched her throat moving. She passed the bottle to him.

"I know I need to say something, but I don't know what it is," Matthew said.

"Take a swallow like I did, and you'll think of what to say while we're walking," said Hannah.

Matthew tilted his head back and downed two large gulps of the champagne. He caught a belch in his throat in deference to her.

"Let's go, then," he said.

"Wait," Hannah said. She reached into the champagne bucket and pulled out the two wilting shards of blessed ice. She rubbed one on her forehead, and, seeing how fast they were melting, she dropped the other shard of ice down the bosom of her dress. She felt the ice water rolling down her stomach.

"I take it you're not fond of Texas springtime," Matthew said. "You should have been here in San Antonio last January."

"I heard there were snow drifts three feet high. The temperture near zero. It's hard to believe."

"Anything you hear about Texas is true," said Matthew.

They walked along the path beside the river going south toward the Commerce Street bridge. Big cypress trees made the slowly moving water dark as the moon popped into the eastern sky like a frozen white ball. The air was clear, and they could see the face of the man in the moon. A whippoorwill began calling from the trees and was soon answered with songs from many birds. A fish jumped and splashed in the river. They heard frogs croaking.

"You have strong hands," Matthew said.

"I have a large family. There was always work to do."

"You busted that cork right out of there," he said, passing her the bottle again.

"Drinking wine and beer is a tradition in my family." She poured a little champagne on her tongue and tasted it, and then she passed the bottle back to

Matthew. "I like to drink, but I'm not very good at it and don't do it often. But this is rather a special occasion."

A canoe glided down the river, its lone paddler dragging a fishing line.

"Is your family in danger in Germany?"

"Yes. The king could have them jailed or even executed if he decides my father is truly a threat."

Matthew paused beneath the overhanging limbs of a pecan tree, with the leaves making a lattice of the moon. He looked at this young woman, who looked straight back at him. She was not one to look away from what might be an uncomfortable situation, he decided.

"Why did you leave them?" he asked.

"Leaving them is the only way I can help them."

"You don't strike me as somebody who would run away."

"I am not running away," she said.

"What do you call it, then?"

Hannah took a step back from the big Ranger and looked up at his swollen nose, his gray eyes. She decided not to be insulted. If she was going to marry this man, he had a right to know her full intentions. She hadn't intended to tell him so soon, but she hadn't expected the direct questions that came natural to him as a Ranger.

"When I make a success of my life in Texas, I will send for my father and mother and two brothers and a sister and bring them here. My father is struggling to bring democracy to Hannover. Many of our people are emigrating to escape tyranny, but he stays. My father can't win against the king. If I stay with my family, there is nothing I can do to make a difference."

"You are willing to marry me so you can bring your family to Texas?"

"Don't worry, they won't live with us. Not even in the same town, if you wish. They might refuse my help, anyway, and stay in Hannover and be shot or jailed. They are full of false pride."

"Why do you say false pride?" Matthew asked.

"Because they're proud of being irrational. I believe in democracy as strongly as my father does, but there are better ways to achieve it than to die trying."

"Have you heard of the Alamo?"

"Yes. It was a heroic battle. Everybody in Europe knows of the Alamo."

"Your father would have liked it there," Matthew said. "It was irrational."

They walked on toward the bridge. Someone on the bridge held a lantern on the end of a stick so that the light wavered in the water.

"Do I disappoint you?" she asked.

"I like your honesty," he said. "I want to know I can trust you."

"You are willing to marry me?"

"Miss Dahlman, we have a legal arrangement," he said.

"Are you going to call me Mrs. Caldwell after we are married?"

He smiled with twisted lips.

"Hannah," he said.

"Matthew," she said.

"All I ask is that you be faithful and smart and work hard so we can bring your family to Texas. But if you ever do feel like you are falling in love with me, I would like to hear about it."

"I will try to love you, Matthew. I will be a good wife," said Hannah.

"Where do you want to do the wedding ceremony?" Matthew asked.

"Is there somewhere you prefer?"

"I thought maybe you being a Jew, we would need to find a temple," he said.

"Matthew, I believe in God and in the Hebrew Bible, but I do not follow the rituals and ceremonies. I would prefer to be married by a rabbi, but I am willing to marry wherever you wish."

"I signed up as a Catholic when I came to Texas. I feel comfortable in the San Fernando Cathedral."

"Will your priest marry you to a Jew in the cathedral?" Hannah asked.

"It never occurred to me that he wouldn't."

"We had better consult with him," said Hannah.

"If he says no, I'll get a different priest."

Matthew felt the impulse to hug her. Suddenly he wrapped his arms around the girl and felt her hair against his chin. She seemed almost weightless, like a bird, and she smelled of soap and a touch of perfume that reminded him of how Dora had smelled the night he met her at the punch table. Hannah's face was mashed against his chest, and she had a sense of his physical power. His arms seemed big as logs to her. She understood that he might squeeze her to death if he continued, though he was just showing affection. His chest smelled of witch hazel and champagne, and there was wet hair against her mouth. With a surge of surprise and fear she wondered if he was going to force himself on her. She wondered how his mouth would taste.

But he released her.

"I hope I didn't hurt you," he said.

"I'm fine. Just let me catch my breath."

"I have forgot how to hug a woman."

Hannah adjusted the shoulders of her borrowed dress.

"Shall we walk on toward the bridge?" she said. "We have so much to talk about. I want to hear your dreams for the future."

"I ain't dreaming, Hannah. You and me and our children are going to have an estate in the hill country. You have my word on it."

# 28

The coffeepot sprang off the embers with a clang as it was struck by a bullet fired from the darkness.

Cullasaja rolled away from the cooking hole and crawled behind a fallen tree trunk. Doc Swift, who was pulling on his boots, ducked into the sheltered arbor where the two Morgan horses and the mule were hobbled. Another blast tore leaves off the pine above Doc's head. It was false dawn, an hour before daylight in the Piney Forest a few miles east of the town of Jefferson in northeast Texas near the Louisiana border. The heavy stands of pine and hardwoods and the abundance of flowing water were similar to old Cherokee lands in North Carolina, although this part of Texas was without mountains or the brisk weather that usually comes with a loftier altitude. Shawnees, Kickapoos, Osage and other tribes—they were being squeezed ever closer together by the whites swarming from the east—roamed this forest, and some of them were thieves and murderers, but Doc sensed this attack was not by Indians, who would have crept in to steal the horses first, and then quietly murdered the brother and sister.

Doc waited and listened. A screech owl cried. Doc listened for movement. Then the third shot struck the mule in the throat. The animal screamed and kicked free of its hobbles, blood spurting from its neck.

Doc lay flat on the brown pine–needled floor of the forest near the Morgans. He gestured to the shadow of Cullasaja to remain motionless. He hadn't located the flashes, but he could smell gunpowder. The horses snorted and shied away from the wheezing mule. The mule dropped forward onto its front knees, genuflecting, muzzle lapping into a puddle of blood. Doc held the single-shot rifle he had borrowed from Gruber. He carefully capped a ball and cocked the hammer, listening for indications of their enemy in the approaching dawn.

A loud pop sounded from across the clearing where they had made camp. Doc saw the flare of exploding powder and heard a thunk as a bullet dug into the log that shielded Cullasaja. There was a tearing noise in the brush near the flash, as if something was being jerked free from a vine. They heard an angry curse. Doc decided there was only one weapon being fired at them. He left the horses and the dying mule and circled swiftly around their camp, dodging between the pines in the darkness. The thrashing noise continued as Doc crept closer to it, and then he heard a man cursing, "Sonofabitch, you come loose of there . . ."

The man was so intent on his problem—his muzzleloading Kentucky long rifle, which was as tall as its owner, was hung in the underbrush—that he did not hear Doc. To load the Kentucky rifle it was necessary to pour powder from a horn, place a greased patch over the muzzle, nestle a ball on the patch and then ram the ball down the barrel, careful to place the ball correctly relative to the charge. Getting off one shot in a minute from a Kentucky rifle could be done only by an expert with freedom of movement. Yet this man had shot at Cullasaja and Doc and their animals four times in no more than five minutes, tangled in the brush much of the while.

"Let go of that rifle," Doc said.

The man squinted into the shadows.

"Who the hell are you?" the man said.

"I'm the fellow whose mule you just killed. Let go of that rifle, or you'll be the next dead beast in this vicinity."

The man took his hands off the rifle, which remained suspended in the brush for a moment and then crashed to the earth. The man stood about ear high to Doc. He wore a shirt and trousers made of homespun hemp cloth that had been torn and stitched many times. The white tail of his skunk fur hat hung down his neck; the black and white hair made Doc remember Caldwell for an instant. The man had red whiskers with two dark tobacco stains spreading from the lower lip. Doc guessed that he was about thirty-five years old, all of it, judging from his scars and crooked fingers, lived in the teeth of nature.

"Hell, you're a white man," the man said. "If I'd known they was a white man there, I never would of shot. I just thought it was a couple of savages."

He spat with digust.

"What are you doing with a damn squaw?" the man said.

Smashing this man's face flickered across Doc's mind.

"Who are you, mister?" Doc asked.

"My name is William Wadsworth Watson. This here is my land. I come to Texas last month from Kentucky and laid claim to this piece of land from where I'm standing all the way to where the bog starts in the east, plus I got a few acres on the bayou. My wife and eleven kids and six cousins and my brother and his eight youngsters—all boys, my brother has always been the lucky one—are about another week or two behind me with our wagons. So I figure that makes you a trespasser."

From his time in Austin with Gruber and among the builders, Doc knew enough about Texas land law, and the confusion of it, that he asked, "Where did you lay claim?"

"Right here."

"What government office?"

"Look, I got a piece of paper that gives me the right to pick two sections of one thousand, two hundred eighty acres of Texas land anyplace I damn please, as long as nobody already owns it, and savages don't count. Savages don't own land. I bought my sections with cash money from a banker in Lexington, Kentucky."

"You've been cheated."

"What would a squaw man know about it?"

Again Doc fought the urge to strike William Wadsworth Watson. Doc gestured with his rifle aimed at the Kentucky man's chest.

"Step into the clearing," Doc said.

Cullasaja was kneeling beside the dying mule, stroking the animal's neck. She looked around at Watson. "You dirty white trash," she said.

"Sorry about killing that mule. A good mule is worth a lot," Watson said. "I got a real fine mule myself."

"What are you going to do with him?" Cullasaja asked her brother, remembering the fate of the lanky man who had attacked her outside Austin.

"I should shoot him," said Doc.

"Hey! I never hurt you!" Watson said.

"Let Chief Bowl decide. This is Cherokee land," said Cullasaja.

"The hell is it!" Watson said.

"Watson, start packing our dead mule's burden on your mule," Doc said. "You're going for a walk."

They approached a forest where cypress trees grew among the pines and hardwoods and ball moss hung off the limbs above lily pads where fish feeding on insects left spreading circles in the morning mist.

Thirty years ago an earthquake in the Missouri Territory had shaken the earth so hard that the Mississippi River reversed its current and flooded its tributaries. The earthquake knocked down so many trees that there had been a logjam one hundred and seventy miles long in the Red River ever since. The river backed up and formed and deepened swamps and marshes and bayous and lakes. Doc and Cullasaja were arriving at Bowl's Town at last.

"You think I'm ignorant, but I know it's a hanging crime to abduct a man and steal his mule," said William Wadsworth Watson. He walked beside his mule, frowning and spitting, the skunk tail swinging on the back of his neck. Doc and Cullasaja were mounted on their Morgans.

"You're a prisoner," Doc said. "You are facing justice."

"What would you know about justice?"

"In the Bible it says if you kill my mule, I keep yours," Doc said.

"The hell it does. I'm a river-baptized Baptist, and I know the Bible don't say nothing like that."

"Am I supposed to overlook that you tried to kill my sister and me?"

"Sister? Haw! I never saw no blue-eyed Indian. I tell you what the law says. The law says if you steal a man's mule, you hang."

A red-shouldered hawk watched from the top of a loblolly. A blue heron spread its wings and flew above a field that had been cleared and planted in corn. They saw a scarecrow beyond a rail fence. A log house with a shingle roof stood near a plank barn and another rail fence that marked a field of beans. A small boy ran out of the door of the cabin and turned toward the center of town to spread the news of the visitors. Doc and Cullasaja began to see more houses and gardens, and the path became a dirt road that led toward a seven-sided meeting house. Now there were Cherokees stepping out of doorways, men dressed in pantaloons and slippers and carrying pipes that had hatchet blades curving down from the smoking bowls.

Cullasaja recognized a relative from North Carolina. "Mother Wren," she cried, jumping down from the Morgan. She hugged a small, stoop-shouldered woman who wore a red cotton dress and silver earrings.

"Cullasaja, what bring you here, girl?" asked Mother Wren.

"I want to live in Bowl's Town," Cullasaja said.

"Who is this man?"

Doc climbed down from the saddle and took off his hat. "I am Romulus Swift, Mother Wren."

"Little Romulus!"

William Wadsworth Watson said, "This man is stealing my mule."

"Oh, Cullasaja, Romulus, you have come at a difficult time," said Mother

Wren. "Long Turkey and Big Mush and John Negro Legs are here from their towns to debate an important matter with Chief Bowl."

"You sound frightened," Cullasaja said.

"Well, I don't want war with the Osage."

Chief Bowl, also known as Duwali, was eighty-two years of age but as erect as a young man. He came out of the lodge wearing a silk turban and silk shirt opened to reveal the medal from Sam Houston on his hairless chest. He wore silk pantaloons that ended at the knee, and there were slippers on his feet. Chief Bowl smiled, baring the false teeth he had bought from a dentist in Little Rock.

"My children," Chief Bowl said.

He embraced Cullasaja first, then Romulus.

"Time goes by so fast," he said. "How is Grandmother Tobacco? How is Knows All Charlie?"

"They are well and send their love and prayer for peace to you," said Cullasaja.

In turn the other chiefs came out of the lodge. Long Turkey, also known as Kunetand, was tall with a sharp chin, a pipe of tobacco clenched in his teeth. Big Mush, also known as Gatunwali, was heavy in the chest and wore a pistol in a holster. John Negro Legs, also known as Nekolakeh, wore a full-length silk robe with only his sandals showing below, and he looked impatient and annoyed during Chief Bowl's introduction of the new arrivals.

"But who is this white man?" John Negro Legs said, pointing at Watson.

"We are using his mule because he killed mine," Doc said.

"I have been abducted," said Watson, "and my mule was stolen."

"Oh, Romulus, the Master of Breath is testing me today," Chief Bowl said.

"If this white man killed Romulus's mule, then Romulus owns the man's mule. It is a clear rule in the code of vengeance," said John Negro Legs. "Just as it is clear that we must kill an Osage because the Osage have killed Velasco Chiltoskie of the Bird clan."

"Our cousin Velasco?" Cullasaja said. "The Osage have killed him?"

"I say we must go kill an Osage," said John Negro Legs. "It is the code of the Cherokee Nation."

"They do not observe the code so firmly in the Eastern Nation anymore," Chief Bowl said. "I think with all our political problems, we must not be rigid in enforcing the code if it will lead us into a war. The Western Nation is abandoning the code in many difficult instances. Texas Cherokees must do the same, for the sake of peace."

"Texas Cherokees, that's us," Big Mush said. "We are the council. It is our decision."

"I say we must set out at once to kill an Osage," said John Negro Legs.

"But Velasco is not even dead yet," Chief Bowl said.

"Where is he?" asked Doc.

"In my house in my other bed," Chief Bowl said.

Chief Bowl's house was sixty feet long, built of cypress logs with a pine plank floor. The house was divided into four rooms—the chief's bedroom, a room with a desk and books, a living room and another bedroom reserved for visitors. Doc and Cullasaja opened the door to the spare bedroom and flinched at the smell. On a cornhusk mattress lay their distant cousin, Velasco Chiltoskie, who was a year older than Cullasaja. His naked body was smeared with blood, and he writhed on the mattress, out of his mind with pain. His upper right chest was torn open by a stinking wound that looked to have been gouged out, perhaps by a broad spear aiming for the heart. The flesh was green and purple with infection, and pus bubbled all through the wound.

"Moist gangrene," Doc said.

"Is there anything we can do?" asked Cullasaja.

Doc turned to Chief Bowl, who had followed them to the door but stopped outside because of the smell.

"Chief Bowl, I need to use the fastest horse in town," Doc said.

"That would be the palomino that belongs to Hog In Pen."

"Would you take me to him?" asked Doc.

Cullasaja watched the two men hurry away. Chief Bowl walked as fast as Romulus, who was less than half his age. She had no idea what her brother was doing, but she trusted him. She opened the shuttered window and left the door open. She poured water from a clay jug on the washing stand into a towel. Cullasaja sat on the edge of the bed and wiped Velasco's face with the wet towel. The wound was hideous. Velasco began weeping.

"Velasco, Velasco, I am here, it's Cullasaja," she said.

He opened his eyes and looked at her. Ten years ago, at the age of nine, Cullasaja had been insanely in love with Velasco. She'd known him for just that one summer in the North Carolina mountains before returning to New York. Velasco and his family moved into the Western Cherokee Nation in Arkansas. She had hardly dared speak to Velasco that summer; he'd seemed so much older and wiser than she, so handsome.

Now his face was stretched with pain. Both Austin pharmacies had run out of laudanum during the town's booming growth, and they had brought nothing in her brother's medical satchel that would ease Velasco's agony. She knew Chief Bowl was a user of herbs, but the old man considered the mental effects of using the poppy as somehow evil. Cullasaja sat on the bed and waved gnats and mosquitoes away from the yawning, putrid wound, and continually bathed Velasco's face and talked to him. "I am Cullasaja, you remember. Cullasaja from the mountains." He opened his eyes and looked at her now and again, but his efforts at speech became gurgling groans.

For more than an hour, Cullasaja sat with Velasco and wiped his forehead and his mouth and held his hand in a room filled with such a foul odor that no one else would approach. When Velasco's head fell back and his body went limp, Cullasaja touched the arteries in his throat to discover he was still alive. He was unconscious, but she felt that he could hear her, that he sensed that she was bathing his face and keeping insects away from his raw, open chest.

She heard a horse galloping to the door, and she looked up to see her brother rushing inside with a clay jar in his hands.

"Rommy!" she said. "Did you find poppy juice? Is it herbs? What do you have?"

Pulling out a wad of cloth which he had used to close the jar, Doc Swift said, "I went back to our dead mule."

Doc reached into the jar and pulled out a handful of what looked like cotton puffs, except they were wiggling. He placed the white puffs deep in the wound, and then he took out another handful of puffs and placed them in the wound along its discolored edges. The puffs began squirming madly, hungrily, chewing the infected flesh.

Cullasaja saw that her brother had spread Velasco's wound with maggots.

# 29

Through the rest of the day and the following night, dozens of legless white grubs born from eggs laid by green blowflies chewed the dead and rotting tissue from Velasco Chiltoskie's wound. Gradually the odor in the room became more that of ammonia from the secreting larvae than the stink of decaying flesh.

Cullasaja spread her pallet on the floor and kept watch over her cousin Velasco. After placing the maggots in the wound, Doc Swift had retired to the

sweat lodge to join Chief Bowl, Big Mush, Long Turkey and John Negro Legs
for an afternoon of purification and meditation. Doc knew he had shocked the
chiefs by putting the maggots in the wound. The Cherokees, whose society
revolved around religion, relied on herbs, prayer, sweat baths and physical
manipulations to cure illness. A medicinal use for maggots was not in their
common knowledge. The healers of Bowl's Town had examined Velasco and
consigned him to the Master of Breath. But the chiefs knew Romulus had been
around the world, and they were willing to see if he had learned something of
value. Romulus had heard discussions at Edinburgh University among surgeons
who had served in the Napoleonic wars, some of whom had observed that
gangrene and battlefield wounds often appeared to be cured by the repulsive
parasites—wounds that, in truth, a battlefield surgeon could only have made
worse. Doc had never tried this remedy, but the instant he saw Velasco, he'd
remembered the Edinburgh discussions and realized this might be the only
option. He also knew where there was a newly dead mule buzzing with blowflies.

Long Turkey threw more water on the hot stones, and the room gushed
with steam. There was no conversation, only grunting and breathing. The afternoon sweat was a time for relaxing and becoming attuned with the Master
of Breath. Big Mush was slumped on a bench with his elbows on his knees,
snoring. John Negro Legs swatted himself with a willow switch to make his
flesh burn. He was eager to resume the debate about the code of vengeance
and then to enforce the code on a particular Osage he believed to be guilty of
spearing Velasco. But for now there was nothing to debate, because Velasco
was still alive. The old code of vengeance called for a death for a death, but
not necessarily a wound for a wound. John Negro Legs scratched his back and
chest with a switch and told himself that Velasco's fate would also decide his
vote on what to do with the white fool and his mule.

Young Romulus had asked to let the man go, which John Negro Legs took
to be a deplorable sign of the weakness of the younger generations. But John
Negro Legs had demanded that William Wadsworth Watson be locked up and
guarded and his mule put into the corral until the issue of what to do with him
could be settled. John Negro Legs remembered the remarkable thing the white
man had said to Romulus. As the white man was being shoved into a house
by a silk-clad Cherokee warrior with a shotgun, William Wadsworth Watson,
his red beard wagging as his mouth flapped in surprise, pointed at Romulus
and shouted, "Sonofabitch, you really are a blue-eyed Indian! Now I've saw
ever' kind of freak in the woods!"

Romulus closed his eyes and inhaled the steam into his lungs. He felt sweat popping out on his brow and his shoulders. His thoughts were racing, sorting themselves out, as he began to concentrate on his breathing. He saw himself at a dinner table with a white cloth and fine crystal and china in his club in London with Lord Pluck. How long ago that now seemed. Only a few months? Was that possible? Between Doc's club and the steam house in Bowl's Town was further than time could measure.

Instead of the meditation which Romulus sought, in his mind a picture began to form.

He saw the man-ape that had first appeared to him in a dream thirty years ago and again on the deck of the ship in the storm, and he felt his nostrils fill with a sour odor.

After the sweat, Romulus walked to Chief Bowl's house, where Cullasaja sat on a chair outside the open bedroom door.

"Is it working?" Doc asked.

"I believe it is, but I can't stand to look at it anymore right now," she said.

Doc left her outside the door and went to Velasco's side. Velasco was unconscious. He had been bathed. A piece of linen lay across his chest and shoulder. Doc lifted the linen and looked down at the wriggling, feeding grubs. The flesh had become pinker, healthier-looking. Doc raised Velasco's eyelids and felt his pulse. Doc lowered the linen cloth back onto the swarming maggots and stepped outside.

"It seems like there's more and more of the hideous things," Cullasaja said.

"A few more eggs got born, I suppose."

"How will we know when the maggots have had enough?" she asked.

Doc said, "I suppose when they come to living tissue, they quit eating. That's when they turn into blowflies and go looking for something else dead or dying they can lay their eggs in."

"What do you truly think, Rommy? Will Velasco live?"

"Pray to the Master of Breath."

"I do."

"I'll come back every hour or so," Romulus said. He kissed his sister's forehead. She put her arms around him and they embraced.

"I love you, brother," she said.

"I love you," Romulus said.

Inside the lodge a meal was being served as Romulus entered. The four chiefs sat at an oak table. They had left an empty chair at the right arm of Chief Bowl in honor of Romulus, their visitor. Two women swept around the room, swishing in their cotton dresses dyed in bright yellow and blue. They were putting platters and bowls of potatoes, venison, fish and greens on the table, along with pears and peaches and jugs of water. Long Turkey filled his tin cup from a bottle of alcoholic spirits blended with grape juice that he had purchased from a traveling whiskey wagon near Jefferson. Chief Bowl did not approve of drinking alcoholic spirits, but Long Turkey was the chief of his own town and an honored delegate.

"The white fool we locked up says he owns hundreds of acres of land west of the bog," Long Turkey was saying.

"His claim is false," said Romulus.

"He says he has a piece of legal paper," Long Turkey said.

"His paper is a fraud. This is Cherokee land," said John Negro Legs.

"It is not so simple," Chief Bowl said.

"In Austin the land developers say Sam Houston gave you this land because you are the father of his late wife," said Romulus.

Chief Bowl carved a curl of peel off a potato and put it on his tongue.

"Sam Houston is one of us as much as a white man can be," Chief Bowl said. "He ran away from his white home as a boy and grew up with us on the Hiwassee River in Tennessee. Chief John Jolly adopted him. We adopted many white runaways in those days. They preferred us to their own people. After Sam Houston quit as governor of white Tennessee, he came to us again and joined our Western Cherokee Nation in Arkansas. We hired him to be our lawyer. He married Talihina Gentry, also called Diana. She was the daughter of John Rogers, who is the brother of John Jolly. But she grew up with me in my family, and Jolly and Rogers and I are closer than brothers, and so Diana was my daughter as much as she was anyone's. Sam Houston treated me like his father-in-law, with great respect. From the time he was a boy, Sam Houston was always restless and on the move. We gave him a name—the Rover— because he would never stay in one place. Eight years ago he left us in Arkansas to go across the border into Mexico to buy land as the agent of white people in New York. Then he took command of men who called themselves rebels against Mexico. He promised us Cherokees the legal ownership of this land provided we didn't interfere while he was fighting the Mexicans. If our people had joined the Mexican side, there would be no Texas, but we stayed out of the fight because our brother Sam Houston wanted us to. He whipped the Mexicans. Now Texas is a free republic, there is nothing simple or easy to understand about any of it."

"But you do own this land," Romulus said.

"This is our land," said Long Turkey.

Chief Bowl tucked the turban up a bit above his right ear, as if it had been making him hard of hearing. In his earlobe hung a silver loop.

"Do you have a deed to this land?" Romulus said.

"Romulus, we have learned to understand and accept the concept of owning land with a piece of paper to prove it in the white man's court," Chief Bowl said. "But we have no paper to prove we own any of our towns in Texas."

"Sam Houston is a famous figure in New York and London. He is known as a man of his word," said Romulus.

"The Texas Congress refused to grant us the land Sam Houston had promised, and now he is no longer in power. If we can hold out until the day Sam Houston is reelected, I believe we could have a peaceful and prosperous future here," Chief Bowl said.

"How can we be at peace when there are so many newcomers like the white fool we just locked up?" said Big Mush.

"Let us stop our arguments and think well of Velasco and pray to the Master of Breath," said Chief Bowl.

"Yes, think of Velasco with your whole mind," Long Turkey said.

"I think of avenging him," said John Negro Legs.

After the meal, Romulus walked along the dirt road between candlelit windows to Bowl's house, where Cullasaja was sitting outside in a chair, looking up at the stars. Inside the room Doc turned up the brightness of the bear oil lamp and saw in the yellow glow that the white grubs appeared to be subsiding, eating less. Doc felt Velasco's pulse. Weak but steady. He went outside and sat on the earth beside his sister's chair and leaned his back against the wall of the house.

"You know the constellations, don't you?" she said.

"I learned the stars as a sailor."

"I learned them from Knows All Charlie, and he can't see."

"That's Orion over there," Romulus said.

"Everyone knows Orion."

"Cully, I don't know what to do," he said.

She looked around and caught his profile in her brown eyes. He was staring at the heavens. She imagined Romulus looking the way their father, Fletcher, would have looked at the same age—curly hair, broad-chested, thoughtful.

"What do you mean?" she said.

"I don't want to leave you here. It is very dangerous. But I must go on my journey into Comancheria now, I feel the time is here. If you can manage with

Chief Bowl for two months, I will come back for you and take you to New York."

"Who do you think you're talking to?" she said angrily.

"My little sister."

"After a flood and a broken leg and everything else that's happened, at last I arrive at my destination, and you say you will be back in two months to yank me up and carry me off to my white home in New York? I am where I want to be, Romulus. You go where you must."

Romulus slapped at a sharp bite on his forearm and then at another one on his cheek. A warm gust from the bayou had blown in the smell of fish along with mosquitoes. Cullasaja leaped up from her chair.

"I must go hang a mosquito net over Velasco," she said.

An hour after daylight, Chief Bowl and Chief Big Mush gathered with Chief John Negro Legs and a red-eyed Chief Long Turkey outside the door of Bowl's extra bedroom while Romulus went inside.

Velasco was conscious, and his chest and shoulder wound was wadded with linen. Cullasaja stood beside the bed. Doc glanced at the dazed expression on Velasco's face and then at the covered wound.

"Where are the maggots?" he said.

"Like you said, they got tired of eating. I scooped them them out of the wound and threw them out the window, so they can turn into flies and start their circle again."

Doc lifted the cloth and saw that Cullasaja had covered the wound with a green poultice that smelled like mud and mint.

"Little Jo Bowl made the poultice," Cullasaja said. "I'm not sure what is in it, but she is a wise person and a healer, and I used it."

Doc snapped his fingers in front of Velasco's eyes.

"Velasco, Velasco, can you hear me?" Doc asked.

"Where am I?" said Velasco.

The smell of cactus in the salve told Doc that Velasco might be hallucinating.

Doc bade the four chiefs to file into the room and gaze upon Velasco, whose eyes were wide and stunned but obviously projected life.

"All right," John Negro Legs said. "Velasco lives. We do not kill the Osage who gave him this terrible wound. If that is how you want it to be, Duwali. I will vote with you."

"I vote with Duwali," said Long Turkey.

Big Mush nodded. He had voted with Duwali all along.

The four chiefs and Romulus left Bowl's house and went to the seven-sided council lodge, where William Wadsworth Watson was waiting in a chair. The Cherokee guard in the silk shirt had remained near Watson with a shotgun pointed at him.

"The decision is yours, Romulus. What do you say?" asked Chief Bowl.

"Let him take his mule and go," Romulus said.

"We should beat him first with sticks and belts," said John Negro Legs.

"No, I request that you let him go unharmed," Romulus said. "With his mule."

William Wadsworth Watson did not understand what they were saying in Cherokee, but he did deduce by Doc's gestures that he was being set free. He sprang up from his chair and crammed his skunk fur cap onto his red hair and started toward the door. He could see his mule in the corral.

"Naw, you're a half-breed sonofabitch. Not no real blue-eyed Indian. You're a damn common mongrel," he said as he passed Romulus.

Braying with laughter, William Wadsworth Watson saddled his mule. John Negro Legs was saddling his own pinto, saying he must return to his town. Watson rode his mule at a trot down the dirt road. He waved his hat at Doc Swift, and his beard glowed red in the sun.

"I'll be back to see you when my family gets here, you can count on it, you savage sonofabitches," Watson yelled.

At the corral gate, Romulus stepped aside so that John Negro Legs, his silk robe pulled up like a woman's dress, could pass on his pinto. "Good health to you, my son, Romulus," said John Negro Legs. Romulus replied, "And good health to you, father John Negro Legs." The pinto began galloping almost at the first steps from the corral. Watson was still in sight.

Romulus saddled the chestnut Morgan. Cullasaja and Bowl's carrying wife, Isobel, loaded his saddlebags with food. Romulus embraced Isobel and Little Jo Bowl, the cooking and healing wife, and he hugged the dignified old chief, who had dressed in his splendid purple velvet pantaloons for this occasion. Then Romulus turned to his sister. She was smiling at him, but her cheeks were wet.

"I'll be back to see you. I promise," he said.

Doc unwrapped a handkerchief and took out a revolver.

"It's loaded," he said, giving her the gun.

"But you said you needed a pistol. I don't need one."

"Cully, you must remember that I'm the doctor," he said.

"Oh, Rommy, please be safe," she said, and hugged him and kissed him on each cheek and his lips. Then she wrapped the cloth around the pistol and turned back toward Bowl's house.

As Doc was leaving Bowl's Town, William Wadsworth Watson was riding his mule at a walk a mile to the south and west, picking a path through a berry thicket, slapping honey flies with his hat. "Sonabitches, Kentucky ain't for shit, but this damn Texas is pure suffering hell full of bugs and snakes and savage red niggers," Watson was saying to the mule and to the earth at large.

Watson became aware of a black and white shape among the trees, and when Watson's mule cleared the berry thicket, there sat John Negro Legs on his pinto with a darkly gleaming bois d'arc bow, its sinew drawn tight and fitted to an Osage arrow. William Wadsworth Watson's mouth made a circle in his red beard. He said, "No."

"We are avenged," John Negro Legs said.

He released the sinew and shot the barbed arrow with Osage markings all the way through Watson's torso.

# 30

Matthew Caldwell and Lawrence Kerr were eating fried eggs, bacon, pinto beans, tortillas and salsa on the Fincus Hotel patio an hour after sunrise the morning after the Ranger arrived in San Antonio.

"I must warn you, Captain, I am a keen negotiator. There is no use you trying to drive the price higher," Lawrence said, sipping hot black Mexican coffee.

"I wasn't planning to sell that old cotton farm," said Matthew. "What do you want with it?"

"I want to establish the Kerr Cattle Company presence in Texas. Until we wrest our land from the Comanches, your six hundred acres is a place to plant our company flag. But I won't pay more than eight thousand in gold dollars, deposited at the Charles Street Bank in New Orleans."

"Lawrence, the farm ain't worth that much," Matthew said.

"Please, Captain. I am the businessman. Let's not haggle."

"Well, then, I guess you've bought yourself a farm," said Matthew.

"Done," said Lawrence. He raised a forefinger toward the waiter. "*Señor, dos mas* of these coffees, *por favor*."

Just before sunrise Matthew had ridden across the river to La Villita. Batista's house was at the top of the hill. The house was dome-shaped, built of mud bricks, wood and animal hides, looking as if it had been patched together rather than constructed. Batista was milking his goats in the shed beside the house when Matthew rode up on the white stallion. Squatting in the straw with his chin on his chest but his eyes open was Rublo. The rope around his neck was tied to a pole that supported the roof of the shed. His empty left sleeve lay across his knee.

"He been any trouble to you?" Matthew asked.

"He scares my wife. Then she scares me."

"I'll take him off your hands soon as I get back from Austin," Matthew said.

"Last time you went to Austin you were gone for months."

"This will be only a few days. I'm showing my fiancée our new house."

"She is a beautiful girl. I congratulate you."

Matthew nodded. The madman had raised his head and was staring at the white horse.

"I do think I have known this man in the past," Batista said.

"Don't think about it. Just keep a watch on him. Remember, if he tries to run away, you shoot him."

After breakfast the Austin expedition gathered in front of the hotel. They had a wagon pulled by four mules and driven by Rafe Cornwell, the teamster. Matthew was mounted on the white Arabian. Lawrence Kerr rode a creaking, new, expensive Mexican saddle on the back of a big palomino. Two Kentucky-bred horses to be used when desired by Hannah Dahlman and Dora Kerr were hitched to the rear of the wagon. Hannah had never ridden a horse—it was a skill Matthew looked forward to teaching her—and Dora, an accomplished rider, chose to begin the journey by keeping Hannah company in the wagon, where they sat on cushions amid supplies of food and water, bedrolls and tenting equipment. The eighty-mile trip in the wagon would require two or three nights spent on the trail. Hannah and Dora both were surprised to learn there were no inns between San Antonio and Austin, and very few farmhouses, where overnight guests sometimes slept six to a room in constant fear of a raid by Comanches. Matthew respected the threat the Comanches represented. He suspected Lawrence might not be useful in a fight, but he knew Rafe Cornwell was a brawler and a killer.

Supper the first night out was cold chicken, cheese, bread and warm white wine. Three bedrolls were spread near the wagon. Matthew put his roll down near the horses, and Rafe tossed his blanket near the mules. If Comanches or bandits did come in the night, the livestock would be the first target.

Hannah and Dora prepared beds for themselves in the wagon. The air at dusk hummed with flies and mosquitoes. Hannah and Dora wore bonnets with veils of fine netting covering their faces. When Hannah had wondered to Dora if the netting was necessary, Dora replied, "Darling, I know you want the captain to be able to gaze upon you, but remember you may have many men in your life, while this is the only face God will give you."

Matthew set Hannah bareback upon one of the Kentucky horses, a mare called Blue. He had searched the corrals of three dealers between San Antonio and Boca Chica Crossing before selecting the horse to buy for Hannah. "Does she feel comfortable to you?" Matthew asked, looking up at Hannah, trying to make out her expression through the netting.

"I think she likes me."

"Now, just press her lightly with your ankles and knees to let her know you like her, too, and you want to be friends. We'll walk a circle around the camp. It is important that you feel relaxed and confident, because Blue can sense it. So we'll go slow until you know each other."

Lawrence sat with his back against a wagon wheel and a bottle of wine in his hand. He was watching Hannah moving on the back of the mare while the Ranger held the bridle and they began a slow circle.

"She has a nice sense of rhythm," Dora said.

"Does she? Oh yes, I hadn't noticed," said Lawrence.

The second evening out of San Antonio, a crisp breeze came from the north and blew away the bugs. Hannah rode bareheaded in great slow circles around the camp while the Ranger held the bridle with his fingers and spoke softly to Hannah and to Blue.

"There's an exact right spot for you to sit in the saddle," Matthew said. "This is not a chair. You want the balls of your feet in the stirrups, and your ankles and knees pressing against Blue's sides, so she feels you are moving together with her. Use your thighs to guide but not to hold on. Riding is balance, not muscle power. If you clamp your thighs for long, you'll be very tired and sore."

Matthew released the bridle. Hannah held the split reins in her left hand, as he had taught her.

"Keep your back straight but soft," said Matthew. "You want to feel Blue's hoofbeats, you want to go with Blue's motion and feel it in the small of your back."

Matthew halted the horse.

"Calm down, Blue," he said. "I'm going to adjust the stirrups a little."

"Shall I get down?" said Hannah.

"No, I need to see your legs against Blue to get the angle. You want your upper legs and your lower legs bent at the same angles, so you don't jam down on the stirrups and wear Blue out before she's given you all she's got."

Hannah felt Matthew's hand around her ankle. He moved her lower leg up a bit and held it there, clutching her ankle, while he shortened the stirrups by an inch or two.

"Now," Matthew said. He stepped back. "With your knees and ankles, let Blue know you're going to pick up the pace a little."

Hannah clicked her mouth as she had learned from Matthew, and nudged the horse with her knees, and she was thrilled to feel Blue go into a fast walk, with Hannah secure and in command. She'd had no idea that horseback riding was so much pleasure.

"This might actually be love," Dora said.

"Well, I suppose it damned well better be," said Lawrence. "After all, she's alone in the wilderness now except for him—and us, to be sure."

Lawrence resisted the urge to rub the burning, exhausted muscles in the backs of his thighs.

Googleye was on the north bank of the Colorado when he saw them coming. In his hazy and distorted vision, what stood out was the black and white spotted beard on the man on the big white horse. Captain Caldwell! Googleye called to his crew to put the *Waterloo Queen* into action. He had hired two strong teenage boys, immigrants from Louisiana, to row and pole his ferry.

"This is rather a lovely location," Lawrence said from his saddle as they looked across the river at the buildings and the sections of stockade fence in the morning sunlight and waited for the *Waterloo Queen*.

"It's so primitive," Dora said. "Even compared to San Antonio."

"Austin is only a few months old. San Antonio has been there for two hundred years," said Lawrence. "I would say this new town shows great promise for a man of enterprise."

Looking across the river at Austin, Hannah felt a thump of realization that she was going deeper into the unpredictible. She saw a field of blue wildflowers, and white clouds above the hills, and the rising structures in the town where she would live and sleep with her new husband.

"Your land is quite close to the city, I recall," Lawrence said.

"See those white cliffs west of the river?"

"So close?" said Lawrence.

Matthew looked at Hannah. "That land is ours."

Austin had grown at a frantic pace in a few weeks. Congress Avenue was now a firm, packed road without a hint of flowing water. The Ranger guided the wagon through the crowds. Even newcomers who didn't know the Ranger gaped at him and then at the two beautiful women and the Mexican-looking fellow riding the palomino. Lawrence wanted his horse to canter, but there was not enough space for a gait, and Lawrence thought about the jarring on his spine. He had grimly hidden the soreness of his muscles from the long ride, the saddle burn inside his thighs. Only Dora could tell, he thought.

Captain Caldwell rode up to the front door, and immediately Richard Bullock evicted customers from three rooms at Bullock's Inn. Matthew and Rafe Cornwell stabled the animals at Boone's Livery. Caldwell tended to the grooming and feeding of Pacer and Blue himself. He didn't trust his own mounts to the care of stable hands.

Caldwell was disappointed to hear that Dr. Swift and his sister had left for the Cherokee village. Matthew wanted to see them again. He wanted them to meet Hannah. While Lawrence and Dora took their siesta—one San Antonio custom they had come to depend on, especially after drinking alcohol in the mornings—Hannah walked with Matthew to the office of Fritz Gruber.

"I think I ought to warn you, Hannah. There's something odd-looking about this fellow we're going to see."

Hannah smiled. Everything she saw around her was the oddest-looking thing she had ever seen. She felt like she was at a circus. She saw some brown men with long black hair wearing only strips of cloth between their legs; they were peddling soft leather moccasins as two of their wives squatted and fed babies at their breasts. Busy white men rushed past them carrying rolled-up architectural plans. She noticed everyone gave Captain Caldwell and her plenty of room to walk. She saw a herd of pigs snorting and honking and clearing a path through the throngs. She saw men who looked European in suits and trousers as they scrambled between blond-haired immigrants in rags with pitchforks and long rifles. The racket of hammering and shouting and of dogs barking was continual.

They turned off at the PARADISE FOR SALE sign, but Gruber was already coming out the door to greet them. Hannah looked for what was supposed to be odd about him. Other than that he was huge and wore a purple scarf on his head, Mr. Gruber didn't looked peculiar to her. He looked German.

Matthew made the introduction. Gruber stiffened his legs, bowed and kissed Hannah's offered hand. The top of his scarf flipped open a bit, and looking down at his bald skull she saw a pink and silver ridge.

"I want to show Hannah our house," Matthew said.

"Yah, Newfield is about done with it. Allow me to escort you."

The afternoon sun was hot when they arrived at the corner of Ash Street and West Avenue. Set amid the three huge oak trees was a framed structure, only partly sided and roofed. The honeysuckle vines had been torn away. The structure was built as two rooms with a dog run between, and there was a separate small house with a brick chimney. The main house seemed tiny to Hannah. It was not even as large as the parlor of her family home in Hanover. Two little boxy rooms—and what was that opening between them?

"She is pretty damn good, yah?" said Gruber.

"What do you think, Hannah?" Matthew asked.

"Is this all there is?" she said.

This was not how she had pictured an empire builder would live. She tried to swallow her disappointment, but she could see she had hurt Matthew's feelings; either that, or he had developed another toothache.

"So far, this is all there is," he said.

"Could I make some changes in the way the house is built?" she asked.

"Mr. Newfield ain't got time for changes," Gruber said.

"You can have changes if you want, Hannah. Where do you start?" asked Matthew.

"The house is facing west. I can already see that it looks straight into a very harsh afternoon sun. Is this wise?"

"Well, it has a view across Shoal Creek and three miles to the Colorado River and the cliff where our land starts," Matthew said.

"Couldn't we face the house south, and build a porch that wraps around to the west side where we can sit and look at our cliff at times when the sun is not in our eyes?" said Hannah.

"Mr. Newfield is busy," Gruber said.

"I will speak to Mr. Newfield," Matthew said.

"Yah. That's the way to get your changes made. Newfield is a tough man, but he's scared to death of you."

"Thank you, Matthew," Hannah said.

"If you're not happy, it ain't likely I will be," he said.

Lawrence and Dora had wakened from siesta and had gone to visit their mansion being constructed on Bois d'Arc Street a block west of Congress

Avenue. Dora turned her wrath on Mr. Newfield because of flaws in the design and building. She used such vehemence that Lawrence feared Mr. Newfield might strike her and provoke Lawrence to shoot the man. They were relieved to see Captain Caldwell and Hannah arrive with Gruber, the big German real estate impresario. Violence was forestalled. In a calm voice, still strained by the bits of chicken wire remaining in his jaw and the two missing upper left jaw teeth, Captain Caldwell persuaded Mr. Newfield to sit down and be quiet and listen to the two women, and at the end to promise them he would do as they said.

Hannah could not help feeling envy that Dora was building a grand house while Hannah was trying to rearrange the plan of an unwieldy cottage. But Hannah believed her husband would provide an estate soon if she worked hard and helped. She watched Dora drawing on Newfield's plans, moving rooms, making new ones, crossing out a couple. The builder sat biting his lower lip and seeming to listen. Developers and businesses were pouring into Austin to be early on the scene of the new capital city, and Newfield was forced to spend precious time on these women.

As they walked back toward Bullock's Inn, Dora asked, "What is there to do here at night for entertainment?"

"Get drunk and play cards at Dutch John's," said Gruber.

"I mean, is there a theater?"

"We have a Masonic lodge hall."

"No place to hear music?"

"The piano player at Dutch John's is good," said Gruber.

"What do you do for amusement at night, Herr Gruber?" asked Hannah.

"I eat a steak and go home to Ruthie. She only eats vegetables. Yah, we find plenty to amuse ourselves."

A man wearing a beaver hat and riding a skinny burro came past them waving a piece of flesh with hair on it. Blood had splashed on his hand. He wobbled and patted the bottle sticking out of his pocket. "Yo ho, here's one fer ya! Two hunderd and fifty dollars' worth of Comanche scalp! Jerked it off with me own bare hands and me keen scalping knife!"

"He's going to see lawyer Bone," Gruber said. "Lawyer Bone is paying a two-hundred-and-fifty-dollar bounty on Comanche scalps. Redback dollars, of course, knowing Bone, the cheap bastard."

"That man there never took a scalp off a Comanche. A Comanche would have sliced him to pieces," said Matthew.

"Yah, that's the trouble. Who can tell a Comanche scalp from a poor Waco or Tonk who lives on Shoal Creek? This is making the Indian Joes very angry and afraid. I think Bone ought to stop, but he says the law is on his side," Gruber said.

Matthew asked Hannah, Lawrence and Dora to meet him later at Bullock's Inn. He and Gruber were going to call on lawyer Bone to verify the story of the scalps.

The Ranger and the Hessian walked into lawyer Bone's office on Colorado Street as the drunk was trying to sell the lawyer the scalp claimed to be authentic Comanche.

"Pure Comanche warrior hair. I shot him off his horse and jerked his scalp while he was still alive. But don't worry, I killed him with a big rock."

For the first time since they had shared a room at Bullock's Inn while Doc Swift and Cullasaja tended their wounds, Matthew and lawyer Bone saw each other. Matthew had never seen Bone with his head unbandaged. He noted the pink bare rectangle in the skull where Bone's flesh bearing hair had been cut off by a Comanche. Bone's eyes glittered in his pale, thin face. He sat in an armchair with a robe across his lap. His slave girl, Chloe, stood behind him. She was dressed in a new gingham gown.

"Where'd you get this scalp?" Matthew said to the drunkard in the beaver hat.

"Off a Comanche I shot."

"Liar. Whose hair is this?"

"You can't prove it ain't a Comanche," the drunk said.

"I don't need to prove it except in my own mind. It looks like you have done a murder," said Matthew.

"Murder! You can't murder a Comanche! There's a damn bounty on 'em!" the drunk cried.

"Lawyer Bone. I am putting you out of the bounty business," said Matthew.

"Yah, me too," Gruber said.

"I have permission from President Lamar," Bone said.

"I don't believe it," said Matthew.

Lawyer Bone lifted his right hand, palm up. Chloe opened a desk drawer and withdrew a sheet of paper.

"Not Lamar himself, but just as good as," said Bone with a tight smile as he handed the paper across to Matthew.

The Ranger read fast and his eyes skipped to the last paragraph. The letter to lawyer Bone, on hemp paper with Republic of Texas embossing, phrased in an official manner, concluded by saying, "... We here close to the President feel we are correct in applauding your enterprise in buying aborigine scalps and paying the bounty out of your own purse. You are indeed the sort of far-seeing patriot we much need in this great and growing Republic."

The letter was signed, "Yours in sincere fellowship, Henry Longfellow."

"The Mexicans are paying scalp bounties, but not you," Matthew said. "I revoke this." He folded the letter and tucked it in his belt.

"On what authority?" said Bone.

"My own authority as captain of the Texas Rangers."

"In what court could a Ranger captain overrule the president of the Republic?" Bone said.

"This is the court of real life, lawyer Bone. Today I am running it." The Ranger captain looked at the drunk, who was almost frightened into sobriety as he clutched the scalp against his breast. "You take that scalp and ride out of this town before I put a rope around your neck and string you up for murder."

The drunk scrambled out the door. He flung the scalp into the road at the feet of the gathering crowd and hauled himself onto his mule.

"What's going on in there?" yelled voices from the crowd.

But the drunk was out of breath from fear and couldn't answer. He scrubbed his right hand on his chest as if he could wipe off the dry blood, and then he kicked his heels into his mule's flanks and fled the city.

# 3 1

Osage Killer, the Talking Man, felt full of the spirit. He drew his blanket around his shoulders because of the chill north wind. To escape the heat, and to avoid for a while the nameless creature who lived near the waterfall, the families had left the Little Pigeon and moved west onto a high, grassy plain dotted with oak groves in sight of the mountains where Apaches were contesting the families for the right to roam the land and hunt the game. The Apaches were hated and respected enemies. There was no greater glory than to tear the scalp off a living Apache warrior. Apaches were fantastic runners. In his prime an Apache warrior could run the distance from San Antonio to Austin in a day and be fresh for a fight when he arrived. Osage Killer's people were different from Apaches in that they tended to be bowlegged, not built for running. But Comanches did have a genius with horses. The families invaded Apache territory on horses and defeated all enemies. Still, as he stood in the crackling firelight and glanced toward the black shapes of the mountains, the thought of chopping up an Apache thrilled him and pumped his spirit; his breastplate, made of dozens of finger bones, rattled as the Talking Man breathed deeply and raised his voice louder in speech, not only to demonstrate gusto, but to rouse several who appeared to be dozing off. The young Isimanica, soon to become a chief, now allowed the white girl Pearl to sit directly behind him in the circle. It annoyed the Talking Man that Pearl often touched Isimanica's hair, even while he sat at a circle. Pearl's blonde hair was hacked off at ear height and painted with a red stripe where it parted in the middle. She had colored her face red, yellow and green. Isimanica's new hairstyle for this day featured a long, braided scalp lock, entwined with Pearl's blonde hair and dec- orated with freshwater pearls and hawk feathers, that hung down over his left ear.

"Oh, Sure Enough Father, powerful over the rocks of the earth and the birds of the sky, powerful over all our families and all our enemies, powerful over the demons that would harm us, give us the wisdom to rule our world and never perish until the sun goes out of the sky forever," the Talking Man said.

They were all listening to him again.

"Now I would like to hear the words of my brother Isimanica."

As he squatted on his haunches, smoking Mexican tobacco in his pipe, Turk's eyes moved to the face of the Talking Man, who was smiling at Isi- manica. Turk, the war chief, understood what was happening. The Talking Man was trying to create an ally. Turk had no fear of Isimanica or of Talking Man. The people did not fight among themselves. If Turk became displeased with what was happening in this family of families, he would take his own family and move. There were plenty of places to go—maybe north, trailing the bison herds. Most of the other families would move with Turk, because he had earned the name Fighting Man for deeds that people recorded in drawings on shields, buffalo hides and cave walls. Some families would stay with Talking Man and Isimanica, if it came to that, siding with the old civil chief and the young warrior. Turk blew a gray trail of Mexican smoke and rested in the euphoric sensation of tobacco. Turk was not concerned with the future. His existence was entirely here with him tonight in each timeless moment, each breath.

"You want me to talk?" Isimanica said, surprised.

"Tell us your words, brother," said the Talking Man. "I will sit and listen."

Isimanica slowly rose. He wore a Mexican cavalry tunic open at the breast and knee-length fringed moccasins. An apron tucked into a belt covered his genitals. He was otherwise naked, despite the coolness of the evening. Pearl gazed up at him proudly, looking at his hard buttocks and then at her own hair braided with his in his scalp lock.

"What do you want to hear words about?" Isimanica asked the Talking Man.

"Tell us about the fight when you killed three Creeks with your hatchet," said the Talking Man.

"Everybody has heard that story more than once," Isimanica said.

"Your new wife has not heard it," said Talking Man.

"My new wife does not know our language yet."

"Then tell us any words that are in your heart," Talking Man said.

"In my heart I know I will lead our people to win a great battle," said Isimanica. He looked at Turk calmly. Turk puffed on his pipe. "In my heart my greatest joy is killing our enemies. That is what is in my heart."

Isimanica glanced at Pearl. He hadn't told the circle that she had found a place in his heart.

"Who will you defeat in this great battle?" Talking Man asked. He didn't like hearing of great battles to come. Talking Man thought great battles were a stupid waste of bodies. Stealth was smarter, killing from ambush.

"The men with hats."

All movement stopped in the circle. Turk froze with the pipe in his mouth. Isimanica was not a member of the group selected to advise the grand council at the great meeting in the coming autumn. There was no rule that Isimanica could not bring up the subject of killing the white invaders, but it was unexpected and presumptuous, seeing that three of the four advisers were sitting in the circle.

"Very well. If that is all that is in your heart . . ." said Talking Man, starting to stand. This was not what he'd wanted Isimanica to say. He had expected Isimanica to mean a big battle with the Shawnees or the Kiowas.

Turk tapped his pipe against a rock and scraped the bowl with a forefinger. Osage Killer began talking again, telling of the countless numbers of big cows that they would soon encounter, and the feasts that would follow. Turk walked around behind the circle, behind where Isimanica now sat as his little white wife leaned closer to him than Turk believed proper at a circle meeting. Going toward his own tepee, Turk saw the sister of Isimanica's white wife. She was softening a wolf skin by rubbing the flesh side with a smooth rock. Her ears and nose had been burned with hot coals by Isimanica's jealous other wife so often that they had become charred meat. Turk passed the open flap of The

Ram's tepee. The Ram was on top of the white slave woman, Wanda Mecom, pumping his body between her legs while she grunted and groaned. The Ram's two Mexican slave women crouched outside, muttering between themselves. They wanted to kill the white woman, but they did not dare.

Turk's main wife, Corn Tassel, was playing a game with her two sisters in front of the primary of their four tepees. They were tossing colored stones at a hole in the ground and giggling as they counted their scores. Corn Tassel's father was the powerful war chief Big Hump. Turk had given Big Hump sixteen hundred horses as a show of respect for the war chief and desire for his daughter. It was a price unheard of before or since and proved that Turk was a warrior of extraordinary power. Now Big Hump was old, no longer in his prime. He had become silly and lived in the lodges of the old men. Some of the old men were wise and would be listened to, but others were silly like Big Hump. When the old men became sick of body, they went off alone to die, or else were thrown away by the families if unable to keep up with the frequent moving of the village. Corn Tassel's mother, Tabitha, was past her prime as well, nearly as old as Big Hump. But Turk took the responsibility of caring for Tabitha, and he accepted Corn Tassel's two younger sisters as his wives so that they would also be under his protection and care.

Like Young Owl Hatching and others, Turk found it a good thing to have wives who were sisters. An important man needed several wives. Women did every bit of the work, including digging roots for food and skinning and butchering the game the men killed as hunters. Sisters got along with each other fairly well as wives of the same husband, Turk observed, and he took good care of all the women around him. The hard time for Corn Tassel and her mother and sisters would come if Turk's body was killed and his spirit passed into the afterlife. In this event on the first morning of the second week after his death—when Turk's women were exhausted from mourning, from slashing their flesh and chopping their hair and wailing in grief and despair—they would be expected, but not required, to share Turk's horse herd—his wealth—among the family of families. Corn Tassel and her mother and sisters would be left poor and without a provider.

Now Corn Tassel playfully moved into her husband's path, and he clutched her breasts. The two sisters laughed, and one called, "She is eager for your sex, husband." Turk massaged her breasts and felt his passion rising and pulled her toward the primary tepee.

"He is in there waiting for you," Corn Tassel said.

"Who?"

"The magician."

"I will send him to another tepee with—which sister do you think? Which one would rather sex him tonight?" Turk said.

"They both would "

"Then they can both have him, and I will have you," said Turk.

"I am always hungry for you," she said.

The Dark Man came out of the tepee, walking on his hands, dragging his legs. He was powered by arms and shoulders that looked carved of mahogany by a sculptor with the classical male torso in mind.

"I have come to tell you that I am leaving this family and moving to the Little Pigeon. You can find me there, at the Little Pigeon, when you need me," the Dark Man said.

"Your *portento* of our deaths? Is it still true?"

"Death!" screamed Corn Tassel. She was horrified and angry, and she spat at Dark Man. "Be gone with your visions of death! Death is far away from my man!"

The two sisters heard the row and joined in.

"Don't speak of death around here, you sorcerer! You demon! Your *portento* is a lie!"

"Be quiet. Everybody," said Turk.

When the war chief of this family of families ordered silence, the whole night became still, as if even the crickets could no longer sing in the grass. A wolfhound, trained since a pup not to bark, flattened on his belly at the sound of Turk's command.

Turk said, "Good. Now I am going to do sex with Corn Tassel in this tepee. Brother, you go with her sisters into the other tepee and do as you wish. Then take whatever horses you want, and all the supplies you want, and go from this place. I will see you on the Little Pigeon before winter."

# 3 2

There were five Spanish missions, each more than a hundred years old, built along a ten-mile stretch of the river running south from San Antonio. The mission oldest and closest to town was the Alamo, aged one hundred and twenty-one, now an almost roofless home to pigs and cows who roamed among the cottonwood trees that were newly grown since the battle. All of the missions were poor and in disrepair, more or less abandoned by the Church of Rome even before the revolutionary war that had established the Republic of Texas. The sabbath was not observed as a religious day in Texas, except in the Catholic Church.

With its front door opening onto Main Plaza and its rear onto Military Plaza, the Cathedral of San Fernando was considered the precise center of San Antonio; all distances were measured from the cross atop its Moorish dome. Though twenty years younger than the Alamo mission, San Fernando was the oldest cathedral in Texas, in the United States, in New Mexico territory or in Mexican California. Beside its Moorish dome rose a higher bell tower with a steeple—a lookout to warn of approaching enemies. Outside the adobe walls that surrounded the cathedral were the two big plazas where people and animals mingled in the dust and sweat of the market.

Inside the cathedral, Father Dominius Rodriguez stood looking up at the carved figure of the Black Christ above its consecrated altar in an alcove off the auditorium. San Fernando had always been a cathedral, never a mission. The Black Christ had come to San Antonio with the Canary Islanders, who had begun building this cathedral to be their parish church. Father Dominius had been twenty-five years old. He had been ordained three years ago by the Bishop of Guadalajara, the city where Dominius had been born to the wife of a shepherd. When his father and mother died of black-tongue, the child Dominius was taken into a Franciscan monastery by two old Spanish monks and taught to read. At times he was not digging in the gardens or scrubbing the kitchen or was not praying or helping to serve the mass, Dominius read over and over the Holy Bible and the seventeen other volumes of religious writings in the monastery library, including a volume of reflections by St. Anthony of Padua, patron saint of Portugal and of finding lost items.

Father Dominius gazed at the sheen on the mahogany cheeks of the Black Christ and at the shadows around the eyes as if they might grant him serenity.

"With all respect, Father Dominius, this is not such a complicated question," said Hannah Dahlman. "Captain Caldwell and I want to get married in this church. Do we have your approval?"

Hannah looked small but imposing as she stood beside the Texas Ranger, who held a straw hat in his big hands. Father Dominius had presided over San Fernando Cathedral for nearly a year and had seen the speckle-bearded Ranger—it was impossible not to notice him—at mass two or three times and sitting alone in a pew in silence another two or three times. This fierce, dark-eyed girl, Hannah, was new to Father Dominius. He crossed himself. Forgive me, Lord, if this is an unworthy emotion, he silently prayed, but this girl has the contentious, disturbing qualities for which her people are reputed, and she is annoying me.

"I have told you the simple solution to a rather complex situation," said Father Dominius.

"That I should convert to Catholicism?" Hannah said.

"We can take care of the necessary rites of conversion in a few short weeks. Then you are free to set your wedding date."

"Father Dominius, I was born a Jew. I am proud to be a Jew. But because I insist upon remaining a Jew, I am not allowed to marry in your church?"

Father Dominius clutched his elbows inside his rough brown robe.

"Not because you are a Jew, Miss Dahlman. If you were a Baptist or a Methodist or a Mohammedan, I would tell you the same rule applies. Only Catholics are allowed to marry other Catholics in this Catholic church."

"That's the damnedest thing I ever heard of," Matthew said.

"You are a widower, Captain?"

"What's that got to do with it, padre?"

"If you are divorced, then I could not let you marry in this church, either."

"Excuse me, padre, but I want to marry this girl here in this cathedral because this feels like a holy place to me. If you say I can't stand here in front of God and swear my love and faith in this girl, then one of us didn't read his Bible right."

Father Dominius looked up into the startling gray eyes of this brute. Father

Dominius had read both the Old and the New Testaments at least a hundred and sixty times in their entirety, and certain passages thousands of times. How dare this hairy animal with a red nose challenge his understanding of the Bible?

"This is not a biblical question. This is a law of the Catholic Church," said Father Dominius.

"I'd like to speak to your chief," Matthew said.

Ah, if only the bishop were here to deal with this creature, thought Father Dominius.

"The bishop is in his summer retreat in the mountains at Lake Chapala."

"In Mexico?

"Indeed. Where the summer is cool."

"When is he coming back?" asked Matthew.

"Oh, come on, Matthew, let's leave the poor man alone," Hannah said.

"I want to know when his chief is coming back," said Matthew.

"Sir, the bishop has never been in San Antonio, much less inside this cathedral, since I have been rector, and I have no reason to expect him to visit in the foreseeable future," Father Dominius said.

Matthew felt Hannah's hair swish against his shoulder as she turned to leave.

"Hannah, please," Matthew said. "The padre here is going to think of something."

"There is one thing we could do," said Father Dominius. "I could perform your wedding service in the rectory."

"Rectory?" Hannah said.

"My office as rector. It's through the door beside the altar, a very nice little space. I have a table in there to do my paperwork on, and I have a chair, and of course I have my bed. It's only a matter of sixty feet from my rectory to the altar, so you would be very much still getting married in this holy place."

"Could we walk up and down the aisle coming and going from the rectory?" asked Matthew.

"Matthew!" said Hannah.

"Wait a moment. Could we, padre?"

"Well, I suppose that would be all right."

"You see, Hannah? What do you think?" Matthew said.

Hannah bobbed her head slightly.

"Thank you very much, Father, for consulting with us," Hannah said, taking Matthew's right arm in both of hers and smiling. In her eyes Father Dominius saw anger that struck him as deeply and ferociously womanlike. "We will discuss this arrangement and be in touch with you again."

Father Dominius watched the German Jewish girl leading the big Texan down the aisle toward the front door. The father hoped they would find somewhere else to be married, but at once he regretted the thought as unworthy. Father Dominius lit a candle at the foot of the Black Christ and prayed to become a better person.

Matthew and Hannah went out the cathedral's tall door and walked across the courtyard to the gate that led into Main Plaza. Hannah looked back at the cathedral and up at its tile dome, now half in shadow from the morning sun.

"Matthew, I'm sorry I was difficult in there," she said. "If this is where you want the ceremony to be, then I agree. There was just something about the man's attitude when he said we could marry in his office but because I'm a Jew, I'm not good enough to marry in the big church."

"It's not because you're a Jew," Matthew said.

"If I were a Protestant, he would marry us in the church," said Hannah.

"If you were a Protestant, you would have signed on to be a Catholic."

"Jews can't do that," she said.

"Well, suppose I become a Jew, then? Where do I go to sign on as a Jew?" said Matthew.

"Oh, Matthew," she said, laughing. "I'll be glad when you meet my father. He'll love your sense of humor."

"Hannah, I'll marry you under a tree by the river if that turns out to be the holy place, but let's give the padre a chance to change his thinking."

"Father Dominius can't change the laws of his church."

"I didn't say change the laws of the church. I said change his thinking."

In the Main Plaza vendors lined up against the walls with their stands of vegetables and fruit and poultry. Red chili peppers and green chili peppers hung in bundles from *vigas* in the adobe. A lane had been cleared, and half a dozen men were betting on a horse race that was about to begin. A donkey coughed. A rooster crowed, and hens set up a general squawking.

As he put his straw planter's hat back on and adjusted the fit, he saw riding into the plaza what he swiftly counted as twenty men including their leader. The men wore the homespun tunics and flat-brimmed hats of the Republic of Texas army. But these were not the slovenly sort of furloughed soldiers who had banded together to become outlaws. These men were relatively clean and most of their buttons were sewn on, and they sat straight in their saddles as if under the military command of their leader. The leader wore a tunic that looked tailor-made, and light glinted from gold stars on his collar. He was a short-legged man with a wide chest and a big head on which he wore a wide-brimmed hat with a snakeskin band.

Matthew stopped Hannah with a tightening of his arm. She looked up in surprise as the leader of the troopers pointed a gloved hand and turned his horse to ride in their direction.

Now Matthew recognized him. He was Felix Huston, a few years younger than Matthew. Huston was a Mississippi cotton grower who had arrived in Texas three years ago at the head of five hundred mounted volunteers from Mississippi to fight for the Texas Republic against Mexico. Matthew considered Huston a murderous hothead but a brave and dangerous fighter. While the Old Chief, Sam Houston, was recuperating from the shrapnel and musket wounds he received at the Battle of San Jacinto, a land speculator from Ohio named David Gouverneur Burnet, who had been serving as the revolutionary ad interim president, sent Mirabeau Buonaparte Lamar to replace Sam Houston as head of the army. But the soldiers, most of whom had never been paid or any longer expected to be, refused to accept Lamar as their leader. Most soldiers wanted to follow Felix Huston, who was clamoring to invade Mexico and conquer their cities and become rich. Lamar resigned from the army to stand election for the office of vice president of the Republic. Sam Houston himself, as soon as he was elected first president of the Republic, assigned Albert Sidney Johnston to be head of the army. But Felix Huston resented the new man's presence. Claiming a slur on his honor, Huston challenged Johnston to a duel. Huston shot Johnston and left him seriously wounded and unfit to serve.

Acting as president, Sam Houston put the entire army, except for six hundred men, on furlough. The Republic could not afford to support an army, but a more important reason was now there would be no army for Felix Huston to become dictator of. Matthew was known as a vigorous supporter of Sam Houston.

"Hello, Matthew," Felix Huston said, reining up in front of them. Huston touched his hat brim as a gesture of courtesy to Hannah.

"Could that be you, Felix?" said Matthew.

"Now tell me, Matthew, would God have made another man like me?" Felix said, showing his teeth.

"I thought you went back to Mississippi for good," Matthew said.

"So you ain't heard the news?"

"Nothing that concerns you, anyhow."

"I am the new commander of the army."

"I don't believe you," Matthew said.

"Tom Rusk resigned and the troops elected me. You are looking at Major

General Felix Huston, the new supreme chief of the army of the Republic of Texas."

"I guess Lamar knows about this?" Matthew said.

"President Lamar swore me in. Johnston is still secretary of war for the time being, but I am the head man of the army."

"I never would have believed you would work for Lamar," said Matthew.

"I could say the same about you."

"I'm a Ranger. It's different," Matthew said.

"Are you going to introduce me to the young lady?" Huston said.

"Not while you're in the saddle," said Matthew.

Huston heaved himself onto the ground and handed his reins to a woolly-bearded man who wore three stripes of a sergeant. Huston removed his hat, unspringing a field of brown curly hair.

"Pardon me, ma'am. I have become such a Texan that I forgot my southern Mississippi manners," Huston said. "My name is Major General Felix Huston."

He bowed his head slightly, and she flexed her knees in return.

"I am Hannah Dahlman."

"A German immigrant?" asked Huston.

"Miss Dahlman is my fiancée," Matthew said.

Hannah felt the confusion among the soldiers and the curiosity of the crowd, but most of all she felt the hostility between Matthew and the general like the freeze of an ice dagger against the back of her neck.

"My compliments," said General Huston.

"Thank you," Hannah said.

"It grieves me to intrude on your wedding plans, ma'am," Huston said. "But I am here to escort your husband to Houston City for a command appearance in front of President Lamar."

Huston's eyes shifted to the sergeant, who ostentatiously loosened the fit of his pistol in its holster. The other troopers sat up straighter, pulling themselves into shape for action.

"Are you going to resist us, Matthew?" asked Huston.

"Am I charged with a crime?" Matthew said.

"Does it matter?"

"The answer might save your life, Felix," said Matthew.

"In fact, you are accused of disobeying the direct order of the President that you arrest a foreign spy and a Cherokee harlot. There is another accusation, that you stole an official document from a presidential representative in Austin. What the President really wants is for you to explain yourself to him, Matthew. We ain't here to put a rope around your neck."

"Tell the President I will be along presently, when it is more convenient," Matthew said. "I'm sure the President wouldn't want to interrupt my wedding."

"Matthew, I am authorized to put you in chains if I have to," said Huston.

"You won't live long enough to see that happen, Felix," Matthew said.

Matthew gently pushed Hannah away and freed his right arm. Though he had dressed to visit the church and not for combat, he wore his two Paterson revolvers, his butcher knife and had the derringer tucked inside his moccasin boot. He regretted that he had left his shotgun, Sweet Lips, locked in the hotel vault. Matthew believed that Huston, if pushed, would give his troopers the order to shoot him, but if Huston was to die before the order passed his lips, the troopers would not fight against a Texas Ranger for the sake of a dead general.

A cry arose from the rear of the crowd and spread across the plaza.

"*Los Rinches! Los Rinches!*"

A wedge-shaped hunk of the crowd opened as Big Foot Wallace, Saginaw Boswell, Fiddle Man, Herman the German and Snake galloped their horses into the plaza. With them was Red Beans, one of the Lipans who scouted for the Rangers at Boca Chica station.

Red Beans was the only one of them who did not have at least one weapon drawn. Although he was a Ranger scout, he knew it was very dangerous for any Indian to draw a weapon in a closed-in place like this plaza with many white people in it.

"Hidy, Matthew!" shouted Big Foot.

Big Foot's great bay horse that he called Old Higgins skidded and threw up dust that settled on Felix Huston and bumped the saddle of Huston's horse, causing the general's canteen to drop off and fall in the dirt.

The troopers shifted in their saddles, looking in awe at the Rangers in their jewelry and beaded vests and hats of various styles, from plug to beaver. Though both groups were charged with defending Texas, they were as different as the army was from the navy. The Rangers obeyed their leader and their president, but not any general. The troopers waited for the sergeant, who waited for Huston to make a move.

"Good to see you, Big Foot," said Matthew.

"Red Beans cut the trail of these bandits, so we followed them here," Big Foot said.

Big Foot sent a squirt of tobacco juice onto the boot of Felix Huston. The major general dared not look at Big Foot. As a friend of Johnston, Big Foot had long ago denounced the duel as attempted murder of a good man by a swaggering bully, and an affront to the Old Chief as well.

"What do you call this, Matthew? Is it a mutiny?" said Huston.

"Huston tells me he is the chief of the army now, Big Foot," Matthew said. "Do you believe it?"

"Shit no. Nobody would follow this sheep's butt," said Big Foot. He looked at the nervous troopers. "Except a bunch of sheep's butt pumpers."

"Let's shoot these sonsabitches," yelled Saginaw Boswell, and the crowd moved back.

"I got my eye on you, you Mississippi bastard," Fiddle Man shouted at Felix Huston. "I hate a Mississippi sonofabitch!"

"You can't kill us all in cold blood," Huston said, keeping his eyes on Matthew.

"Don't give me cause to do it," said Matthew.

"Matthew, if you believe in this republic, if you believe the elected president of this republic has authority at law over the people, you have to come with me," Huston said. "If you don't believe the President has authority, then the Republic is in chaos. During a total breakdown of law the army will take over, and it will become my responsibility to reestablish authority. That is, unless you murder me here today in cold blood before five hundred witnesses."

The Republic must endure and prosper, Matthew believed; it must survive men like Felix Huston and Lamar until next year's election, when the Old Chief could be voted back into power as president.

As Texas Ranger senior captain, Matthew was directly responsible only to his conscience and to the president of the Republic.

Matthew scratched his beard. The crowd hushed. People ducked behind stalls or burros to escape a possible storm of bullets. Dora stood close beside Lawrence, who hugged her with one arm and gazed from beneath his sombrero. If he got the chance, Lawrence would shoot one of the soldiers, he thought. That would show Dora not to laugh at his frontier behavior.

Hannah stood three feet from the Ranger and glared at Felix Huston.

"Matthew, I have grown up around men like this, officers of the king," she said. "I know he may not deserve to live, but it would be a folly to kill him."

"A folly, eh?" Matthew said.

"By God, you know she's right," said Huston.

Matthew turned his broad back on the general and put both hands on Hannah's elbows.

"Would you mind if we don't get married for a week or two?" he said.

"I would understand," she said.

"And you promise not to run off with a young, handsome stranger while I am gone?"

Hannah smiled. She rose on her toes and kissed him on the lips.

"I will be here, I promise," she said.

# 33

M r. Maurice felt his heart flutter. Since the baron had died in his arms in Houston City, Mr. Maurice had never felt attracted to another man his own age, which he maintained was somewhat short of forty. But he saw this wide-shouldered, graceful person striding across the tiles toward the registration counter, and he noticed the athletic body, the pleasant, blue-eyed Irish face with an aristocratic structure to it.

Mr. Maurice very much liked the looks of this stranger, enough so that he was glad his young assistant had not been there to observe the flush in his cheeks. He was already preparing to tell the man that the Fincus Hotel was full, but Mr. Maurice would somehow find a room, when, to his astonishment, he heard the stranger address him in easy if imperfect French.

"I know, my good sir, that a bed in your fine hotel is difficult to obtain, but I do have gold dollars," said the stranger in French.

"Why, however do you happen to speak such wonderful French?" replied Mr. Maurice in French.

"You flatter me. I speak French like the student I was. I am more comfortable in English," said Doc Swift, changing languages.

"I would not have guessed," Mr. Maurice replied. "You made me homesick for Paris."

"A beautiful, romantic city," said Doc. "My favorite city in the world, I believe."

"How true and how peculiar," Mr. Maurice said. "I had gone for many months here in Texas without hearing Paris mentioned, and now you arrive speaking my own language."

"My name is Doctor Romulus Swift. I am a physician. I am passing through your city and need a room for a week or two while I have some special equipment prepared."

"There she goes now," said Mr. Maurice.

"Who?"

"The other person I met recently who loves Paris. Her name is Hannah Dahlman."

Doc turned and saw her on the other side of the lobby. She was wearing a robe and was about to enter the canvas flap of the Pataki Bath House. He saw the pale flash of her knee as the robe parted, and he raised his eyes to find that she was staring at him—her dark, wet eyes fastened upon him—and Doc was jolted. He felt slightly sideways. He knew he had never seen this young woman before—she must have been about the age of his sister—but he felt that he had known her always. Another robed woman, taller, with red hair, crossed Doc's vision, paused to examine him boldly and then disappeared behind the canvas flap, following the young woman into the bath.

"She is beautiful," Doc said.

Mr. Maurice tapped his skull with two fingers. "And up here? The brains? This one is a musician, a linguist, a philosopher. She is shrewd as a Jew must be to do well in this world. I predict she will become one of the great women of Texas."

As a young man Doc had decided it was better for him to live alone or in the company of men than to live with a woman who made him wish he were alone.

Doc believed the power of love to be the energy that held the stars in the heavens and kept the human spirit alive. But romantic love such as his friends the poets wrote about, this always seemed to lead to pain. Love poems were about yearning, which is suffering. The love poems—and the behavior of Doc's literary friends—testified that not much needs to be consciously known for two people to fall in love. Lovers will find a way to love. It happens all the time. It happens in an instant. The result is nearly always a disaster sooner than later. But there were exceptions, the rare pairs like Doc's father and mother, well married for forty years. Considering his father was a vigorous eighty-nine and his mother strong and unwrinkled in her sixties, Romulus figured that he at thirty-nine was about halfway through the life his body was engineered to function, barring disease or violence. He loved life, though he did not love people in general. He loved healing, which was reaching into the core of the mystery of life. Buried inside himself, he loved the other side of healing, which was violence and death. But to love a woman, romantically and for a lifetime, had been for Romulus a fantasy.

He realized Mr. Maurice was speaking to him.

"Your room is ready now, Doctor Swift," said Mr. Maurice. "It's one of our finest rooms, view of the river, delightful. Its regular tenant has gone to Houston City on business. By the time he returns, I will have another room for you, if you are still with us."

"Thank you," Doc said. "Now I need to care for my horse and have a bath."

"Fincus Livery is the best. We can draw you a tub here, but I would recommend Rupert's Barber Shop and Tub Bath on the opposite side of the plaza."

Mr. Maurice watched the doctor walk toward the door, his hips moving so gracefully, and then Mr. Maurice saw his young assistant, Arias, watching the same sight.

"Arias!" he said. "Do I pay you to stand around gaping?"

"Yes sir, if it's you I am gaping at," replied Arias.

"Insolence has killed many a joker," Mr. Maurice said, reading the register signed by the physician: New York City was his given residence. A sophisticated man, a gentleman. This was the sort of encounter that made the hotel business fascinating to Mr. Maurice.

Doc groomed and stabled the Morgan. He had a haircut and bath at Rupert's. Doc asked that his hair be cut short, no more than two inches at its longest. This was part of the preparation for his journey. Tomorrow he would visit Pope, the gun maker, to order an accurate, reliable fast-loading rifle with real power. Doc envisioned a breech-loading rifle, such as he had fired in France, in which the chamber had a central pillar. The conical bullets, which Pope would have to mold specially, could be loaded in the breech to rest on the pillar, and a tap or two from the rod, if needed, would settle the bullet into the grooves of the barrel. Doc had brought the French designer's drawings of the rifle to Texas, but they'd been lost in the flood months ago. He and Pope would have to re-create them.

Doc's room at the Fincus was large and pleasant, and he could hear the river and the birds. He lay across the bed, wondering about the tenant who was clearly rich and powerful enough to keep a hotel room reserved in Texas.

He thought again of the pale flash of the inside of the knee of the dark-haired girl he had seen entering the ladies' bath. He rested and tried to meditate for an hour before dinner.

Hannah was having dinner that night with Dora and Lawrence in the Fincus dining room when Mr. Maurice, his cheeks puffed with pride, escorted the newcomer to a table for one. Hannah had noticed the man in the lobby, had thought him attractive and mysterious, but she had put him out of her mind until now. He wore a black cotton coat that reached halfway down his thighs, and a white shirt, and his short brown hair lay close on his skull—like a Greek statue, Hannah thought. His skin was pale on his forehead, but his face and hands were reddened by the sun. His expression was lively; his blue eyes examined the room. Hannah felt his eyes fall upon her. It was as if hot fluids stirred in her heart and pelvis. She turned her gaze on Lawrence, who had dressed for dinner in a white cotton pullover shirt, white trousers and sandals, and was telling the two women of his scheme to drive beef cattle east to the Mississippi River and then ship the cattle to northeastern markets.

Lawence stopped in the middle of a sentence when he saw the new man enter.

"That's the man I saw in the lobby today, Hannah. The one I was talking about in the bath. Isn't he divine?" said Dora. "Let's invite him to join our table."

"Now, Dora, do you think that would look proper? Everyone knows our Hannah is engaged," Lawrence said.

Hannah thought she saw resentment, perhaps jealousy, cross Lawrence's face before he covered his expression with a swig from his ceramic mug of beer.

"For God's sake, Lawrence, who are you to be talking about looking proper? In those ridiculous sandals? This man is alone and new in town. He looks quite interesting. You and I are here to chaperone Hannah. What could possibly be wrong with behaving cordially to a stranger?" said Dora.

"Why don't we ask Hannah her opinion?" Lawrence said.

Hannah allowed herself another peek at the stranger, who was looking at the label on a bottle of wine being offered by Mr. Maurice. She looked back at Lawrence, who had begun tapping his fork on the table.

"You can trust her, Lawrence. Her heart is pure," said Dora.

"Would you please let her speak for herself?"

"Yes. Invite him," Hannah said.

Lawrence sighed and pushed back his chair, took another nip from his ceramic mug, and walked toward the stranger's table.

Doc saw him coming. A tall, bony man, a high-born–looking fellow, comfortable in his adopted dress. Doc would not have been surprised to hear him speak with the accent of an Oxford man who had gone native.

"Pardon my intrusion, sir," said Lawrence. As a top operator in New York financial circles, Lawrence was smooth at introducing himself to strangers who might have something to offer. "My name is Lawrence Kerr."

Doc stood up and shook hands with Lawrence.

"Pleased to meet you," Doc said. "My name is Swift."

"We see that you are alone and newly arrived and would like for you to join our table for dinner," Lawrence said. He leaned closer. "Frankly, the ladies are dying to meet you. Where are you from?"

"From?"

"Excuse me. I don't mean to be rude. It's just that everybody in Texas is from someplace else, and we grow accustomed to asking," said Lawrence.

"I am from New York," Doc said.

Lawrence brightened.

"A fellow New Yorker! Splendid. My wife is Dora Kerr. You probably have seen her if you are a theater fan in New York or London."

"Did she sing the role of Birdie in *The Rose of Brighton* at the Eighth Street Theater in New York three seasons ago?" Doc said.

"Did she! Wasn't she smashing? Please, you must join us."

"Thank you, I will," said Doc.

The other diners looked around as Lawrence led the stranger across the room.

"Dora, I have found one of your fans," said Lawrence. "This is. . . . ah. . . . Mr. Swift."

Doc bowed at Dora and said, "My name is Dr. Romulus Swift. I heard you sing Birdie in *The Rose of Brighton* in New York and enjoyed your performance immensely."

"How kind of you to remember. You beautiful man." Dora beamed. "Please sit down."

Doc looked at Hannah, waiting to be introduced. At first her eyes were fixed on the middle of his chest, but she looked up to his mouth when Lawrence said, "And may I present Miss Hannah Dahlman?"

"Delighted, Miss Dahlman."

"Doctor," she said, lowering her eyes. She was thinking, how can this be happening? I have hardly finished kissing Matthew Caldwell passionately and swearing my love for him when suddenly my heart is turned upside down by a stranger. Hannah had been in love only once before, four years ago at age sixteen, with an intellectual boy who led a student protest strike that her father was responsible for secretly organizing. Hannah and the boy were never lovers, but a piece of her heart had died when he was killed by a blow from a soldier's baton. Now here she was, declaring her love to one man one day and falling in love with another man the next. It must be the heat in this tropical place, she thought, that is making me crazy.

When they had ordered dinner—there were two entrees tonight, catfish and rabbit—Lawrence said, "I am Yale, class of '21."

"King's College, Columbia, class of '22," said Doc. "University of Edinburgh medical school, '26." Doc mentioned Edinburgh to see if this information made a good impression on Hannah Dahlman, for she spoke English with a slight German accent and appeared well educated by her bearing.

Hannah felt awe. This handsome physician with the confident demeanor was an experienced, polished adult who was at ease in the world—from Europe to New York to a world so raw and peculiar as Texas. Captain Caldwell had frightened her at first with his shaggy manliness, but this doctor made her feel somehow inadequate, an unfamiliar feeling.

"So what brings you to Texas?" Lawrence asked. "That's the second thing we say here, right after 'Where are you from?' "

"I am exploring," Doc said.

"You mean, you're not here to gain a large piece of land, like most everyone else?" said Dora.

"No," Doc said. "I don't want land."

"Exploring where?" asked Lawrence.

"West of the Colorado," Doc said.

"In Comancheria?"

"As it is called, yes," said Doc.

"Well, by God, I own two hundred fifty thousand acres of Comancheria. The Kerr Land and Cattle Company will be a flourishing industry as soon as we kill these damn Comanches," Lawrence said.

"Sorry, Lawrence, but I'm not going out there to kill Comanches," said Doc.

"To heal them, perhaps?" Hannah asked.

"What?"

She had spoken so softly that he hadn't heard. She was surprised at herself that she had spoken aloud at all.

"I said, perhaps the doctor is going into Comancheria as a healer," Hannah said.

Doc smiled at her, and this time she did not look away.

"No," he said. "But that is a perceptive comment."

"I'm glad to hear you don't want land," Lawrence said, leaning back to allow the waiter to serve his platter of fried catfish. "That makes you a rare bird in Texas. I daresay that outside of Mr. Maurice and some of these peons in aprons, you are the only person in this room who is not here to grab land."

"Is land what brings you here, Miss Dahlman?" asked Doc.

She nodded.

"Hannah soon will own at least half of a ten-thousand-acre spread in Comancheria, not so far from the Kerr Land and Cattle Company headquarters," Lawrence said. "The land is deeded to her fiancé, Captain Caldwell."

"Oh," said Doc. He remembered the Ranger had sent for a bride from Germany. Doc was stunned to realize this lovely, sensitive girl was the one.

"You sound as if you know Captain Caldwell," Dora said.

"I knew him in Austin," said Doc.

Lawrence enjoyed the disappointment he saw in the doctor's expression at the news that Hannah was engaged to the famous Texas Ranger captain. Lawrence was jealous of the way his wife and Hannah looked at this fellow.

"Yes, she is engaged to Captain Caldwell. In fact, you are sleeping in his room, in his bed," Lawrence said.

Doc smiled.

"Powerful man, the captain. Skilled as I am at fencing and pistol shooting, I would hate to go up against Caldwell with my life on the line," Lawrence said.

"Yes," said Doc, looking at Hannah. She tore a bit of rabbit off the bone with her knife and fork and pretended to be hungry. "He is a powerful man."

Dora sensed the feelings that were passing between Hannah and Doc. She only wished this adorable, intelligent, sophisticated physician would demonstrate a desire for a mature woman who was more experienced in giving and getting pleasure. Dora touched her lips to her wine and patted her mouth, smiling behind her napkin. She loved intrigue, and now she could feel it being born.

# F O U R

## THE COUNCIL HOUSE

There may be changes indeed
in dress and seeming, but the
heart of the Indian is still his own.

*—James Mooney*

# 34

Henry Longfellow was embarrassed and angry. To hear the suggestion from his old colleague and current president that he should leave Houston City at once, maybe go to Galveston Island for a refreshing dip in the salt water of the gulf, and make his exit tout de suite before Captain Caldwell arrived, this brought to the base of Henry's crane-like neck a pain that he associated with the feeling he used to get as a boy when the girls laughed at him and the other boys called him ugly.

"Do you suppose, sir, that I am afraid to face this brute of a lawman who refused to arrest the Cherokee whore and her thug?" said Henry. "It is I who am cursed for life with a mangled shin bone. It is I who burn with fury. I demand to hear the explanation from this spotted freak who disgraces his responsibility to our government."

"You demand?" President Lamar said.

"My apologies, sir. I mean I request, sir."

"Henry, I have a matter of vital importance to discuss with Captain Caldwell. Not that your brutalization is unimportant, or this Ranger roughing up your friend in Austin and stealing his private documents are of no consequence. These things will be dealt with in good time, I promise," said Lamar. The President was becoming irritated by Henry Longfellow. Henry's gawky frame and constant twitching were becoming a nuisance to the President's eye. "You would not demand that I put your personal affairs above those of the Republic?"

"I would never request that my personal affairs be put above the Republic," Henry said. Using a copper-knobbed cane of polished ebony which concealed a sword blade of Damascus steel inside, he propelled himself toward the door of the President's office. "I am merely saying that I deserve a hearing with Captain Caldwell, once you have preserved the Republic, of course."

Henry ducked under the doorjamb and met Albert Sidney Johnston smoking a cigar in the hallway.

"Why are you still here?" asked the general. "Didn't he tell you Old Paint is not far from town?"

"What makes you think I would avoid him?" Henry said.

"Self-preservation," said the general. "I'm sure Captain Caldwell has good reason for all he has done, and I doubt it will reflect well on you."

"Explain yourself, General."

"I am saying you don't want Old Paint for an enemy."

Johnston entered the President's office and shut the door. Henry jerked his beak back and forth, squinting up and down the hallway to see if he should behave as if publicly offended, but no one had heard. Henry hurried toward the steps, scraping his right shoe against the planks. One of his slave boys was waiting with the carriage downstairs to drive him back to the plantation. He might, indeed, take a trip to the seacoast. It was a more sensible idea than confronting the Ranger and offending the President all at the same time. If this Old Paint should become a menace, Henry would deal with him. But for now he would have himself bathed and massaged by his slaves, and drink a bottle of Jamaican rum to still the ache in his leg bone and the burning tension in his groin.

Henry cackled inside his chest as his mind called up pictures he remembered through slits in the canvas at the bathhouse. He recalled watching Captain Caldwell's young, beautiful fiancée undressing and posing naked and slowly stepping into the water, with her lovely breasts, her luscious hips. Henry saw in her soul the devil lover. Her lust to sin floated off her like the stench of Henry's late wife's cologne.

Henry had seen the Ranger's bride naked. He would bet he had been first to see her naked, before Caldwell. That is how the evil bitch meant it to be, thought Henry. She exposed her body to him. He was pleased and agitated as he hobbled toward his carriage.

It was an entrance the equal of which was seldom seen, even in Houston City. Major General Felix Huston rode at the head of his troopers, sitting proudly in his saddle. Behind the snorting, farting horses of the troopers came the big speckle-bearded Ranger riding a white Arabian stallion abreast with three savage-looking white men. The summer air was thick with the sweet-sour aroma of manure. There were hundreds of horses on the continually damp streets of Houston City, and even more mules, oxen, pigs, dogs, ducks, gulls and chickens. Their excretions drew snarling swarms of flies. The gas from decomposing turds rose into perfume in the white afternoon heat. Loafers left bottles and card games and came to the doors of saloons to peer at the troopers and the Rangers as they passed on horseback. Girls in cotton vests, their hair flowing loose, looked down and smiled from second-floor windows of the Ritz Hotel.

"I'm going to get me a whore," said Saginaw Boswell.

."I expect we could all use at least one whore apiece," Big Foot said. "Except for you, Matthew. I don't suppose men who are engaged to be married should consort with whores, should they?"

"Big Foot, for once in your life, you are correct," said Matthew.

The other Rangers laughed.

"She got you whipped already, Captain," Saginaw Boswell said. As the youngest and newest of the Boca Chica Rangers, Saginaw had learned that the Ranger social order was based on the rule that the strongest and smartest were in charge, but not even the captain was above being joked with.

"Look sharp now, men," called General Huston back to his troopers as they approached the capitol.

"I'm liable to stomp his head in, that Mississippi sonofabitch," Fiddle Man said.

"Troopers, dismount," yelled the sergeant.

The nineteen weary, worried troopers, dripping with sweat, climbed from their horses and glanced at the Rangers and then stood at ragged attention. General Huston, his chest erect, walked onto the front step of the capitol, his sword tapping against his leg.

"Captain Caldwell?" the general said.

"What do you want us to do now, Matthew?" asked Big Foot.

"I'd appreciate it if you'd hold off on the whores until I'm sure if there's going to be any shooting," Matthew said, swinging down from the white horse. He pulled Sweet Lips from its saddle holster and tucked the shotgun under his right arm.

# 35

The muddy boots of Felix Huston climbed the eight steps to the second floor of the capitol, followed by the almost silent feet of Matthew in his moccasins. Albert Sidney Johnston, the secretary of war, waited for them outside the President's office. Johnston nodded abruptly to General Huston, the man who'd shot him in a duel three years ago, then smiled and shook hands with Matthew.

"Nice to see you, Matthew," said Johnston.

"Same to you, Albert. I've been wanting to ask whatever happened when you sent the army down to Cristolph Rublo's old place to look for General Savariego's Mexican soldiers," Matthew said.

"Matthew, there is nothing to tell, because I couldn't round up a large enough force to justify sending them. If General Savariego had been there waiting, he would have slaughtered the few soldiers I could send. My God, most of our men were on foot!"

President Lamar opened his office door and interrupted the generals. The President's dark hair was brushed back past his ears to collar length, and he was showing much forehead in front. His eyes were far apart and melancholy. He had a wide mouth with thin lips, and he wore a silk cravat and a high-collared linen shirt with pearl studs. In his left hand was a handkerchief, which he used to pat the sweat off his face. The underarms of his shirt were wet.

"Captain Caldwell, it pleasures me that you are here," said Lamar.

"Right now I can't say I agree with you," Matthew said.

"When you hear me out, you will change your mind. Come in," said Lamar.

"You're not carrying that shotgun into the President's office," General Huston said.

"Yes, I am, Felix," said Matthew.

"It is quite all right, General Huston," Lamar said. "In fact, I wish you would wait here in the hall."

"If Johnston is coming in, I'm coming in," said General Huston.

"General Johnston will wait out here with you, won't you, Albert?" Lamar said.

"I'll wait out here, but not with this bastard," Johnston said.

"Do you want to test me in the field again?" said Huston.

"Gentlemen, please," Lamar said. Johnston turned and moved stiffly away from them, favoring the old dueling wound in his left hip, making a cloud of cigar smoke. "Thank you for your patience, Felix. We won't be long."

Lamar shut the door and was alone in his office with Matthew Caldwell.

"I have big news for you, a great scheme," said Lamar. "I am not angry about this Henry Longfellow situation."

"I damn sure am," Matthew said. "He lied about the girl and that assault in Austin, among other things."

"Somebody broke poor Henry's leg, that's plain enough."

"Look at this."

Matthew unfolded the letter encouraging lawyer Bone to pay a $250 bounty for Comanche scalps.

"Did you authorize this?" asked Matthew.

"Let's go up on the roof," Lamar said.

Inside a closet was a wooden staircase that led up through a third-floor attic with two windows in each wall and opened onto a rooftop that had a twenty-by-sixty-foot flat deck, protected by a railing, from which the President could see most of Houston City.

Although it had scarcely rained in three months in the San Antonio and Austin areas, there had been two floods in Houston City in the same period. Buffalo Bayou had risen eight feet, and large ponds of water stood in the prairies beyond the cleared building lots that fringed the downtown area. Shanties and tents crouched between saloons and hotels and mercantile stores and dozens of empty or partly constructed lots. The trees had all been cut down and used up. Much of the city was a muddy bog. Drunks stumbled in the streets amid countless piles of wet horse apples.

"Look around and tell me what you see, Matthew," said Lamar.

Matthew noticed a brawl down at the corner of Main Street and Texas Avenue beside the hotel, and he hoped it wasn't his boys whipping troopers.

"I am serious. What do you see?"

"I see a hell of a mess," Matthew said.

"Would you smoke with me?"

"Sure," said Matthew.

Lamar produced two Cuban cigars. The men clipped the tips and lit the tobacco.

"You have spent quite a while in Austin," the President said. "I am not asking you why you did not arrest the Cherokee woman and her boyfriend, the spy who claims to be a doctor. I say if Henry Longfellow has a complaint with those people, he can go settle it himself, man to man. You and I have more important affairs."

"What about the scalp bounty?"

"I did not authorize it. Henry has such a hatred for these aborigines that he goes too far sometimes."

"Where can I find Henry Longfellow?"

"I believe he is in New Orleans. Forget him, Matthew. Just tell me this—from your experience in Austin, do you not agree that Austin is a much happier place for our government to meet than in this godforsaken, fever-ridden swamp?"

"Yes, I agree," said Matthew.

"But our serious danger in moving our capital is that we might bring the Comanche Nation down on our heads."

"I would say it is a certainty," Matthew said. "We're going to have to fight the Comanches if we're going to stay in Austin."

"And you are building a house in Austin, I am told, for your beautiful German bride-to-be. My congratulations. I know you want her to be safe in her home in Austin. But we have these damned savage Comanches sitting right in our face across the river, and I don't need to tell you what shape our army is in. You can look at General Huston and tell we are desperate."

President Lamar admired a half inch of glowing ash on his cigar.

"Captain, you say we are going to have to fight the Comanches if we intend to plant our capital in Austin. To that end, you have seen the pitiful stockade fence they tried and failed to build in Austin. Austin has no defense against the Comanches. We have General Savariego and his Mexican army marching somewhere in Texas, and more Mexican armies with more generals behind them, and trouble with savages everywhere, even with the Cherokees, who were supposed to be our allies."

"What about the Cherokees?" asked Matthew.

"I have heard Chief Bowl is in the pay of the Mexicans and will turn against us at a signal and slaughter our northeastern settlers."

"I wouldn't believe that of him," Matthew said.

"Well, we need pay some attention to the rumor. But our most urgent problem is the Comanches. I say our army—even fighting beside you Rangers—could not defeat the Comanches should war break out today. The Mexicans would attack us, the Cherokees would attack us, all the savage tribes would attack us—because they know the Comanches alone are more than we can deal with in a war. But I have an idea of a way we can avoid a war with the Comanches and expand and solidify our Republic at the same time."

Matthew waited, a foot on the railing, smoking the Cuban cigar and looking at the desolate prairies dotted with pools of water outside the city. For an instant Matthew feared Lamar might be suggesting a union with the United States.

"The Republic is going to buy all the land up to a line fifty miles west of San Antonio," Lamar said.

"We already own it," said Matthew, who was relieved to hear Lamar's plan was to expand the Republic.

"Yes, but we have this problem with it, don't we? Matthew, our five-million-dollar loan is soon to come in from the government of France. Count Alphonse Dubois de Saligny, the French consul assigned to Austin, was here in my office not a week ago, assuring me this money is coming. I am prepared to pay the Comanches a fortune if they will move back fifty miles west of San Antonio."

Matthew was seeing a map in his mind: San Antonio was about fifty miles farther west than Austin. A line such as the one proposed by the President would open up nearly a hundred miles of wilderness west of Austin for use by the Republic, including Matthew's ten-thousand-acre estate for Hannah and himself, and the two hundred fifty thousand acres for the Kerr Land & Cattle Company.

"This line would start at the Rio Grande and extend to one hundred miles north of Austin. We can negotiate a little on the southern end," the President said.

"What if the French loan doesn't go through? How will we pay for this?" said Caldwell.

"Taxes."

"The people don't want taxes. They're having hard times as it is."

"Matthew, you are an elected member of Congress. I have faith that the leaders of Texas will find a way to do what must be done," the President said.

"What makes you think the Comanches will sell?"

"This is gold I am offering. Not even a savage would turn down gold."

"Indians have the peculiar idea that nobody owns the ground they walk on."

With two fingers President Lamar plucked his snuff box from his shirt pocket, but the powder he tapped onto the back of his wrist became a glob absorbing the humidity, and he wiped it off on the railing.

"Savages are very different from you and me, but they are similar to us in that they like things," said Lamar. "They like to have beautiful things to wear and things that are fun to play with. They will learn that gold will buy these things. If they don't believe anyone owns the land, anyway, then why not take our gold and move back fifty miles?"

"How do you intend to present your plan to the Comanches?"

"Matthew, I am counting on you to do it."

"I thought as much."

"You're the only man who can. Everybody knows of Old Paint. All the Mexicans, all the savages—they know of your spotted beard and your uncanny prowess, they fear you, they respect you. If there is one white man the Comanches will listen to, it is you."

"What would I tell them?"

"You would bring their big chiefs, their leaders who have the power to make deals, to San Antonio, where we will have a meeting with them at the Council House to negotiate the amount of gold they are to receive for moving back fifty miles. They make their X on the paper, we pay them the gold—and our new capital is safe, our Republic expands, and the land claims west of the Colorado River suddenly become reality. This will be a great step forward on our expansion all the way to the Pacific Ocean, Matthew."

Matthew thought of Hannah, of her kiss on his lips, of their future. Lamar's plan might be historically sound. Two hundred years ago natives had sold Manhattan Island for a string of beads, two axe heads and a handful of nails, it was said. Two years ago the Sioux had sold all land east of the Mississippi River to the United States government, as if the Sioux owned it. Neither side in this Texas negotiation would trust Comancheros to arrange a meeting. A military expedition led by Felix Huston to carry the message would be massacred. Matthew knew the Comanches admired courage above all. One man might be allowed to ride into Comancheria. If there was such a man, Matthew had to agree that Lamar had picked the right one.

# 36

**C**ristolphe Rublo was a mind connected tenuously to a body by a spiral of spirit. His mind was off in a long, moonstruck dream. He swirled among ghosts, was shined upon by the eyes of angels. Phantoms moved through his dreams. He saw a muscular figure that looked like himself crouched on a rock, watching as someone claiming to be other than he himself gouged through the flesh and bone of his left arm with a small knife. Pain ate his nerves, but it was fear that disconnected his mind from his body.

He knew in his dream that his body was being horribly abused, that he was being poked and tormented and led by a rope, but it didn't matter what happened to his body now that his mind was no longer living inside it

In Rublo's dreams his worlds were constantly changing from red fields of demons to giant silver fish under blue waters, from a boy riding a pony across a wide plain to the hiss of a panther in the night. He heard gurgling sounds, like rushing water over rocks, or like crowds of people talking all at once, and then he would hear music, a violin sonata from the salon room in the hacienda after dinner, or the accordions of street musicians. Pictures passed through his dream, halting and sharpening; he saw a magnificent white Arabian stallion.

"Of course," Rublo said aloud. "Of course."

Batista was passing by the goat shed and heard the madman speak for the first time since the loon had been tethered to the pole.

"Where is my horse?" the madman said.

"You don't have a horse," said Batista.

The clouds in Rublo's dream whirled apart and left a clearing into which more pieces of memory moved. Yes, he did have a horse, a fine white Arabian. And he remembered his own name—Cristolphe Rublo—and his family's plight, their million acres stolen by the Texans. But where was his horse? His mind told him he had seen his horse recently, but where?

"Where is my damn horse, you impudent goat keeper?" Rublo said.

Cautiously, Batista edged closer. He knew this madman from someplace. The arrogant tone of voice, the haughty lifting of his whiskery chin—these were very familiar.

"You are a crippled lunatic without even a name, much less a horse," said Batista.

"You will tremble when you hear my name," the madman said.

"Tell me."

"My name is Cristolphe Rublo," said the madman. More information was returning to his mind now. He remembered his family was powerful and rich and dangerous to their enemies. "See! You tremble. Your hands are shaking."

Batista stared at the gaunt, scabby face. Yes, this madman was Cristolphe Rublo.

"Rosie!" Batista called. His wife appeared in the doorway of their *jacale*. "Rosie, come out here."

She fetched her machete from inside and walked toward her husband and the madman.

"Is he giving you trouble?" Rosie asked.

"Rosie, this is Cristolphe Rublo."

Rosie looked at the madman, who was licking his lips as if he had developed a painful thirst.

"He does look a little like Cristolphe Rublo," said Rosie.

"Woman, I am Cristolphe Rublo!" the madman said, bringing his attention back to the moment. "I can make you rich. You and your husband cut me loose and take me back to my family estate in Mexico. I am too weak to make the journey by myself. I need your help. If you do this for me, I will pay you beyond what you can imagine, more money than you have ever seen, and when I get my family estates back from the Texans, I will make you two the overseers of the hacienda, the kitchen, the grounds. What do you say?"

"Do you know me?" asked Batista.

Rublo studied the squat brown man with the flattened features. No, he looked like so many others. Rublo looked at the woman. Heavy, big-breasted, fat-lipped. They were peons. They would never do to be in charge of a hacienda or anything more important than a herd of goats. The image of the white Arabian stallion kept intruding, and suddenly Rublo remembered that he had confronted Old Paint and had lost his horse, his arm and almost his life.

"It doesn't matter if I know you," Rublo said. "I need your help to escape to Mexico, and I will make you rich. Our Mexican armies will come and destroy these Texans, and I will make you the king and queen of San Antonio. How does that sound?"

"Don't you remember me?" asked Rosie.

Rublo looked at her again. He felt a tug at his memory, a strain, something familiar about her voice. He was very tired and weak. He needed food and water. There was a long way to go to reach Mexico. Rublo had to trust these people.

"Such a lovely woman as you, I should remember. It will come to me, I am sure," Rublo said. "Please tell me where we met."

Rosie squeezed her fingers around the handle of the machete.

"Three years ago you raped me," she said.

# 37

Antonio Rocca, master carver, had worked off and on for half a dozen years fashioning the big rosewood armchair, planing and sanding, cutting and polishing, examining it from all aspects. Sometimes he would sit almost motionless in the chair for hours, shifting his buttocks and his thighs and back and elbows in subtle movements, trying to find the exact shape and points of contact in which the chair and his body would blend and the nature of the rosewood would absorb all the tensions of his system and make him invisible.

But just as Antonio was sensing that he was finally about to learn to be absorbed at will into the universe of the rosewood, his landlord came to the door demanding money. Antonio had begun using so much time and passion on the rosewood chair that he had neglected the carving jobs—the table legs, the gates, the angels—that paid his way in the world. His three grandchildren helped him load the rosewood chair onto his cart, drawn by an old black mule. The oldest boy walked beside his grandfather and the switchy-tail mule as they took the rosewood chair up the mission road for eight miles into Military Plaza in San Antonio for the Saturday morning market.

Dora Kerr saw the old man and the boy plod into the plaza. The black mule pulled a cart in which a large object was draped by a red and blue blanket woven in the dancer patterns of the Mayan mountain tribe that were Antonio's ancestors.

"What a gorgeous blanket. Oh, I simply must own that blanket," Dora said, tugging Hannah's shoulder and pointing. Hannah had been looking at crockery, baked clay in rust color with a high sheen. She was buying serving ware for the house she and Matthew Caldwell would soon occupy in Austin. The Saturday market in Military Plaza was the premier shopping place in all of Texas, Dora assured her. Desperate pilgrims on their search for utopia had sold Dora their pipe organ at the market a few weeks ago; the organ, now meant for the Kerrs' mansion in Austin, was being stored at the Fincus warehouse, a stone building near the hotel.

"That blanket is Central American Indian of some sort, I know it is," Dora said. "I saw one like it at an exhibition in New York City. It's a work of folk art. The perfect thing to hang on a wall in one of our guest bedrooms. Let's go bargain with the old man."

Hannah was the interpreter. She could make herself understood in her formal, classical Spanish, and other than native idioms or Mexican Indian dialects, she could understand the sense of the words she was hearing.

Hannah instructed the vendor to crate the crockery and deliver it to the Fincus warehouse, where Mr. Maurice would pay from the Caldwell coffers in the hotel vault. Dora took her hand and led her across the plaza, dodging vendors and horsemen, avoiding hordes of black, glittery grackles that made a nerve-ripping racket in the cottonwoods in the middle of the plaza, peppering the benches with their excretions.

Doc Swift watched the two women through the window of Pope's gun shop.

He and Pope had worked through several nights to make a breech-loading rifle of a French design that was known to both of them. But no amount of hammering or prying would force their home-fashioned breech to fit properly. Pope had sold Doc a Colts revolver of .31 caliber with two extra cylinders—a total of fifteen loaded shots—but there was no way to build the rifle to Doc's specifications without sending for the needed breech, perhaps to New Orleans, perhaps to Delvigne in France, and the return might take six months or a year, if it came at all. Doc was looking at a breech-loading rifle of Pope's design. It fired an elongated .40-caliber bullet and had a handsome polished rosewood stock and body. Doc was weighing buying this Pope rifle against the possibility of waiting to search for a Delvigne breech when he looked out the window and saw what was putting him in the humor for stopping a while longer in San Antonio.

It was Hannah Dahlman, crossing the plaza with the wealthy actress Dora Kerr. Doc had been truthful when he told Dora he had seen her on stage and enjoyed her performance. She was a saucy redhead with a powerful projection of herself. Beside her, the smaller and younger black-haired Hannah looked like a girl, a student, determined and curious and vulnerable. Hannah fascinated Doc. As he rested in Captain Caldwell's bed at the Fincus Hotel, the image of the Ranger's bride-to-be would not leave his mind. Doc had been avoiding her. He was powerfully drawn to her, but an arrangement had been made between Hannah and Caldwell. Doc stayed away from her, yet he wanted her more each hour that passed.

What was it about her? He had barely met her. Why should he think this was the woman he had been waiting for? Was it partly because her age and her long, shining black hair made him think of his sister, Cullasaja? He had always loved Cully. Had she not been his sister, he would have admitted she was sexually desirable to him.

Antonio Rocca and his grandson halted their black mule near the governor's palace. Vendors with stalls and wagons and baskets of poultry and rabbits were packed three deep at the front door of the palace. Flies were darting from piles of manure to hands and faces, from the rumps of oxen to sacks of beans, from puddles of urine to slabs of beef. Hornets swarmed around an Indian woman who was selling pieces of beeswax. Three Mexican dandies wearing black pants decorated with silver *conchos* and black sombreros trimmed in gold rode past on fine horses. If three such roosters rode out in the *campo* and met a crazy Texan, thought Antonio, men would die. Here in San Antonio, the population was more than half Mexican, but everybody called themselves Texans now, and the three dandies were relatively safe.

"Don't look," Dora said to Hannah as they approached the cart decked with the glorious blanket, "but that gorgeous Dr. Swift has stepped into a doorway to our right and is keeping us under observation. I intended to save this gossip for lunch, but I'll tell you now, before he might join us."

Hannah felt a sudden fear.

"Gossip?"

"Lawrence had a chat with Dr. Swift. Them both being New York gentlemen, university boys, they began comparing histories, and what do you know? Dr. Swift is the scion of the Swift Shipping Company, quite a flourishing business. He is a descendant of the Irish writer Jonathan Swift."

"*The Travels of Gulliver?*"

"Yes, the very same. Why, even Lawrence has heard of *Gulliver's Travels*. Of course, Lawrence had to have learned something at Yale besides drinking and gambling and chasing about looking for sex. So, my dear, besides being gorgeous and unmarried, our Dr. Swift is heir to a shipping fortune."

Hannah caught her breath. It was the connection with the great writer—whose masterpiece was a favorite she had heard read aloud and quoted by her father, the professor, who was witty in his despisal of the hypocrisies and inequities and foolishness of European society. Hannah heard what Dora said about the shipping fortune, too. That this physician should be rich as well as beautiful and intellectual, this was more than she dared allow herself to comprehend. Hannah was pledged to be married to Matthew Caldwell. If indeed Dr. Swift had come into her life, he had come too late.

"*Quanto cuesta el blanketo*, please?" Dora said. "Oh, Hannah, you take over. Ask him the story of that blanket, then how much he wants for it. Offer him half of that."

Antonio Rocca was surprised to hear that the red-haired woman wanted to buy this old blanket. One of his brothers had left it in Antonio's house years ago while visiting from the mountains. Antonio owned much finer blankets than this. The woman wished to hear a story about the blanket. Antonio invented a story. He told her the blanket was woven by his grandmother, a princess, in his ancestral village in the jungles on the south slope of El Popo. What did the figures of the dancers mean? Antonio studied the dancers and said they mean happiness. They are little gods of happiness. Very quick and light on their feet, full of joy. How lovely, and how much would he sell the blanket for? Antonio began to reckon. He owed his landlord for back rent and would like to pay up for a year in advance. Then there were the necessities—food, tobacco and wine. And the three grandchildren to feed and care for. This red-haired woman looked prosperous. He chose a sum that would carry him and his grandchildren for the rest of their lives.

"I must have two hundred for it. In gold," Antonio said.

"We will pay you twenty-five dollars, and we will pay in silver, not gold," said Hannah.

"You are a hard-hearted girl to bargain with a poor old man. All right, silver. But I must have one hundred," Antonio said.

"Thirty-five."

"Beautiful young lady, have a grace toward those of us who are not so fortunate. This blanket is without a price in gold or silver. It is the work of the fingers of my own grandmother. This blanket has warmed me all my life. I would never sell it, except my village is starving and disease has killed our cattle."

"Give him whatever he wants," said Dora, who understood bits of the discussion. She knew where El Popo was.

"Fifty," Hannah said.

Antonio lowered his eyes, peered at his toenails sticking out of his sandals, then looked lovingly at the blanket and sighed, "All right. Fifty."

"You have bought the blanket for fifty dollars in silver, quite a high price in this part of the world," Hannah said to Dora.

"This is art, darling. I have an eye, and money is money everywhere. Tell the old man and the boy to fold up the blanket and put it with our other goods."

Antonio's grandson hopped onto the cart and peeled the Mayan blanket off the big rosewood armchair.

The instant she saw the rosewood armchair, Hannah imagined Matthew Caldwell sitting in it.

Most of the chairs she had seen in Texas were too small for Matthew. He had to sit with his knees up to his chin in the brown and white calfskin chairs in the Fincus lobby.

And never in her experience from hearing about the baronial halls of Germany and the great houses of France could she have imagined a more beautifully carved chair. The chair sat on the cart exuding its own majestic light.

"Dora, you have offered to lend me money. Now I must ask you to do so," Hannah said.

Dora was examining a tray of small stone figures held by an Indian wearing a sombrero and a breechclout. She had bought her furniture in New Orleans and was having it freighted to Austin, but she needed clever frontier artifacts to place about the house. Dora looked up and saw the rosewood chair.

"I am going to buy that chair for Matthew for a wedding present," Hannah said.

"How much are you going to pay?"

"Whatever the old carver asks."

"That's not very smart of you, dear."

"Nevertheless, may I borrow the money? I can't have this put on Matthew's bill."

"Of course," said Dora. "Anything you wish."

But Antonio did not want to sell the chair. He no longer needed money.

"Honored sir, why did you bring the chair to market if not to sell it?" Hannah asked.

"Things are always changing," said Antonio.

"I must have this chair," Hannah said.

"I am sorry, gentle lady, but there is not a price that would buy this chair from me."

From Pope's, Doc had watched vendors and other shoppers form a semicircle around the two women and Antonio and the boy at the cart with the rosewood chair on it. Doc was drawn to the scene. He joined at the back of the crowd and shouldered his way toward the front.

Hannah flushed as she heard herself say, "I will pay you two hundred dollars in gold."

Cries of astonishment went up from the crowd. Antonio was stunned. He could pass the rest of his life on two hundred dollars in gold. He looked at the rosewood chair that was nearly ready to make him invisible. Instead, the chair was giving him a different gift—freedom to do the work that he loved the most. Antonio was an artist. He would carve another rosewood chair.

"Gracious lady, I pray this chair brings you great happiness," Antonio said.

As Antonio and the boy lifted the chair down from the cart, Hannah said, "Dora, I don't know what came over me. I have never spent such a sum. It's as if I have a fever."

Dora laughed. "Oh, darling Hannah, spending money is one of the great pleasures in life. I'll have the hotel boys carry the chair to the warehouse and wrap it in linen in the Kerr storage bins so Captain Caldwell won't know until the proper time."

Doc Swift stepped out of the crowd and nodded to Hannah and Dora. He touched his hat brim with his right hand, as was the custom in the South and in Texas. He looked toward the rosewood chair, which had its four carved legs now in the dirt of the plaza as two white-shirted servants from the hotel waited to be told what to do.

"Captain Caldwell is a fortunate man," Doc said.

# 38

**D**ora had invited Doc Swift to join them for lunch at the Café Sanchez. While Hannah went to supervise the storage of the rosewood chair in the Fincus warehouse, Dora ordered for all of them—plates of quesadillas with goat cheese folded into the tortillas, scrambled eggs on the side, a mug of beer for herself and for the doctor a jug of pure artesian water cold-fresh from Ingrid Sanchez's well. Dora felt she had the doctor's rapt attention, a sense that she had developed from communing with her audiences.

She told him stories of London and New York theater life backstage, gossip of actors he knew from having sat in the boxes and watched them perform. Dr. Swift said he had no patients in London or New York who were from the theater world, but he wished he did because he found them fascinating.

"But now you will have me, of course," Dora said. "When Lawrence gets this frontier madness out of his head and we return to New York, I will be at your office at the slightest twitch of pain."

"My office in New York is so informal that it is usually closed," the doctor laughed. "But in London I do keep a proper office in Chelsea and a flat in Cheyne Place. If you should turn up at my door in pain, I would do my best on your behalf."

Dora gave him a deep study and an amused smile.

"I would suppose your bedside manner is quite accomplished," she said.

Romulus could smell the musk coming off her. He wondered how intimately she knew Matthew Caldwell.

"I'm quite confident of it," he said. If he had met this woman even a few days earlier in his life, she would have had her legs wrapped around him in another hour, but now she could mean nothing to him.

He saw a flicker of annoyance cross Dora's face and heard Hannah say, "Dora, I'm so sorry. I didn't mean to be gone so long."

Doc rose and stepped aside so his back would not be toward the girl. He saw that her cheeks were lightly sunburned, or blood had rushed to her skin from exertion and excitement.

"Happy to see you, dear," Dora said, and Romulus heard the ice crunching beneath the pleasantness of her tone. Hannah heard it, too, but she swallowed and plunged into her explanation and her plea that Dora must go to the hotel and sign the bill for the rosewood chair. As Dora listened, she glanced at the doctor. She had aroused him. She could feel that she had been close to an adventure.

"Very well, but you stay and keep our good doctor company while I do this signing matter," said Dora. "Keep him here. Don't let him escape me."

"I should go back to the hotel," Hannah said.

"Nonsense. I'll be back in a few minutes," said Dora.

"Please, Miss Dahlman. Sit and talk to me," Romulus said.

"This man is a physician, Hannah. He is perfectly safe company," said Dora, sending a seductive smile toward those blue eyes that now were intent upon the German girl. The doctor should be quite ripe for adventure by the time I return, Dora thought as she left the café.

Hannah felt a tingling shock from the doctor's fingers touching her shoulders as he pushed her chair close to the table. She was sitting where Dora had been. He sat down and took a drink of artesian water. Hannah realized she was staring at him. She looked down, picked up a tortilla with her fingers and bit into it. A strip of cheese clung to her lower lip until she pushed the cheese into her mouth. She realized he was watching the way she ate. If he was going to continue examining her, she thought, she would speak sharply to him about it. Because he was a physician did not mean that he could treat her like someone who had requested a diagnosis.

"That is an extraordinary chair you bought today," he said. "Mexicans are brilliant wood-carvers and masons, every bit the match of the finest in Europe."

"I am pleased that you approve of it," she said.

"But there is nothing else on this frontier to match the finest in Europe," said Romulus. "How will you ever get along out here? Dora will have her fun and then go back to New York. I will do what I must do and then return to London. But you? You are here for life. How will you ever stand it?"

"When you speak of Europe, Dr. Swift, you are speaking of the Europe of wealth and sophistication. The Germany I left is crowded and filthy and brutal. In Texas I have hope for a grand new life. In Germany I had no hope."

"Forgive me. When I speak of Europe these days, I usually mean London or Paris. A sign of age. Getting set in my ways."

Hannah smiled, and he wondered how she kept her teeth so white, brushing them with leaves and cobs and salt and soda. Strong white teeth must run in her family.

"If you are old and set in your ways, you are certainly in a strange place to show it," Hannah said. "Going exploring in Comancheria is hardly a sedentary act. What on earth are you looking for out there? A treasure?"

"Perhaps."

"I am sorry if you think me overly curious. In my family, being curious is a virtue."

"Maybe I am going into this exotic place for no better reason than to see what is there? Being the curious sort, you would understand that."

"You and I are doing very much the same thing," she said.

"I would love to see your favorite places in Paris with you," said Romulus.

Her cheese stuck to her teeth and burned her lip. She drank from Dora's beer mug. She felt sweat on her forehead and in her armpits. She could hardly believe what she had heard.

"I have a confession," she said. "I have never been to Paris. I have only read about it and seen pictures and heard it described by my father."

"Then I will take you to Paris," said Romulus.

"Maybe Captain Caldwell and I will encounter you there someday."

"I want you not to marry Caldwell," Romulus said. "I can't imagine you would rather be with him than with me."

Hannah felt as if a fist had punched her in the chest.

"You know very well I am pledged."

"That matters not at all to me. I love you," he said.

"I must go," she said.

He grasped her forearms and kept her from rising.

"You are crazy. You don't even know me," she said.

"But you don't deny that you feel the love for me that I feel for you?"

"Yes, I deny it. What an insane, impertinent thing to say. I don't care if you are a physician, you had better mind your etiquette."

Romulus released her and sat back against the leather of his chair. Maybe she was right. He was insane for her. What had happened? Had he changed worlds too abruptly? He looked at Hannah, who brushed a hank of black hair off her forehead. Yes, he was right. She was the one meant for him.

They heard Dora's voice at the doorway.

"Here I am, you two, back again! And look—what a surprise!"

Filling the doorway behind Dora they saw the broad body of Matthew Caldwell and the gray glint in his eyes as he looked at them.

# 39

The five of them met at sundown at a table in the Fincus patio. After finding Hannah with Dr. Swift at the café, Matthew had escorted her back to the hotel even before stabling and grooming Pacer. Matthew hadn't liked what he'd seen in the faces of Hannah or the doctor, but he accepted the greeting kiss of the startled girl, and then told Dr. Swift he had best find himself a new room, and to meet him with Hannah and the Kerrs in the patio when the lobby clock said seven. Matthew had something important and secret to tell them.

Hannah spent much of the afternoon relieving her nerves by bathing in the river with Dora and some other women from the town and being massaged by Maria de Bethencourt, who had learned the art of facial and anatomical manipulation in Madrid. Dora and Maria and Mary Maverick quizzed her about wedding plans and about the intentions of Dr. Swift, but Hannah dared not tell them of the offer of marriage by the physician. She felt a powerful connection to this man, there was no denying it, but big, hairy, rough, honest Matthew Caldwell was her bridegroom and her future. A part of her did appreciate the irony of her situation—from no husbands and a life of oppression and doom to two potential husbands and new possibilities in life that she could not have imagined.

Mr. Maurice ejected two hardware salesmen from a second-story room so that Dr. Swift could move into it. Doc passed the afternoon reading Deuteronomy—the story of deliverance—in the hotel Bible and writing a long letter to his parents in New York, another to Lord Pluck in London and a third to his sister, Cullasaja, at Bowl's Town. In every letter he mentioned meeting Hannah Dahlman.

As drinks were served on the patio, Lawrence Kerr told them of how he had that day killed a wild boar with a spear. It was an Indian lance—a Comanche lance, fourteen feet long, Big Foot had told him—and admittedly the beast had been wounded by shots from Big Foot, Saginaw Boswell and Lawrence himself, but the light of life never left the animal's eyes until Lawrence on foot drove the spear point into its throat.

"Congratulations, darling. Today you are a warrior," Dora said.

"Don't be tart with me, dear. This is not some theatrical make believe. This is life and death on the frontier. Man against animal," Lawrence said. He was into his third tequila, and his blood was still rushing from the thrill of the kill.

Hannah kept her eyes away from Dr. Swift, an action that did not go unnoticed by Matthew. The Ranger had bathed and put on his lightest beaded doeskin jacket for the summer evening, and he had brushed his hair and his beard. Blackbirds could be heard rustling in the cottonwoods while bullfrogs croaked from the river. Matthew drank tequila with a mug of beer, as did everyone at the table but Dr. Swift, who drank only water. Under the table Hannah felt her knee touching Matthew's knee. It was solid. She had begun to think of the doctor as an etching she imagined, beautiful but unreal. She drank more beer than she should have. She supposed Matthew's announcement would be about their wedding, and she was frightened.

After a dinner of beefsteak, refried beans, rice and avocados, coffee was poured all around. Lawrence was fairly drunk, and Dora was drunk enough to have begun flirting with Dr. Swift, who favored her with polite smiles and small talk. But soon the interest turned to what Matthew had to say.

"The first thing I have to tell you," said Matthew, "is that Hannah and I are going to put off our wedding for a few weeks."

Hannah looked around, surprised, as her husband-to-be rubbed the back of his hand across his black and white beard, smoothing the hair. Doc kept his eyes on the sunset and the cloud mountains, but he felt a leap of joy. A few weeks. Much could happen in a few weeks.

"But, Matthew, why?" Hannah asked. She was feeling that the marriage had best be soon, before she fell to temptation with the doctor.

"I am going into Comancheria on a mission for the Republic," said Matthew. "I am going to invite the Comanche chiefs to a council here in San Antonio. If this succeeds, Hannah, our land will be open for our use. The same for the Kerr Cattle Company. This is a secret for now. We don't want to start a rush in land speculation before we see what the outcome of this council will be. I am telling you, Hannah, for obvious reasons. Lawrence and Dora, I am telling you because you are Hannah's friends, and I want you to continue to help her with whatever she needs until I get back."

"I say, Captain Caldwell, I find it hard to believe you will get back. I understand no white man has ever gone out and crossed Comancheria among the savages and returned. Sorry to be a realist, but I have learned a lot about the Comanches from Big Foot and the Rangers. I should guess the odds against you are like betting your fortune you can hit a thirteen on a single wheel at roulette," Lawrence said.

"Captain, why tell me?" asked Doc.

"Doctor Swift, you are going with me," Matthew said.

"What? Me?" said Doc.

"You've been curious to see what's in Comancheria. You come along and find out," Matthew said. "With me and Sweet Lips to look after you."

"But when?" said Doc.

"At daylight."

"I can't be ready by then. My rifle is not finished. I don't have supplies," Doc said.

"Is there some reason you want to stay here while I am gone?" asked Matthew.

"No. No, of course not," Doc said.

"Doctor Swift, get your supplies together and find a good rifle and a strong horse, because you and me are heading west at first light. You'll find out all you want to know about Comancheria."

# 40

Doc Swift rose and tossed his napkin on the table. Caldwell's words were a sign, a reminder that Doc had come to Texas on a quest. He nodded to each of them, smiled at Hannah, and then walked out of the hotel gate.

He strode across the plaza toward Blue's Tavern, where he knew he would find Pope, the gun maker, downing a quart of ale. Doc was making a mental list of what he would need—a mustang horse, a mule, the breech-loading rifle of Pope's design, powder, lead and fish hooks. The three-pound Cherokee Bowie knife from Velasco's cousin in Bowl's Town would be handy. He would tuck his medicine kit—restocked with cutting instruments and with opium and morphine tincture even more powerful than laudanum—inside his bedroll. For food, he would buy smoked, jerked meat in the plaza and buy coffee and tortillas and salt from Mr. Maurice. He would wear his Colt's pistol and carry his spyglass, both newly purchased from Pope. He would wear his black coat and wide-brimmed black hat—the knee-length coat he'd received in barter for medical services in Austin, and the hat that had been presented to him as a gift by the citizens of the new capital—as protection from the sun—far better to be sweating than burned. He would need a large water bag made out of a cow's stomach. He would bring his journal with two pens and six nibs and a tin of carbon to be mixed with water to make ink, so that he could record in words and drawings the factuality of the man-ape and life among the native peoples, and, of course, the cavern of treasure that Knows All Charlie and Fritz Gruber said was there—and the wisdom he was seeking for his mother's people. He needed rigging for the mule and new canvas for tenting. He was excited to be crossing the frontier into the unknown.

Hannah felt as she had felt when she first laid eyes on Matthew Caldwell, stunned and speechless. This big wild man with the long black hair and spotted beard, pledged to be her husband, was suddenly leaving her again, this time going into unexplored wilderness filled with Huns. He could disappear from her life forever. And the blue-eyed physician with the keen passion for her—he was leaving her as well. The frontier was swallowing them up and might not give them back. Everything in Texas changed the moment she thought she had a grasp on it.

Dora and Lawrence got up to dance to the music of guitar and accordion. They were the only dancers in the patio and were happily drunk and amorous. Hannah shifted in her chair.

"Matthew, there is nothing between Dr. Swift and me. I can tell you think so, but there isn't," she said.

"I believe you."

"Why do I feel otherwise?"

"I wouldn't know. Hannah, I have to go take care of some things for a couple of hours. I'll knock on your door to say good night."

"Please stay and talk to me, Matthew. We've had so little time together."

"Tonight. We'll talk tonight."

"But you're going across the frontier, and you don't even know what is out there. Surely, you can talk to me for a while first."

"Would you do me a favor?"

"Yes."

"Kiss me on the lips."

"Everyone is watching."

"That's all right. You are my woman."

His lips felt like grainy leather as she pressed her lips against them for a moment, and his lips parted slightly and his tongue touched her teeth.

Hannah pulled away, smiling. Everyone had seen that she was loyal.

"I'll knock on your door tonight. We'll talk then," Matthew said, and moved his large body gracefully and quickly through the patio gate, his leather fringes waving.

At the livery he put his saddle on the white Arabian and rode across the river on the Commerce Street bridge toward Batista's *jacale* up in La Villita. Matthew couldn't go into Comancheria and leave the mad Cristolphe Rublo as a perhaps lifelong burden on Batista and his wife. Matthew would need to decide at once what to do with Rublo. There were no prisons or hospitals. He could turn Rublo loose to natural predators, or he could ship him back to Mexico, or he could choose the most final solution and shoot him.

The full moon was rising above the hill where Batista's *jacale* stood. Matthew rode at a slow walk. From behind the shed Matthew could hear the thunk of a spade and the chink of a hoe. He knew the Batista garden was back there. Then he heard scraping sounds in the earth. Matthew slid down off the white Arabian and led the horse around the shed. Batista with a long-handled spade and his wife with a hoe were working in their garden in the moonlight. There were beans growing in rows.

"Planting by moonlight?" Matthew said.

Batista tapped the earth with his shovel and looked around at Matthew.

"You came softly," said Batista. "The dogs didn't bark."

"Good evening, *señora*," Matthew said.

Rosie Batista scraped a smooth path in the dirt with her hoe, like a trail, and Matthew stepped closer to them, leaving moccasin prints.

"I'm here to pay what I owe you and to take that lunatic off your hands," said Matthew.

"You owe us eight dollars," Rosie Batista said.

"I'll make it ten for good measure. I know he has been a bother to you," said Matthew.

He handed her a gold piece which she squinted at and then deposited in her bosom.

"Where is the lunatic?" Matthew said.

"You are standing on him," said Batista.

Matthew looked down at his shadow in the moonlight across the freshly dug and turned-over earth, a low mound.

"Why did you tell me I didn't recognize the madman? He was Cristolphe Rublo," Batista said. "He was very rich and powerful. One time his family owned all the land for miles and miles around here."

"Well, then he is home," said Matthew.

"Rublo loved that white horse you are riding," Batista said.

"I give him credit for good taste in horses," said Matthew.

"I wish I could dig him up and kill him a thousand more times," Rosie Batista said.

*A migration. The fortunate circumstances of our lives are generally found at last to be of our own procuring.*

Hannah was trying to pass this horribly anxious evening by at least pretending to read *The Vicar of Wakefield* by Oliver Goldsmith, a book she had borrowed from Dora Kerr. But Hannah's eyes and thoughts kept getting stuck on the heading of chapter three.

*A migration. The fortunate circumstances of our lives are generally found at last to be of our own procuring.*

Hannah felt these words were written directly to her.

From her window she could see the full moon climbing above the cypress trees along the river. The light from her bear oil lamp shone across the pages of Goldsmith and attracted moths. She sat in a chair beside the window. Her bed was tightly made, her clothes put away on shelves hidden behind a drape of blue velvet. Nothing was out of place.

She missed her father tonight.

She missed all of them from home tonight. Her mother, her sister, her brothers, the unfortunate, romantic younger brother Justinian, who was right now lying on the cold, wet stones of Hannover prison. She missed her gray Persian cat, whose eyes reminded her of Matthew Caldwell's eyes.

And what of Matthew Caldwell? Was she beginning to miss him? Or was it only that she was depending on him, and if he vanished into the wilderness she would be alone and penniless in a foreign country. Well, not alone entirely. She felt she had made a friend in Dora. But she had not laid eyes upon a man in Texas she would consider for matrimony once she had seen Matthew Caldwell. Except for Dr. Swift. But why had such a choice man reached the age of thirty-nine unmarried? It made no sense that he would then suddenly declare that he had been saving his love all that time for Hannah. She felt a jolt in her stomach at the thought of him, but she took a breath and tried to return to Oliver Goldsmith. This was her own procuring. She must forget Romulus Swift. Matthew Caldwell would be her husband. If he returns. What would be the chance of a New York physician returning from a journey into an unknown land filled with savage barbarians? But it was true that Romulus seemed to have attributes that would serve him well among the Comanches. He might even return to tell the tale, as his ancestor Jonathan had done, at least in his imagination. But even if he did return, he would surely have forgotten his mad declaration of passion for Hannah. A thirty-nine-year-old bachelor with such charm and education and money must encounter gullible young women as a regular thing. Hannah told herself to be strong and to concentrate on her forthcoming marriage to Matthew. He was her future, the object of her procuring. She had to believe he would come back from this journey across the frontier. He was a Cossack, a fierce warrior, respected by all, and yet Hannah had seen a soft, boyish part to him. She loved his pleasure when she kissed him, and the warmth in his gray eyes when he thanked her for saying she loved him. Like Hannah, he was a displaced person of strong character, looking to put down roots in Texas and grow a family. He was a man of action, always moving toward a glorious future.

What of the doctor? She wished him health and success and happiness, of course, but she was conflicted about his return to San Antonio.

Better she should forget the doctor.

Hannah heard a rapping at the door. She put down her book, stood up and looked at herself in the mirror. She was wearing a muslin dress, borrowed from

Dora, in the color of Egyptian sand, which contrasted with her black hair. The skirt was full, the waist tiny, her shoulders bare and sprinkled with sweat. She had no idea what to expect from Matthew Caldwell as a farewell-for-now speech or action. It occurred to her that he might demand a husband's favors in advance of the ceremony, his life being at risk. The thought excited her, but she would not give in to such a demand, nor did she really expect it even from such a woolly wild man. The mirror assured her that she looked her best. This was the picture of her he would carry in his mind into the wilderness. She heard the rapping again, softly even though it was early in the sultry evening.

She opened the door and looked into the lively blue eyes of Dr. Romulus Swift. His cropped hair was flat against his skull, and drops of sweat rolled down his forehead. His right arm was behind his back.

"You can't come in," she said.

"I am not asking to come in," he said.

"Go away. I am expecting Captain Caldwell at any moment."

"I'm not afraid of Captain Caldwell."

"What do you want?"

"I want to remember how especially beautiful you are tonight, Hannah."

She felt her cheeks flushing.

"Dr. Swift, you must go away. I will say good-bye to you at daylight when you and Matthew ride out."

His right hand came into view. In it he held a cluster of bright pink roses growing on a single stem. Hannah recognized them as China roses of the type called Old Blush, because the color became deeper and bloodier each day after the roses were cut. She knew he must have snipped them from Mary Maverick's garden. His right hand also held a pale blue envelope.

"Please," he said.

Hannah accepted the roses and the envelope, which had no name on it and was sealed with candle wax.

"Thank you," she said. "Now you must go."

"I would like one kiss," said Romulus.

"I can't do it," she said. "Please go."

"Just one kiss."

Hannah shut the door in his face. She turned and leaned her back against the door and breathed rapidly until she heard his boot steps receding down the hallway. A kiss! How impudent of him. What did he take her for? Would she have kissed him if she hadn't expected Matthew to come upon the scene? Certainly not. Why should he even consider that she might?

She sniffed the roses. With her thumbnail she tore through the candle wax and opened the envelope. Inside was a piece of linen paper on which he had written the words *I love you. Wait for me. Romulus.*

Hannah gasped. She put the paper back inside the envelope. Pulling aside the drape, she hid the roses and the envelope beneath a stack of lace-trimmed underwear. She closed the drape and sat back down in her chair. Goldsmith lay open beside the lamp, and the full moon had climbed above the window.

Hannah got her breathing under control and forced her mind to begin trying to read at page thirty-three of *The Vicar of Wakefield.*

One hundred and eighty four pages later, she read, "... *all my cares were over, my pleasure was unspeakable. It now only remained that my gratitude in good fortune should exceed my former submission in adversity.*

*THE END.*"

A whippoorwill called from a cypress tree. Bullfrogs croaked, and crickets sang. The night air was heavy and dark. Oil was low in her lamp and the wick sputtered. It had been hours since Dr. Swift left. What could have happened to Matthew? Hannah knew it was very late, but how late? She went into the lobby, where the young assistant manager was sleeping on top of the front desk. Hannah looked at the clock.

It was two-fifteen in the morning.

Her apprehension vanished and anger overwhelmed her. She imagined Matthew Caldwell drinking at Blue's Tavern with his rough companions and probably with Lawrence Kerr. She'd heard tales of Matthew's epic drinking bout with Sam Houston. Though the Ranger had not been drunk in her presence, the women in the bath whispered stories of his ferocious drunken conduct on several occasions. Yes, this was what a Texas man would do—stay out drinking, and the hell with what the woman felt. What could Hannah do about it, anyway? She could lecture him sternly and order him to change his behavior. She was furious.

Hannah went back to her room and took off the Egyptian sand-colored muslin dress and hung it on a nail behind the drape. She glimpsed her naked body in the mirror. Matthew Caldwell would never see this body, she told herself in anger. Hannah pulled on a gingham gown that covered her from throat to ankle. She blew out the lamp and crawled into bed. It was too hot for a sheet, too hot for clothing of any kind, but she needed to be covered. She pictured the Ranger in his planter's hat pouring whiskey into the hole between his beard and mustache while drunkards contended for his approval. Hannah felt abused and hurt. If he thought no more of her than to get drunk instead of visiting her on what might be their last night together, then she didn't want him. It was better she find out now what kind of man he was rather than after the wedding ceremony that Hannah now swore to herself would never take place. He could never have her, not even if he came begging. Let him go get himself killed.

"Hannah."

The crown of Matthew's hat was at the window, which was six feet above the ground, as the rear of the hotel was built on stilts because of flooding. She pretended to sleep.

"Hannah," he said a little louder.

She made a point of breathing deeply and regularly with her eyes shut.

Hannah heard a rustling, scratching sound, and then a heaving, and she thought she felt the room tilt and a board creak. She sat up and saw the bulky dark figure of Matthew Caldwell, who had hauled himself up the six feet and jumped through the window.

"Hannah, look, I know I haven't made a real big success with you yet," he said. She was listening for a slurred tongue and sniffing for liquor, but as yet could detect neither.

"Is this the time to try to make it up to me—three in the morning?" she said angrily. "I have been waiting in this room since shortly after dinner. Where have you been?"

"Don't be mad at me, Hannah," he said.

"Why not? How can you explain this careless disregard of my feelings?"

"It took me a long time to find the *alcalde*. He was down the river, fishing. Then I had to wake up Sam Maverick to get a trustworthy witness."

"What are you talking about?"

"Can you read this?"

Matthew handed her a piece of paper that had a red official stamp at the bottom with two sprigs of yellow ribbon.

"It's too dark," she said.

Matthew lit a candle and looked at the light moving across Hannah's strong features as she read the document. Her dark eyes grew wider.

"Matthew!" she said.

"Hannah, I know it ain't fair to you, to bring you here all the way from Germany and then me go off and maybe get killed and leave you abandoned in Texas. So I saw a lawyer tonight and made a provisional deed of five thousand acres, half our land, for you and the other five thousand to be split up among the boys at Boca Chica Station. They'll make sure you are safe."

"I can't take your land," she said.

"The land is what you came over here for. You have earned it. It's yours.

You accepted me at my word. Now no matter what happens to me, you'll have a place to bring that family of yours someday."

"Matthew, I don't know what to say."

"Yes, you do," he said.

"I love you."

He moved closer. His large, hairy body bent down toward her, and she moved the candle so as not to set his chest afire. She got the feeling that he was going to climb upon her, mount her.

But he stopped and said, "I love you, Hannah. You get busy with our wedding plans, because when I come back from Comancheria there is nothing more that can prevent us from getting what we want."

Matthew returned to the window and put a moccasin on the sill and his two hands on the sides, turning his shoulders so they would fit through the space.

"Why don't you use the door?" Hannah said.

"My horse and mule are loaded and waiting down below."

"But you're not leaving until daybreak."

"I decided to be gone before the town wakes up."

"Are you leaving without Dr. Swift?"

"No, Doctor Swift is packed and waiting down below, too."

Hannah leaped up and ran to the window. She grabbed Matthew's beard and twisted his face around and kissed him on the lips. She was aware of movement, heard leather creaking and horses breathing below, and she wondered if Dr. Swift could see her kissing Matthew.

"All right," she said. "Go on, now."

Matthew slid through the window and landed lightly on the ground. Hannah leaned out and looked down into the darkness in the shadows of the cypress trees, where she could see Matthew swinging into the saddle of his big white horse. Farther back against the trees she could make out another man on horseback with a pack mule.

"I'll be waiting for you," Hannah called as the two riders passed from her sight.

# 4 2

The sun rose above the low hills to their left as the two men rode at a trot toward the forbidden realm of Comancheria. The Moorish walls of San Antonio had long ago disappeared behind them. Doc Swift rode a few paces in front, bending over the neck of the mustang he had traded the Morgan for, keeping his eyes on the wagon ruts that formed the road called the Camino Real. Matthew Caldwell had tied the lead ropes of both mules to the saddle of his white Arabian. A trot was as fast as the mules would willingly go, and not for long at that. But Matthew believed the mules would be worth the trouble. He looked back at the two canvas bags on his own mule. The load rode well. Matthew looked at the burlap, canvas and leather containers and the cow's stomach full of water that were strapped to Doc's mule. Matthew admired the packing job, which showed the economy and tight hitches of the physician's sailor background, and he approved of Swift's handling of the mustang. Trading for the mustang was a good idea, Matthew thought. The Ranger had considered riding a mustang into the wilderness because of the feral breed's fabulous toughness and endurance, but he had elected to stay with his white Arabian stallion. A big white horse was a thing of awe and desire, a possessor of magic, for Comanches. Everything Matthew was bringing with him was something the Comanches would seriously want, including his chest pelt, beard and scalp, and shotgun, Sweet Lips.

"We're veering off to the west right about here," Matthew said.

"Fritz Gruber came down this northern track when he escaped Comancheria," said Romulus, reining back his mustang.

"This is the old royal road from Saltillo to Nacogdoches. If you backtrack on this road you'll find yourself in deep east Texas, not far from Bowl's Town. How is your sister doing up there?"

"She is searching for peace."

"She's a special person, your sister. I'd hate to see her come to grief." The Ranger twisted around in the saddle and threw one brawny leg over the horn while he felt in his shirt pocket and came up with a cigar. Matthew sucked the end of the cigar and spat the bitter brown fluid. He lit the cigar and blew a smoke ring. "Right about here is where Fritz Gruber was found."

Doc smiled.

"You know the story?" Doc said.

"I was in Military Plaza when they brought Gruber in with that axe blade sticking out of his skull. He was hugging the gold bars to his chest." The Ranger pointed at an animal trail that led toward the west through the scrubby brush. "I figure Gruber must have walked onto the Camino Real from that path. If we backtrack on that path, Doctor Swift, it will take us straight into Comancheria."

"Where are the white cliffs we see in Austin?"

"The cliffs curve off to the east a few miles north of here, and the ground gets lower and flatter south all the way to the Gulf. This is our best route into Comancheria, I figure. We'll climb the cliffs from the south. We'll come up from the southeast and cross the Guadalupe River where it cuts through the cliffs, and there won't be any doubt about whose country it is from then on. The first person we see will be a Comanche, or else dead."

Matthew licked his cigar and looked around to find Doc staring at him in that way he had of appearing to be making a diagnosis.

"What the hell are you looking at?" Matthew said.

"Your nose, actually. I was marveling at how well it has healed. And I can't see any trace of your fractured jaw, but distortion could be hidden by your Appaloosian beard."

"What do you figure, as a medical man, caused my beard to break out in white and black patches like this?"

"I don't know. Could be an inherited characteristic. I've ridden through the town of Coldwell in north England, or Scotland, rather. Is that where you are from?"

"My father and my grandfathers are from that part of the world, yes. My father used to tell us our family history once a year when I was a little boy."

"I don't remember seeing any, but there may be an unusual number of mottled beards in Coldwell."

"What would that have to do with it, Doctor Swift?"

"I'm just trying to answer your question. This condition could be inherited. It could also be a dysfunction of the mind, some sort of trauma. When did your beard become spotted?"

"I never had a beard until my wife and children were killed three years and three months ago. After that, I didn't give a damn about shaving, and the beard grew out full and spotted black and white."

"Then this mottling might be an emotional reaction. Of course, it could be simply the aging process that affects some follicles differently. Since old hair is always falling out and new hair replacing it, and your colors stay the same, I'm going to guess this condition is God's way of marking you out from the herd."

Matthew turned and lowered his leg back to the side of Pacer and stuck his moccasins into the stirrups.

"Doctor Swift, you are a strange fish," Matthew said. "You're an educated man, a fistfighter, a Yankee, a rich half-breed who lives in London—and you come all this way to find a pot of gold like you're some common grub."

"If I tell you what I am really searching for, you will laugh."

"I can always use a good laugh," Matthew said.

"Fritz Gruber says his life was saved by a creature that looks like an ape but seems almost human. That's what I'm searching for."

"Now, why would I laugh about something like that?" said Matthew. "For all we know, we might run into dozens of creatures no white people ever heard of. You might can fill the whole London zoo."

They covered thirty-five miles the first day and forded the Guadalupe at a gap in the cliffs at dusk. Weeks without rain in the hills had left the river a string of blue and green pools connected by thin clear water over the rocks on which the two riders and their mules crossed. Beyond the river they were on high ground, across the frontier into Comancheria. They made camp in a pecan grove and unloaded their animals. Matthew watched the physician's strong fingers adroitly undoing the many sailor knots. There was an art to tying and untying knots, Matthew believed, and this doctor was the best he had ever seen. Matthew heaved the two canvas bags off his mule and laid them on the ground. The horses were unsaddled, and in a few minutes Matthew would tell the doctor to take them down to water while the Ranger and Sweet Lips kept guard.

Romulus took a stiff brush out of a bag and began stroking the tan mustang's neck and long brown mane. The front of the mane lay like a woman's hair arrangement across the mustang's forehead between her two almond eyes with thick lashes. Doc was trying to make friends with this still half wild horse, and he spoke gently and crooned and breathed into the mustang's ears until her ears quit twitching back and forth and she began listening to his voice and reading his breath.

"How come you are so good with horses?" Matthew asked.

"I love horses."

"It must be the Indian in you."

"I find myself wondering if I hear a hint of an insult."

"Doctor Swift, don't get your bile hot. I ain't trying to insult you. If I want to insult you, you won't have to wonder. I'm just speaking my mind."

"Maybe it is the Indian in me," Doc said. "I grew up with horses in New York, but I first learned to love them as a child at my Cherokee grandmother's farm in North Carolina. This mustang here, she doesn't trust me yet. But the more I touch her and rub her and sing to her, the more she will let me into her heart. I want her to realize she and I are partners, bound together by fate."

"She's a fine-looking mare. Intelligent eyes. What do you call her?"

"I think I'll call her Gaucha. She looks very much like my favorite polo pony I had in college, an Argentine mare named Gaucha. Gaucha could turn in a wink and be off at high speed in a different direction, and she could run all day. She won many matches for me by thinking faster than I did."

Doc led the animals down the sandy bank to drink from a pool in the Guadalupe while Matthew prowled the area with his ten gauge shotgun in his arms. The two men groomed their horses and hobbled all four animals to graze inside the grove. Matthew opened one of his canvas bags and scooped out two handfuls of oats to supplement the Arabian's nutrition. The mustang was self-bred to thrive on wild grasses. Doc assumed both canvas bags were full of oats—the Ranger had already laid out his bedroll and produced a cold meal of tortillas and jerked meat from his saddlebags. But Doc heard a clank from one of the bags, an odd scratch and scrape as Matthew retied the top of the bag of oats.

"Damn, I hope I didn't break any of them," Matthew said.

"What are they?" asked Doc.

"Mirrors. Mirrors and hairbrushes."

Matthew opened the bag and removed several mirrors and wooden brushes with pig bristles.

"They look all right," he said.

"I take it these are gifts for the Comanches," Doc said.

"I cleaned out the town of what people could spare. This brush here belongs to Mary Maverick. Some buck warrior is going to get a thrill brushing his hair with it. See the little MM scratched in the wood? This brush goes to a chief."

"You think you can buy the Comanches' friendship with mirrors and brushes? Like giving toys to children?"

"Never underestimate how strong a Comanche man feels about his hair and his appearance," Matthew said. "No, I can't buy their friendship. I don't even want their friendship. But I can sure get their attention with these mirrors and brushes. I don't confuse the Comanches with being like children, Dr. Swift, and I damn sure don't treat them like children. But they ain't the same kind of human being as you or me. Well, they must be somewhat like you."

"Comanches are ancient enemies of Cherokees."

"Comanches are ancient enemies of everybody. I mean, you and them do share Indian blood."

"I know what you mean."

They heard the howl of a wolf from a distant hill and then an answering howl from nearby, close enough to cause the horses to snort and dance. Coyotes began yipping at the moon. Doc unstrapped one of his bundles and unfolded it into a narrow canvas tent. He propped up each end and the middle of the tent with sticks carried for that purpose.

The Ranger grinned. The physician had brought a funny-looking tent. He had more Yankee than Indian blood, after all.

"We'll do up a small fire in the morning to make coffee," Matthew said. "No fires at night."

Doc swatted a mosquito on his cheek and looked at the blood on his fingers. After a few seconds he smashed another on top of his left hand. He looked at the Ranger, who was chewing a piece of dry meat, carefully avoiding the painful sockets where teeth were missing. Caldwell sat quietly, cross-legged, listening to the sounds of the night.

Doc slapped his cheek again and smashed another fat mosquito.

"My uncle Charlie makes a salve of garlic that drives mosquitoes away and doesn't stink so much it keeps you awake, but that's in North Carolina. There's not enough garlic in Texas to defeat these vicious little pests," Doc said. "So I'm going into my tent."

Matthew's eyes followed the scene as Doc crawled into the canvas tent and lowered at the foot end a flap that held mosquito netting. There were two net-covered windows on either side of Doc's head.

"How can you stand it out there, Captain? My Lord, I see mosquitoes in black bands around your face."

Matthew picked up the stub of his cigar from a rock and rolled the tobacco with his tongue. The acrid saliva seemed to soothe the hurting in his teeth.

"Tell you the truth, Doctor Swift, mosquitoes don't like the taste of me. They whine all around me, but I kind of enjoy that, like listening to singing. Every so often a mosquito will bite me and die. To hear the rest of them carry on when that happens, it's like an opera. One died just now, and it sounds like *Don Giovanni* out here."

"*Don Giovanni?*"

"It's an opera. By Mozart."

There was a wriggling in the tent and Doc's face appeared at the foot, peering through the mesh at the Ranger, who sat on a log watching the horses and listening to Mozart being sung by mosquitoes.

"Forgive me, Captain. I didn't realize you are a person of education."

"I ain't educated, Doctor Swift. My late wife's mother was an Italian countess. She made me start attending the St. Louis Opera House if I was going to marry her daughter. I saw *The Marriage of Figaro* and *Cosi Fan Tutte*, that I remember from Mozart. The last opera we saw in St. Louis before we packed off to Texas was *William Tell*. It was written by a fellow named Rossini, who the countess said was bound to be kin to her. I like good singing, but everything I know about opera is because of my late wife and her deceased mother, not because I'm educated."

"What did you do to support your family in St. Louis?" Doc asked.

"I had a dairy farm that did right well. And I hired out as a guide and guard to survey crews going west in Missouri to Independence. That was a high-paying job, because the crews were so scared of the Shawnee and the Sioux."

"You weren't afraid of the Shawnee and the Sioux?"

"I ain't afraid of anything except my Maker, Doctor Swift. But I do respect the Shawnee and the Sioux. They are fierce, proud people, and they will die to protect their hunting grounds. I treated them decent and tried to avoid violence. I grew up among Indians on the frontier in Kentucky and Missouri. I know Indians."

"Native peoples are different from each other. To know one tribe is not to know them all."

"Indians are all of one heart, Doctor Swift," Matthew said, rising and picking up Sweet Lips. "I'm going to stroll around our area. You catch some sleep. If I get tired, I'll wake you to take over. I'd hate for us to get our horses stolen and our heads cut off the first night out. The boys at the station would hooraw my ghost about that."

Romulus rested his head on his arm and closed his eyes. His muscles ached. It felt good to be tired and now cozy in the tent he had bought last night at Pappas Mercantile, after pulling the owner out of a card game to open the store so Romulus could inspect his wares. The sleeping tent was the latest item to arrive from New York sporting goods store Abercrombie & Fitch, a novelty that looked to Doc as if it might be handy. Already, it was saving him from mosquitoes. Romulus closed his eyes. Immediately he saw Hannah. He saw her profile and smelled the sweat on her forehead. He saw the question in her eyes when he asked for a kiss. She had wanted to kiss him. Romulus wondered if he should tell Matthew Caldwell of his desire for Hannah. The Ranger had shown him respect as an honorable man in Austin and believed him when the doctor said he was not a spy. The Ranger had refused to arrest Romulus and his sister despite an order from the President. Did Romulus, then, as an honorable man, not owe it to Caldwell to confess his feelings?

No, he thought. Certainly not. Not at this stage of the game. There was really no misdeed to confess. There was only his passion, and that had not been overtly returned. It would be stupid to turn the Ranger against him at this part of the journey. He must stay with the Ranger and find the Comanches, who would know of the Little Pigeon River and perhaps of the man-ape. Still Romulus felt Hannah close to him, and he kissed his own elbow as if it were Hannah's cheek.

A scream sounded out there in the night, followed by another scream and a loud moaning, crying wail. Some animal was dying out there. Being torn apart by a bear or a mountain lion or a panther. The coyotes left off their yapping for a few moments, and the wolves ceased to howl, out of a natural respect, while the creature died. Then the night was again taken over by mosquitoes humming and owls hooting. At the tension caused by the screaming, Hannah's presence had faded away. Romulus concentrated upon making her return. He was falling deeper into an exhausted sleep, concentrating on bringing back Hannah's face and flesh.

He smelled an old, familiar rotting meat stench, and in his dream appeared the face of the man-ape, the eyes full of curiosity, the forehead bulging, the gray complexion, the foul breath; the man-ape lifted his upper lip and showed his teeth sharp as ivory awls, and the sensation that Romulus felt throughout his mind and body was that he was being summoned, and it was urgent that he arrive before the next wisdom vanished.

# 43

In mid-afternoon of the second day after they crossed the Guadalupe and climbed into the hills, they watched a small herd of eight hundred bison pass between two clusters of oaks and rumble across a valley that was turning yellow with summer grass. Beyond the herd, on a long ridge line half a mile away, Matthew saw three or four riders appear. He gestured to Doc and pointed. The original riders were joined by another dozen. Doc mouthed the word "Comanches?"—there was no use trying to converse because of the thundering hooves and growling bellies of the traveling bison—and the Ranger nodded.

When Doc looked back again, the riders had increased to a hundred. And within minutes there were five hundred, then a thousand. Matthew squinted at the riders and frowned. Could it be that many Comanche villages had communed in order to hunt, and these passing beasts were all that remained of a mighty herd? Otherwise a thousand—and now they saw two thousand riders on the ridge—was an extraordinarily powerful assembly of Comanches. Never had a Texas farmhouse or settlement been raided by more than forty or fifty Comanches. This was an incredible number of Comanches that faced them from half a mile away. Why would so many have gathered? Matthew wondered. Were they warring against Mexico? Was Texas their goal?

Doc dug into his saddlebags and found the spyglass he had bought from Pope. He put the six-power lens to his eye and studied the far ridge as if sweeping a shoreline from the deck of a ship. Doc spoke in amazement and handed the spyglass to the Ranger. Matthew looked through the lens and also muttered in wonder.

Standing in a rank with their heads raised, giving the impression they were carrying riders, were two thousand wild mustangs, the forward scouts of a vast party. The mustangs came over the ridge and down onto the plain and were followed by untold thousands of wild horses, showering dust, hooves pounding the earth, heading in the direction of the Ranger and the physician, not in a chaotic stampede but in an orderly gallop, their tails and manes flying.

Doc felt Gaucha tremble against his knees. He knew she felt the call to join the herd. With difficulty Doc urged Gaucha off to the north, following Matthew on his stallion with the mules in tow. Both men urged the mules to move faster. Doc and Matthew estimated the angle of approach and the speed of the herd of mustangs, and they pointed their animals toward a stand of live oaks that should be about at the edge of the mustang passing.

But the mules refused to move faster than a halfhearted canter.

The Ranger saw that there was not enough time. His Arabian would be overrun by the oncoming galloping herd. He glanced back and saw Doc a few yards behind him, struggling with his mustang. Matthew let go of the ropes of the mules and hauled Sweet Lips out of its sheath.

Looking at the charging eyeballs and frothing lips and flared nostrils of the wild horses that were racing upon him, their front ranks fifty yards away, Matthew fired both barrels of Sweet Lips into the air with one pull.

The explosions and fire from the shotgun made the Arabian rear up on its hind legs, and the kick of the butt of Sweet Lips hurled the Ranger backward out of the saddle. Matthew felt a rock gouge his shoulder as he landed and rolled over to see the booming of the shotgun influence the flowing herd of mustangs to veer south by a few yards and the thousands of wild, free horses hammer past.

The two mules were caught in the sweep of the galloping herd and were carried along, running as they had never run before in their lives, trying desperately to keep up with the mustangs and not be trampled.

Gaucha resisted Doc's reins and knees and voice and joined the herd, running at the very edge, running wild like the feral colt she once was. It was an exhilarating shock for Swift, like a cold wave at sea that rises and sprays over the prow into the face, to be running wild and free with thousands of wild horses. He caught a glimpse of the two mules, obvious by the packs they carried, bobbing along in the midst of the herd, and for an instant Doc thought of his Thoroughbred Donnybrook and Cullasaja's horse and all their belongings washing down the Colorado River valley in the flood. But Romulus released himself to the primal ecstasy that burst from within his soul as, mounted on Gaucha, he ran with the wild horses.

Romulus dropped the reins and clutched Gaucha around the neck with both arms, crooning into the mustang's ears and breathing warm air into her aural passages. Gaucha ran with the herd for three miles, until the horses reached a creek with a steep bank, where they flowed out like syrup to pour down the bank into the water. Gradually Romulus felt Gaucha coming back into their partnership. As the main surge of thousands of horses plunged down and across the creek to continue their run in the direction of Mexico—a run, Romulus felt, that was born of the joy of running more than any other reason—Gaucha allowed her rider to turn her away from the herd. They were becoming partners again. Gaucha's wild runaway life was back under human guidance, as was the wild runaway life Romulus had been experiencing.

A dust cloud hung over the trampled earth all the way to where Doc met the remounted Matthew Caldwell, riding toward him through the red haze, his straw planter's hat crushed at the crown.

"You see our mules?" the Ranger asked.

"In the middle of the herd, running for their lives."

"Maybe we got lucky and the mules broke loose somehow. We better take a look."

"That was quick thinking to fire your shotgun," Doc said.

"It turned the herd, all right. But you can bet the Comanches heard it."

The two riders followed the beaten track of the horse herd. Grass was flattened for half a mile from side to side, and into the distance out of sight under the dust cloud along the line of the running.

"That's what we want, isn't it?" asked Doc.

"I'd rather we find the Comanches on our own terms than they find us on theirs," Matthew said.

The tree line of the creek came into view.

"There's your mule, Doctor Swift," said Matthew.

They could identify the mule from a distance by the cargo that was still strapped on—clearly it was Doc's, and the packing had held when the mule ran headlong into a pecan tree and almost folded around it. From the hang of the mule's head, they could tell its neck was broken.

Then they saw a figure come up over the edge of the bank and hurry to the mule and pull a knife to begin sawing through the harness. The figure had not noticed the two riders. The Ranger had already reloaded Sweet Lips—his shotgun was always loaded except when he had just shot it or when he was cleaning it—and now he slid Sweet Lips out of its sheath again and gigged the white stallion into a gallop, followed instantly by Romulus on Gaucha.

The figure looked around at the oncoming riders, and they saw he was a black man wearing city clothes.

# 44

Jefferson Antone's spirits rose in perverse amusement as he considered the increasing absurdity of his situation. While surviving incredible hardship and brutality—and the smashing of a dream—he had traveled nearly two thousand miles to reach this wilderness creek bank where he was about to be murdered.

A great speckled man and a man in a black hat and coat had appeared on horseback from out of the dust. What were white men doing up here? Jefferson wondered. This was said to be Comancheria, where white men dared not venture.

Jefferson was thirty-five years old, born in Boston, a harpooner and the son of a harpooner in the whaling fleet. His mother was a housekeeper at the Ritz Hotel. Both of his parents were second-generation citizens of the United States. Jefferson's grandfather was born in Boston the son of a free man, went to sea and became a harpooner, and his grandmother took in laundry. His great-grandparents were natives of West Africa, but Jefferson felt more a product of New England's cold salt water and deep harbors and granite than of ancestors whose true names he did not even know.

He wore a derby hat and the ruin of what had once been a fashionable suit, now out at knees and elbows.

Jefferson folded his frog sticker, slipped it into his pocket and lifted his hands into the air.

"I've got no money," he said.

"Who are you?" asked the man in the black coat who was mounted on the mustang. The great speckled man on the white horse kept his long shotgun aimed in Jefferson's direction.

"Jefferson Antone."

"How in the hell did you get here?" asked speckled beard. Jefferson was impressed by the speckle-bearded man's bearing, as if he were a boss on a dock gang or a bosun on a whaler. The other white man was wide-shouldered and strong, but he looked to Jefferson like the more reasonable of the two. Jefferson knew from the knots on the packing that one of the strangers had served at sea. He decided to invest his hopes with the man in black.

"I got here all kinds of ways. Lately it's been walking."

Jefferson lifted one foot to show them his leather soles were barely hanging on around holes that revealed blisters and bruises on the swollen flesh beneath.

The man in black dismounted and looked at the twisted neck of the dead mule and then turned his gaze upon Jefferson Antone, who noted the sea-blue eyes.

"I want to compliment whoever tied the knots in the packing on this mule," Jefferson said. "I hated to be cutting instead of untying them, but I was in more of a hurry than I realized."

"You see another mule anywhere?" asked speckle beard. Jefferson noticed he had a thin white scar down the middle of his nose.

"No, sir."

"What do you know about knots? Are you a seaman, Antone?" asked the man in black.

"Eighteen years a harpooner with the Wilcox whaling fleet out of Boston, sir," Jefferson said. "My daddy was a harpooner, and so was his daddy before him."

"Untie those knots," said the man in black.

"Yes, sir," Jefferson said. The two white men watched the black man's fingers manipulating the ropes. "I am not a thief, you understand. I thought this cargo was, ah, lost at sea, more or less."

The bundles slipped off the mule and fell to the ground.

"I see you truly are a seaman," said the man in black.

"A harpooner, sir, not merely a seaman. You are a former officer on a ship of major importance, I would wager, a master of knots."

Jefferson saw a gray edge of hard biscuit poking out of a flap from the bundles that had been on the mule. He couldn't help licking his lips.

"Go ahead and eat," the man in black said.

As Jefferson cracked the hard biscuit and began to chew on a segment of it, the hairy man dismounted and walked over so close that Jefferson was looking down at beaded patterns on buckskin moccasins.

"Try again telling me how you came to be here," the big man said.

"About six months ago, in the middle of a blizzard in Boston, my wife and I was reading in *The Boston Globe* that there was land in the Republic of Texas that was practically being given away, twenty-five cents for an acre of prime country, and if we was to become citizens of the Republic we would get a nice homestead to start. That sounded good to us. Owning some land of our own. I could stay home from sea at last and be among my family."

"What happened to your family?" asked the man in black.

Jefferson squinted and judged the kindly expression on the man's face. "Serenity!" he called. "You come on out here now."

A chocolate-skinned woman of thirty, wearing a torn calico dress, edged out of the brush. She aimed at the two strangers with a Mexican *escopeta*, a scattergun that had an effective range of thirty feet.

"You let my man go," she said.

"Please, Serenity, put that gun down. Please," said Jefferson

The woman lowered the gun but continued to stare angrily at the two strangers.

"Ephraim!" Jefferson called. "Desdemona! You come out here now."

From deeper in the brush came Ephraim, a twelve-year-old boy who was dressed as if he were about to go off to school, except his clothes were frayed and dirty. Peeking around behind him was his sister, Desdemona, a tiny girl of six who was dragging a canvas pouch.

"This is my family," said Jefferson.

"Come here, little girl. Desdemona. Let me see that canvas bag," said the great hairy man.

"Show it to him, darling," Jefferson said.

The Ranger took the canvas pouch from the girl's hands. The strap that had attached it to its companion pouch was ripped in half. He shook the pouch and listened to it jingle. He untied the pouch and looked inside. "I set out with twenty mirrors and now I've got five hundred," he said. "Look here at the only thing that came through unhurt."

He showed the other stranger an ebony hairbrush with MM initials on the handle.

"Help yourself to the food in the packs," said the man in black to the Antones. "There's jerky and biscuits and coffee and sugar and lard and salt. And some corn and beans."

The Antone family fell hungrily to eating from the packs.

"Why aren't you in Texas on your own land?" asked the man in black.

"Sir, I wish to heaven that was possible. Let me tell you, Serenity and the children and I made it through a fearful journey from Boston by coach and by steamer—a Negro family traveling is an annoying sight for most whites, especially the farther south we came, where they started to act like we was runaway slaves and continually threatened us with arrest. Serenity had saved us a batch of greenback dollars from her wages as a seamstress and my pay as a harpooner, and we thought with the whole United States in a money panic, and Texas even worse, this was a good time to buy us a piece of land cheap. After we left the steamships, we bought our own horses and a wagon and drove into what we hoped would be our own version of Tahiti—you as a sailing officer, sir, will know what I am trying to say—where we would be free and safe and the masters of our own lives."

"What happened?" asked the man in black.

"We got arrested in the first Texas town we came to—Nacogdoches."

"Arrested for what?" asked the man in black.

"Sir," Jefferson said, "there is a law in Texas that makes it a criminal act to be a free Negro anywhere in the Republic. I am a free man and the son and grandson of free men. Slaves are the only Negro people who are allowed in Texas."

The man in black glanced at the big hairy man, who was tying the pouch of broken mirrors and hairbrush bits onto his saddle roll.

"Is this true?" asked the man in black.

"Oh, yes sir," Jefferson said.

"Captain Caldwell, is this true?"

"It's true," the hairy man said.

"Show him your back," said Serenity.

Jefferson peeled off his tattered coat and shirt. Hard muscles knotted in his belly, and his shoulders were mountains of muscle that had thrown thousands of harpoons. He turned his back to the two white men. "Look what they done to him," Serenity said.

Jefferson's wide back looked as if it had been fried like strips of bacon.

"They whipped him in Nacogdoches and stole our money and made us ride out of town in our wagon with just the clothes on our backs," said Serenity.

"Was it a lawman stole your money?" the hairy man asked.

"No, sir. It was a crowd of rough men who said they had fought to make Texas a place where there wasn't no Negroes. Some of them did have on old soldier jackets, but they looked like a gang of robbers, not soldiers to me," said Serenity.

Jefferson put his shirt and coat on and said, "We was rightly afraid to run to the east, because we know gangs of white men hang and burn Negroes over that way, and so we ran to the west, out here where we heard there wasn't any white men."

"Why didn't you run north and go back to Boston?" asked the man in black.

"We talked it over as a family and decided to go to Mexico," Serenity said.

"Mexico? You want to go live under Santa Anna?" said the hairy man.

"Negroes have full rights as citizens of Mexico," Jefferson said.

"You had full rights as a citizen back in Boston," said the man in black.

"But we couldn't afford to own no land in Boston," Jefferson said. "Down in Mexico there is beaucoups of land available for Negroes."

"You're being swindled," said the hairy man.

"Begging your pardon, sir. But swindled of what? Our money and possessions were stolen in Nacogdoches. Our horses died and wrecked our wagon when they fell trying to climb the cliffs up to this high ground. We have nothing to be swindled out of."

"Bandits will kill you," the hairy man said.

"What for? We've got nothing bandits could want. I'll take my chances with bandits before I will try to cross Texas again," said Jefferson.

"That *escopeta* is a poor weapon," the Ranger said.

"It's broken. We found it this morning. The hammer is broken off, and we don't have any powder, anyways."

"Antone, I want you and your family to take my packs and provisions for yourselves," said the man in black. He unbuckled from his saddle the scabbard that held the breech-loading rifle Pope had built. He unstrapped a pouch and then handed the rosewood rifle and the pouch to Jefferson.

"This is a breech loader. You know how it works?"

"Yes, sir. We had one on ship. I shot sharks with it."

"Here are shaped bullets and powder."

"You are a saint," said Jefferson.

"There's a canvas tent you should unroll and cut up to repair your shoes," the man in black said.

Serenity, Ephraim and Desdemona—their mouths stuffed with jerky and dry biscuit—picked up the bundles that had been strapped on the mule.

"How far is it to Mexico?" Jefferson asked.

"Keep heading southwest and you'll reach the Rio Grande in another hundred and fifty miles or so," said the hairy man.

"Then we better butcher this mule before we proceed, hoping you gentlemen don't take it as an insult if we eat your property," Jefferson said.

"You got a good rifle now. Why don't you shoot a buffalo or a deer? You're going to walk past thousands of them," said the hairy man.

"Right. Good idea, sir." Jefferson turned to the man in black and bowed smartly. "Much beholden to you, Admiral." Jefferson gave a flapping motion to his wife and children. "We'll be gone then, kind gentlemen. God's blessings be upon you. If you ever need a friend in Mexico, look me up—Jefferson Lafayette Antone."

The Antone family scrambled down the bank carrying Doc Swift's packs and provisions and rosewood rifle. Matthew Caldwell mounted the white stallion.

"It was a foolish thing, Doctor Swift, to give that man your rifle," said Matthew.

"He needs it worse than I do."

Matthew sat up straight in the saddle and leaned back, stretching his chest and shoulders and yawning. Other than the dull ache in his jaw, he felt healthy and ready for whatever life might present next. The thrilling, glorious sight of thousands of mustangs running free was one that had pumped him full of energy. He took off his straw planter's hat. The crown was crushed, but the hat still had plenty of life.

"Is that what I suspect it is?" Doc said.

Matthew looked up and saw rising from the hills on the horizon three separate balls of smoke that floated in the air like small black clouds.

# 45

From the journal of Dr. Romulus Swift—
July 9, 1839

By my reckoning we have come ninety miles deeper into Comancheria in the two days since we lost our mules in the running of the wild horses. What a grand adventure that was! In the crucial matter of my yearning for God, which is intense, I consider myself a Christian-roseybuddhitarian, a light-headed way to explain my theology—Christian, Rosicrucian, Buddhist, Presbyterian, all mixed into one cosmological scheme. This theology broadens to include my soul's allegiance to the Master of Breath, and to my own spirit, which stirred me gloriously while riding Gaucha with the wild horses. I became a free-feeling, exultant, primitive spirit. I felt like wild laughter sounds. I was a strange being that is no stranger to me. Was I this in a former life? Is this another aspect of the life I am now living? Who was I? Who am I? Who is writing in this journal? Who is thinking these thoughts? What will become of Who is thinking these thoughts?

The man-ape appeared in my dreams again last night. It has been the same the last few times—the stench, the curiosity in the eyes, the baring of the canines and premolars where fangs should have been on an ape. When he appeared from inside me in my hallucination on the ship during the storm years ago, I felt he was protecting me. I don't have that feeling now. I have the feeling he wants something from me, but not to protect me. He may want my life.

This is a wondrous country we are in, a high plateau. We are more than two thousand feet higher than San Antonio. The earth is limestone with a light layer of soil. There are stands of oak and juniper and vast patches of grass mixed with shrubs and cactus. The trees are short and the plants of the almost arid type that indicate erratic rainfall, but the land around us is like a fountain. Springs burst from cracks in the limestone and form many deep pools and streams. These streams flow north and south and east through canyons lined with sycamores and pecans. The limestone caves are home to beehives and sweet honey. Caldwell—who seems unstingable—grabbed us a large honeycomb to eat—excellent for energy. With a fish hook, a piece of twine and the sacrifice of a few grasshoppers, I caught four nice bass out of the pool beside which we are camped. Caldwell cleaned the fish and cooked them on a spit. No restaurant in Paris could offer as great a taste as those bass.

I hear more wolves tonight than usual. They are some distance away, but there are a great many of them. It is as if they are at a gathering of wolves for some festive banquet. Caldwell is keenly listening. The stars are so bright and close tonight that I feel I could jump up and touch them. We have seen no more smoke signals. Caldwell appears to grow more intent upon his task the deeper we go into Comancheria.

Caldwell says a pack of wolves began following us several hours before sundown. He says they are watching us now and are silent because they think we don't know they are there. The night is bright enough that I can see to write in this journal, and I have seen no sign of wolves nearby, but Captain C says he has seen the flashes of their eyes. He says our horses smell the wolves. I look at Gaucha's flaring nostrils and twitching ears and nervous eyes. I agree.

Are we leading these wolves toward their kin that we hear in the distance, or do these wolves think they are driving us there?

A mist settled in during the night, while Doc was writing in his journal. In the morning Matthew and Romulus rode through a wet gray fog that covered the junipers on the hills. Steam rose from the cold-water springs. Romulus studied the ground as he rode. The earth was littered with clamshells and oyster shells and snails of many sizes. They lay in the mist as if sucking up the moisture. Romulus was reflecting on the time before time when this country had been at the bottom of an ocean. The thought was almost incomprehensible, but it was plainly true. The evidence was everywhere.

The doctor glanced to his right and saw six gray wolves come padding out of a patch of tall grass, their tongues lolling. The wolves remained at a distance of thirty yards, dark shapes in the fog, keeping pace with Gaucha. Romulus looked to his left. There were four more gray wolves forty yards away, idling along with the mustang's walk.

He saw the large figure of the Ranger on the stallion up ahead, entering what appeared in the ghostly terrain to be the opening to a valley. Water could be heard pouring from a spring into a pool. Doc's gaze returned to the ground, searching among the ancient remains of shelled creatures—and there, sparkling with pearls of dew, he saw a human skull.

Doc dismounted and picked up the skull and brushed off a few ants and beetles that fell onto tufts of black hair on the grass. The skull had been picked clean by scavengers and insects; not a patch of flesh remained. The strong, uneven teeth indicated a young person, probably around twenty. From the size of the skull, Doc presumed it to be a man. There was a fracture running across the temporal bone over the middle ear. This was a blow that would have caused hearing loss and perhaps paralysis but not death, Doc thought, but of course the skull being detached from its body was hardly a survivable circumstance. Doc looked around for more bones. The wolves both on his right and his left crouched down and watched him.

Doc saw scattered in a patch of cactus what looked to be the full complement of twenty-four vertebra that could have been attached to this skull. He examined the base of the skull and found a smooth axis where the cervical vertebrae would have been connected. No sign that the skull had been removed from the neck by a chopping or snapping. Doc studied the axis again and saw tiny white scratches that would have been teeth marks. This skull had been dragged away from its body after death.

Near the cactus lay a clavicle, twelve pairs of ribs that looked like spider legs clinging to the sternum, and several more bones he identified as scapula, humerus, radius, pelvis, femur, tibia and fibula. But he saw no metatarsals or metacarpals, which indicated the body's hands and feet had been removed, whether by an enemy using force or by some creature like a buzzard or a coyote—or a wolf, Doc thought, glancing at the two places in the fog where wolves crouched and waited.

But where were the clothes?

Scavengers and insects would have cleaned every bit of fluid and pulps and meat and flesh from the body, but they would not have eaten the clothes.

Walking slowly through the fog with Gaucha's reins in one hand and the skull in the other, the wolves creeping apace, Doc felt a fine tension, his senses increasingly acute, as he approached the head of the valley where he could hear water pouring.

"Draw this in your sketchbook, Doctor Swift," said Matthew Caldwell.

Before them were three skeletons tied to three live oak trees with arms outstretched as if in crucifixion, the radius and ulna bones lashed to tree limbs by rawhide thongs.

A dozen arrows had punctured the three bodies that were now skeletons. The arrows stuck into the trunks of the live oak trees.

"This is odd," the Ranger said.

"I should say so," said Doc.

"I mean, leaving the arrows. Look at those shafts. You got any idea how long it takes to make a straight shaft that will fly true out of mulberry or dogwood or ash? The feathers in these arrows are turkey and owl, not all that easy to come by. Comanches put a lot of work into making these arrows. To my knowledge they always try to retrieve their arrows when they can. Might be they were having such a grand time that they just said the hell with these fellows here."

Walking their horses, the wolves padding along silently in the fog, the two white men advanced farther into the valley. The valley floor looked cluttered with stones and weird plants in the grayness. They heard water rushing in a stream hidden by fog. The air on their skin felt cool and wet even though it was the middle of summer. Matthew slid Sweet Lips out of its saddle sheath. For a moment Doc wished he had Pope's rosewood rifle in his hands; the Ranger had been right, it was foolish to give the rifle to a family so obviously doomed. Doc smiled at the thought. Why should he think Jefferson Antone's family was so obviously doomed when the two of them could be in an even more ominous situation than the Antones?

As they proceeded into the valley, they began to make out the shapes in the mist on the ground, and then they realized they were standing in the midst of what they now recognized as a vast bone yard.

Skeletons of humans and horses were scattered across the valley floor.

"How many would you guess?" Matthew asked.

"Two hundred humans. Maybe more. The bones are so jumbled about I doubt if we could ever count them all."

The only arrows left sticking in the bone yard were those with broken shafts. There were no guns lying about, except for a few broken *escopetas* like the one the Antones had found.

They came to the black remains of six charred wagons. Burnt human bones stuck out of the wreckage. Matthew glanced left and right, his eyes moving swiftly to detect any movement. He saw there were more wolves now, a good fifty of them. Matthew remembered the wolves had prowled the field and torn apart the bodies of dead Mexicans on Peggy McCormick's farm after the Texans slaughtered Santa Anna's army. In his heart he felt a certain kinship with wolves, an admiration for them. But he did not fool himself that these were amiable beasts aimlessly licking their teeth in the fog. He remembered the legend on his family shield: *Homo Homini Lupus*. Man is a wolf to man. These wolves prowling in the fog had tasted human flesh.

"In your medical opinion, how long have these bones been here, Doctor Swift?"

"I'm going to say six months," said Doc.

"Four months maybe?"

"Could be. Did the Comanches strip these bodies?"

"They did."

"Why?"

"Made it a better show when they cut their peckers off and mutilated their flesh. The Comanches kept what clothes caught their fancy and burned the rest, I would guess. See that black circle over there on the ground? That was probably clothes."

Beyond the black circle, Doc saw an apparition in the fog. It looked like a man standing, but the figure was unnaturally still. Unlike the skeletons all around, this figure was dressed in a brown uniform. But under the uniform were bones. The skeleton stood upright on a sharpened stake that rose from the ground. The stake reached up to pierce the grinning skull. The stake had gone up through the anus all the way up the torso and neck and into the brain.

Matthew looked at the red tabs on the epaulets of the uniform jacket. Then he opened the first three buttons and pulled the jacket away from the bones so that he could read the tailor's label inside. Matthew knew what he was going to see.

The label read: *General Domingo Savariego.*

These were the remains of the Volunteers of Monclova, the Mexican battalion whose scouts had chased Matthew and delivered his enemy Christolphe Rublo into his hands.

# 46

The fog and mist thickened and grew chill as the two white men continued up the valley in a northwesterly direction, leaving behind the bones of General Savariego and his army.

They heard a deep rumbling, a gargantuan throat-clearing from behind them somewhere in the mist. Suddenly with a fantastic white, electric splatter, the scene flamed up, like flaring phosphorus, and an explosion blasted chunks of rock that fell all around them. Gaucha bucked, but Doc held his seat in the saddle with grace, a skill that Matthew noted.

Then cold raindrops big as gold pieces hammered down on them with such ferocity that the two men lost sight of each other at a distance of ten feet. Another flash of white light and an explosion. Doc and Matthew saw it at the same moment—a gash of black in the side of the hill. Bowing under the fierce weight of the rain, the two men let their horses struggle toward the shelter of the cave.

Inside the cave, which extended forty feet into the limestone and narrowed into a tunnel large enough for a child to slip through, they unsaddled and unpacked their horses to remove the water-sodden burdens. The two men were so thoroughly soaked there was no use undressing and trying to get dry. The thunderstorm crashed outside the cave mouth. The sound of the rain was like the breaking of thirty-foot waves.

In the smears of white lightning that washed the cave walls near the mouth, they saw drawings scratched into the rock. Using ochre and botanical dyes, unknown artists had rendered bison and bears and warriors. Some warriors were hunting and some were fighting each other. Doc studied one of the bears. The hang of the creature's arms, the tilt of its head, the black pits of its eyes, excited him. This creature could have been a bear, but to Doc's view it could also have been an ape.

"You're a poetry-loving fellow, Doctor Swift," said Matthew, looking over Doc's shoulder at the pictographs. "Ain't there some famous poem about the powerful and pompous turning into dirt? Like we all come into this life dirt and we all go out of this life as dirt? Something like that?"

" 'I am ashes where once I was fire,' " Doc said.

"That's sort of the idea. Who said that?"

"George Gordon, Lord Byron."

"Do you know him?"

"I saw him a few times in London when I was young. He became ashes fifteen years ago."

"Well, I suppose 'once I was fire' was the last words that went through General Savariego's mind as he felt that sharp stake sliding up his butt," Matthew said.

"You knew that fellow?" asked Doc.

"I fought against his cavalry three years ago along the Nueces, and a few months ago his scouts chased me across the Warloop. Some were alarmed that he was going to attack Austin, but he was looking for Comanches. Found them, too."

"I've never seen such a display of anthropophagy," Doc said.

"I guess I never have, either," said Matthew.

"I mean, so many men having been eaten. Those bones were clean as dinner plates."

"I never had seen Savariego face to face until today. I heard he was a real favorite with the ladies."

"I noticed many of the skeletons had their hands and feet missing. The Comanches do that?"

"Probably some did. Most of the hands and feet were carried off by coyotes and rodents, is my guess. Little bones, easy to run off with and hide from the competition."

Both men were shouting over the noise of the storm.

"It's peculiar to me how these savages take such joy in tearing bodies apart," Caldwell said. "But I guess you might understand, you being a surgeon."

Doc grinned. "We learn to be ruthlessly immune to screams."

"I mean tearing a body apart for pleasure only. This is what I find peculiar with these savages."

"Two years ago I saw a public execution in London," Doc said. "Three young men condemned for treason. The sheriffs dragged the three traitors behind horses over the cobblestones for a mile while crowds cheered. At the gallows, the three traitors were half hanged, strangled until they were in agony. Then their genitals were cut off and burned. Next the sheriffs split the three bodies from crotch to chest, and ripped out their bowels. The traitors were still conscious."

"White men did this?" Caldwell said.

"Yes, very normal-looking white men. Then they chopped each body into four parts, and placed the three traitors' heads on poles. In a prize fight I saw in Liverpool, one pugilist knocked his opponent's eyeball out, scooped it up and ate it," Doc said.

"You telling me white men are the same as savages?" said Caldwell.

Another explosion blasted near the mouth of the cave, and lightning illuminated the wall of pictographs.

"What do you think this is?" Doc asked, pointing.

"An ape."

"The truth."

"Doctor Swift, I believe that is some primitive's best effort at drawing a bear. But if you want to think it's the ape you are looking for, then you might be right."

Doc rolled his black felt hat and twisted it, wringing out a stream of water. His monk's hair was mashed so flat against his skull that it looked as if he were wearing a red-gold bathing cap.

"Why did you bring me with you?" asked Doc.

"You're a handy fellow, with your medical knowledge and all. You'll come in useful, if the Comanches don't kill us the moment they get close enough. And you're fairly good company. Why do you ask? I thought you were eager to cross the frontier."

"I know what I want to find here. Curiosity's got the best of me. But what is it drives you to leave your fiancée and go on this mission, Captain?" asked Doc.

"Just as sure as I believe my soul is eternal, I believe in the Republic of Texas. I believe what I am doing is good for the Republic."

"All right." Doc nodded.

"Now you tell me something," said Matthew. "Why did you bring that beautiful young sister of yours to Texas? I can hardly think of a worse place for her to be."

"You were Cully's patient long enough to know she gets what she wants. She has her heart set on Bowl's Town."

A stab of pain struck Matthew's lower jawbone and whirled in his empty tooth sockets. He squinted hard and made himself accept the pain. "She don't belong in Bowl's Town with a bunch of doomed Cherokees. Did she grow up a churchgoer or a heathen?"

The sound of rain was lower now, a continual hum. The rain was still falling hard, but it was toward the tail of the storm that was passing up from the Gulf of Mexico.

Doc looked over at the Ranger's eyes and knew that pain was hitting him.

"She was raised Presbyterian in New York City, and in North Carolina she followed the teaching of the people she has now gone to live with. I have never heard you express any interest in theology. What religion are you?"

"Catholic."

Sitting on the ground with his back against a bison drawing, Doc strained to pull off his boots and pour water out of them.

"Well, Catholic more or less. I was a Protestant as a boy and young man," said Matthew.

"You constantly surprise me," Doc said.

Matthew was digging into his saddle pouches and learning that most of their powder was wet.

"You don't expect to hear a wild barbarian on the frontier talking about soul?" said Matthew.

"My uncle in North Carolina says the Master of Breath wanted to hide the secret of the soul until human beings grew wise enough to understand it, so the Master of Breath hid the secret of the soul inside us."

"What would you call your religion?"

"Have you studied the Bible?"

"I've never read the Bible," said Matthew.

"The Old Testament is about God creating the world and all natural life, and then creating humans, and God telling humans the correct way to live in this world is to love your neighbor as yourself. But humans wouldn't do it. So in the New Testament, Jesus came to us and said God wants you to love your neighbor. God is love. Love is the only way to have a perfect world. But you know what we did to Jesus. God has told us how to have a perfect world. We

refuse to obey. We make our own catastrophes in this natural world. We think
we can dominate nature, but I don't believe we can. Somewhere in there is my
religion, as you call it."

The Ranger laughed and his mottled beard streamed straight down from
the water. It reminded Doc of the beards of Jewish diamond merchants in New
York or London, and Hannah appeared in his mind at the thought. Doc knew
an instant of fear when he thought he might have spoken her name out loud at
the memory of her face.

"I believe my soul is eternal, as I was first taught as a Protestant in Kentucky. I don't know where my soul was before now, but it was somewhere.
And when my body dies, I don't believe my soul is going to hell for eternity,
although heaven sounds like a good place to strive for. Ain't that what your
uncle was saying?" said Caldwell.

"I don't know."

"Well, with your half-Indian, half-white outlook, Doctor Swift, you got the
hereafter covered from all angles."

Matthew began scratching the ears of the big white stallion. The horse's
eyeballs rolled back in pleasure.

"What does the Catholic Church say about you marrying a Jew?" asked
Doc.

"You got something against Jews?"

"I was thinking about the Church, and the Texans you'll be dealing with
from day to day."

"I'm going to marry Hannah regardless of what the Catholic Church says.
As for our Texas citizens, I don't think many of them know what a Jew is, or
give a damn. The Allen brothers, who built Houston City, are Jews, I believe.
People here don't hold a grudge against Jews. There's too much else to worry
about."

"I understand you have killed a number of men," Doc said.

Matthew gave the physician a look of curiosity but did not answer; he
continued scratching Pacer's ears.

"I have killed one," Doc said.

"That's not many for a doctor."

"I beat a sailor to death in a saloon because it thrilled me. How do you
feel when you kill a man? Do you find it thrilling?"

"I never killed anybody for the thrill of it, Doctor Swift, but I will say that
causing the death of another person is an interesting experience, to see how
they take it, and an experience I have never grown accustomed to, nor have I
ever hesitated to do it—if I think it is the right thing to do."

The rain had ebbed to a pattering, and a yellow glow of sun was burning away the mist and fog at the mouth of the cave. Both men began repacking their bedrolls and preparing to saddle their horses. The smells of wet wool and wet hair and wet leather mingled in the cave with the odor of ripe horse manure.

"So your conscience is clear, Captain?"

"I try to do the right thing, Doctor Swift."

Emerging from the cave into the sun, they walked into waves of steam. The thunderstorm was a blue bruise in the sky to the north, but in the valley outside the cave it was a steamy July day again. Captain Caldwell and Doc Swift were still backtracking, near as they could reckon, on the path that might have brought the German stumbling onto the Camino Real. That seemed a good plan for locating a Comanche village. The Comanches were horse nomads, but they returned regularly to their favorite places, such as the valley of the Little Pigeon River that the German had spoken of. The site where Austin was rising had been one of their most highly favored places, Matthew was thinking. The Comanches must be prevented from ever again returning to Austin.

From a hill above, the Fighting Man and the Dark Man looked down on the two white men whose horses were picking a route between the cactus thorns and the rocks and the overhanging cottonwood limbs.

"That is him on the big white horse," said the Dark Man. "That is Old Paint."

# 47

The buffalo cow stood knee deep in grass, chewing her cud and keeping an eye on her calf. Like ranging cattle and domestic milk cows, the buffalo cow had front teeth on her bottom gum only. She would reach her head down into the grass, wrap her tongue around a clump of stems and break them off between her bottom teeth and her fleshy top gum. Then she would grind the grass between her big flat teeth on both upper and lower gums in the back of her mouth, and swallow the mass into the first of her four stomachs. In a few minutes she would cough up the partially digested food, chew this cud for a while, ruminating, and swallow it again. This could go on all day. Flies buzzed around her ears and mouth, crawled across her face, stung her rump.

Captain Caldwell and Doc Swift stood beside their horses fifty yards downwind of the wandering group of eight buffalo cows, six calves and one stud bison that was six feet high at the shoulder and weighed more than a ton. The stud was moving slowly around the perimeter of the group, nearsighted but alert for sounds or smells of wolves or other dangers.

"That bull thinks the world of himself," Matthew said. "He thinks he can take care of his harem and his offspring on his own, with no need of a big herd around them. We need to show that bull how wrong he is. I'm hungry for a steak. It's nature's way, as your Cherokee uncle would say."

The Ranger removed his hat and shirt and hung them on his saddle horn. He stripped off his two pistols and draped his pistol belt across the stock of Sweet Lips in its sheath. For weapons he was left with his butcher knife and the derringer hidden in the barrel of his right moccasin boot. Observing the Ranger's massive, hairy torso and beard and long hair, the physician was struck by the thought of how much Caldwell looked like a wild beast, or like some savage hybrid.

Matthew went down on all fours and crept into the high grass. Doc Swift could hardly detect a ripple. Even in the ocean the fin of an approaching shark would have shown, but in this lake of grass there was no sign. The powerful aroma of the shaggies increased as Matthew edged closer to the cow. He heard her drooling and slobbering as she ruminated on her cud. She snorted and flinched at the bites of flies and fleas. Matthew smelled the dust that covered the cow's back and hump; she had recently wallowed to try to destroy her insect tormentors.

The Ranger felt heavy steps on the earth and knew the stud shaggy was making his rounds of his harem. This was the beginning of rutting season. Matthew hoped the bull would not suddenly decide to make sex with this target cow. The Ranger flattened against the ground and froze as the bull passed by him twenty feet away, paused a moment to sniff the air, and then proceeded.

Matthew came upon the tawny calf, which danced about as if the hairy stranger were a relative that wanted to play. It had crossed Matthew's mind that killing the calf would be simple and would provide enough meat for a meal. But now that he was so close to the cow, whose bulk rose above the grass like a breathing boulder, some deeper urge took over Matthew's heart, and he pushed away the calf and crawled beneath the cow. The Ranger sat up, clenched both hands on the handle of the butcher knife—and slammed the knife under the cow's ribs, driving the blade into her lungs.

The cow lifted her head abruptly, startled, and blood flew from her nostrils.

Other shaggies looked at her. The cow coughed and gasped but stood still, calming the other shaggies' sudden instinct to run. In a moment the other shaggies went back to their cuds. Matthew's cow wobbled a bit, sighed, and knelt down. Then the cow rolled onto her side and died.

The calf began bawling.

Matthew smacked the calf on her flank to drive her away, but she kept bawling. The other shaggies were interested again. Matthew saw the bull turn and peer in his direction. The bull began to trot forward, shaking his head as if unloosing his horns.

Matthew stood up, a hairy creature rearing out of the grass, and howled like a wolf.

The bull stopped. Matthew howled again, a long howl, menacing. He felt the howl tear something loose in him. He heard answering wolf howls from three hundred yards away, beyond the bull's perimeter. The bull made a grumbling, bellowing sound, and the cows began to run, the calves running with them, and the bull brought up the rear, looking back to turn and fight if this tall wolf-like thing chose to pursue.

Still the calf bawled for her mother.

"Go on. Get out of here!" Matthew said.

He spanked the calf across the nose and kicked her tail until, still bawling, the calf ran through the grass to catch up with her family of shaggies as they fled.

Doc helped Matthew heave the dead cow onto her belly and spread her legs.

The Ranger glanced at the three-pound Cherokee knife in Doc's hand and said, "I'm just going to cut out her tongue and take a few rib steaks. I can handle it."

"I'm a surgeon," Doc said. "I've hacked more carcasses than you can imagine. But never one of these bison. Let's do a good job of it."

They cut her at the neck and across the brisket, pulled back her hide and carved out her forequarters. Doc cut out her elaborate system of stomachs and removed it with her brisket. Matthew scraped out her guts. They broke off four rib steaks. Doc sliced off a hunk of her hump. They had forty pounds of meat piled in front of them, and they had hardly started with the harvest that would come from just one cow.

"Leave the rest for our wolf brothers," Matthew said.

Matthew started a flame with the sun, a broken mirror from his bag, dry grass, tinder and twigs. Doc cut branches from a stand of live oaks. They built a fire in a shallow pit lined with stones. They dug marrow from bones and spread it like butter on buffalo steaks they roasted on spits.

Long before their meat was cooked they saw a hundred yards away a pack of wolves ripping at the dead cow, and coyotes circling beyond the wolves, and foxes poking their noses through the grass.

His stomach full, sucking bloody juice from his fingers, Doc leaned against a live oak trunk and began writing in his journal. The feat he had seen the Ranger perform had to be recorded. It was a match for any display of primal cunning in Doc's experience.

"How long do you think it will be before we contact the Comanches?" Doc asked.

"This afternoon maybe. More likely tomorrow."

"Why?"

"See those birds in the far north? That little tiny black swarm, way off? Could be another kill of shaggies, but my guess is the birds are eating the garbage at a big Comanche camp. I know the Comanches know we are here. They're watching us right now. So when we start getting close to that bird swarm, the Comanches will make a move. Either they'll kill us right off, or else they'll talk to us first."

"If they want to kill us, why haven't they done it already?" asked Doc.

"You're half Indian. Why do you think it is?"

"Curiosity."

**48**

Twenty young warriors had ridden off with Isimanica three days ago on his first raid as leader, but in the camp of two hundred lodges there were one hundred and fifty prime men who were preening themselves for the forthcoming adventure. They slipped silver and copper rings into the lobes of their ears. They combed and brushed their hair and shined it with bear grease. They draped necklaces of porcupine quills and lion's teeth around their necks. Several produced full feather headdresses with trains of eagle feathers that would reach the ground if the wearer was mounted on his finest war horse. Each warrior had strapped his medicine pouch, his magic, beside his genitals.

The warriors were watching Turk, the Fighting Man, as he mixed red dye in one stone bowl and black in another.

If he painted his face red and black, it meant death for anyone who opposed him.

The Talking Man squatted with Young Owl Hatching, studying Turk. The Dark Man dragged his legs with his hands until he could maintain a sitting position. Like all the others, he was watching the Fighting Man.

Though he was not directly addressing the Fighting Man, the Talking Man spoke loudly enough to be overheard by Turk, whose chest, with its curious growth of hair, was bare and unpainted, but his biceps and forearms were decorated with copper bands. His necklace of bear claws hung from his neck as he bent toward the two bowls of dye that he was stirring. He wore a brooch of pearls clasped in his hair. His lips were tight and his eyes were solemn. He did not look around when he heard Osage Killer's voice.

"To me it is more sensible to see what these men with hats want. To kill them straight off is not wise. Maybe they want to give us presents. I have heard of such things being done," said the Talking Man. "But no, I believe Turk wants to skin Old Paint so he will own the longest body scalp any family has ever seen. Turk can make a hairy rug out of Old Paint. If that is what Turk wants, I will not oppose him," said the Talking Man, whose deadly protégé, Isimanica, was away from the camp. "What do you think?"

"I have not decided," said Young Owl Hatching, touching the stringy hairs that grew out of his chin.

"Should we have a council to talk this over?" the Talking Man said.

"Turk said he is going to do what he is going to do no matter what a council says," said Young Owl Hatching.

Turk daubed a finger into the bowl of red dye and the watchers thought he was about to begin painting his face, but he was only testing the substance for consistency. He scraped off his finger on the bowl.

"What do you think, Magician?" the Talking Man asked.

The Dark Man fluttered his eyelids so that his eyes looked white and blank.

"Do you hear me?" asked the Talking Man. "Is this another *portento* you are having?"

The Dark Man rubbed his lightning-scorched cheeks with his long, powerful fingers, as if bringing his spirit back from somewhere.

"The other white man with Old Paint," the Dark Man said, and then fell silent.

"Yes? Yes? What about him? Does he bring gifts?" asked the Talking Man. "I think he does. But he is no stranger here."

"How could he have been here before? Nonsense. The last white men to reach this part of our land were those traders who brought us the sex rot sickness. We killed all of them—except for that big ox that I buried my axe in his head before your monkey god dragged him away from me as tribute. I would imagine your monkey god ate that big man long ago and added his bones to the piles in his cave. So how could this man with a hat riding with Old Paint have been here before?"

"I feel his spirit has been here," said the Dark Man.

Turk beckoned for a wife to bring him a pipe with the bowl filled by Mexican tobacco. She held a burning stick to the tobacco and Turk breathed deeply, sending out puffs of smoke. He settled back to sit on his heels and smoke his pipe and think. His enemy was riding into his country to meet him. Turk knew of Old Paint. The people told stories about this Ranger who looked like a paint horse. Old Paint was a big war chief among the men with hats. Old Paint riding into his country was crazy. Bringing one companion—the Dark Man had already told him this spirit feeling that the white stranger with Old Paint was different from other Texans—was crazy. That Mexican general a few moons ago had brought many soldiers into Turk's country, and that was crazy, too. Any outsider who rode into Turk's family country was crazy or stupid. As a famous war chief, Old Paint must understand what he was facing.

# 49

From the journal of Dr. Romulus Swift—
July 14, 1839

Caldwell saw them before I did. I had my eyes on the ground, examining the plants and the rocks as specimens and watching for herbs I might recognize. I heard him suck in his breath across his teeth. I looked up and saw sixty or seventy Comanche warriors on horseback.

What a vision! I wish my fellows at the Explorers Club could see it. The warriors were dressed in their finery—bison helmets with the horns, like the Huns wore, caught my eye, along with feathered bonnets and sixteen-foot lances and colored shields made of bison hide and ribbons in the horses' manes. Caldwell said this was good. No paint, he said. They were dressed for guests but were not wearing war paint. He said it was vital that we exhibit no fear as we rode to meet them. He said we were doing what the Comanches least expected by riding into their country, and this would disarm them.

Three men rode out to meet us halfway. In the middle was a tall, powerful man, rather Mediterranean in appearance, with copper bracelets on his arms. His long hair was combed back and held in place by jewelry, but his head was bare, as if he was of such eminence that he needed no further adornment. To his right was an older man, going toward fat, wearing a full train of eagle feathers; to his left a strange-looking creature—built like a boxer from the waist up, but with legs wasted by what I took to be some bone disease, and his flesh was dark as if scorched. The dark man looked straight at me, and I almost felt we had met before; he looked straight at Caldwell and began to speak in frontier Mexican.

I was not surprised to hear the Indian call Caldwell by the name Old Paint. I believe everybody I have met since we reached Texas knows Old Paint.

The dark man asked if either of us had a disease or if we came from a place of disease.

Caldwell replied that we were clean and healthy and we'd come in peace to bring presents and to tell of great things to come.

The older man in eagle feathers said we must surrender our weapons. Caldwell said we were guests, and we trusted our hosts and we expected to be trusted in return, as is the custom. We would keep our weapons.

Going with them toward the Comanche camp, the powerful man they called Turk, clearly a chief of a high order, rode in the middle beside Caldwell. The older man in feathers was on the outside. The dark man rode beside me. He smelled of sulphur, of something burnt, of sage. He asked if we had brought whiskey. I said no. That pleased him. He is the most peculiar-looking man, with sharp, gaunt features and wide eyes that show large white globes and irises that are like shiny black stones.

The rest of the warriors folded around behind us, and we rode into the camp. There was a strong odor of unwashed flesh, of blood and entrails and excrement on the fringe of the camp where ravens and vultures picked at the garbage. There are hundreds of tepees in this camp, spread out for miles along a stream. Each family has its own lodge, which might be one or two tepees or even more if the head man is powerful. Naked children stared at us. Young girls in buckskin gazed boldly. Dogs frisked about, playing games with the children, or lay panting in the shade. Women wearing leather dresses, some ornamented with beads, watched us appraisingly. There was something going on everywhere—roots being cleaned, hides tanned, meat ground in stone vessels to mix with dry corn for pemmican, just as I remember my grandmother doing. I saw an angelic girl with chopped blonde hair, about twelve years of age, a white captive I was sure, and she smiled sweetly at me. Near her was another white girl close in age but showing burns and bruises; I made a note to treat her burns when I am able. The two girls were chopping onions to be put into a stew pot on a bank of coals at their bare feet.

This Comanche camp is a paradise for flies, with meat and Mexican sugar candies hanging from racks.

They brought us to this large tepee and told us to wait. I saw the big chief, Turk, admiring Caldwell's white stallion as the older man shut the flap to prevent us from seeing out. I admire the structure of this tepee. These eight lodge poles are twenty feet long and true as if shaved by a master carpenter. We heard drumming, then flutes, joined by voices that took up chanting—a sort of aaayaaaaa aaaayaaaa, over and over. We heard stomping, shuffling feet.

Caldwell peeked out the flap and saw several warriors going past carrying long brass ceremonial pipes. Caldwell says this is good. Smoking indicates thoughtfulness and hospitality. He is amused that I am writing in this journal. He says more than seven hundred Texans, including many men of education, defeated Santa Anna's army in the bloody, glorious battle of San Jacinto, but not a single Texan has written about the experience as yet. Meaning no disrespect for the art of writing, but in Texas we rely on deeds, he says.

Caldwell rattles his bag of hairbrushes and broken mirrors.

Minutes later—
The Dark Man pushes open our flap and drags himself inside our

tepee. He moves very strongly with his hands, arms, shoulders and chest, his thin legs trailing behind. He asks if he can see my instruments of healing. I open my kit and show him scissors, forceps, twine, needles, bottles of opium tincture. He picks up each item and studies it. In Spanish I ask if he is a healer. He says no, he is a prophet. He is glad the gift of healing is not for him. He laughs and says the healers are sometimes badly treated when their magic fails. I ask how prophets are treated when they are wrong. His eyes pierce me. He says he is never wrong.

# 50

**M**atthew and Romulus were invited to a meal at dusk. While women and children and men past their prime pressed forward from the background, being careful not to cross closely behind a feeding warrior—a slip in protocol that could ruin the warrior's personal magic and force him to go alone into the wilderness to seek another vision and refill his medicine pouch—a hundred and fifty prime men gathered with Caldwell and Doc Swift in and around the roasting fires and ate a stew of buffalo entrails and chopped onions, colored with green bile, followed by hunks of meat and bowls of dry corn and an array of onions that had been washed but not peeled or sliced.

After the meal the men crowded around the patch of earth that had been marked off for a council. Caldwell and Doc Swift were invited into the center of the square, where they sat cross-legged and listened as Osage Killer, the Talking Man, stepped into the square and began to speak. Doc noticed a bulge in the flesh of the Talking Man's belly—a sign of blockage of the colon.

After half an hour of boasting of the tribe's success with him as the civil chief, and praise for Turk's victories as primary war chief, the Talking Man said he spoke for all families in wondering why Old Paint, a war chief of the men with hats, had come so far to place his life in their hands. Was Old Paint trying to throw his body away?

Osage Killer sat down heavily. Matthew rose and opened his saddlebags and presented to Turk the hairbrush with the initials MM carved in the handle. The Comanches crowded in closer. Doc caught a glimpse of the angelic blonde girl before the gap was closed again. Matthew passed out the rest of the hairbrushes and the pieces of broken mirrors until his bag was empty. The Talking Man received a palm-sized piece of mirror, in which he began examining an insect bite on his face. The Dark Man politely brushed aside the gifts; he had no need of a mirror or a hairbrush.

Although those who received pieces of mirror or a hairbrush appeared to be happy with their gifts, Talking Man tucked his mirror into the waistband of his leather leggins and said, "These are very poor gifts, and not enough of them."

Caldwell said, "These are tokens from me. I could not carry more. Your real prize will come from the big chief of Texas."

"What does your big chief ask in return?" said Turk.

"Peace."

"Tell him to move his new town out of our valley on the Colorado," Turk said.

"It is too late for that," said Matthew. "The town is built. Our people cannot pick up and move their camps at will as your people do."

"We can have no peace if you place a town in our Colorado River valley," Turk said.

"What kind of gifts does your big chief offer?" asked Young Owl Hatching, stroking his chin hairs.

With a slight bow the Turk acknowledged the question from the Thinking Man, even though it was improper to be interrupted.

"My chief will tell you," Matthew said.

"No. You tell us," said Turk.

"He will give you wagons loaded with gold," Matthew said.

"What? Gold?" said Young Owl Hatching. "What good is gold? We don't want gold."

"My chief will give you whatever you want," Matthew said.

"We want guns and powder and bullets. We want blankets and cooking pots. We want knives and hatchets. We want iron for making arrowheads," said the Talking Man.

"Also we want sugar and coffee and salt," the Thinking Man said.

"Gold will buy you all these things from the Comancheros at Santa Fe," said Matthew.

"No gold. Gold is no good. Comancheros will cheat us for gold. No, we want our gifts from your chief himself. We want wagons piled high with gifts," the Talking Man said.

"It will be as you want," Matthew said.

"White men don't give gifts freely, as our people do, expecting nothing in return," said Young Owl Hatching. "What do you want from us?"

"We want to buy the land from San Antonio for one day's ride toward the setting sun," Matthew said.

"What do you mean, 'buy' the land?" asked the Talking Man, scowling, his scalp lock dripping sweat and pearls of sweat running down his belly. He had sat too close to the fire and had eaten too much, he told himself. "Do you think you can 'buy' the air, or 'buy' the water?"

"Come and meet with my chief," Matthew said.

"I can't read the white man's mind. What does he want? He says one thing and does another. Our people do not change. We live in our own way, and our promise is good and strong. We don't understand the promises from the men with hats. This 'peace' you mention. What does this mean?" said the Talking Man.

"No fighting with Texas. Mexicans are your enemies."

"I don't trust you," Turk said.

"I will ride beside you to the Council House. You will meet my chief. He will make you happy. He wants peace," said Matthew.

Turk did not like what he was hearing.

"Why should we ride with you into your town where you can ambush us and kill us? Why should we trust you?" Turk said.

"I give you my word you will be safe at the council and safe to return to this country after the council. I am Old Paint. My word is honored. Your people know I have fought you fairly and have never lied to you."

"The Sure Enough Father created the land. White men cannot own it. What is the harm if we take wagon loads of presents from the men with hats so they may think they can own land that nobody can own? I am holding in my laughter at such a joke," said Young Owl Hatching in Comanche.

They heard yips and hoots of celebration coming toward them down the streambank. Women of the men who had gone on Isimanica's raid began to laugh and sing and dash about, pausing to dance. Blonde Pearl was ecstatic. She clutched her elbows and twirled and raced to greet her husband.

Isimanica galloped his pony through the camp, almost to the council ground, where he pulled back sharply on the bridle and the pony reared with his forelegs, scattering dirt, and Isimanica, wearing a Mexican cavalry tunic, brandished a rosewood rifle. He screamed and waved a willow wand that had four pieces of hairy flesh tied to it.

Romulus felt something reborn in his heart. His ancient antagonist, his primal ferocity that he tried to keep buried under layers of learning, rose in a rush and flooded his brain. His thinking was cold and clear, his bearing was athletic, his intent predatory. In his mind he saw Jefferson Antone in his city suit, and the brave Serenity, and their children, Desdemona and Ephraim, struggling to find freedom and land in Mexico. He saw in his imagination the butcher blows and heard the screams, and the howls of glee and whoops of triumph. He slowly and gracefully got to his feet. Until now he had not spoken a word at the council.

Feeling the anger growing inside, he said calmly in frontier Mexican, "That is my rifle. You stole it. I want it."

Isimanica waited for the translation. Men in the council gazed in curiosity at Romulus, interested that he somehow misunderstood how the world works. Matthew looked at the mounted, painted, scowling Isimanica and saw the scalps. Matthew looked back to Romulus and said, "Don't get your bile hot, Doctor Swift."

"This man has massacred the Antone family," said Romulus.

"We're close to talking them into coming to the Council House," Matthew said.

Isimanica's translator said, "He killed a black man and took this rifle."

Romulus walked across the patch of earth in the center of the council, stepping over legs and around bodies of warriors who were watching with curiosity as he made his way toward Isimanica.

"I will fight you for that rifle," Romulus said.

Isimanica handed to the blonde girl the willow limb from which dangled the bloody scalps of the four Antones. To a warrior standing nearby he gave his fourteen-foot lance. Isimanica dismounted from his pony, which was slashed by war paint. He held the rosewood rifle across his chest. The wide-shouldered white man was an odd-looking creature with hardly enough hair to be worth tearing off his head. The white man must be a crazy animal, Isimanica thought, incapable of understanding the situation.

"I challenge you to fight me man to man for that rifle. If you win, you get our white Arabian stallion as well as the rifle," said Romulus.

Matthew spat a squirt of mesquite bean tea onto the dirt.

The translator spoke to Isimanica, who glanced at the Ranger captain and then again at the other white man. They must both be crazy, Isimanica thought, but this one with the blue-eyed skull face was the worst and closest and most annoying.

Romulus closed the space between himself and Isimanica, measuring his opponent as he would a boxer in the ring, noting the position of the young Comanche's limbs, the center of his body gravity, his tension.

Isimanica did not accept the unreality that his territory was being invaded swiftly and confidently by a white man until the rosewood rifle was snatched out of the raid leader's hands by the insane one.

"Fight me or be known to your family as a coward," Romulus said.

# 5 1

The young members of the Gentleman's Boxing Club in Edinburgh were encouraged to study Greco-Roman wrestling to learn footwork and balance and leverages of the bones and muscles. As a physician with knowledge of anatomy, Romulus quickly learned which hinges control the reactions of the limbs, and how easily they could become unhinged with the swift, proper application of strength. This knowledge was valuable on the boxing ground, but it was indispensable in a serious fight. Romulus laid his pistol on a log but carried his Cherokee knife in his right hand. He stayed on the balls of his feet, his hands close to his chest, the knife held in a slashing position. He watched the eyes of Isimanica and watched the warrior's midsection, his center of balance.

Isimanica shed his Mexican cavalry tunic. His sculpted torso gleamed with sweat. His long, oily hair glistened; watching, Pearl wished she'd had time to comb it for him. Isimanica looked at the white man, saw the pistol put away. The Comanche pulled a butcher knife from his waist wrap. The blade was red with the blood of the Antones.

This was a weird and surprising encounter in the camp of the families. The people were forbidden from ever challenging each other to fight, or from fighting at all among the men of their families. If a man was wronged, he might demand payment of arrowheads or horses or food from the one who harmed him, and the council would see that the matter was settled without blood. But for a newly anointed raid leader like Isimanica to be challenged to fight by a white man, a guest—this was great drama for the people. Isimanica could never survive the humiliation of turning down a challenge from any man, much less a white man, but there was never any fear or thought not to fight in his mind. People pushed close around the council patch, where the fight was about to take place. The big hairy Ranger stood in one corner, beside the Talking Man. Turk was watching with a small smile. The only noises were heavy breathing, the yapping of the dogs, a few crying babies.

Romulus watched the right hand of Isimanica, which waved the butcher knife, indicating a sudden plunge and sweep of the blade could be expected. The instant it came, Romulus stepped aside. He was judging Isimanica's speed. The Comanche was quick, but now Romulus knew just how quick. Romulus circled right, away from Isimanica's knife but moving closer to it. He heard a shrill cry of encouragement for Isimanica in mountain English and recognized the blonde girl's voice. Romulus shifted his Cherokee knife into his left hand.

Isimanica cursed. Sweat ran down through the black paint under his eyes, which were red from riding all night. He was in no mood to play with this white fool. Whatever this challenge was about, it must end now. He would cut the white man bad, maybe kill him, with one spinning dive and flash of his blade.

Romulus blocked Isimanica's sweeping right arm with his own left arm, bone to bone. Swiftly Romulus's right hand grabbed Isimanica's right thumb and twisted the digit backward and down where it was structurally weakest and on down toward the ground, leverage carrying the warrior along so his right wrist and thumb would not break and be torn out of their sockets. Isimanica's knife fell from his hand. With his left hand Romulus clamped Isimanica's right elbow, which greatly increased the power of the lever. Isimanica had to go to the ground to prevent his shoulder from being ripped apart. It was simple anatomy.

The Indian sat on his knees, blinking, in pain, gathering himself.

Romulus stood over him with the Cherokee knife poised to strike.

"He'll never quit, Doctor Swift. You're going to have to finish him," said Matthew. "Don't let him get up."

Romulus dropped his Cherokee knife. He stood with his hands at his sides. Isimanica slowly rose, trying not to show the pain in his right shoulder, and turned toward his challenger.

The fists of Romulus moved so fast the watchers could hardly see them and later argued how many blows had been struck. First there was a left that landed under Isimanica's heart, then a right that smashed against his temple, and then another left that dug below the rib cage and bruised Isimanica's liver. Isimanica was unconscious by then and already falling. He crumpled into the dirt, his mouth open and drooling, letting forth a long sigh.

So that's what happened to me in Austin, thought Matthew, feeling a runner of pain race along his jawbone.

Pearl smiled sweetly at Romulus—it unsettled him to see such sexual allure in an angelic face—and joined Isimanica's other wives and her sister, Rose, with the burns on her body in dragging their husband out of the council patch. The warriors and crowd of spectators opened a path for them and looked on in wonder as the tough fighting man's heels left trails in the dirt.

Romulus felt refreshed and powerful. The explosion of violence had drained his tension. His anger receded, though he still felt a fine edge of it pumping his glands. He picked up his rosewood rifle. He stuck the Cherokee knife back into his belt. He walked over to the log and fetched his pistol.

Turk and the Talking Man and the hundred and fifty warriors looked at Romulus with respect. They had never seen such a style of fighting. The Dark Man watched from his seat on a log. Romulus dusted his pants and flexed the fingers of his right hand. The middle knuckle was beginning to swell. His blood was rushing and he took a deep breath and he felt invincible.

"Here is Mookwaruh!" cried the Thinking Man. "Welcome, brother."

Into the circle swaggered Mookwaruh, a squat, ugly war chief who had come from a family miles away because he had heard there was to be a discussion about dealing with the men with hats. Mookwaruh wanted presents. He thought he would sell the Texans his captive for a good price.

"Look at her," Mookwaruh said proudly in Comanche, pointing at a fifteen-year-old white girl. Her face and arms were hideously disfigured. "I caught her maybe two handfuls of moons ago, while she was picking pecans. Look how one of my wives burned off her nose with a flaming buffalo chip. The Texans will have to pay a lot for her."

Romulus didn't understand the language, but as a healer he started toward the unfortunate girl to see if he could help her.

Mookwaruh barred him with a lance.

"Stay away!" Mookwaruh said in Comanche.

"Stand back, Doctor Swift," said Matthew in English. "Let me say my piece."

Matthew Caldwell stepped into the center of the council patch and addressed the warriors, most pointedly Turk and the Talking Man.

"If you agree to ride in with me to the Council House for a council with my big chief, I will leave Doctor Swift here in your camp as your hostage to prove we are men of good faith and not liars. If any harm should come to your delegation at the Council House, you can have the life of Doctor Swift in return."

Romulus stared at the Ranger.

"But I want an answer now," said Matthew to the council.

"Very well. We will debate and give you an answer," the Talking Man said.

Matthew and Romulus were escorted back to the tepee in which they had previously waited. As the flap was being closed, they could hear the Talking Man's voice rising in oratory.

"This is rather extreme," Romulus said as the Ranger flopped down and searched his pockets for the shreds of his last cigar. "I bet your horse, so you retaliate by betting my life?"

Matthew scraped a hot coal out of the fire hole in the middle of the tepee and lit his stub of cigar. He inhaled and then blew out a stream of white smoke.

"You're going to abandon me out here?" Romulus said.

"I figured it would please you to have time to chase your big monkey."

"You planned to leave me," said Romulus.

"You were never going back to Austin with me, Doctor Swift," the Ranger said. "I saw the way you and Hannah looked at each other. You were shaping up to become a real problem. By leaving you here with these Comanches, I'm giving you a chance. If this Council House meeting goes well, the Comanches will keep their word and let you go."

"You're very clever, Captain," said Romulus.

"I didn't plan it exactly this way. I just planned that you would never return to Austin. If you get out of here, go straight to Bowl's Town and fetch your sister and take her back to New York. Make a wide circle around Austin, because if I see you near Hannah again, I'm going to kill you."

"I'm going to take Hannah away from you. Hannah is too good for you," Romulus said.

"But she's mine," said Matthew. "Good-bye, Doctor Swift."

# 52

The freight wagon was parked in front of the new Maverick home. Now that Sam Maverick had been assured by President Lamar that General Felix Huston would not order San Antonio abandoned to Mexicans and Indians, the new limestone residence with three bedrooms had been built at the intersection of Soledad and Commerce streets, with a view of Main Plaza in front and the river in the back. On either side of the main house were small houses for the servants. A cook house—the kitchen—made of limestone with a shingle roof, stood between the main house and the river. Closer to the river were the stable and the corral. Mary Maverick's garden, conspicuous because of sixteen fig trees and rows of pomegranates, grew between the main house and the stable. A wooden picket fence surrounded the backyard. Chinaberry trees and a giant cypress spread from the fence to the river, making a shady walk beside the water.

Hannah Dahlman, Dora Kerr, Mary Maverick and Lawrence Kerr watched as two Mexican servants loaded an armoire onto the wagon. The armoire was a house gift from Sam and Mary Maverick to Hannah and Captain Matthew Caldwell. Hannah was careful to prevent the servants from putting the armoire on top of the magical rosewood chair, carved by Antonio Rocca, that was to be her wedding gift to Matthew. The chair had been loaded onto the wagon at the Fincus Hotel warehouse and covered by blankets, but Hannah was nervous about keeping it pristine. Other household items like a tin bathtub, a Franklin stove, curtain rods, footstools, bed frames and a dining table were already on the wagon. Word had come that construction was complete on the future home of the Caldwells in Austin. The builder, Newfield, had moved the front doors to the south and added two porches as Hannah had requested. She was getting ready to ride to Austin with the furniture in the wagon driven by the teamster Rafe Cornwell with an escort of two Texas Rangers—Big Foot Wallace and Saginaw Boswell.

The two Rangers had not yet arrived, which was just as well because the wagon was three hours late in being loaded. Still, the absence of the Rangers made Hannah nervous.

"If they don't show up, I will escort you myself," Lawrence said.

"Thank you, Lawrence," said Hannah, knowing she would never start on the road to Austin with only Rafe Cornwell and Lawrence Kerr to guard her.

"Oh, I would like to get my hands around the throat of that Newfield wretch, that so-called architect. Our house should have been finished by now. We should be transporting our furnishings to Austin today with Hannah," Dora said.

"Mr. Newfield would have finished our house ages ago if you would desist from altering the design every week or two," said Lawrence.

"Lawrence, don't you dare defend that son of a bitch. You know from the start I told him Greek Revival, I drew the facade for him on his plans, and still he brings us Roman columns and French windows."

"Here comes Mr. Wallace," Mary said.

Galloping across Main Plaza on Old Higgins, Big Foot dodged between the carts and vendors and reined up beside the freight wagon. Old Higgins was lathered and slinging foam. Wind and sun had burned Big Foot's face, and he squinted down at them through watery eyes red with dust. He touched his hat brim but did not dismount.

"The captain is on his way," Big Foot said.

Hannah's heart leaped. "Matthew is here? How far?"

"Eight miles out. Matthew has about a hundred Comanches with him. Saginaw is keeping an eye on them. Excuse me, ladies, but I got to go wake up the bell ringer."

A hundred Comanches? Lawrence thought with anticipation. His fingers touched the handle of his Colts pistol. God, what he would give to kill a savage. He would be the envy of Wall Street, the toast of the Metropolitan Club. Girls would chase him.

Hannah wanted to ask if Dr. Swift was in the approaching procession, but she choked back the question, and Big Foot disappeared toward the San Fernando church. Within moments they heard the bell in the tower clanging loudly, and they felt vibrations from the stone and adobe buildings.

Out on the plain west of town, Matthew and the Comanches heard the bell ringing.

"Don't worry. This is a greeting," Matthew told the Talking Man and Isimanica, who rode with him at the head of a column that trailed behind them for half a mile. In the column were fourteen war chiefs and another thirty warriors in their prime. Following were fifty-nine women and children. Pearl and her sister, Rose, rode ponies that dragged travois and Isimanica's lodge poles. Riding near them was the white girl slave of Muukwaruh. She had told them her name was Matilda Lockhart. Matilda was leathery from exposure to the weather, yet pale and blue as if near death. Her body was covered by bruises and burns. Matthew wondered how her life would be back in white society as a scarred freak who had been raped by aborigines.

Turk had voted not to follow Matthew to the Council House. The Thinking Man and the Dark Man and another two hundred men in their prime who had come from camps in the hills to get in on the debate had also voted against the journey. The Talking Man was the leader of the position that the families deserved to take presents from the big chief of the men with hats. The Talking Man built word pictures of camps that were full of food and new cooking pots and vermilion, with rifles and pistols and ammunition and good woolen blankets to supplement their buffalo robes. The Talking Man said he trusted Old Paint, and he praised the gesture of leaving the white fist-fighting man as their hostage. When Isimanica stood and voted to go with the Talking Man to the Council House, Turk could not help but smile.

The Moorish walls and roofs of San Antonio came into view. The bell was still ringing. Matthew saw Saginaw Boswell a mile away. Big Foot must have been with Saginaw and had gone to warn the lookouts, since the bells had begun before the column could be seen from town.

When the column was yet a hundred yards from San Antonio, Hannah Dahlman ran across the field crying, "Matthew." He felt a burst of love and relief. She was still here, waiting for him. The emotion of seeing her loyalty made tears come to his eyes. He watched her long black hair flying as she ran, and he saw happiness and a wide smile on her face. Matthew leaned down from his saddle and swept Hannah up in his arms. She hugged him and kissed him. He felt her trembling.

"I love you, Matthew. I've missed you so," she said, kissing him again.

"I love you," said Matthew.

Hannah's head moved away from his shoulder, and her eyes swept from Talking Man and Isimanica back along the column. Matthew knew she was looking for Dr. Swift. Without making her ask, Matthew said, "The doctor stayed behind with the Comanches. He's on some kind of scientific expedition. He said to tell you he's going on back to New York and then London, but he enjoyed meeting you."

Matthew felt her body tense with disappointment, or did he imagine it?

# 53

With Hannah in his arms, mounted on the white stallion, Matthew entered the streets of San Antonio at the head of the Comanches. Osage Killer looked at the residents—Mexicans, most of them, it seemed to him—and at the new buildings they had erected since the years-ago autumn moon when he had ridden these streets in the lead of a raiding party. The men with hats had just lost a big fight to the Mexicans then and were dead or on the run. The Talking Man had ridden up to the front door of Blue's Tavern and shouted, "Look at me! Look at a man! Come out and fight!" And from inside a voice had answered in Spanish, "If you want to fight, go down to the San Juan mission. There's some Texans hiding there." Talking Man had led his party to the San Juan mission and repeated his challenge. But no Texans were hiding there, not even a priest.

Big Foot rode up on Old Higgins.

"This don't look good, Matthew," he said.

Caldwell noticed soldiers at the near end of Main Plaza, beside the one-room limestone courthouse that was connected by a wall to the jail and a courtyard. The soldiers were ragged and dirty, and their uniforms were inconsistent, but Matthew recognized their commander, Colonel William Fisher, and assumed this must be the First Texas Regulars, the genuine army, at least two hundred of them. That was about a third of the entire Texas army. The whole southwestern frontier must be unguarded, except for the fifty or sixty Rangers who would be patrolling the Nueces.

Two men in uniform stepped out of the courthouse. Matthew recognized General Hugh McLeod, a twenty-five-year-old graduate of West Point, and William G. Cooke, the quartermaster of the Texas army. Matthew lifted Hannah to the ground and then dismounted. He glanced back at the Comanches following him into Main Plaza with their tent poles and horses. Though they came for a council and not for war, the men held bows in their hands, and at the sight of the soldiers they notched arrows into the sinews.

"How long will it take the President to get here?" Matthew asked.

"President Lamar has appointed Mr. Cooke and myself as Indian commissioners," said General McLeod.

"That's not the question I asked," Matthew said.

"General McLeod and I are to conduct the meeting with the Indians," said Cooke.

"The hell you are," Matthew said. "I'm going to tell these people to pitch their tepees outside of town instead of here in the plaza, and then we'll settle down and wait for Lamar."

"President Lamar is not coming, and there will be no waiting," General McLeod said. To Matthew the general looked like a schoolboy preposterously dressed up like a gazette picture of an officer in a crisp red tunic with epaulets. "We are to start the council immediately in the courthouse."

Matthew said, "These people have traveled far. They are tired and edgy. We need to throw a feast for them tonight and smoke with them and let the council take place tomorrow or the next day when everybody is in a better humor."

"You're not in charge here, old man. Your mission is done. You may as well leave," said General McLeod. "Take your Ranger comrades and go back to patrolling."

"Big Foot, is there any legal penalty for breaking a general's neck?" Matthew said.

"I believe it is the same as spitting in the dirt," said Big Foot.

"I smell something funny here, McLeod," Matthew said. "I gave my word to these Comanches. Are you intending to make a liar out of me?"

"I am following the orders of President Lamar," said McLeod.

General McLeod lifted a gloved hand. They heard Colonel Fisher shout commands. His troops formed into three ragged companies and began to march toward the courthouse.

"Are we to talk or fight?" Osage Killer asked in frontier Mexican.

"Our big chief is not here. He is sick. These two chiefs will speak on his behalf. They want to begin the council now," Matthew said.

"Now?" said the Talking Man.

"That is their wish."

"Why do you have so many soldiers?" asked the Talking Man.

"The Texans are very much afraid of the Comanches," Matthew said.

Reassured and flattered, the Talking Man nodded.

"We can start the council now, without even the civility of a smoke, if that is what these two men with hats desire. I am eager to get our presents and go back into our own country. I do not like this town. Let us talk to the white men and get this thing finished."

Fourteen war chiefs and thirty men in their prime entered the courtroom, now called the Council House, with Matthew and the Talking Man and Isimanica. The Comanches squatted on the packed earth floor with their bows in their hands. Matthew leaned against the wall beside the door. He could see Hannah waiting near a wagon with Mary Maverick and Dora Kerr at a house with a picket fence on the other side of the plaza. He saw Lawrence Kerr swaggering across the plaza with his pistol in his belt. Out in the plaza, the Comanche women sat with their bundles and waited, but the children began playing with the townspeople. A circuit court judge was setting up targets that the Comanche boys shot down with arrows. The mood was friendly. Then Matthew noticed a disturbance. Some of the townspeople had seen Matilda Lockhart. Their horrrified report was passing from mouth to mouth.

General McLeod and William Cooke sat on the only chairs at the only table in the Council House. The room was stifling with the smells of leather and sweat and foul breath. Beside the table stood Red Beans, the Lipan who scouted for the Rangers at the Boca Chica Station and could speak both English and Comanche. McLeod knew no Spanish or border Mexican.

"First let me welcome you on behalf of my president and the people of our great republic," McLeod said to the assembled Indians. He waited for Red Beans to translate. The Talking Man relaxed a bit. This sounded like it would be a long, elaborate talk fest, the sort he thrived upon.

"Here are our terms," McLeod said. "You people must remain west of a line to be drawn no closer than a full day's ride to the west of San Antonio. You must never again approach white settlements or communities. You must never interfere with white efforts to settle on vacant lands anywhere in Texas. What do you say to that?"

Soldiers of the First Texas began filing into the courtroom, carrying rifles and sidearms.

"What are these soldiers doing in here, McLeod?" Matthew said.

"This is not your affair, old man," said the general.

"This damn sure is my affair," Matthew said. In frontier Mexican he spoke to the Comanches. "Don't worry. They are afraid of you."

Soldiers shuffled in until they lined all four walls. The Comanches muttered and many notched their arrows into sinews. Matthew noticed that the soldier nearest him, a boy of about sixteen, was fascinated and terrified at the appearance of the savages squatting on their heels on the dirt floor. The young soldier was breathing in gasps. Feeling that the heightened anxiety in the room was to his advantage, because it would be his masterful oratory that would win the day, the Talking Man stood up and faced the two white men at their table.

"We have set our lodges in these groves and swung our children from these boughs from time immemorial," said the Talking Man. "When the game beats away from us, we pull down our lodges and move away, leaving no trace to frighten it, and in a while it comes back. But the white man comes and cuts down the trees, building houses and fences, and the buffalos get frightened and leave and never come back, and we are left to starve, or if we follow the game we trespass on the hunting grounds of other people, and there is war."

McLeod and Cooke exchanged a glance. The Talking Man's haughty tone offended them.

"We know the white man does not understand our ways," said the Talking Man, speaking frontier Mexican, which he assumed the white chiefs would understand. "One portion of the land is the same to the white man as the next, for he is a stranger that comes in the night and takes from the land whatever he needs. The earth is not his brother but his enemy, and when he has conquered it, he moves on. He leaves his fathers' graves, and his children's birthright is forgotten. The sight of your towns pains the eyes of our people. But perhaps it is because you think our people are stupid and understand nothing about the world."

McLeod and Cooke waited impatiently for Red Beans to translate. The boy soldier beside Caldwell moved his lips as if praying.

"There is no quiet place in your towns. I am told that in your big towns there is always a loud clatter. There is no place in your big towns to hear the leaves of spring or the rustle of insects' wings," the Talking Man said. "But perhaps I am stupid and do not understand, and your noise only seems to insult my ears because I don't know any better than to prefer the soft sound of the wind darting over the face of a pond, the smell of the wind cleaned by rain or scented with flowers. The air is precious to our families. For all things share the same breath—the beasts, the trees, the man. Like a man sick and dying for many days, we can allow ourselves to become accustomed to the stench if we take the wrong path and stay on it too long."

Matthew was impressed by the Talking Man's eloquence. The Ranger found himself wishing for an instant that Dr. Swift could hear this speech. The doctor would want to write it in his journal.

"What is man without the beasts?" continued the Talking Man. "If the beasts were gone, men would die from great loneliness of the spirit, for whatever happens to the beasts also happens to man. All things are connected. Whatever befalls the earth befalls the children of the earth."

"Tell him to hurry it along," General McLeod said.

"Sir, a great civil chief is never to be interrupted at council," said Red Beans.

"All right, then. Proceed."

The Talking Man pulled back his vest to bare his chest and his drooping breasts. "It matters little where we pass the rest of our days, they are not many," he said. "A few more hours, a few more winters, and none of the children of the great tribes that once lived on this earth will be left to mourn except our families, the Comanches as you call us. You whites, too, shall pass—perhaps sooner than we will. Continue to contaminate your bed, and you will one night suffocate in your own waste. If we allow you to slaughter all the beasts and tame all the wild horses and make the secret corners of the forest thick with the scent of many men, and the view of the ripe hills is blotted out by your towns, then where would our families be? Gone. Where would the eagle be? Gone. And what is it to say good-bye to the swift and the hunt, the end of living and the beginning of survival? We might understand it if we knew what it is that the white man dreams, what he describes to his children on long winter nights, what visions he plants in their minds so they will wish for tomorrow. But we are savages. The white man's dreams are hidden from us. So we are here to accept our presents from your big chief, and if the presents are many and of good quality, those of us who are here today will withdraw to one day's ride toward the setting sun, and we will leave you in peace so long as you leave us in peace."

"What did he say about presents?" asked McLeod.

"Sir, they expect to be given presents," Red Beans said.

"I told them there will be presents," said Matthew from the wall.

"There will be no presents. The custom of giving gifts to savages has been dispensed with," McLeod said.

"Sir, I am not going to tell him there will be no presents," said Red Beans.

"President Lamar intends to offer them gold," Matthew said.

"Preposterous," said McLeod. "Let's get on with this. No presents."

The Talking Man, Isimanica, Mookwaruh and the other warriors were growing more anxious. They did not need to understand English to tell the situation was not going as they wanted.

"Tell the white fool we want our presents, and plenty of them, or we will fight a war against Texas forever," the Talking Man said.

"I'm not telling him that," said Red Beans, who began stepping among the Comanches and heading toward the door.

In the doorway, flinching back as if expecting a blow, appeared the tormented figure of Matilda Lockhart, who was being pushed into the room by several of the angry townspeople.

At the sight of Matilda, the boy soldier beside Matthew shouted with horror. Angry and terrified, the boy lifted his rifle and shot into the Comanches.

In an instant the room was clouded in smoke and flashes of flames and the booming of rifles and handguns and the smell of sulphur powder and the howls and whoops of the Comanches and the clanking of knives and the whizzing thumps of arrows and the whining of bullets ricocheting off the walls. A ball struck Matthew in the thigh. He felt as he if had been slammed by a club. He fell back against the wall, unable to put weight on his right leg. Suddenly appearing in the smoke above him, he saw the fierce eyes and tattoos and grinning mouth of Isimanica, who was plunging his knife toward Matthew's chest. Matthew rolled over and swung Sweet Lips up beneath Isimanica's chin and the shotgun roared and there was a shower of blood and bone and bits of meat.

The fighting inside the Council House was brutal, face to face, and then the fight spilled into Main Plaza, where the Comanche women and children had seen what was happening and had started attacking the townspeople and chili vendors. The circuit judge who had been propping up targets for the Comanche children to shoot was killed by an arrow fired into his heart by a six-year-old boy.

Warriors who burst out of the Council House ran toward their women and children, but suddenly they were all running toward the river. The soldiers of the First Texas and the townspeople, who had come armed from their houses, chased the Comanche men, women and children across the plaza. As the Comanches ran past the wagon at the Maverick house, Lawrence Kerr propped his pistol on the tailgate and took aim at a nearby savage and fired. The Comanche fell, rolled over and tumbled against a wagon wheel. Lawrence now saw the Comanche was a woman, a large red hole blown in her breast, showing her meat. But how could he have known? When he told this story in Manhattan, she would become a chief who had been charging him.

Hannah tried to run across the plaza toward the courthouse because she had not seen Matthew come out, but she was restrained by Dora and Mary. There was howling and screaming all around, the blasting of caps, the shrieks of butchery. A big Indian ran at them. He was a large man wearing leggins and a vest. Lawrence aimed the pistol at him, but the hammer snapped on an ill-prepared chamber. The Indian's eyes were big as grapes as he reached them— but he then ran on past, going along the picket fence, making for the cypress tree and the water. A soldier fired a ball that struck the Indian in the arm. The Indian staggered, circled the tree, leaped the picket fence and ran into the cook house.

Sam Maverick, who had been at his law and land office when the fighting began, entered the main house at the same time as half a dozen soldiers trotted along the outside walls. Hannah, Dora and Mary gathered at the back door, looking at the cook house and wondering what to do.

"There's a big savage hiding in the cook house," Lawrence shouted.

The soldiers crouched and ran to the cook house. They battered on the door with their rifle butts and with a log, but the door was oak and thick. They chattered among themselves, making a plan. One soldier found a candlewick ball and soaked it in a bucket of turpentine which had been destined for the stable. The soldier climbed onto the roof of the cook house with the candlewick ball.

"What the devil are you doing?" shouted Sam Maverick.

The shingle roof of the cook house erupted in flames and black smoke.

The soldier jumped down and picked up a hatchet that had been used for trimming the fig trees in Mary's garden. When Osage Killer, the Talking Man, screamed and rushed out of the burning cook house, the soldier split the Comanche chief's skull with the blade of the hatchet. The Talking Man had thrown away his body, as had been foreseen in the Dark Man's *portento*.

# 54

President Mirabeau Lamar picked his steps with care in Houston City as he crossed Main Street by treading on planks that were laid in the mud. Rain was falling again—how he hated this place—a warm gray shower that dripped from his parasol and spattered the baggy trousers that he favored. His thinning hair was stuck to his ears by the humidity. A wagon wheel rolling past slung a syrup of mud across the President's boots. He longed to be gone from this dreadful city. A few more weeks, he told himself, and I will be a hundred and eighty miles north of here in Austin, on a hill breathing refreshing clean breezes in a mansion with a wonderful view of the white cliffs and the river and creeks and forest. What a difference from this steaming slush.

Lamar was meeting a dinner invitation from his old comrade, Henry Long-fellow. It had been weeks since Longfellow had called upon Lamar at the capitol, or had been seen in the restaurants, racetracks or saloons of Houston City. Lamar was relieved to have a respite from his former fellow Georgia legislator, who was more and more of a trial. Unseemly tall and gawky, enormously unattractive and awkward, gimping about with his copper-knobbed, ebony sword cane, always leering at women, the scent of a dirty sort of sex exuding from his pores, Henry was a clever lawyer and businessman, a moneymaker, a valuable adviser, but he could certainly be a pain and an embarrassment, especially if there were females in company.

The restaurant was called the White Swan. The President closed his parasol as he entered. He shook like a dog, spraying water from his person, and accepted the greeting of the owner, a French immigrant who wore a pencil mustache and ruffles at his collar and cuffs. The owner, M. Beauclair, glanced at the President's muddy boots and at the rain dripping from the trousers which appeared to fit Lamar comfortably around the waist but had room inside each pants leg for another leg or two. M. Beauclair had been told the President wore such trousers on purpose, for freedom of movement and perhaps with the curious notion that this might one day become stylish.

"May I take your parasol, Mr. President?" asked M. Beauclair, who was anxious that the wet bumbershoot not be tossed onto his new mahogany hair sofa or onto the two red velvet rocking chairs that sat in the alcove in which patrons of the White Swan could drink spirits and smoke cigars while their tables in the dining room were being prepared. Protecting the chairs and sofa was a losing effort—these Texans tracked mud every place and crushed their cigars into the carpet and left mysterious stains on the furniture—but M. Beauclair refused to give up, not yet.

"Mr. Longfellow and another gentleman are expecting you," Beauclair said, passing the parasol on to a serving boy.

Another gentleman? thought Lamar. Henry had not mentioned another gentleman.

Lamar saw them at a table at the far end of the room. Longfellow struggled to his feet, leaning heavily on his cane. Overdoing it a bit, the President thought. A little too well considered. The other man also stood up. The sandy hair on top of his head barely reached Longfellow's shoulder. Though it was not yet dark outside—the rain and clouds made the hour seem later—half of the ten tables in the White Swan were occupied. Spaniards believed in dinner at ten

P.M., but Beauclair had learned that Texans wanted to eat dinner early. The White Swan served its evening meal beginning at five in the afternoon.

Nodding and smiling a practiced political grimace at the diners, and stopping to shake the hand of a cotton buyer from New Orleans, the President reached the table and found his fingers enclosed in the grip of talons. Longfellow pumped the President's hand and said, "Wonderful to see you, Mr. President. You are looking fit."

"My pleasure, Henry, and thank you," said Lamar, looking at Longfellow and wondering whether to return the compliment. He decided against it.

Without seeming to notice, Henry gestured toward the young man at his side.

"President Lamar, may I introduce Joshua Watson from Lexington, Kentucky."

"I'm a Texan now, Mr. President," Joshua Watson said.

"We can always use another good man," Lamar said. He shook hands with Joshua Watson and allowed a waiter to slide a chair beneath him. "What do you recommend tonight, Obediah?"

Obediah, the black waiter who belonged to M. Beauclair, smiled brightly, enjoying the bond of what he and the President considered their own private joke. On the east wall of the restaurant was a large framed corkboard with the dinner of the day written on paper in calligraphy that was slave Obediah's special hobby but was almost indecipherable. The White Swan served no breakfast, one lunch and one dinner. Lamar wiped his spectacles on the tablecloth and squinted at the menu board: tonight's meal, near as he could tell, was black bean soup with chili peppers, stewed tomatoes, baked potatoes, fresh sea trout or beef steak (fish or meat was the one choice M. Beauclair gave his customers), apple pie and coffee.

"Oh, never mind, Obediah. Bring me what you judge I will like," said the President.

"Yas sah. Be that trout or beef?"

"The fish."

Obediah bowed and chuckled at their joke and began to pour the President a glass of white wine from the bottle in the bucket beside the table.

"What is your business in Texas, Mr. Watson?" Lamar asked.

"Land," said Watson. He had that freckled, wide-eyed gaze of an idiot, thought Lamar, smiling, hoping this Watson had a lot more money than he appeared to have. Lamar reminded himself it was unlikely Henry Longfellow would have invited the man to dinner unless there was a financial opportunity for Henry and for the President.

"Splendid opportunity. Choice land we offer in abundance." Lamar looked at Henry Longfellow's beak as it dipped over the edge of a wineglass. Hideous manners. Lamar was growing annoyed observing such things. The President forced himself to show his teeth in a smile again. He wanted to get this dinner behind him, find out what favor Henry wanted or what inside knowledge he could share, and return to his bedroom in the dismal presidential shack and work at his writing desk. This was the perfect place to compose the melancholy poem that he was eager to continue. When the muse gripped him, Lamar had little patience with the world outside his imagination. "Where have you been keeping yourself, my dear Henry?"

"Austin," Longfellow said.

"Ah, Austin, lucky man."

"Yes, an agreeable town," said Longfellow, spreading apple butter on a piece of French bread. "I'm hanging out my law shingle there. Building a house. Going to deal in real estate. Money to be made in Austin, Mr. President. New citizens are pouring in. The roads are a madhouse of crowds, but your acres on Guadalupe Street and Congress Avenue are soaring in value."

"What about your rice and cotton fields down in this area?"

"Why, I'll do it all, I'll keep it all. There are great fortunes to be made here for those who grasp and hold," Longfellow said.

Obediah and a lesser waiter served the dinners—two beefsteaks and one sea trout that was deftly fried in cornmeal.

"Sir, I've got to get my family land back," said the young Watson.

Lamar was rhyming a sonnet in his mind and reveling in the taste of the trout. He looked up, irritated. Was this to be a problem dinner? He glared at Henry Longfellow. He hoped Longfellow's house in Austin would not be close enough to the governor's mansion that Henry could drop in at odd hours, but the President knew it would be.

"Mr. Watson is my client," Longfellow said.

"Bring him to my office tomorrow. I don't want to intrude upon this trout and wine with business matters."

"Looka here," said Watson. He unwrapped a package and laid an Osage arrow on the table. "This here Cherokee arrow killed my brother."

"Please take that thing off the table," the President said.

"It's still got his blood on it," said Watson.

"I have lost my appetite. Excuse me, Henry. I am going back to my rooms," said the President.

"Mr. President, please. I promise you will be interested in what Mr. Watson and I propose. Joshua, put that damned arrow away.

"I beg you to listen, Mr. President. This is very important to the Republic. My client is being barred from his rightful land by the Cherokees," Longfellow said, taking on his courtroom voice, which had an edge of the bully in it.

"How does Mr. Watson come to own this land?" asked the President.

Henry Longfellow slid a document from his breast pocket.

"This is his legal claim, filed at the courthouse in Nacogdoches. You will notice his property certification, purchased from a bank in Lexington, Kentucky, that had bought the title from a land speculator who had received title from the land office of the Republic right here in Houston City."

Lamar studied the documents with closer attention.

"Yes. I see. Templeman sold the titles." The President wondered if money from the sale had gone into the Treasury. He recalled no such transaction. Lamar reminded himself to look into this matter. Templeman was gone now, dead of the cholera in this damned swamp. But the documents had the appearance of authenticity.

"Tell him how you know the Cherokees killed your brother," Longfellow said.

"Me and our family—two women and nineteen kids and six cousins— found his body in a thicket not far from the Cherokee town that sits on our twelve hundred eighty acres. My brother's body was so ate up we recognized him by his clothes. We found this Cherokee arrow sticking in a tree a few feet behind where he fell."

Lamar chewed his trout with renewed pleasure. The murder didn't interest him. But the fact that the Cherokees were squatting on private land was worth a prominent space in his thoughts.

They heard the voice of Albert Sidney Johnston, and Lamar turned to see his secretary of war, limping from the pain of the ball that had been shot into his left hip in his duel with Felix Huston. The wound hurt him in particular on damp days, which was almost every day in Houston City. He could barely constrain his excitement at the news he had come to deliver. Johnston told M. Beauclair to bring a bottle of cognac to the table, and he stood grinning down at the President while Obediah brought another chair. Johnston ignored the presence of Henry Longfellow and Joshua Watson, another affront Henry would store in his mental records for a day of reckoning.

"Caldwell did it," Johnston said.

"He contacted the Comanches?" asked Lamar, beginning to feel the thrill of good fortune.

"He brought them into San Antonio," Johnston said.

"To the Council House!" said Lamar.

"But that's not the best news," Johnston said.

"Out with it, man!"

"The Comanches are already dead."

"God bless Matthew Caldwell," said the President. "How did it happen?"

Cognac was poured all around. Joshua Watson found this strange drink a little harsh, but weak in comparison to some of the spirits they distilled in the Kentucky mountains. Johnston downed his glass and had it refilled.

"I don't mean to say all the Comanches are dead. The figure I get is fifty-seven are dead. But this includes fourteen chiefs and thirty warriors. Our side lost two dead and eight wounded. Caldwell was accidentally shot in the thigh by one of Fisher's boys, but I am told Captain Caldwell has left for Austin, so his injury is not so serious."

Henry Longfellow knew Caldwell and the Jew girl he had seen naked were building a house in Austin, but he did not like the idea of the Ranger living in the same town where Longfellow would practice law and trade in land. Caldwell would have to be dealt with.

"But how did it happen?" the President asked. He had hoped the Council House meeting would end in a battle, but this was better than he could have expected.

"One of their big chiefs got up in court and gave a rambling, half-witted speech that made McLeod mad, and then some citizens brought in a white girl captive whose nose had been burned off—and the fight started."

"There are surviving savages?" asked the President.

"Yes, sir. We are holding forty-some women and children and one old blind man as prisoners. They're in the courtyard beside the jail. I hear they just sit there crying and wailing. It's music to our ears."

"What will we do with the prisoners?" asked the President.

"I don't know," Johnston said. "Some people want to shoot them, but Sam and Mary Maverick have stopped that plan. Probably just as well. The New York papers would make it into a scandal and maybe cost the Republic some investors. On the other hand, executing the savages might bring even more investors. I don't know what to do with them."

"Make them slaves," Henry Longfellow said. "I'll buy some of the children."

General Johnston acted as if he had not heard.

"Mr. President, you remember Dr. Wiedeman, the Russian who was sent here by the emperor?"

"Yes. To study us? That fellow?"

Johnston began laughing deep in his chest, wheezing and sputtering.

"I hear—you know how snooty Mary Maverick is—well, I hear the Russian doctor cut off the heads of two Comanches, a man and woman, and left them on Mary Maverick's windowsill." The men laughed. "Wait, there's more. Doctor Weideman boiled the flesh off the bones of many savages and dumped the soupy mess into the main *acequia*, where the town's drinking water comes from. He barely escaped being lynched."

"Why would he boil their bones?" asked Joshua Watson.

"He is putting together two perfect aborigine skeletons to ship home to St. Petersburg," Johnston said, wondering who was this latest person Henry Longfellow had inserted into the President's life.

Johnston waved away slave Obediah, who had come to ask if he preferred beef or fish.

"I'm too happy tonight to eat. I'll just drink this cognac," said Johnston. He leaned his elbows on the table and looked into the eyes of the President, whose cheeks were flushed with excitement and liquor.

"And what else do you think Captain Caldwell did?" Johnston said. "He took that foreign agent, that false doctor from New York who broke Longfellow's leg, into Comancheria and left him there as a hostage at the mercy of the savages."

"A toast to Captain Caldwell," the President said, raising his glass.

"Here's to Old Paint," said Johnston. "He always comes through."

Henry Longfellow joined the others in clinking their glasses and swilling cognac in honor of Captain Caldwell. Bad politics to scorn a hero, Henry thought. He should be happy that Caldwell had gotten rid of the ambusher who had smashed Henry's leg. But it would have been sweeter if Henry could have seen the death of the thug with his own eyes.

# 55

The Bishop of Guadalajara ruled that Matthew Caldwell would not be allowed to marry an unbaptized person in the Cathedral of San Fernando, and that included in the rectory. However, the bishop issued a dispensation that allowed Father Dominius to perform the Catholic marriage ceremony upon Caldwell and his bride at any venue other than a Catholic church.

One hundred and nine years ago the Franciscan fathers had built a mission on a hill near what was now known as Barton's Springs, but the mission was abandoned to the wilderness and became a pile of stones buried under the brush. There had never been another church of any sort built in the Comanche valley that had become Austin.

Matthew lay on the bed in their new home with his leg bandaged from being shot by a soldier at the Council House fight. He wondered if the battle had been a betrayal by Lamar, or if it was caused by the stupidity of the two army officers who presided.

Hannah tended his wound and brought him laudanum from the pharmacy. He knew she was wondering about the fate of Dr. Swift, but she did not mention him. Instead, she busied herself planning their wedding. With no church in town, she went looking for a suitable location.

Hannah wandered the busy streets, avoiding a squadron of Bullock's pigs, listening to the shouting and the hammering, smelling the aroma of horse manure that permeated the town. The builder Newfield suggested she walk down Bois d'Arc Street to East Avenue to look at the new French Legation, which had been completed on a hill with a splendid view of the flowing Waller Creek and the frantic construction activity below.

She went past the temporary capitol, which was almost ready on Colorado Street between Hickory and Ash. Carpenters were nailing rough pine planks from Bastrop onto the walls of the one-story building. Other workers prepared the roof of cedar and cypress shakes weighted by logs. The drive to protect the entire city of Austin with a fence had long ago been abandoned as futile, and the fence had fallen into disrepair. But men were digging a moat around the temporary capitol to protect it from Comanches and the Mexican army. Inside the moat they built a stockade fence made of twelve-inch logs ten feet high.

The capitol faced east, and Hannah kept going in that direction until she crossed the broad dirt road, East Avenue, and climbed the path up the hill, following the direction indicated by a wooden sign that said FRENCH LEGATION.

As she neared the top, she heard a voice speaking French on the other side of the hedges that grew in clumps along a white picket fence.

"What is this nonsense?" the voice cried. "One dollar for each carriage horse? One dollar per wheel for any carriage or cart that is used for pleasure? One dollar for a silver watch but three dollars for a gold watch? Crazy. Texans are crazy!"

Hannah walked to the gate. Pacing the grass in front of the two-story house and legation, which had a hipped roof and French doors opening onto a gallery with Doric piers, she saw a small man, overdressed for the heat in a satin jacket and waistcoat and a silk cravat. A thin strip of beard ran along the jaw of his almond-shaped head. Spit curls were pasted to his forehead with pomade as well as sweat. His mustache curled up at the tips and moved with each wide pronouncement that came from his mouth. He was speaking to his male secretary, reading aloud from a piece of paper, which he slapped with disdain.

"Three dollars per deck for playing cards? Hah! There would not be enough magistrates in all of France to collect such a tax from gamblers! These Texans tax a person for taking pleasure!"

"But certainly they would not dare to tax you, Excellency," Hannah said in French.

Count Alphonse Dubois de Saligny whirled and stared at her. She saw his eyes appraising her breasts first and then arriving at her mouth and face and hair.

"That accent!" he said. "A hint of the Prussian?"

"Hannoverian," said Hannah.

"Delightful! Delightful! Please come in. It lifts my spirits wondrously to hear French spoken in this wilderness, even with a German accent." He wiggled a finger at his secretary. "Go and fetch us a pitcher of tea."

After chatting with de Saligny, drinking iced tea on the porch in the shade, Hannah said, "I hope I am not being ridiculous, but Captain Caldwell and I would like to have our wedding here at the French Legation."

The count stirred more sugar into his tea and smiled at the girl from Hannover. Her request offered him the advantage of inflating his reputation among the citizens of Austin. A true Texas hero, Captain Caldwell, marrying at the French Legation would belittle the damned Richard Bullock, who had been heard to boast that the wedding would be at Bullock's Inn. Already the count's servants had used a hundred and forty pounds of nails repairing Legation fences after raids by Bullock's hogs, who gorged on corn meant for de Saligny's horses. The locals appeared to regard the count as merely a foreigner with money to spend.

"Why would you choose the French Legation?"

"This is the most beautiful building in Austin," Hannah said.

"Indeed."

"Mr. Newfield says you plan to bring eight thousand French immigrants to settle in Texas. I should think news of your relationship with a man of Captain

Caldwell's stature would be quite good for your business in Texas and in France," Hannah said.

"A wonderful idea. You are a shrewd and charming girl. When do you wish to be married?"

"One week from today," Hannah said.

# 56

O n the afternoon of the wedding, Matthew and his best man, Big Foot Wallace, went to Rupert's Bath House for a scrubbing. Matthew propped his right heel on a stool beside the tub to keep his wounded thigh out of the water.

"Are you scared?" asked Big Foot.

"I'm wondering if I ought to shave off my beard. What do you think?"

"How do you know what your face looks like underneath?" asked Big Foot. "You might look old and ugly."

"I'll only get a trim."

"You are scared of women, ain't you, Matthew?"

"Ain't you?" Matthew said.

"Sure am. And I never even married one. I always keep me from four to six good dogs instead. I'm scared enough just thinking about having a woman in my life every day."

"I'm going to marry this girl, Big Foot," said Matthew. He would never tell even his friend Big Foot that he had fallen in love with his contracted bride. Men did not talk about love to other men, and seldom to women. Matthew rose up on his elbows in the tub and shouted to the bath boy, "Raymond, come in here and cut Mr. Wallace's toenails! It hurts my teeth to hear them scraping on the tin."

While waiting for their mansion to be finished, the Kerrs had rented a two-room bungalow on the grounds of Bullock's Inn. Dora spent the afternoon at the inn fussing over Hannah, seeing to the details of her wedding gown, a tissue white silk with a bodice that verged on being immodest, but her breasts were concealed and made more titillating by lace. Hannah would wear a lace veil as well. Dora was thrilled to be the matron of honor at this ceremony at the French Legation. Since Lawrence had killed the Comanche, he had begun wearing his pistol outside his trousers, in a holster, like his Ranger friends. A university chum and business partner had sent him three works of imaginative fiction—Cooper's *Last of the Mohicans*, Hugo's *The Hunchback of Notre Dame*, and a *Burton's Gentlemen's Magazine* containing Poe's *The Fall of the House of Usher*—and Lawrence turned the pages with a smug feeling. Out here on the frontier he was living a daring, adventuresome life of his own and had no need for this secondhand guessing.

"I do so envy you, my darling, your happiness," Dora said. "How thrilling! In a few hours you will be in the arms and in the bed of a glorious dream of a man."

Hannah tried to smile. She swallowed hard to drown her fear. She was excited about the wedding, about the ceremonial part of it, about the future once they could set up housekeeping and begin to build their estate—but the thought of being in his arms in bed in a few hours was daunting. Tantalizing but alarming, appealing but still repulsive. Her wifely duties would be expected this night. She pictured Matthew naked, that great furry chest, and she shut the sight out of her mind, not sure whether she found it enticing or disgusting. But at least one thing was now utterly clear, and that was that fleeing to her family in Hannover was no longer a possibility. Since her arrival in Texas, not one of her numerous letters home had been answered, and she feared the worst. Her family could be in prison in Hannover. She needed to begin making inquiries, and this she would do immediately. But after she married Matthew Caldwell.

Dr. Swift remained in her thoughts. He was an extraordinary man, brilliant, educated, a world traveler, and he had made an indelible impression on her. Hannah remembered the blue-eyed man who had brought her roses and a love note and asked her to wait for him. She had believed then that he loved her. But if he had loved her, he would have come back, wouldn't he? She wondered whether Matthew and Dr. Swift had had a conflict in the wilderness that was being kept from her.

As the sunset approached, a parade of wagons and pedestrians climbed Legation Hill. Fritz Gruber, who had once owned the twenty-one-acre hill but had sold it to Anson Jones, the Republic's ambassador to Washington, arrived early with his wife, Ruthie. They accepted glasses of wine from de Saligny's butler and listened to the tuner gauging the spinet. Everyone in Austin who mattered—except for the reclusive lawyer Bone—gathered on the hill. This wedding was the biggest social event in the brief history of Austin.

Father Dominius, wearing his black linen vestment, took up his position on the porch at the front door of the Legation at six in the evening, with nearly an hour left of summer sunlight, which the building shielded from the eyes of the guests who stood on the grass and earth. The musician played Mozart on the spinet as Matthew and Big Foot came around the house from the north, and Hannah and Dora from the south. The four met before Father Dominius, who stood on the porch a step above them. Matthew wore a new white doeskin jacket that had been made for him by Lipan women in a village near Boca Chica Crossing. The blue and red beadwork—a star over each breast—was by a Canary Islander artist in San Antonio. Matthew's long black hair was cut to the bottom of his neck, and his mottled beard had been trimmed by three inches. His weather-burned face shone with power and with good health for a forty-three-year-old man whose body carried many wounds. He wore soft brown leather trousers with silver *conchos* down the outside of the legs, and new moccasins with a beaded star on each. The sight of him in his wedding garments quickened Hannah's heartbeat. The moment is here, she thought. Looking at his bride, Matthew was overwhelmed by her spirit, her beauty and her youth. It occurred to him to thank God for bringing her to him, and his lips moved in a silent prayer.

Dora stepped up onto the porch beside Father Dominius. She looked like a glamorous visitor to the frontier from another world. Her red hair was swept up into ringlets to reveal her beautiful neck. She glanced at the sweating musician who sat at the spinet. The fool knew only classical music, no show songs at all. Dora had spent an hour teaching him the song she would sing at the wedding. She could have played it on the spinet herself, but she wanted to be standing on the porch in full view of all when she performed.

She sang "I Shall Ere Be True," from the musical *The Garden of Romance*, in which she had starred on the New York stage.

Dora looked out across the crowd and knew she was a sensation. People hushed their whispering to listen to her every note. She drew out the closing words in a thrilling soprano.

The audience applauded loudly, and some cheered—a reception rarely heard by wedding singers. Lawrence was proud of her, and sexually aroused as he clapped and felt the weight of his pistol against his right thigh.

Father Dominius performed the service in Latin, which did not please Hannah. She had told him she would prefer it in Spanish, in deference to where they were. The veterans who had been in Texas for two or three years had picked up a working knowledge of frontier Mexican. Certainly there were few who understood Latin. Hannah knew Latin well enough to follow the service. Romulus Swift would have known what was being said in Latin, she thought. Hannah wondered if Father Dominius was hiding his nervousness behind words he counted on no one but his God to understand.

As Matthew's closest friend, Big Foot was honored to be best man, but he was afraid he had lost the ring. He fumbled in his pocket until he found the gold wedding band Matthew had bought in San Antonio. Embarrassed, Big Foot avoided Matthew's eyes. Matthew took Hannah's hand and slid the band onto the ring finger of her left hand. It was a perfect fit. Blood was pounding in Matthew's ears. He heard Father Dominius pronounce them married—this much he could understand—and he lifted Hannah's lace veil from her face and kissed her, not roughly but tenderly and for long enough that the audience began laughing and clapping.

In his desire to be known for lavish entertainment Count Dubois de Saligny saw to it that wine and whiskey flowed. A buffet of meats and vegetables and cheeses was laid out. Two guitar players and one accordionist replaced the spinet. Guests danced on the grass and dirt in front of the Legation. Matthew and Hannah danced a Mexican waltz. He felt her so light in his arms, and she was pleased by his gracefulness. Dora and Lawrence danced theatrically, with spins and whirls, but Matthew and Hannah waltzed plainly and looked into each other's eyes.

Matthew knew that from the amount of liquor being consumed, it would not be long before Big Foot took over and organized the dancers into a Stompede, in which the men would paw like stallions and the women would whinny like mares and two drunken sexes would collide. After the first waltz Matthew whispered to Hannah, "Ready to go?"

"I'm ready," she said.

They slipped through the crowd, nodding and smiling and shaking hands, being wished well, and then they were out the gate to a buggy Matthew had waiting. They climbed into the buggy, and Matthew took the reins and clicked his lips. The horse began trotting. Hannah looked at her husband's profile in the last red light of day, and she told herself she must continue to please him. She must bear children for them both. From now on, their lives were one. At their new house, hearing the water rushing in Shoal Creek, Matthew lifted Hannah from the buggy and carried her across their threshold.

# 5 7

From the journal of Dr. Romulus Swift—
Summer, 1839

The strange fellow called Dark Man tells me he has not only seen the man-ape, but he is a frequent visitor to the secret cavern. He says it was the man-ape's demand that set the German, Gruber, free on the road to San Antonio with an armload of gold.

I must meet this man-ape, I tell him. I must visit the cavern, I say.

The Dark Man says I want to steal the gold.

I say no, I am a doctor, a student of the human race, and I want to see the creature purely for the sake of knowledge. This is true, but I do not mention my quest from Knows All Charlie that I strive to find the next wisdom. The Dark Man is a very mystical sort, who believes almost everything, but he is a Comanche. I had rather he and the others believe I am white than know I have the blood of their ancient enemy, the Cherokees.

The Dark Man refuses to take me to the man-ape. The Dark Man says he is waiting for a sign.

No word from those who followed Caldwell. I feel the people growing more hostile.

They are making magic now—shaking gourd rattles and dancing to flutes and drums—to protect Turk and the small scouting party he is leading to San Antonio to look for his missing people. I have contemplated escape, but I am closely guarded.

This lovely stretch of water along which lodges are pitched for two or three miles is called by Comanche words that Dark Man tells me translate into the Little Pigeon River.

I am allowed to swim in the river if Dark Man is with me. Today

I ask how he understands the man-ape, and makes his own thoughts known to the creature.

The Dark Man says information is transplanted from one brain to another—I recognize what we call telepathy.

The Dark Man says, We talk with lightning.

It struck me that this is how the man-ape spoke to me in my dreams aboard the ship during the storm—by lightning, by telepathy.

Who is he? What is he? I ask the Dark Man.

Who are you? What are you? the Dark Man replies.

My sister and Hannah are always in my heart.

# 58

From their house, which had been built among cypress and oak trees that dripped with moss, Cullasaja could look across the water to the small islands rising from the lake that lapped into the far shore and became a reedy swamp. She heard fish flopping and spanking the water, and she saw blue herons gliding into the mist. Cullasaja loved the serenity and the smell and swishing of the water. She watched life on the lake, portrayed in ripples or the flapping wings of a wood duck or the wail of a loon or the call of a bullfrog. Everything had its purpose here. When Cullasaja and Velasco were married by Chief Bowl in the old way—by knotting their two blankets together, declaring to the town their desire to live as husband and wife and receiving, through old Duwali, the blessing of the Master of Breath—the people of the town joined to build the new couple a house out of pine logs with a dog run and a shake roof, and in a flowing of good spirit the people built a barn and corral as well and started on the cooking room. Velasco had lost much of the use of his right arm because of his wound, but he worked as hard as anyone, except perhaps Cullasaja, who was carried lightly in her labors by a profound happiness.

Velasco brought to the partnership six goats, five horses, three milk cows, a young bull, a dozen laying hens and a loud rooster. He milked the cows left-handed and mucked the barn and corral. Cullasaja tended the other animals—

including her Morgan—and gathered the eggs and fed the chickens and the goats and kept the two-room house clean and cooked for Velasco, who worked in the town's corn fields and vegetable gardens during the day and built up their share of the harvest.

This morning as she listened to the bell on the neck of the goat who led the others to the clear spring that flowed near the house, Cullasaja watched a red-shouldered hawk swaying in the top of a loblolly pine, and she felt a rush of happiness and peace. She smiled to remember the girls who had been her friends and classmates at Miss Finch's Academy in New York City. Where were they today? Summering on Long Island. Dancing under Japanese paper lanterns. Sailboating with their suitors. What would they think if they could see Cullasaja standing barefoot on the bank of a lake in Texas in her calico dress, with a pocketful of grapevine clippings, the bride of a full-blood Cherokee?

And pregnant. She felt she was pregnant. It was too soon to be sure, but she and Velasco had both had the instinctive feeling after a long, driving orgasm on one particular evening of lovemaking. They had looked at each other and known that another life had just entered her body. He slept with a hand on her belly the rest of the night, while she swelled with happiness and thought of her parents in New York and Grandmother Tobacco and Knows All Charlie in North Carolina, and of how she must take the baby to see them and introduce Velasco to them—but all in good time. There was no hurry, no anxiety. She would follow the rhythms of nature and keep herself open to the care and guidance of the Master of Breath, who was telling her to relish each moment.

She thought of her brother.

She worried that he had crossed the river into Comancheria and that something had happened to him. But another part of her thought that her brother was invincible. Cullasaja loved her brother more than anyone, even more than she loved Velasco. Her brother had been her idol all her life. She wished Romulus would find the joy that she had found with Velasco. Several times Romulus had seemed close to getting married in New York or in London, but Cullasaja had found herself to be strangely relieved when each romance broke off. In Cullasaja's mind, none of those women was good enough for her brother. But now all that would change; she wished for Romulus the happiness she had found.

As a child she had heard their father, Captain Fletcher Swift, telling Romulus that he must wait for the right woman, and that Romulus would know when he saw her.

As Cullasaja looked across the lake, at the morning sun in the water, she thought how peaceful her life had become. Bowl's Town was where she belonged.

"Cullasaja!"

Velasco trotted into the clearing, leaned his hoe against a log wall of the house and went inside.

"Why are you back so early?" she asked.

Velasco stepped out of the house with an old muzzle-loading rifle and bags of powder, patches, caps and balls.

"The word is going out," Velasco said. "The Texas army is here. Chief Bowl is speaking to them now. All men are bringing their weapons to meet the Texans."

"I'm coming," she said. She had placed on a top shelf, wrapped in an oily rag, the loaded pistol Romulus gave her before he rode away.

"You had better stay here. We don't know what might happen," Velasco said. He started to mention the baby, but Cullasaja was already inside the house, fetching her pistol.

They ran through the dirt streets of Bowl's Town, past neatly trimmed houses and barns and gardens. Dogs were barking. Roosters were crowing. Men wearing turbans and leggins stitched with beads were rushing from doorways carrying shotguns and rifles and bows and arrows. Women and children ran with them, carrying knives and clubs. Cullasaja heard the news cried out from many voices—Big Mush, Long Turkey and John Negro Legs were coming with their people. Warriors were coming from the Delawares, the Shawnees, the Kickapoos and the Creeks . . . and the Caddoans, too, they were coming. All the tribes in northeast Texas were coming to stand against the Texan army.

In a field that was being cleared for next spring's planting, Chief Bowl faced three men in brown Texas army uniforms. Cullasaja looked for signs of rank and judged the men to be colonels at least, maybe generals. The three men wore wide-brimmed hats. Cullasaja, her pistol hidden behind her back, thrust her way forward through the gathering crowd until she could hear what the white men were saying to Duwali.

She heard a young Texas officer with an erect bearing, like a West Pointer, say, "Maybe you don't understand English, Chief. I am ordering you off this land. I am ordering you to depart from the Republic of Texas with all your people. We will give you twenty-four hours. You must remove the locks from your guns and give them to me. When our soldiers have escorted you through the unfriendly Indians around here, you may have your gun locks back. Do you understand that? Do you speak English that well?"

"I have been speaking English three times as long as you have been alive," Chief Bowl said. "Who gives you the right to order my people off their land?"

"President Lamar."

"President General Sam Houston gave this land to my people. I cannot agree with you that we must leave it."

"What Sam Houston told you doesn't matter anymore," said a red-faced Texan, a portly older man who walked with a limp. Cullasaja noted he was sweating heavily in his wool jacket with tabs on the collar. "You people are a menace to the Republic of Texas. We know you plan to join the Mexicans when they invade us again."

The third Texan spoke. "I am authorized to approve payment for your houses and other improvements to the land, but no payment for the land itself, since you do not own the land."

The man with the limp said, "You are between three fires here, Chief. The wild Indians, the Mexicans and us. You will be destroyed if you try to stay here. We're doing you a big favor to escort you to a safer place."

"We could not leave before we harvest our crops," said Chief Bowl.

"You will leave tomorrow morning at the latest," the young officer said.

"I must come and address your Congress," said Chief Bowl. "They must hear me. We have built this place and lived here in peace. This is our land. I will explain it to your Congress with the help of our lawyer, President General Sam Houston. He is my son and my son-in-law. He will hold my hand."

"The Congress has nothing to say about this. The Republic does not own this land. You are on private property," said the sweating officer with the limp.

Cullasaja's eyes followed a wave of the officer's hand. She saw a carriage two hundred yards away. A very tall, gawky figure leaned on a cane beside the carriage, and a short man carrying a long rifle stood beside him.

"You have one hour to think it over, old man," the young officer said.

As Duwali turned to lead the growing crowd back into the town for a council, Cullasaja saw horsemen in brown uniforms, hundreds of them, moving out of the pine forest that bordered the cleared field. She looked again at the tall figure beside the carriage. There was something familiar about his ungainliness.

Big Mush, John Negro Legs, Long Turkey and other chiefs rode with their warriors into the town as Duwali emerged from his house in his green velvet jacket and his blue silk turban and his purple velvet trousers that ballooned and stopped at mid-calf. On his feet were Persian slippers. Around his neck hung the medal of valor he had been given by Sam Houston. He carried a saber and a pistol. The eighty-three-year-old chief threw back his shoulders and fifty years flew away; Cullasaja saw a flash of how handsome and powerful he had been before she first knew and admired him, when he was already in his sixties.

Duwali yelled to the crowd, "They demand we give up our homes and go away or they will destroy us. What do you say? Is there any use talking about it?"

"We fight!" cried Big Mush.

"We fight! We fight!" screamed the people. Cullasaja saw strange tribes among them now. She guessed there must be eight hundred men here, all of them armed. She was frightened, but anger and the roar of the crowd overcame her fear. "We fight!" she yelled.

Under the direction of Bowl and the other Cherokee chiefs, who had observed the tactics of the U.S. Army for years, the warriors formed into ranks that made up a regular battle line. Cullasaja saw the Kickapoos and Shawnees breaking away from the group in disgust. A Shawnee chief shouted, "You are fighting the white man's way! Have you forgotten how our people make war?"

Bowl raised his saber and led the battle formation marching out of the town and across the field toward where the three officers waited. Cullasaja and Velasco were in the front rank. She held her pistol in her right hand. With her free hand Cullasaja clutched Velasco's weakened right hand, and he squeezed her fingers.

"Are you crazy? What the hell are you doing?" shouted the portly officer with the limp.

"We are your friends. We have done you no harm. We could have done you great harm in your war with the Mexicans, but we did not. This is our land that President Sam Houston gave us in reward for service to Texas. You have no right to threaten us. We will not leave here," Duwali replied.

"You intend to fight us?" asked the young officer, who appeared pleased at the idea.

"If you force us to fight, we will fight. We will not leave here," Duwali said.

"Very well, then. We will return to our troops," said the young officer.

"Chief, I regret what is about to happen," the officer with the limp said as he heaved himself into his saddle.

The three Texas officers cantered to the far end of the field, where their troopers were now spread across the line of pine trees.

"Get on your horse and go," Velasco said to his wife.

"This is where I belong," said Cullasaja.

"Please. Go. Save our baby. I will find you when this is done," Velasco said.

They heard the Texans shouting at the end of the field. They came on screaming at a gallop, waving sabers and rifles and pistols, some men with reins held in their teeth. Duwali roared his war cry, and the hundreds of Cherokees and others still in the ranks made their own individual cries of fierceness. Cullasaja heard Velasco's shrill, yelping howl and was surprised and thrilled. She screamed, imitating him. Her heart seemed to stop with anticipation. Her soul seemed to be observing her body. She saw smoke and heard the Texans begin to shoot, and Duwali was hit but did not fall. The Cherokees were shooting back. Dust and powder obscured the air. She heard shouts of people whose flesh was torn by lead or chopped with blade. Then the Texans charged among them, horses trampling, guns firing, the smell sour and sickening.

With people falling around her, Cullasaja felt as though time had no reality. She saw bullets strike Chief Bowl twice more. He fell to his knees. Beside her she heard a sound like a boot kicking a door, and she felt Velasco's brains spatter onto her arm and hand. She fell under the hooves of a Texan horse and rolled away, sloshed with blood, passing for dead. Around her Cherokee bodies were piling up. She saw the young officer ride up to badly wounded old Duwali, who knelt but defiantly clutched his saber, though his eyes were glazing. The young officer aimed his pistol and shot the old chief in the throat. The force of the ball flung the old chief sideways onto the bloody earth. "I got the son of a bitch," Cullasaja heard the young officer say. Another Texan rode up and shot Duwali again. "So did I. I got the son of a bitch, too," he said.

The Texan charge passed over and left Cullasaja, dazed, behind with the bodies of the dead and wounded. Cherokees were running and being hacked down by Texas sabers and shot with pistols. Shawnees and Kickapoos shot balls and arrows from the forest, and many Texans peeled off to pursue them. The main Texas force galloped straight into the town, squawling and yipping with the thrill of conquering. Cullasaja saw black smoke rising and orange flames bursting from the houses. Bowl's Town was being burned to the ground.

Cullasaja rose to a crouch. She looked at Velasco, but there was nothing of his face left to see. She heard gunfire and screams from the town, and the flames grew wilder. Bending low, with the unfired pistol still in her hand, Cullasaja ran for the pines. The house she had shared with Velasco was outside of town, on the bank of the lake. It would take the soldiers a few minutes to find the house, she hoped.

Chickens scattered as Cullasaja ran to the corral. Without waiting for a saddle, she swung onto the Morgan and rode away from the flames and torment of the town. She decided she would ride to Austin. She had friends there, she thought. She felt she could depend on Fritz Gruber for help. She had cared for many sick people in Austin. Surely they would come to her aid. If she could find Captain Caldwell, he would protect her. Her dearest hope was that she would find her brother.

She let the Morgan pick a path cautiously through the pine forest, where Texans were searching for and killing those who had fled. She saw many plumes of smoke as Delaware, Shawnee, Kickapoo, Creek and Caddoan villages were put to the torch. The Morgan splashed across a stream, and she saw a line of mounted Texans riding south. They had not seen her, so Cullasaja steered the Morgan beneath an overhanging bank in the deep shadows, and hid there for hours while the screams and shots diminished, but the whole sky looked ablaze as the villages were being razed. Her life had become even simpler than it had been during the loving days and nights with Velasco. Now she had only two goals—to see that this baby inside her was born, and to find her brother.

Behind her the Cherokee dream was destroyed. Nobody was left.

Cullasaja rode by night and hid in the forest during daylight. She avoided the roads, which were crowded with soldiers and with people curious to see the dead Indians and burned villages. Cullasaja traveled on paths made by animals through the forest and used by her people. She ate roots and berries. There was grass enough for the Morgan. But the journey was slow and careful. Her brother, Romulus, was always in her mind now. She could hear him telling her what to do next, which path to follow. She drew strength from him.

At dusk of the third day, with Austin in reach by morning, Cullasaja awoke from an exhausted sleep and found a man standing over her. He was naked except for a breechclout and moccasins, and he carried a rifle and knife and had feathers in his hair. He was grinning at her with all his front teeth missing.

He spoke to her in a language she did not understand. He made a gesture that was understood everywhere. He grabbed his scrotum and motioned for her to spread her legs.

Cullasaja had slept with her pistol in the crook of her arm. She rose up with the pistol in hand and saw the shock in the man's eyes, and then she shot him in the chest. Blood flew out of his back. He stumbled and sat down hard. He looked at the hole in his chest and sighed. Echoes of the explosion vibrated in the leaves. The smell of powder drifted.

She heard a voice say, "I believe the bitch has killed our scout."

Three Texas soldiers appeared from among the trees.

"I told him not to stop and take a shit here. That's what he gets," said a plump man with a red mustache. He wore homespun trousers and a cotton shirt, but on his black felt hat Cullasaja saw tabs that indicated he was an officer. The other two men were dresssed like farmers, with no hint of the military, but they aimed their pistols at Cullasaja and admired her womanhood with sneers and licking of the lips.

"He was trying to rape me," Cullasaja said. There were three shots left in her revolving pistol.

"She speaks good English," said the plump officer in the black hat.

"My name is Cullasaja Swift. I am a United States citizen, born in New York City. I am a friend of Captain Matthew Caldwell," Cullasaja said, still holding her pistol on them.

"You a friend of Old Paint?" said the officer.

"I was his nurse. I know him well. I have many friends in Austin. Please let me go to them," Cullasaja said.

"Girl, you being a friend of Old Paint does carry weight with me. These other boys ain't been in Texas long enough to know they ought to be scared of him," the officer said. He was chewing a piece of sweetgum that stuck in his mustache. "But I can't let you go. You killed my Lipan scout that was issued to me by the army."

"Captain Caldwell will kill you if you touch me," Cullasaja said.

The officer spat out his sweetgum and lifted a hand to block the other two, who were taking a step toward Cullasaja.

"Boys, she is telling you the truth about Caldwell," said the officer. "You don't want no part of him." He squinted at Cullasaja, trying to decide whether to believe her. "Me and these boys are militia, not regular army."

"I want go home. I'm sick of killing Indians for now," said the second man.

"If we ain't going to jump her, I am leaving, too," said the other man, whose pistol had crept closer to her breasts. "I got cows to milk."

"Well, hell, you can ride along to Austin with me," the officer said. "But you got to give me your pistol."

"No," she said.

"How can I trust you won't run off? Or shoot me?"

"I give you my word," she said.

"Will you tell Old Paint how good I was to you? Will you tell him there's some horse thieves in Bastrop that need to be killed? I can point them out. My name is Captain John Carver."

The other two militia soldiers took the dead Lipan's gun and knife and horse and disappeared into the forest, going back to their farms. Cullasaja mounted her Morgan and rode onto the road with Captain Carver. She recognized the country, the flat blacklands that led to the river and the white limestone cliffs in the distance in the moonlight. Her heart soared. They were approaching Austin; in the blue night she could detect sparkles of light that came from cabins on the outskirts of the city.

Her Morgan stepped into a wagon rut, almost fell, and then began limping badly in the right leg.

"Might be a stone got caught in the hoof," said Captain Carver. "You want I should look and see if I can pry it out?"

Cullasaja slid down from the Morgan. She shoved her pistol into the dress pocket that had held grapevine clippings not so long ago. Captain Carver dismounted and lifted the Morgan's hoof, feeling with his fingers for a stone.

"You say you're from New York City?" he said.

"Yes. I was born there," she said.

"I'm from Penn's Grove, New Jersey," he said.

Cullasaja stroked the brave Morgan's neck and scratched the horse's ears. She did not heed the plodding hooves or the rolling wheels coming down the road in the darkness. The carriage was upon them before she looked up. She was thinking about a good meal and a bath at Bullock's or at Fritz and Ruth Gruber's house. Maybe Romulus would be in Austin.

"Was you at Bowl's Town?" asked Captain Carver.

"Yes," she said, remembering the hot, wet splash of Velasco's brain on her arm and the smell of burning bacon as the town died in flames.

"I'm sorry for what happened there. I didn't know that was going to be the outcome. Will you tell Old Paint I said so?"

"I will tell him," said Cullasaja, aware the carriage had stopped, its horses blowing loudly, and a dark figure was at the window.

The carriage door was flung open, and a beaked head on a long neck bobbed out, a long arm pointing with an ebony cane.

"Captain, arrest that Indian," the crane of a figure said.

"Mr. Longfellow!" said Captain Carver. "What can I do for you, sir?"

"That woman is a spy and a robber. Arrest her."

Cullasaja froze for an instant, chilled by the remembrance. This was the lunatic who had attacked her, whose leg Romulus had broken. Then she grabbed for the pistol in her pocket. The hammer caught on the hem, and as she jerked it loose, she felt a slam on the back of her head. She tumbled forward, aware that the officer had struck her with his rifle butt. She cried out for her brother before her conscious mind went blank.

"She told me she's a friend of Captain Caldwell," said the officer.

"She's a liar. Caldwell is trying to arrest her on orders from President Lamar. She's a whore and a spy for the Mexicans."

The militia officer sensed that he was in a dangerous situation. If the breed girl was telling the truth, as his instinct told him she was, Captain Carver was in desperate fear of Old Paint's retaliation. Carver wished he hadn't hit the girl so hard. But he couldn't allow an Indian to shoot Mr. Longfellow, a wealthy citizen and presidential adviser.

"Adam, Franklin, you boys lift her into the carriage," Longfellow said.

The two young black slaves jumped down from the driver's seat of the carriage. One picked up Cullasaja under the shoulders, and the other took her feet. Carver saw her bare legs as her dress bunched, and he thought the Negro at her shoulders was clasping her breasts unnecessarily. They heaved her unconscious body into the carriage and heard it thump. Then the carriage door snapped shut. The dice was rolled now, thought Carver. He wanted to go home to Bastrop and do chores at his farm. It was better he should forget he ever saw this half-breed girl. Mr. Longfellow could have her. The hell with trying to help a person.

# F I V E

## PLUM CREEK

Of what use is all the lands in Texas
or the figures on a Bank book to a
dead man?

*—letter from Samuel
Maverick, the elder,
to his son, Sam, of Texas*

# 59

Stripped to the waist and sweating in the afternoon heat, Romulus helped two painted warriors lift Antonio down from his horse and lay him on a buffalo robe in the shade of a lean-to.

An Apache arrow stuck out of the warrior's upper right chest. The arrow had penetrated the pectoralis major, but from the slight wobble of the shaft in his fingers Romulus had reason to hope the barbed tip was not buried in Antonio's scapula. Blood oozed around the entry wound, and the purple swelling told of internal bleeding. Antonio's two wives wept and wailed and begged their husband to stay alive. Without him the women and their children would have no provider, as they had no relatives in Turk's camp. The mighty Turk himself had made Antonio and family welcome, but now many people were missing and Turk was gone to search for them.

Romulus unwrapped his medical tools. The Dark Man, Young Owl Hatching and two dozen warriors, with scores of women and children behind them, crowded around to watch the white healer at his art.

Twirler, the shaman, ran to his tepee and returned wearing his magical healing quartzes, his headband with a mirror on it, his wand from which waved eagle and owl feathers, and shaking his gourd rattle. While Romulus raised Antonio and felt underneath his back to see if he could touch the arrow point under the skin, Twirler began chanting and calling upon the spirits that are in the known and in the unknown. The wives had not paid Twirler for his service, but he felt an obligation to a dweller in this village, even one from a faraway and unfamiliar family. Too, there was the dim possibility that Antonio would recover and reward him.

In frontier Mexican, Romulus asked the Dark Man to use his powerful hands to assist in turning Antonio onto his left. side. With a scalpel Romulus opened the flesh below Antonio's right shoulder blade.

"He is lucky," Romulus said. "The arrow missed his lung, and it's far enough in that we can push it on through." Removing a barbed war arrow from human flesh was like ripping a handful of fishhooks out of the body, tearing through nerves with each awful inch. If this arrow had demanded pulling out, a large chunk of Antonio's chest would have had to come with it, and he would die.

Twirler tapped his feet and spun in place and chanted *ayeayeayea,* and the wives wailed and scratched bloody rips into their arms in grief that would turn far worse should their man perish. Romulus wiped sweat off his forehead with his forearm and brushed away swarms of gathering green flies while he prepared to cut again with the scalpel.

Antonio's lips ran with blood as he bit through them in order to hold his cries. He shut his eyes to keep pain from showing. Romulus felt among his medical tools for the brown bottle of opium tincture. At first he wouldn't accept it, but it was true—the bottle of opium was missing. Romulus stared at the Dark Man, who spoke calmly.

"I drank it."

"You drank the whole bottle?"

"Yes."

"When?"

"I don't know."

"But this was opium. Not really for drinking. It's to cure pain and bring about a dream state."

"I know that now," said the Dark Man.

"Antonio, I'm sorry, young buck, but this is going to hurt like hell," Romulus said in English.

With a sudden lunge Romulus powered the Apache shaft deeper into Antonio's chest, and then deeper still, muscles taut in the doctor's right arm and shoving harder while Antonio looked straight ahead, his teeth protruding through his gums, blood soaking his chin—and then Romulus felt a lightening of resistance and knew he had punched through to the other side of Antonio's body.

A bloody blob of flesh formed around the point of the barbed Apache arrowhead that poked out of Antonio's back. With his Cherokee knife from Bowl's Town, Romulus sliced the arrowhead off the shaft. Swiftly Romulus stepped around in front of Antonio, looked the man in the eyes, grasped the feathered end and pulled the shaft out of the torso with one smooth yank.

Askara, a woman of Turk's family who was known for her herb and root healing, crept forward and began to stuff Antonio's wounds with a doughy paste made of the meat of prickly pears and ingredients she found in trees and under rocks. Antonio's blood flow was slowing. He lay mute and looked at Romulus and at the arrow. His women and relatives realized that maybe he was going to live. They howled with joy. They grouped tightly around their fallen hero and crooned about the miracle of life.

Twirler danced up and down, singing *ayeayeaye* and shaking his rattle.

Romulus wrapped his medical tools and started back toward his tepee, which was located among those that made up Turk's lodge. The Dark Man walked on his hands, his body wavering behind like a reptile, leaving an S path in the dirt.

"It makes me angry that you drank my opium," Romulus said.

"I felt very great. Then I got sick and lost my bowels. Then I felt very, very great again for who knows how long, and I understood the entire reason for the earth and the stars in the heavens."

"But I suppose now you have forgotten what it is?"

"You have done the same?"

Romulus laid his medical tools with his kit inside his tepee and left again quickly, causing the Dark Man to make a difficult turn. Romulus walked between the tepees and the busy people to the bank of the Little Pigeon River. The water was clear enough that he could see stones on the bottom, and fish hovering. It would be cool underwater in this heat. Romulus pulled off his boots and stepped out of his trousers. He stood naked on a boulder on the bank while many of the people glanced at the strange white man, averting their eyes as though not really spying on him. His body hit the river with a thunk and a shower of water flew as Romulus relished the shock. Behind him, wriggling, the Dark Man slid into the river. Here in the water the two were equals at motion. The Dark Man's legs adapted to the water as well as the tail of a fish, and with his powerful shoulders he slithered like a cottonmouth, spreading a wake at his chin.

"When will I see the creature?" Romulus asked, floating in a blue pool.

"I have no messages," said the Dark Man.

"Will you take me to the cave?"

"When I am told to do so."

"Why is it called the Singing Rock?"

"You will hear it."

The Dark Man ducked below the surface and came up with water streaming down his long black hair, eyes blinking in his charred face.

"You did well with Antonio," said the Dark Man. "Our families are grateful to you."

"Why won't you take me to the creature?"

"It is good that you saved Antonio, because there has been talk spreading up and down the lodges on the river that you should be skinned alive."

"I am a hostage."

"Yes, but Talking Man's party has been gone for too many days, and now Turk has been gone for too many days, and the families are growing uneasy. The story is spreading that something bad has taken place, and you must pay."

"You're the prophet," said Romulus. "When are they coming back?"

"I don't see them coming back," the Dark Man said.

They heard a clamor that began half a mile downriver and grew as it raced among the lodges. People were running downriver, the men grabbing weapons. Romulus swam to the shore and put on his boots and trousers. The Dark Man crawled up the bank like an otter.

Riding along the path upriver past the lodges that spilled out people came Pearl, the angelic blonde child, mounted bareback on a stolen Texas army horse. In the delicate girlish fingers of her right hand she held a piece of flint that she was using to chop bleeding cuts in her left arm. Behind her formed a wave of people, all of them beginning to mourn. A woman ripped open her dress and slashed her breasts with a skinning knife. The number one wife of the Talking Man sliced off two fingers of her left hand. Others hacked their hair, pounded their legs with sticks, bashed their faces with their hands. All were crying and wailing with desperate sadness, the sound rising from the valley like a wind.

Pearl was crying in English, "All dead. All dead."

None of the families spoke English. Pearl knew little Comanche and no frontier Mexican, but it was clear to all what she was saying. They had seen her ride away with her husband, Isimanica, and with Talking Man and many others, going to the Council House.

"All dead. All dead," she cried.

"What happened?" asked Romulus.

"Hello." Pearl smiled sweetly at him.

"What happened in San Antonio?"

"My husband was killed."

"What does she say?" asked Dark Man.

"How did it happen?" Romulus asked.

Pearl had quit abusing her arm, but the howling around her became louder, and she lost her air of sweetness and angrily said, "They killed all our people."

"Who did?" asked Romulus.

"The men with hats," she said, using the Comanche term and then slipping back into her mountain drawl. "They put our people in the schoolhouse and killed them. They killed us in the road, too."

"All are dead?" asked Romulus.

"Some women and children are behind the fence. My sister is behind the fence. I found a horse in the dark. The rest are dead or behind the fence."

The howl became a roar as Romulus translated.

From each side angry warriors closed in on Romulus and grasped his arms so he could not launch blows as he had done to Isimanica.

# 6 □

Using a long-handled wooden paddle, Hannah scooped a loaf of dough onto the hot bricks in the window of the outside bread oven which was used on warm days. There was another bread oven inside the kitchen building, where meals were taken, and the fireplace in the kitchen always flamed or smoldered, furnishing the coals that made the bricks hot inside the bread oven.

She saw Matthew carrying his rosewood chair onto the west porch. On a clear morning, while the sun was in the east, Matthew would sit in his chair in the shade on the porch and drink coffee and look three miles across West Avenue and Shoal Creek and the forest and the river to the white cliffs of Comancheria, and she could tell he was dreaming and planning of the castle they would build up there.

In these early, honeymoon days of their marriage, he would carry his chair indoors when the sun passed high noon to protect the rosewood from the harsh afternoon glare, and then would bring it back to the west porch again at sunset to sit and watch the sun go down behind the white cliffs. After dark, Matthew would carry the rosewood chair into the parlor and buff the dust off with a soft cloth. He had been drawn at once to the magic of the chair, another emotion he shared with his wife.

As she baked bread, it struck her how much her husband looked like a bearded Celtic king sitting on his rosewood throne. Hannah felt a rush of happiness. Matthew was a good husband for her. He was gentle and tender with her. She found, in intimate moments, a little boy inside the scarred skin of a warrior. She was deeply pleased by him. She felt moments of giddiness, of romantic lust and silliness, but more she felt wanted and appreciated, and she loved her husband. She found his presence thrilling and comforting, and she discovered that he paid attention when she talked, and his own conversation had not come close to boring her. He could be quite intelligently amusing, and he knew dramatic and amazing stories about the frontier. He had a powerful ambition to serve his term in Congress before quitting politics and beginning to establish their Caldwell land empire. She had safely and secretly tucked away under a sheet of linoleum in the bottom of her underwear drawer the dried Old Blush roses and the declaration of love from Romulus Swift. They were souvenirs of an encounter she could hardly believe had happened. Matthew had told her Dr. Swift could handle himself among the savages, even after the fight at the Council House, and she believed it. The marriage contract between Hannah and Matthew was a good one. She tried nearly every night to make a child for them.

Hannah saw that her husband had brought a large piece of builders paper and spread it on the west porch table and was drawing on the paper with a pen dipped into an inkwell, leaning back to sip coffee and examine his work.

She scraped cornmeal dough off the paddle, leaned it against the kitchen wall and walked toward the house, scattering ducks. Their mastiff panted in the shade of the giant oaks. She heard water flowing in the creek and a shout from some distant fisherman. The morning smelled of baking bread and warm grass.

"What are you drawing?" she asked.

She stepped onto the porch and looked over his shoulder. In bold black lines Matthew was drawing a large house with a great gallery, huge windows striped with mullions, peaked roofs, crossed planks as decoration and bracing on outside walls. She scratched her nails lightly into his scalp—she knew he was fond of a head scratch—and kissed him on the ear.

"My daddy used to tell me and my brothers some of the history of our grandfathers. This is how I picture their houses to have looked, from what Daddy said."

"Tudor," she said.

"No, this is just what I see in my mind."

"I mean, the house you are drawing is in the Tudor style, which has been popular in England for hundreds of years. I have seen paintings of the great Tudor houses. This is their style."

"How would you and me look in a house like this?" he asked.

"Like we belong in it."

A Mexican boy who worked as a fetcher at Bullock's Inn kicked up dust running toward them down the Ash Street hill and swung himself between the trees and past the stable, where the white stallion and the Kentucky thorough bred swished their tails. The boy, who was barely tall enough to see over the edge of the porch, rushed up, his eyes round with excitement, and cried, "Captain Caldwell, sir! Mr. Bullock needs you at the hotel right now, sir."

"Tell him I'll be along in a few minutes," said Matthew.

"Sir, he says please you should come now. It is very important."

Hannah brought out a cotton sheet and covered the rosewood chair against dust while Matthew strapped on his pistols and his knife and picked up Sweet Lips.

"I'm going with you," she said.

"I'm not riding. I'm going to run."

"Do you think I can't keep up with you?"

Matthew grinned and began trotting up the hill on Ash Street, heading east into the sun. Hannah stayed beside him, her head bobbing at his shoulder height, her knees churning smoothly as she lifted her skirts and ran. He was not a regular at praying, but several times a day he was moved to a silent prayer of gratitude that God had sent Hannah to him. It almost seemed like treachery to Nancy and their two sons for Matthew to realize these days of living with Hannah were the happiest of his life. Memory was an illusion that we built for ourselves, and he meant no dishonor to the memory of his beloved Nancy, but he felt he had never been happier than now, and he was old enough to appreciate that it was happening.

The common morning sounds of the growing city spread all around them— hammering, sawing, cursing, dogs barking, roosters crowing, wagon wheels creaking—as they reached the crest of the Ash Street hill and started back toward the south. Matthew noted that Hannah's breathing was still unlabored. Below them a crowd of men was gathering around a ditch beside Pecan Street near Bullock's Inn. Matthew saw Richard Bullock and Mayor Waller in the inner circle, and Fritz Gruber came riding down Congress Avenue on his big palomino in the company of a guide from the Shoal Creek Wacos and two young surveyors, whose instruments were loaded onto a mule. The German dismounted and shouldered through the crowd. Matthew heard a howl of anguish and anger from Gruber.

Men stepped aside for the Ranger and his wife.

A naked woman lay on her back in the ditch, her arms outflung and her fingers curled and stiff.

"She's so messed up it's hard to tell, but I believe she was that Cherokee nurse," Mayor Waller said.

Seeing the crowd of men staring at the nude body as if examining a cow that had fallen dead, Hannah broke away and ran a few yards east to Bullock's Inn. She knocked on the door of a bungalow until Dora opened. Dora's eyes were red from the five bottles of wine she and the snoring Lawrence had drunk at dinner.

"Yah! That's her. That's Doc Swift's sister," said Gruber.

"How about it, Captain?" Mayor Waller asked.

"That's Cullasaja," Matthew said, his gut turning cold with growing rage.

Hannah hurried inside the circle carrying Dora's bedspread, which she draped across the body to cover Cullasaja from the eyes of the men.

"How long has she been here?" said Matthew.

Bullock shrugged. "My kitchen swamper told me she was laying here when he come to work at dawn. But he didn't tell me until a few minutes ago. He said a number of people passed by, but they didn't pay much attention because she's only an Indian."

"She's supposed to be in Bowl's Town," Gruber said. "Doc took her to live with the Cherokees."

"No more!" the Waco said. He looked down at them between the ears of his horse.

"What do you mean?" said Matthew.

"No more Cherokees. Army come and burn Bowl's Town. Burn all the people's towns. Kill many," the Waco said.

"How the hell do you know?" asked Mayor Waller.

"The word is on the wind," the Waco said.

"When was Bowl's Town destroyed?" asked Matthew.

"Not yesterday. Maybe the day before that," the Waco said. Scouting for surveying crews, he had tried to learn to measure time with a white man's precision.

Matthew realized that Cullasaja must have fled Bowl's Town and been searching for her brother or himself.

"I thought someone said this girl is a dead Indian," said Lawrence Kerr, tying the belt of his bathrobe.

"She's half Cherokee, like him," Matthew said.

"You mean she really is Doc's sister?" said Bullock. "I thought that was just their little story."

"Me, too," Waller said.

"Hero's sister murdered," said the reporter from the *Sentinel*.

Dora moved in close and put an arm around Hannah's shoulders. Hannah was stunned to discover Romulus Swift had a sister who looked to be the same age as she. And he was half Cherokee; she had been taught that meant he was half savage. But that notion did not penetrate the horror of the young woman's mutilated corpse. For Dora, hugging Hannah, this was a horrible turn of events and she felt sympathy, but she recognized it as melodrama she would use in her New York stage show about Texas, should it occur.

"I think I might of seen this body last night, Captain," a carpenter said. "I was walking along here about midnight after a few nips at Dutch John's. I seen somebody laying out here, but I thought it was just another drunk."

"A naked woman?" said Gruber.

"Hell, I said I had a few nips. It was dark. If I'd known it was a naked woman, I would of tooken a closer look."

Matthew looked at his wife.

"Hannah, I want you to see Cullasaja to the mortuary," he said. "You and Dora make sure he fixes her as good as possible before we ship her body home. Lawrence, you know where in New York her body should go?"

"They're a prominent family. Yes, I'll know how to address it," said Lawrence.

"I am paying the expenses," Gruber said. "This was one fine woman, yah. We pack her in ice."

"We must notify her brother," said Hannah.

"When we find him," Matthew said. "Stick a prod in these fellows, Hannah. Make them treat Cullasaja with respect and get her body out of that ditch."

Matthew set out trotting toward the Bois d'Arc Street home of Henry Longfellow. He had a feeling about who was responsible for this terrible event.

# 61

Rather than building yet another southern plantation-style house to add to the city of Austin—the Kerrs were setting the standard in that area, though their mansion was not yet finished—Henry Longfellow had changed his mind and asked Newfield to erect for him a house that would be called Longfellow, made of logs that had been hewn and counter-hewn until they were smooth as glass and no longer looked like wood. A wide porch supported by columns of polished walnut ran the eighty-foot length of the house. On the second floor were four bedrooms, each with its own sandstone fireplace, and a bathing room with a marble tub. The President and the Kerrs were having their mansions painted white. Henry chose to have the Longfellow house painted fresh peach.

On his palomino, Gruber caught up with the trotting Ranger.

"You think it was Longfellow that killed her?" Gruber asked.

"That's the idea."

"Why would he do it?"

"He's crazy. He tried to rape her last spring."

"Longfellow ain't been in Austin since before your wedding. He's scared of you."

The Ranger climbed the four steps onto the porch of the Longfellow house. The front door and all the windows were open because of the heat. Mosquito nets hung across the openings. Matthew banged his fist on the wall.

"Yassuh?"

Matthew looked down at a tiny Negro girl, maybe twelve years old but short for her age. She stood behind the netting wearing a short polka-dot dress.

"I want to see Henry Longfellow," the Ranger said.

"He gone."

"Who is in charge of the house?" asked Matthew.

"I is."

"There must be somebody older than you," Matthew said.

"Old Root, he older. But he work de yard and de stable. I in charge of de house. Massah, he not move he into dis house yet. When he move he, he bring Florence and Liberty and dey be in charge of de house. But now I in charge."

"Was Longfellow here last night?" asked Matthew.

The little girl drew a circle with her toe. "Waaal . . ."

"He was here, wasn't he?"

"Who you be?" the girl said.

"A friend of his," said Matthew.

"You doan look like no fren to he."

"Was he here last night?" Matthew asked.

"Nossuh."

"How long has he been gone?" asked Matthew.

The little girl ran deep into the house. They heard her bare feet on the wooden floors.

Matthew walked around the house to the stable. Gruber followed, leading the palomino. Inside the corral they saw two standard-bred saddle horses, a heavy-hipped work horse, and four gray Holsteins. The Holsteins were big horses with muscular, beautifully formed necks and powerful legs bred in Europe for long striding and war. They turned their large eyes onto the strangers at the gate.

"Matched coach horses," Gruber said.

Matthew entered the corral and spoke soothingly to the Holsteins as he approached. He rubbed the back and neck and ears of each horse and let them smell and nibble his beard. He felt the muscles in their forelegs and looked at their feet. He sniffed their breath and looked at their manure. Matthew eased himself out of the gate again and walked around to the stable door, looking at the ground. The entrance to the stable had been swept by a broom, but Matthew could see the marks of wheels.

They heard a banging inside a horse stall, as if someone had stumbled.

Matthew aimed Sweet Lips at the stall door and said, "Come out of there."

A bald, fat Negro with gray hair staggered out of the stall, holding a hand to his forehead.

"Damn," he said.

"You Old Root?" asked Matthew.

"Yassuh."

"Henry Longfellow stopped here last night and changed coach horses. Those four Holsteins have been driven hard. What you tell me, Old Root, is when Longfellow left here and where was he going."

"Suh, I didn't see no Massuh Longfellow."

"Don't lie to me, Old Root."

"Nossuh. Last night I went off to the flats by the river and drunk a lot of jug whiskey and played dice, and two Mexicans whipped me. Looka here."

Old Root tilted his head for inspection.

"See how they bunged up my eye and phlabotomized my nose?"

Matthew nodded. Old Root had been punched around, and he reeked of alcohol.

"So I didn't wake up and come back here until sunup, and I didn't see no Massuh Longfellow," the Negro said.

"How many Holstein coach horses does Longfellow own?" asked Matthew.

"He got eight. Four grays and four bays. He mighty proud of them horses."

"Are any of the Holsteins here in Austin?"

"Yassuh. I keeping care of the four bays."

"How did the four grays get in your corral?" Matthew said.

"Is they? I doan know."

The Ranger and the German walked back around to the front of the house on Bois d'Arc Street.

"Maybe the old drunk is wrong about what color horses," said Gruber.

"He changed horses here. My hunch is he's running to Houston City for Lamar to protect him. I'm going to catch the son of a bitch before he gets there," Matthew said.

"But he's got a head start of ten or twelve hours."

"He's got rivers to cross," Matthew said. "I'll get him."

"Yah. You're right. I go with you. She was my friend."

"Appreciate it, Gruber. But I can make better distance alone."

"Then let me ride you back to your house. Save you some time."

Matthew mounted behind the German on the palomino, and they rode into the traffic of wagons and livestock and people on Congress Avenue. A herd of Bullock's pigs trotted up Bois d'Arc in the direction of the French Legation. The two young surveyors and the Waco guide waited for Gruber near Bullock's Inn, but Cullasaja's body was gone and the spectators had joined the general mass along the streets.

"Where you surveying?" Matthew said into the German's ear.

"Southwest, past Bone's Spring. Beautiful valley, yah."

"Be careful."

"Hah, you killed all the Comanches, Captain. But I'll be careful to choose valuable land."

In a moment Gruber said, "What do you think happened to Doc Swift?"

"He's sitting on a golden throne in that cavern you told him about."

Gruber brightened. "Yah. Yah. That's what he's doing! With the big ape!"

In their corral, Matthew was throwing a saddle onto the white Arabian when Hannah entered the gate. She looked at his packed saddlebags, which leaned against a pitchfork.

"I'm going to catch Henry Longfellow," he said.

"Lawrence says you're wrong to suspect him. He says Longfellow is a harmless peeper."

"Lawrence wants to be in business with him."

"Matthew, I think we should not ship her body home."

He tightened the cinch on Pacer and looked around at his wife.

"She is so mutilated and so badly beaten. The bones in her face are crushed. There's nothing to do that can fix her into a daughter for her mother and father to see."

"What do you suggest?" Matthew said.

"Lawrence will write a letter of condolence to her mother and father and say she died of a contagious illness. Lawrence and Dora will call upon the Swift family when they return to New York City."

"Bury Cullasaja here?"

"We will bury her in the new cemetery on the other side of East Avenue. It's a beautiful place, very green and shady. Mayor Waller wants to do the service. He says she once cut the ingrown nail off his big toe."

Matthew smiled, remembering how Waller had howled until Cullasaja dosed him with laudanum.

"What kind of service should it be?" Hannah said.

"Tell the mayor to make it a general, all-purpose consigning this creation back to God kind of service. Cullasaja's good soul is already someplace else, but we need to pay tribute to the body that carried it. Hold off the service until I get back. Pack her in the ice house, like Gruber said."

Matthew picked Hannah up in his arms and held her so that their noses were on a plane, his gray cat eyes locked on her dark, exotic ones. Slowly she moved her head forward and kissed him on the lips.

"What if her brother comes and claims her body?" she said. "He'll know it was no contagious disease."

"I love you, Hannah," he said.

"I love you, husband."

Matthew lowered her to the ground.

"If Doctor Swift should show up here, don't let him leave. I will be back to discuss things with him."

The Ranger mounted the white Arabian, threw a two-finger kiss at his wife, and set off down West Avenue, south toward the river, at a canter, his straw hat brim turned up, his hairy torso bare except for the suspenders that helped to support his two pistols and his butcher knife. Sweet Lips was tucked into its scabbard near his right leg.

Suddenly left alone again by her husband's call to duty, Hannah sat down in a rocking chair under a great oak and spread her legs and threw back her arms and sighed loudly. Her Texas life was almost unreal, like a dream.

Thinking of strangeness, of unreality, she remembered Romulus. Hannah rushed into the house. She opened her armoire and pulled out a drawer. She tossed undergarments onto the floor. She lifted the linoleum and pulled out the blue envelope and the dried Old Blush roses that she had wrapped in paper. She read the doctor's vow of love and his plea for her to wait for him. A feeling of wistfulness rose in her, and tears surged to her eyes as she felt the petal of a rose crumble in her fingers. She should destroy these things. Burn them. The doctor was a romantic phantom. But she stopped in her path toward the kitchen fireplace. She turned around and went back into the house and hid the roses and the letter, a secret part of her, again under the linoleum at the bottom of her underwear drawer.

It was a hundred and eighty miles from Austin to Houston City, through swamp and forest, crossing dozens of bodies of flowing water, some called rivers, fed by springs and keeping up their flow in the late summer. By the time Matthew rode into the outskirts of Houston City, he realized Longfellow was not running to the President but to the steamboat docks.

The B. J. Biggs Steamship Company was a one-room pine building, painted blue, on the bank of Buffalo Bayou. Biggs hurried to show the Ranger his manifests. The steamboat *Gulf Coast Belle* had left six hours ago, bound for New Orleans after a stop in Galveston. On the passenger list Matthew saw the names Henry Longfellow of Houston City and Joshua Watson of Lexington, Kentucky. They were accompanied by "2 Negra slave boys, names unknown."

"Where is Longfellow's carriage?" Matthew asked.

"Mr. Longfellow had us load his coach aboard the *Belle*, and he took it with him. His horses went with him, too."

"Four matched bays?"

"Yes, sir. Beautiful animals."

Matthew had hoped to inspect the carriage and look inside for blood or hair lost when Cullasaja fought for her life, but now that was beyond his grasp also. He shut the ledger, gave Biggs a friendly smile that the shipowner found alarming, and then he mounted Pacer and rode along Main Street toward the capitol. As crowded as Austin had grown in the past six months, Houston City had grown even more. A lesser figure than a Texas Ranger on a white Arabian stallion would have found it difficult to negotiate through the people, wagons and livestock. It had not rained in a week, and Main Street was oddly dusty rather than muddy. A haze of mosquitoes, flies and methane gas from decomposing manure made a rust-colored light fall across the city.

The clerk at the entrance to the capitol was sleeping, his elbows in pools of sweat on the desk. Matthew climbed the stairs to the second floor, hardly making a squeak in his moccasin boots, and had turned into the hall when he heard the clomping of boots and saw Albert Sidney Johnston limping toward him.

"At least let me beat you to his door so I can announce you, Matthew," Johnston said.

In his shirtsleeves, his armpits black with sweat, Johnston limped in front of the Ranger and rapped twice on the door to Lamar's office. All the other doors—and windows—on the second floor were open to catch any breeze, but a swamp-like stench floated through instead.

They heard the President's voice say, "What do you want?"

"Captain Caldwell is here to see you, sir."

"Come in, come in."

As he pushed open the door, Johnston said, "Nice job you did on the Comanches, Matthew."

"Who sent Fisher and the regulars to San Antonio?"

"I did."

"Albert, you're an idiot, or else you betrayed me," Matthew said. "Was this a plot?"

"What is this, now?" said Lamar, entering from his inner office, where his pen lay on top of a stack of papers that he was cursed to read and either sign or not sign.

"Sending the regulars to San Antonio was the act of a fool," Matthew said. "It was treachery that has started a war. Did you do it on purpose?"

"I resent your tone, Captain," said President Lamar.

"You made me out a liar to the Comanches. I don't take that lightly," Matthew said.

"You don't really think we started that fight with the Comanches on purpose?" Lamar said.

"Maybe it was stupidity," Matthew said.

"Why, Matthew, I was about to tell you I am having a medal struck to commend your noble success at bringing in the Comanche chiefs. You have done a great service for the Republic," Lamar said.

"You were supposed to come to the Council House," Matthew said. "We had a chance to make a peace."

"I'm not good at that sort of thing. The two fellows I sent are expert at dealing with savages."

"You have started a war with the Comanches that we are not strong enough to win," Matthew said.

"Nonsense," said Johnston. "The Comanches are no threat. We have killed seventeen of their chiefs. You may call it stupidity. I say it is good fortune."

"You have stirred up thousands of Comanches out in the hills," Matthew said. "We will need at least three battalions of regulars in Austin and as many in San Antonio. Pronto."

"We can't afford that many soldiers," said Johnston.

"You found enough soldiers to wipe out Bowl's Town," Matthew said. "Albert, you treacherous bastard, you knew General Houston had promised Bowl's Cherokees they could settle there. What gave you the right to destroy them?"

Johnston's face was red, and he unbuttoned another button on his shirt. "The Cherokees fired the first shot. We gave them plenty of warning to move peaceably, but they attacked us," he said.

"We were legally evicting old Chief Bowl from privately owned land, and things got out of hand," the President said. He poured himself a glass of water from a crystal pitcher. "But look what this lucky, accidental violence has done for us. We have cleared out the whole rats' nest up there. We have opened a thousand square miles to settlement. I call that a great thing for the Republic of Texas. Yes, of course we had regular troopers up there—a few cavalry— but most of our fighters were militia from east Texas. If you fear the Comanches haven't learned their lesson, we need to put together a strong militia in Austin and one in San Antonio."

"We need an army," Matthew said.

"When Congress meets in October, we will levy taxes to pay for a large army," said Lamar. Caldwell's words were of deep concern to the President. In a few weeks Lamar would begin moving the capital to Austin, and he felt that Caldwell was now warning him that Austin would not be safe. "Albert, tell General Huston to move his troops into the Austin area. No, Felix won't listen to you. I will write him an executive command."

"You have millions of dollars the French loaned us," Matthew said. " Pay for six battalions out of that money."

"The loan from France has not come through," said the President. "The chargé d'affaires in Austin keeps complaining about pigs eating his corn. But we'll get the money. If there's no loan from France, our citizens will be willing to pay taxes for their own protection and the expansion of our Republic. In the meantime, I'll send General Huston to help you Rangers safeguard San Antonio and Austin."

Matthew plucked a cigar from the humidor on the table. He lit the cigar from a tallow lamp that was kept burning in the hope its smoke would drive away cholera.

"You lied to me," Matthew said.

"Be careful, Captain. I could take offense."

"With no French loan, how were you going to pay the Comanches? Is that why you used bullets on them instead?"

"As president, I have learned that every day brings a new reality," said Lamar. "If I needed gold, I would have found it. But the new reality is, I do not need gold to pay the Comanches, because they are dead, and the Republic of Texas will honor you as a hero in October."

Matthew looked at Johnston, who continued to flush and glare at the Ranger.

"Was Henry Longfellow with you at Bowl's Town?" Matthew asked.

"He was there representing his client who owns the land," said Johnston.

The President carefully turned up his cuffs one more fold.

"I know you don't like Henry," Lamar said. "But the violence at Bowl's Town cannot be blamed on him. The Cherokees charged our men, who were attempting to serve a lawful order. Well, the damned savages picked on the wrong bunch this time. Just like they did at the Council House. We have a big fight with the Comanches and a big fight with the Cherokees, and we crushed them. I believe the red men are on the run, due to heroes like yourself, Captain."

"I serve the Republic of Texas, but I ain't doing any more special jobs for you, Lamar," Matthew said. "You're a four-flusher. If the Comanches catch you in Austin and cut your throat, you deserve it."

"You're out of line, Matthew. You can't talk to the President that way," Johnston said.

Matthew had propped Sweet Lips against the table while he lit the cigar. Now he picked up his shotgun and regarded Lamar and Johnston. The President was idly pulling at locks of hair above his ears and looked at Matthew as if waiting for the funny part of the joke. The secretary of war wiped his sweaty face with a handkerchief.

"Caldwell, what do you want from me?" asked Lamar.

That the Comanches would come across the Texas frontier for revenge was as inevitable as the coming of winter. Matthew puffed his cigar and looked at the President. This war would have to be won if the Republic was to survive, much less expand.

"Why are you silent? What are you staring at?" the President asked. "I don't like this." Lamar hurried into his inner office, where piles of papers lay for his examination. He slammed the door behind him. "Go away, both of you!" he shouted through the pine.

Johnston limped beside Matthew to the top of the steps.

"If I was younger, I would call you out for naming me a fool and an idiot in front of the President," Johnston said.

"Albert, I'm older than you are," said Matthew.

"I'm not going to fight you, Matthew. But if you don't like taking orders from the President, I can officially accept your resignation."

"It's not up to you, Albert. I don't work for you. Doesn't Lamar realize his new capital is barely defended? Doesn't he know how many Comanches are in the hills?"

"I have told him over and over. I don't want to move the government to Austin. We're much better off here in Houston City. You damn politicians should have voted against Lamar on this issue," Johnston said.

Matthew moved quietly down the stairs and passed the clerk, who was now awake but uncurious, and took the reins of the white stallion from the hitching pole. He would find a good stable for Pacer and get a room for himself in the Palace Hotel. He had a powerful desire to go to the Palace saloon, where he had last seen the Old Chief, and drink all the whiskey behind the bar, and sing "Come to the Bower," and blot out the memory of Cullasaja's body lying naked in an Austin ditch.

# 6 2

In a show of grief unsurpassed in the memories of any family, the widows of the Talking Man offered his entire herd of fifteen hundred horses to be sacrificed in his honor. The horse herd was nearly every bit of the widows' earthly wealth, but their bereavement was extreme, and the widows had three sons entering their prime who would be called upon to care for their mothers. Young Owl Hatching and two hundred warriors and chiefs walked among the herd in a meadow downwind of the village and cut the horses' throats. Then they covered the field of dead horses with logs and brush and set it afire. To kill and burn the horses took three days. The tower of black smoke could be seen for fifty miles. For this family of families, the distress at the events of the Council House dug into their communal heart even deeper than the deaths of the Talking Man and Isimanica and the others. Death was always to be expected at any moment, but death because of treachery was an unbearable insult.

Pearl had rushed into the arms of her mother, Wanda Mecom, now known as wife of The Ram. Pearl spoke her tale of the Council House in her mountain drawl, and her mother translated it as best she could into the language of the families. Pearl's version of the ambush was known in every lodge of the encampment in the valley of the Little Pigeon, and soon spread across the plains to the snowy mountains. For Pearl there was no difference between imagination and reality. She related what she had seen and what she had imagined as though they were equally true.

In her addled mind, Pearl imagined she had seen the Talking Man with his hands tied behind his back kneeling in the middle of the road as the big man with the black and white beard took a two-handed grip on a sword and chopped off the Talking Man's head. She told it to her mother, who repeated it as the truth.

And the word went across the plains to the snowy mountains—Old Paint must die.

Every family in Comancheria felt insulted by the Texans. Peace was sacred during an arranged council between even the worst of foes. To violate a council by betrayal and ambush was inconceivable.

At family councils on the high plains, warriors promised to kill the Texans. There were curses and threats and wails of mourning in camps from the Comanche Trace, west of San Antonio, north seven hundred miles to the North Canadian River, northwest eight hundred miles to near Bent's Fort on the Santa Fe Trail, farther west to the snowy mountains.

Thirty thousand members of the family spoke and sang at the many councils and demonstrated hatred for the men with hats. The families were buzzing angrily, like swarms of disturbed bees, ready to attack but not yet certain how to begin. They lacked the leader who could inspire them to follow him.

During this time Romulus sat cross-legged on the earth floor of his tepee, his torso bare, his wrists crossed before him and wrapped together by rawhide straps. Each of the widows of the Talking Man entered his tepee separately and beat his bare head and chest and shoulders with peach tree switches. Groups of women came in and sat and looked at him and reached over to pinch him or to gouge out a piece of skin with the point of a knife. One of Isimanica's widows brought in a branch burning with live coals and extinguished it on his back with a sizzle as if into snow. He was given no food and only enough liquid to keep him alive until the council decided his fate.

Romulus withdrew into himself and withstood his ordeal stoically, accepting the pain, concentrating on each breath, allowing each thought that came into his mind to float gently by. After a day of this he reached a state that seemed to be suspended animation. He felt that love is not what holds the universe together—imagination does it.

So he sat during the burning of the Comanche chief's horses and lived in imagination and did not speak or flinch from the blows, and the women grew bored with abusing him. They brought water in a buffalo stomach and squirted it between his lips.

"We want you to be healthy for the fire," a woman told him.

Pearl came to see him. She slapped his face.

The Dark Man looked through the flap, took in the sight of the cross-legged healer, switched and bloody, who seemed to be in a trance, and then went away to pray to the band of stars that crossed the night for guidance in the council that was soon to begin. Dark Man expected a message to appear in his mind from the creature, but none had come.

Romulus became aware of the thumping of axes into the earth and knew a pit was being dug to hold the flames that would roast his body. His soul seemed to remember this event from a time long ago, and the feeling somehow kept him from being afraid.

The shriek of an eagle-bone whistle awoke his conscious mind.

Romulus began to hear tooting and fluting and cries of happiness growing closer, like a breeze blowing into the village.

The clamor proceeded toward him—Romulus understood from the screams and shouts that Turk had come home, and something exciting had happened. He heard horses thumping the dirt, the voices of women raised in scorn and menace, and the whack of a body falling heavily, and groaning.

His tepee flap was raised, and a half dozen warriors rolled a large naked man inside. The man's arms were strapped behind his back, arms that were broad and laced with old whip wounds. His body came to rest facedown. Romulus found himself staring at his own handiwork in the form of an iron fin on the crown of the man's bald head, surrounded by flesh as smooth and healthy pink as baby skin.

"Fritz Gruber," Romulus said, the first words he had uttered in days.

The figure moaned. The head turned sideways to get its mouth out of the dirt. Blood had congealed around a gash in the left eyebrow.

"Fritz. It's me. It's Doc Swift."

"Doc?"

Romulus uncrossed his legs and stood up, needles running through his nerves, and with his bound wrists helped Gruber turn over onto his back and sit, propped on his elbows.

Other than the blow to his left forehead and the many cuts and bruises that had been caused by the women throwing rocks and stabbing with sharp sticks, no injury was apparent on the German.

"Oompossible. Oompossible," Gruber said. "It's really you, Doc."

"How did they get you?"

"I was with two surveyors and a Waco guide crossing the Warloop. They shot us from ambush. That savage called Turk has the scalps of the others. He brought me here for special treatment, because these animals and me are old friends." Gruber tried to spit, but his mouth was too dry. "But I have the satisfaction of knowing that bastard who buried his axe in my head was killed in San Antonio."

"Caldwell led the Comanches into a trap," Romulus said.

"You've heard about it?"

"Every Comanche has heard about it."

"I don't know if trapping them was Old Paint's purpose or not, Doc. Listen, I can't see out of my left eye. Is my eyeball still in my face?"

"You have blood caked in your eye. I wish I could clean it for you."

Gruber breathed deeply, his hairy belly heaving, as if mining for air to feed his system.

"What are you doing a prisoner? Caldwell told me you stayed out here to look for the ape and the cave of gold. I warned you to forget about that gold, Doc."

"Caldwell left me to die," Romulus said.

Gruber struggled until he could raise his knees and sit in a more modest position, his testicles dangling in the dirt.

"Doc, I don't know if I ought to tell you this, seeing the fix we're in, but I think you should hear it."

"What?" Romulus said.

"The army burned Bowl's Town and killed old Chief Bowl."

A dagger of fear dove through the layers of peace that had formed during Romulus's meditations.

"Cullasaja?"

"God forgive me for telling you, Doc. Your sister is dead."

Romulus was aware his breathing became rapid and shallow, and his pulse went weak, as if in shock. His eyes glazed and his cheeks pinched in. With his new beard and the growing out of his monk's cut, and the burns and bruises on his wide, bare shoulders, this man looked far different from the Doc Swift that Gruber had known in Austin, the healer who had saved Gruber's life.

Looking at Doc, who was trying to refuse to believe what he had heard, Gruber regretted telling about the girl. If Doc was going to die at the hands of these savages, why increase his suffering?

"I'm sorry," Gruber said.

"Tell me. How did it happen? Who killed her?"

"Caldwell thinks it was Henry Longfellow that killed her and dropped her body in the middle of town, but there's no proof. His slaves say Longfellow wasn't in Austin."

Yes, Romulus could imagine that the ugly pervert Longfellow would have killed Cullasaja and put her body on display.

"What is Caldwell doing about it?"

"When I left, he was chasing Longfellow."

"Where is my sister's body?"

"We were going to bury her in the cemetery when Old Paint and I got back. His wife was making the arrangements. Caldwell's wife is a nice girl, Doc. Only young Jews are pretty like her. She's been caring for his bullet wound, but you don't hear her complain. He got lucky with this wife."

They heard drums pounding outside the tepee. Flutes and whistles shrilled again, and they heard chanting and whooping. Through the tepee's smoke hole they could see the sky darkening.

"It's a big circle. Yah," said Gruber. "For me Texas is a big circle from savages to riches and back to savages." He inspected a seeping puncture wound on his chest, made by a child's pointed stick. "I got lucky with Ruthie, Doc. She's a good woman. If you should get away from these savages, tell Ruthie I love her. Help her get a mean lawyer, like Ridgewood Bone, and collect what's coming to her."

"I'll take care of it, Fritz."

"You and your sister have been good to me, Doc. I hope I see you in heaven."

For the first time since he had encountered Gruber beneath the stairs at the Redbud Hotel nearly eight months ago, he saw fear in the German's eyes.

"They're going to finish me off slow," Gruber said. "What can I do, Doc? How can I endure the pain? I'm afraid."

Romulus shook his head. There was nothing adequate to say.

"They're going to chop off Big Willy. I know they are," said Gruber. "Hey, where is that ape? Did you find that ape? Maybe he will come save me again."

"You could pray," Romulus said.

"Doc, I'm really scared. I need help, not just praying."

"I could kill you," Romulus said. "I could break your neck and make it painless."

Gruber chewed his upper lip as he thought it over.

"Not yet, Doc. Maybe something will save me."

The flap flew open and Turk entered the tepee. The hairy-chested chief carried a wreath woven from sage and dry twigs.

"We do not need a council to decide what to do with you," Turk said in frontier Mexican, looking down at Gruber. "You brought us the sex sickness. You should have been killed long ago."

"It wasn't me that brought the sickness. It was one of my partners, not me. I never had the sickness."

The Dark Man crept to the edge of the flap and looked in.

"You!" Gruber saw him and said, "Where's the ape? Call the ape! Save me!"

"Stop calling the name of the creature!" said Turk.

Turk leaned forward and placed the wreath around the German's neck. Out of curiosity, Turk touched a fingertip to the iron blade that protruded from Gruber's skull. Then Turk accepted a burning branch from a warrior and lit the wreath. With a puff of wind, like a ghost breath, the sage and twigs roared into flames that roasted and split open the flesh on the German's face. Gruber started screaming and kicking. Four warriors grabbed him by the ankles and dragged him out of the tepee as his belly left a rut in the dirt and he yowled like an angry tomcat and Romulus saw the burning flesh peeling and curling away from the iron blade. Black smoke hung in the air as the warriors dragged Gruber from the tepee and toward the area the families had prepared for the spectacle of torture.

Turk looked at Romulus.

"We will decide what to do with you," Turk said. Turk glanced at the Dark Man. "Climb up, my brother."

The Dark Man reached up with two sinewy arms. Turk grasped the Dark Man and lifted him so that the magician's arms were around the chief's neck and the noodle legs were clear of the ground. The Dark Man pressed his knees into Turk's sides, as if mounted on a horse. The drumming and the tooting increased in volume and rapidity, and they could hear the German screaming through the chanting and laughing and fierce whoops as the families danced in the firelight.

Romulus saw through the open flap that Gruber lay spread-eagled, face-down, his arms and legs held by a dozen warriors, women and children poking him with sticks, as if testing how done a piece of meat might be. In a shallow trough below Gruber's belly burned a red and yellow bed of coals, the heat eating into his guts.

Turk and the Dark Man went out and shut the flap. Romulus sat in the dirt, seeing the picture of his sister lying naked and dead in the middle of Austin painted on a white canvas in the center of his mind, chilling him. He buried his forehead against his bound wrists and wept.

But now something coursed through him. Suddenly he tasted the blood, the pure joy of vengeance. The meditative pose he had adopted to endure his ordeal melted away. Now he had a powerful purpose, written large in his mind in Old Testament letters. He saw it clearer than he had ever seen anything. His purpose was to kill Henry Longfellow. Romulus would kill Longfellow, then would beat Matthew Caldwell to death for betraying him. He would take Hannah Dahlman away to Paris. The Master of Breath had removed Cullasaja from this life. But Romulus knew Hannah was waiting for him. He thought of old Chief Bowl dying to defend his people from the Texas army. In the code of retribution Knows All Charlie had taught him, Longfellow and Caldwell had to die.

All his previous meditation and philosophizing meant nothing now that he had a purpose. Now, while the families were murdering Gruber, Romulus would make his escape.

With a new focus, his seaman's skill and his surgeon's fingers, Romulus began working on the knots in the rawhide that bound his wrists.

The German's screams sounded in his ears as Romulus lifted the rear hide of the tepee and crawled out into the night.

# 63

Eight women, two carrying babies, entered the camp as survivors of the fight at the Council House while Fritz Gruber's screams tore through the firelight. The survivors were greeted with shouts of joy. The women had found the gate unlocked in the stockade fence beside the Council House and had walked out. Strung along behind them for three or four days of walking from San Antonio, in straggling groups, were the rest of the women and children survivors who had crept out of the stockade. The San Antonio Texans had been more than careless; many were eager for the Comanches to be gone from their town. A few girls and women had been given to San Antonio citizens to use as servants, but these Comanches, too, had little trouble escaping.

Turk had become civil chief as well as war chief. He had proposed Young Owl Hatching as civil chief, but the council had voted against the Thinking Man as not being forceful enough to lead them, a relief to Young Owl Hatching. Turk sent a dozen warriors with forty horses to bring in the rest of the survivors.

One hundred and twelve men in their prime—all of them warriors, some of them chiefs—gathered in the open space reserved for meetings. While women and children helped warriors extend the torture of Fritz Gruber, these men sat in a circle, smoking pipes filled with Mexican tobacco. They waited to hear the debate on the fate of Romulus Swift, the white healer. He was liked by many. He had befriended them, been eager to learn their language, had saved the life of Antonio from the Apache arrow. The people were divided in their opinions of what should be done with him. But the prevailing view was that Doc Swift had been a conspirator in the ambush and murder and humiliation at the Council House, and therefore should be tortured and killed.

Turk stepped into the center of the circle and peered into the faces of the men, searching their eyes for a reading of their emotions. He wore a leather vest and was bare-chested, his necklace lying in curls of chest hair. The men in the circle saw in Turk a fierce leader, hook-nosed, hot-eyed.

He swept the faces until he found the Dark Man, who had crawled into the far side of the circle, between two pipe smokers, and was leaning on his elbows, watching.

Addressing the Dark Man, Turk said, "Send for the white healer, brother. We will put him in the middle of the circle while we talk about him."

"The white healer is gone," said the Dark Man.

"How can he be gone?"

"I don't know. But I see him gone."

They heard a shout from behind the healer's tepee, and then more voices yelping through the screams of Gruber.

"He's escaping!"

The warriors leaped up from the council and ran toward the healer's tepee. Men of the families were not comfortable running. Most of the men were bowlegged, meant for the saddle. Warriors trotted to their horses and mounted.

"Climb on your pony, brother," Turk said to the Dark Man. "Lead me to the white deceiver."

Romulus heard them yelping behind him like hounds as he ran like a fox.

In the moonlight Romulus could pick out blotches amid the shadows on the footpath that went beside the giant Singing Rock, and though his legs were weak from sitting for days, his feet now found their way as if they had trod this path for ages. The rock appeared to be pink granite, an anomaly that sat on this ancient seabed as if dropped from heaven. Romulus heard the moaning sighs that came from the rock after sundown; as a scientist, he would have said the sound was caused by the night air cooling the rock and changing the pitch of its electrical vibrations. But now it seemed to Romulus that the rock contained the moaning of spirits, of ghosts, crying for deliverance and redemption.

As a Comanche arrow buzzed past his head and hammered into a tree trunk, Romulus came to the ledge above the waterfall that roared in the night, pounding the rocks below and pouring into a pond that caught a shine from the moon.

He saw a boulder that appeared to guard the entrance to a cavern, and he smelled the putrid meat scent of the man-ape. While the Comanches emerged from the night—he saw Turk and the Dark Man on their ponies—Romulus crawled onto the ledge. He looked down and saw the galloping horses and the running warriors skid to a halt. They feared coming closer to the creature's cave. The boulder concealed a crack two feet wide, enough for Romulus to squeeze through sideways. He paused at the entrance, listening, and heard the waterfall and the songs of the night birds. Then he edged into the cavern.

"Go in there and get him," Turk said, looking up angrily as the healer disappeared behind the boulder.

"I dare not. The creature is furious," said the Dark Man.

"We have paid our tribute," Turk said.

"No, not enough," said the Dark Man.

An odd blue light illuminated the main room of the cavern and glowed faintly in the passageways and vaults, a light that seemed without source except from the energy of the matter in the rocks of the cavern itself, a sort of blue quartz blush.

Romulus descended worn stone steps. Cones of lime dripped like icicles from the darkness of the ceiling and plunged down the sides of the main room. Romulus heard a low hum from below the cavern, and the sudden sound of something, an animal, crashed in one of the passageways, causing a clanking as of metal falling over, and then there was silence once more. Romulus walked into the main room and looked at the golden altar. Carved in the gold were inscriptions in hieroglyphics, and he noted the adornment on the altar of a fish swallowing a fish swallowing a fish in a circle, the symbol that Knows All Charlie had tattooed on his biceps and wore as a band on his bowler hat.

Ignoring the vaults stacked with gold bars, the niches full of crowns and jewels, Romulus followed a passage that was lined with armor. Helmets, torso plates, breastplates, steel-backed gloves, shin guards. The weapons that lay among the armor were Spanish swords and daggers and lances and flintlock guns, preserved without rust in the atmosphere of the cavern. The farther into the passage Romulus went, the older the weapons became until the passage began revealing bone axes carved with unknown symbols, and the armor of Spain became the copper-plated shields of unknown peoples, and then Romulus saw what he now knew he had been looking for all along—the sword.

The sword was of Mediterranean origin. The bright blade was three feet long and curved artististically from an ivory handle that had a silver finger guard and an emerald set in the tip of its grip. The sword lay in dust that had not shown a footprint other than that of scorpions for centuries until now.

Romulus bent to pick up the sword. He scraped the sharp edge of the blade against his forearm and hairs fell off. It was a sword made especially menacing and deadly and beautiful by the curve in its blade, a pure merging of art and function.

Yes, this was the sword that would defend him against the man-ape, the figure of his nightmares.

Romulus retraced his steps out of the passageway, along the rows of armor and weapons, carrying the sword in his right hand. He walked across the main room, past the golden altar, until he came to a closed door.

Romulus pulled the handle and the door slid open.

Inside was a room as big as a polo field, whose far walls vanished in darkness. The blue glow was dimmer than in the main room, and there was a pulsating sensation, as of blood pumping. Romulus slowly began to see that the walls were made up of layers of crypts dug into the mountain. There were hundreds of crypts, perhaps thousands, filled with bones and open to the air. He had stepped into an enormous mausoleum. A movement yanked Romulus's attention away from the crypts and onto the figure of the man-ape.

The creature knelt in front of an empty crypt in a posture of worship, looking weary, centuries old.

Romulus understood that all his dreams of the man-ape had brought him to this moment. He walked up behind the kneeling creature.

*I will give you what you want,* the creature communicated to Romulus. *Then you must give me what I want.*

# 64

The white healer, his bare chest smeared with blood, his ginger beard and long hair matted with blood, his eyes wild as though he had lost his wits, appeared from behind the boulder and held his left hand high in the moonlight, displaying the dripping head of the creature.

In his right hand was a curved sword, its blade bloody.

The warriors and families gathered below the ledge gave out a wail of dread and amazement.

Romulus hoisted the creature's head as high as his arm would stretch and slowly turned so that all could see. The bravest of warriors recoiled from the otherworldly menace in the creature's white eyeballs and dangling tongue.

The healer climbed down from the ledge and walked to Turk and the Dark Man.

Romulus held out the creature's head to Turk.

"I give you this power," Romulus said.

"Why?"

"In return for my life, my horse and my rifle," said Romulus.

Turk accepted the head. He held it aloft and the families gazed on it with shock and reverence.

"Now we own the power!" Turk shouted.

The families stared in stupefaction, then broke into whoops and cries of approval.

"We will use this power to kill the men with hats!" Turk shouted. "We will gather our families from all our places, and we will destroy their new town in our valley as we should have done long ago! We will kill Old Paint!"

The warriors cheered.

"Climb up behind me," the Dark Man said to Romulus from the pad saddle of his pinto. "I will take you back to your tepee."

"Take me to the horse herd," Romulus said.

"No, take him to his tepee," said Turk. "Give him food."

Romulus pulled himself up behind the Dark Man, mounting from the right side as the Comanches did because they had adopted the custom from Spaniards, who had learned from Moors.

"After the food, I want my horse and my rifle," Romulus said.

"Healer, you are staying with us. You can have your horse and gun, but you must promise not to run away," said Turk. "If you refuse to promise, I will kill you right now, myself. Do you give me your word?"

Romulus nodded. Turk turned to display the creature's head to the families again.

"He has never seen such powerful magic," the Dark Man whispered. "But who has?"

In the morning Romulus awoke in his tepee to find Pearl kneeling beside him. She smiled like a cherub. He got up and walked to the Little Pigeon River. Pearl followed.

Romulus stripped off his boots and trousers and tossed them onto the bank. Pearl picked them up. He waded into the cold, spring-fed water and began to wash the blood from the blade of the sword. He scraped the blood with his thumbnail. Pearl brought a bowl of deer fat mixed with powdered limestone. Using the abrasive mixture as soap, he scrubbed his body and his head clean. Romulus scratched his beard and arched his brows at Pearl, who squatted on a rock on the bank. She jumped up and ran away. Romulus climbed out of the water, shook his wet hair and lay down on a stone ledge in the sunlight. He heard voices from the council in the distance and smelled cooking fires. Crows and buzzards circled in the west, diving into refuse heaps.

In two minutes Pearl was back. She gave him a piece of mirror that he recognized as having come from Caldwell's bag. Her strong fingers began rubbing deer fat into his beard to soften it. "Not long ago, you were slapping my face," Romulus said. Pearl smiled, remembering. She produced a skinning knife and demonstrated how sharp it was by slicing a tuft of grass. Using the knife and the mirror, and gourds of water Pearl brought up from the river, Romulus shaved off his beard. Then he sat naked on the ledge and watched perch striking at bugs making bubbles in the water while Pearl cut his hair, taking great care with it as she had done for Isimanica.

Romulus thought of his mother, Carrie, and of his father, the captain, who would be at the horse farm on Long Island now, near the end of summer. He pictured the captain, with his strong Irish face, cheeks drawn by time, standing with globes and charts in his office on Hudson Street, keeping up with his fleet, or standing on the deck in command of a sailing ship, a hundred men moving smartly as he spoke his orders. The captain loved his family and his ships. He was not able to forgive harm to either. Romulus thought of his mother, her lovely brown face glowing healthy and plump, her eyes large and dark like those of Cullasaja. Carrie was a gentle person, forgiving, but she would not forgive the murder of Cullasaja. He remembered Grandmother Tobacco and Knows All Charlie vowing that vengeance must always be taken against offenders of the clans. It was the code that sustained their existence. Romulus thought of his studies in the Cherokee mountains and with the philosophers at Columbia and the surgeons at Edinburgh. He thought of the many ships he had sailed over much of the world, and of Hannah and Caldwell, and Henry Longfellow, and all the seemingly random and purposeless choices that had brought Romulus to this moment at this place.

He remembered the man-ape's last message: *Love must replace fear or you are lost, like I am.* Then the creature had knelt and offered his neck to the sword. Was this the so-called Third Wisdom?

He heard hoofs and looked around to see the Dark Man, mounted on his paint pony, leading Romulus's mustang by a twisted hemp rope. Beside the mustang walked Turk, who carried Romulus's rosewood rifle and his Cherokee-styled Bowie knife. More than two hundred people followed close behind them. One gaunt woman in deerskin was Wanda Mecom, who was happy to see that her daughter Pearl had been accepted by a powerful man. Wanda's other daughter, poor scarred and abused Rose, had not been among those who'd returned from the Council House stockade, and none of the others knew for sure what had become of her. But Pearl was a survivor.

"Be ready to ride at sundown," Turk said.

"Where?"

"We are going among our families all over our nation," said Turk.

In the afternoon, Romulus put on his boots, which Pearl had polished with fat and mended with rawhide, and the trousers she had washed and sewn, along with the cotton shirt and black coat that Pearl had scrubbed in the Little Pigeon River and dried in the sun and breeze. She buffed specks of dirt off his black hat brim with her elbow and then handed him the hat and smiled. She looked like a radiant Giotto painting of an Italian peasant girl, lighted by heaven.

In London he would have said this child suffered from dementia praecox. No grasp of reality. Out here it really didn't matter. He gave her the curved sword with the emerald in the tip of the handle.

"I give you this in return for your kindness. The sword's magic will keep you safe."

Pearl smiled and rubbed the emerald. She wanted Romulus to come back to her. But if he did not, she would remember him fondly.

The party left the camp and rode northwest. Turk, Young Owl Hatching and Romulus rode in front. Next came the Dark Man, who carried the creature's head on the tip of a lance. The head had been slathered with grease to protect it from decomposing, and the sight of it was powerful enough that children ran and covered their eyes. Twenty warriors armed for battle but not wearing war paint rode in the rear as a guard, and four scouts ranged far ahead and on the flanks to watch for their ancient enemies, the Apaches.

The party was riding across Comancheria to gather enough warriors to howl down upon Austin like a blizzard.

# 65

The caravan of eighty-four wagons, drawn by oxen, that bore the archives of the Republic of Texas, made a steady pace of nine miles a day for the journey that was moving the capital from Houston City to Austin.

Two companies of Texas army regular infantry walked guard, dressed in new blue jackets that had been furnished them by the secretary of war on the command of President Lamar. He wanted his soldiers to look utterly professional when they marched into the new, temporary capitol building, which was being called Fort Austin because of its surrounding stockade fence that was in turn surrounded by a moat six feet deep.

President Lamar traveled on horseback with the archives caravan. His aim was to ride into Austin as the head of government in a most tangible and symbolic fashion. He was nostalgic for a view of the violet hills that he recalled from an earlier visit to the place that had become Austin. Then he had been shooting for sport with buffalo hunters, and they had come across this hilly location that had plenty of flowing water and so many lovely vistas that Lamar had been inspired to jot poems in his notebook. At that time the local settlement had been called Waterloo. It was Lamar's inspiration to locate his new capital on the north side of the river in the valley with the crown of violet hills—he loved the image of "violet hills" and used it often in writing about Austin— and his request to the congress to move the capital from Houston City to Austin had started people swarming into the Colorado River valley and caused the sounds of saws and hammers and wagon wheels to become the dominant noises of the town, much louder than the piano playing at Dutch John's or cattle bawling in their pens. The President yearned to see his new mansion, the White House, built to the specifications he had drawn up and sent to Mayor Waller, his agent in the matter. On the night before the Fourth Texas Congress would convene for the first time at the new capitol, the President would hold the grandest party ever known in the new city. He would open his White House to members of the House and the Senate, to all local citizens of repute, to his cabinet and government workers, to visitors who were looking for investment opportunities in the Republic. The White House would be a beacon that shone for all friends of Texas.

The President rode his horse—the bay that had carried Henry Longfellow back to San Antonio after the assault near Austin months ago—and sat his big leather saddle studded with *conchos*. He made conversation with the infantry, most of whom were suffering blisters from their new boots and had begun to travel barefoot. He studied the coarse countenances of the teamsters as they prodded their animals. Lamar traded remarks about the poet William Wordsworth with young Abernathy, an assistant land clerk who had immigrated from England. Lamar didn't care for what he called Wordsworth's lyrical flatulence in the early work and the moralistic tone of the latter, and the President detested blank verse though he did love nature writing, so all in all, what did Abernathy think of Wordsworth? Abernathy, a public school boy in London, spoke up brightly and recited a verse from *The White Doe of Rylstone*. Abernathy said he thought Wordsworth was overpraised in some areas but underappreciated in others. How thoughtful an answer. Lamar wrote in his notebook to interview Abernathy for promotion to secretary.

They slept under the stars on their bedrolls. Farmhouses offered shelter for the President, but this was early October and the nights were cool and the skies were clear. Lamar loved lying wrapped in his blankets on the grass near a camp fire. The summer had been beastly hot, and now the crisp evenings gave the premonition of an early winter. These perfect autumn evenings were to be taken advantage of, to thrill in, to let one's soul fly upward; this was energizing, emotionally uplifting weather such as the Republic ought to be famous for, weather that was almost unknown in Houston City.

The President was proud that he was near to establishing the new capital. It was his defining move toward expanding the Republic, and he felt secure— even under what the locals called a Comanche moon—because he was in command of hundreds of soldiers and teamsters who would scare the savages away.

Lamar knew there were Rangers out there in the night patrolling between the caravan and the Comanches. He hoped Captain Matthew Caldwell was among them.

Lamar had read Caldwell's report that General Savariego and his Mexican army had been slaughtered by the Comanches. The deaths of hundreds of Mexican soldiers was a wonderful event for the Republic of Texas, blessed as was the killing of the Comanche chiefs in San Antonio. More good tidings from Caldwell. It was too bad the captain disagreed with Lamar's tactics. If Caldwell had not been laid up with a bullet wound and had found out that action was about to be taken to throw the Cherokees out of Bowl's Town, he would have caused trouble. Caldwell was a Cherokee lover like Sam Houston. He would have protested the presence of Henry Longfellow, doing his duty as a lawyer. Lamar didn't fully understand Caldwell's hatred of Longfellow. The President knew it had something to do with that old assault claim, and the death later of the Cherokee woman. He felt the captain could be mollified with an important political appointment, perhaps as land commissioner? A land commissioner who did not become rich was stupid.

# 6 6

The Kerr mansion in Austin was still largely unpainted, and there was carpentry yet to do, but Dora and Lawrence had moved in, bringing their furnishings that had been stored in New Orleans and in the Fincus Hotel warehouse. Dora spent her first day in Austin scolding Newfield, the builder, and directing the positioning of the Duncan Phyfe sofas and the rest of the furniture. From her porch she could see workers preparing the President's White House for tonight's party. Newfield found himself apologizing to Dora for painting the President's house before getting around to doing hers.

Late in the afternoon Dora soaked in a tub of warm water and napped for half an hour. Then she wrapped herself in a light wool robe and went into the bedroom she shared with Lawrence. As she weaved through the still packed boxes, she noticed the quarterly publication of the Ladies Physiological Society.

She was a regular at attending meetings of the society in New York, and she missed that companionship. At these gatherings women spoke freely about matters they could never share with men or discuss in public. Dora recalled discussing how one time in preparing for a grand New York ball she had had her corset cinched so tight that her liver ached and she'd felt burning pains in her stomach. Other Ladies Physiological Society members exchanged stories of punishment by fashion even worse than her own. Several had suffered ribs broken by corsets while others had placed hollow ceramic inserts into their vaginas to prevent the pressure of their tight corsets from collapsing their interior passages. One winter night the Duke's wife had worn forty pounds of clothes, thirty pounds of which were the skirt that pulled down from her waist. She had worn a tight corset for so long that her uterus had been squeezed out through her vagina.

All around Dora in New York, women were dying of tuberculosis, cholera, fevers and a wasting away called the vapors. But Dora had remained healthy, pink of cheek and full of energy with the vitality of the New Bedford Sweeneys, a whaling family known for vigor, temper, and singing voices.

Dora took the Ladies Physiological Society magazine with her and climbed into the oversize four-poster bed. She would start to get dressed for the President's Ball in an hour or so. The invitation had said seven o'clock in the evening for refreshments and dinner followed by entertainment and dancing to the music of an orchestra. Dora wondered if she would be asked to sing tonight. Oh, of course she would. If no one else asked her, Lawrence certainly would.

She felt a chill and pulled her robe tightly around her body. She could see through the tall windows that the sky in the north was turning dark plum blue, and a gust of cool air brushed her face. Dora looked at a drawing of a female body in the magazine. There were arrows pointing to areas of the anatomy and notations of the damage that was done by high-heeled footwear, corsets and nipple-pinching engineering of bosom display. Dora thought of Hannah Caldwell. Dora had overseen sewing Hannah's gown for the President's Ball. Hannah would show plenty of breast, but no pinching would be needed. Dora smiled, allowing herself to imagine Hannah naked with Matthew Caldwell and to wonder about their sexual life. Was it as thrilling as Dora imagined it was? At the Ladies Physiological Society, women would know these things about one another.

For herself tonight, Dora had chosen an Empire gown that would announce her bosoms while hiding the few extra pounds that here in Texas she would not wear a corset to conceal.

"My turn to bathe?" Lawrence said.

He was wearing his greasy leather frontier garb with his pistol in a holster. Since leaving San Antonio, Lawrence had started wearing stovepipe flat-heel boots instead of Mexican sandals. He had replaced his sombrero with a wide-brimmed hat like many of the fellows wore at Dutch John's.

"Lulu is filling your tub." Dora glanced at her lanky frontiersman. She would enjoy seeing him in satin lapels again. Lawrence had the bearing and the slender body that looked wonderful in elegant clothes. In their social crowd in New York, Lawrence was a star. Dressed in evening clothes at a Metropolitan Club Ball, Lawrence looked like a romantic lead. Here in Texas, when he stood beside Matthew Caldwell, her husband looked, Dora thought, like a minor player who dressed well and could dance.

"I thought I might not wear the evening jacket tonight," Lawrence said.
"What?"
"I might wear my new buckskins."
She sat up. "Lawrence, please do not start a quarrel with me."
Lawrence winced.
"All right, then," he said. "But may I wear my pistol?"
"To the President's house? Where you do think we are—in the middle of Africa?"
He shrugged. He would carry his derringer in his boot, as Caldwell did. Dora would never know.
"Ladies Physiological Society," Lawrence said, bending near to read the title of the magazine as he stripped off his shirt. "Isn't that the club you used to go to?" He clasped his arms across his chest, shivering in the cold that was blowing in. "What does physiological mean?" he asked.
"The study of living organisms and their parts and organs."
"Living organisms? Like frogs?"
"Like women."
"Really? Women?"
"And women's parts and organs."
"It's funny to think of you women meeting to discuss your arms and kidneys."
"A vagina is an organ."
"Pardon?" Lawrence dropped out of his trousers and reached for a sheet to protect himself from the increasing cold.
"We talk about sex at our Physiological Society meetings."
"Surely not."
"We do."
"Rubbish. You're trying to shock me. You're acting the role of some wa-

terfront tart. You're not interested in sex. Wives are not interested in sex," he said. "I mean, outside the marriage bed."

"Lawrence, darling, you impregnated your partner's wife. Do you think that was strictly an act of boredom on her part?"

"No, but I'm different."

Dora laughed.

Lawrence said, "Women don't want sex the way men do. Women just do it to make men like them. Women are meant to be devoted to finer things."

"Sit down here on this footstool," Dora said.

Lawrence pulled the sheet around his shoulders and sat on the stool. He was becoming aroused. Dora swung her body around in the bed so that she faced him, looking down at his patrician nose and watching his eyes widen as she opened her robe and spread her legs.

"My darling Dora," Lawrence said.

"Sit back down, Lawrence. Look at me."

"I am looking."

"Don't look at my face. Come closer. Look down here." He scooted the footstool closer and peered between his wife's legs. "At the society we study each other's vaginas," she said, opening herself with her fingers.

"No, you don't," he said.

"Do you know what a clitoris is?"

"It's a type of flower."

"I masturbate by rubbing my clitoris."

"Women do not masturbate," he said. "Stop all this playacting."

Lawrence stood up and let the sheet fall to the floor. He no longer felt the cold. His face was flushed, and his erection pulled his foreskin so tight that it hurt.

"Do you want to watch me—" she said.

Lawrence was on top of her before she could finish the question.

Afterward, Lawrence bathed while Dora's hair was brushed by Lulu, the Mexican maid she had brought from San Antonio. Dora was wearing her hair long and full tonight. Sitting in front of her mirror, Dora touched rouge to her cheeks, smiling that she hardly needed the artificial color now, after the rush of excitement from bouncing with Lawrence, who had been inspired, pounding her with an urgency that made him seem like a stranger at a party, meeting her in the carriage house for a passionate encounter. The mirror loved Dora. She didn't look a day over twenty-eight, she told herself, and her teeth were white from being scrubbed with baking soda and salt. She smiled at herself in the mirror, pleased by her reflection. It would be amusing to share with the women at the Ladies Physiological Society the story of this afternoon's discussion and sex with Lawrence. She could hear them laughing.

Promptly at fifteen minutes after seven, their carriage was brought around to drive Dora and Lawrence across the road to the President's house. The temperature had fallen twenty-five degrees in the past three hours. Dora covered her shoulders with a mink stole. Lawrence went back inside to fetch a cloak to wear over his evening jacket. They heard rising wind rattling the trees. The northern sky was black. At the President's house, every window was aglow.

# 67

On the western horizon above the white cliffs, splashes of orange and red pushed against the rumbling blackness approaching from the north. Sitting in his rosewood chair on the porch looking across West Avenue, smoking a stout Cuban cigar that Lawrence Kerr had given him, Matthew Caldwell felt a gush of happiness. He had convinced himself not to look back upon the joys he had known with Nancy and their family before the revolution. He had loved them and had done the best he could for them, but they had perished through no fault of his own. His happiness now, with Hannah, was a gift he was growing to appreciate more each moment.

A gust of cool breeze ruffled his newly washed hair and beard. Matthew was already dressed for Lamar's party. Because of his dislike of Lamar, Matthew would have avoided the party. But Hannah was excited about attending, and he liked making her happy. He wore one of his familiar white doeskin jackets with the fringes on the sleeves and the red and blue beaded stars on each breast. His shirt was blue cotton with a high collar. Matthew would not wear a tie around his neck. He wore creamy soft leather trousers and moccasin boots with beaded stars on the tops of his feet. When ready to go to Lamar's, Matthew would top himself off with a new wide-brimmed, nut brown beaver hat from which his long black hair, threaded now with gray, would stream down to his shoulders. Matthew was aware of the devastating impression he would create when he entered the President's house; he took it for granted that people, especially newcomers who had never seen him before, would gape and whisper and be wary of him as if he was a bull bear on the rut. But tonight he expected most eyes would fasten upon his wife, Hannah. His wife, he repeated. Matthew touched the tips of his fingers together and thanked God for her. He was learning to accept his blessing of life with Hannah. She pleased him in every way.

Blackness fell swiftly and the stars disappeared. Chill air brought squawks of protest from chickens who nested in tree limbs. Matthew's body fit so well into his rosewood chair that he could believe the woodcarver's claim that the chair could make him invisible. He picked up the chair and carried it into the parlor. He closed the shutters on the north windows, and in the light of the whale oil lamp he inspected once again the mysteries of the grain in the rosewood and the genius of the carver to create such a chair. Each time he looked at this chair, it reminded him of Hannah. He had been given powerful gifts in this chair and the woman who chose it for him. His heart was warm with love for her.

Matthew had spent two nights away from Hannah this week, riding with the Rangers from Boca Chica Crossing in a screen between the archives caravan and the Comanches. He had argued that Hannah should stay in the middle of town—at Bullock's or with the Kerrs—while he was gone. West Avenue was only a few blocks from the town center, but it was that much nearer Comancheria and was exposed to menace from the Indian Joes on Shoal Creek and the furloughed soldiers who skirted the edges of civilization looking for plunder. Hannah refused to leave their house. "I am not going to be put under guard each time you ride off to do your duty for the Republic," she told him. "I faced dangers before I ever came to Texas. Now you have taught me how to shoot and ride. We have a mastiff to patrol outside our house. I am not afraid." Matthew was proud of her, but he cut short his night-riding time with the Rangers, partly because he worried about her, but mostly because he missed her and yearned for the comfort of Hannah lying with him in bed.

He decided he would lock Sweet Lips and his pistols in the iron vault in their storm cellar. Matthew would carry only his derringer in his boot. He might put his butcher knife in his belt. It would be covered by his jacket. But no, the butcher knife would make dancing awkward. When he had wiped his rosewood chair with a soft cloth and locked away his guns, Matthew opened their bedroom door.

Hannah was standing naked with her back toward him, looking at herself in a tall mirror. He saw the front of her body in the glass, and their eyes met.

"Excuse me," he said.

Matthew shut the door. Seeing her was a picture he would never forget.

"Matthew, don't be silly. Come in," she said.

He opened the door again. She now was wearing pantalettes on her legs and was about to pull on a muslin petticoat.

"I should have knocked," he said.

"My father and mother taught us not to be shy about our bodies. There were too many of us in too few rooms. My brother, Aaron, is a nudist. He goes to camps on the North Sea coast."

Hannah looked at her dress that was hung on a rack beside the mirror. She hoped her husband would approve. She watched Matthew as he leaned against the wall, his arms folded across his chest, gray eyes gleaming in his sun-wrinkled skin in the forest of black and white hair. What a spectacular-looking man he is, she thought once again. There were times when the sight of him made her gasp with awe and animal attraction. He had delighted her last night at dinner in the kitchen house by talking about Rossini's operas. In the candle-light she had looked fondly at the thin white scar on his nose. There were so many marks on his body. Hannah could no longer imagine a life without Mat-thew Caldwell in it. She would always remember Romulus Swift as a secret fantasy, but she was proud to be married to Matthew.

"What do you think? Do you like it?"

Matthew looked at his wife wearing a dark green tissue silk gown as she fastened around her neck a gold chain that supported a gold locket he had bought for her in San Antonio. The chain and locket lay against white skin and the swelling of her breasts.

"You're the most beautiful thing I ever saw," he said.

"After this party tonight, we will make a baby," she said.

They could see vapor in the breath of the buggy horse as Matthew drove Hannah up the Ash Street hill. Houses and stores groaned in the wind. People clutched themselves and hunched as they walked, as if they had forgotten that winter came every year. A black veil was falling across the bowl of Austin.

"This is what we call a blue norther," he said. "This wind blows straight downhill from Canada."

"It's the first time I can remember being cool since I came to Texas," she said.

Lamar's White House dominated a hill facing south toward Bois d'Arc Street a block east of Congress Avenue. The Caldwells could see lights in the windows of the Kerr mansion a block away, west of Congress as they hitched their horse and buggy and walked up the flagstone path to the front porch of the White House. Lamar had offered his own person to shake hands with guests until the weather became too chill and he retreated just inside the door.

"Ah, Captain Caldwell. I am so happy you could attend," the President said as Matthew and Hannah entered. Lamar wore a purple velvet coat with high-cut lapels, ruffles at wrist and neck, an Ascot tie, and a pair of black wool trousers in the baggy style he preferred. Tufts of hair framed his ears. His eyes swept at once toward Hannah, even as he was extending his right hand to her husband.

"This is my wife, Hannah. President Lamar," Matthew said, shaking hands.

"My honor," said Lamar, releasing Matthew's hand. He reached for Hannah's hand and grasped her gently by the fingers. "Welcome to Texas, Mrs. Caldwell. May I congratulate you both on your marriage?"

"Thank you, Mr. President," she said.

"In your opinion, who is the greatest German writer—Schiller or Goethe?" asked Lamar.

"Schiller is a great poet and dramatist," Hannah said. "But Goethe is a religion in Germany."

Lamar laughed with appreciation. "Exactly so! *Faust! The Sorrows of Young Werther!* He is a towering genius. Are you familiar with his studies of the occult?"

"Germans are attracted by the supernatural. My father is a scholar of the Kaballah."

"Ranking them strictly as poets—poetry is an obsession of mine—I say Schiller might have become the greatest had he not fallen into blank verse, which is the sign of a failing imagination," said the President.

"In my opinion, the greatest German poet is Heinrich Heine," Hannah said.

"He's a romantic, radical Jew, isn't he? Dreaming of overthrowing governments with the power of his pen? But we are all romantically radical in Texas, Mrs. Caldwell. We overthrew one of the great governments of the world only three years ago. But not with the power of the pen. We did it with the bayonet, didn't we, Captain Caldwell?"

"We did," Matthew said.

Lamar took a glass of champagne off a tray being passed by a Negro slave dressed in a wing collar and black suit. The President insisted Matthew and Hannah each accept a glass. "It is real champagne, from France. Confidentially, I bought it as a sop for that disagreeable French consul who refuses to lend us money because the pigs eat his corn. Matthew, my old comrade, I have something in mind for you that will prove quite rewarding."

"I ain't running any more errands for you," said Matthew.

Hannah was astonished to hear her husband speak to his president in such a way. If an officer had spoken thus to Ernest Augustus, the hangman would be busy before the hour was out.

"No, nothing like that. No more Comanches to bring in, not for you. I have in mind a high political post."

"You know I am solid for the Old Chief. I am his man, not yours."

"I am thinking of land commissioner."

"I won't betray the Old Chief by joining your administration. No, sir. I will continue to wear my badge, but I am your political opponent."

The President whiffed snuff off the back of his wrist and wiped his nose, holding his champagne glass out for a refill.

"Matthew, you and I want the same thing. We want the savages exterminated and our Texas open for settlement all the way to the Pacific Ocean. I would never expect you to betray Sam Houston. Work for me as land commissioner for the rest of my term. I need your ideas and your strength."

"No."

"Then please excuse me so I may chat with other, more friendly guests. So nice to meet you, Mrs. Caldwell. You must come to my house for coffee and we will talk poetry. I would like to get your opinion of my new collection of poems."

Matthew took Hannah's pale elbow, observing her shining black hair and the whiteness of her bosoms, and steered her toward the ballroom, where they saw Dora and Lawrence at a table eating from plates of food that came from the buffet. The walls were lined with counters piled with roast wild turkey, venison, fresh fish, ham, vegetables from the President's gardens. In the front of the room was a bar where three uniformed Negroes poured glasses of wine and whiskey and beer for the crowd. On the small stage at the north end of the room was the orchestra, playing dinner music. Dora was listening to the talent of the piano player, judging whether he could accompany her when the crowd called upon her to sing.

"The President is an educated man," Hannah said.

"He's a lying bastard," said Matthew.

For the next two hours Lamar's party was nearly everything he hoped it would be. All the prominent citizens were there, including the notoriously mysterious lawyer Ridgewood Bone with his slave-nurse, Chloc. Every legislator in town for tomorrow's Fourth Congress shook hands with the President and praised the White House and the new capital city. A few congressmen had brought their wives to Austin and to the party, a few more would have brought their wives if the town had not become overcrowded and expensive, but most had left their wives home to care for the children and the house, or else they had no wives and were looking forward to frolics at Dutch John's and romps with the whores at the Redbud. The orchestra played. People danced. Dora Kerr sang two numbers from *The Gay Pretender* to wild applause. Food and liquor were being consumed in staggering quantities. Matthew danced with his wife and then turned her over to the cut-in crowd, the first of whom was Lawrence. While Matthew admired the sight of Hannah whirling about the floor, he was tapped on the shoulder by Dora. Matthew and Dora waltzed, and the crowd gaped at them—these two theatrical creatures.

My party would be perfect if only the weather were not so fickle, Lamar was thinking as he smoothly separated Richard Bullock and Dubois de Saligny from what could have become a shooting over an argument about Bullock's pigs. He persuaded Bullock to present his views on defending the city to Albert Sidney Johnston, and he introduced Dubois de Saligny to the French-speaking senator from Galveston. The President had wanted to hold much of his party on the grounds of the White House, with candles burning in paper sacks and orchestra music floating through open windows. The north wind had unexpectedly ruined that plan, but otherwise it was a superb evening.

Lamar himself opened the front door and gave an effusive good night to Dubois de Saligny, who decided to leave as the party was reaching the stage when the drunks were starting to laugh too loudly and looking for someone to fight. As Richard Bullock glared from the bar, Dubois de Saligny made a courteous bow to the President and muttered, "I am going to kill those damned pigs."

Lamar smiled and assured the Frenchman the matter would be settled to his satisfaction, and with a hand in the small of de Saligny's back the President stepped onto the front porch and saw to his shock the gawky figure of Henry Longfellow clumping up the top step, leaning on his copper-knobbed black ebony sword cane, wearing a fur hat and a cape over the shoulders of black wool formal evening attire. Lamar had been told that Longfellow was traveling to New Orleans and Kentucky on business. He had been gone for a month.

In the ballroom, Hannah and Dora were returned to their chairs by admirers. Matthew and Lawrence stood while their smiling, perspiring wives took their seats and waved off new invitations. The two men sat down again. Both men were drinking bourbon whiskey, and Lawrence was showing the effects. The Kerr Land & Cattle Company had grown by half a million acres in the last four ounces of liquor.

"A toast to the two most beautiful women in Texas," Lawrence said, lifting his glass.

"Look who is here," said Dora. "It's the Peeper."

Matthew saw the familiar beak on the long neck that bobbed as Longfellow peered around at the paintings and allowed a servant to take his cape and hat. Instantly the Ranger was out of his chair and striding across the ballroom.

"Captain, wait!" Lawrence said. Then Lawrence sat back and finished his drink and looked at the women. "Nothing I can do about it now. He's going to give Longfellow a beating at the very least. Not a wise idea, from a business perspective. As party entertainment, though, it's hard to top."

Henry Longfellow was sniffing the women at the party, smelling their stinking flesh, when he saw Captain Caldwell coming toward him, with his Jew bitch of a wife running right behind. Henry remembered the thrill of spying on her naked body, and the evil in her eyes as she had looked up at him through the rip in the canvas of the bathing tent. Henry's pecker twitched and felt wet. The Jew wanted him, and she would have him, he told himself. He would take her straight back to the devil, where she wanted to go.

Henry had known he would have to confront Caldwell sooner or later, and he had decided that the President's party at the White House was the place to do it.

Lamar moved quickly to step between Longfellow and the Ranger, who was approaching with a wild glistening in his gray eyes.

"Longfellow, you are under arrest," Matthew said.

The clamor of the party ceased. The orchestra stopped playing and the musicians joined the crowd that followed Caldwell across the ball room. They knew from the thrust of the Ranger's walk that there was about to be violence. Death so often smelled like cigars and whiskey. The chance to see Old Paint in action was not to be missed.

"On what charge?" said Longfellow.

"The murder of Cullasaja Swift."

"Preposterous. What evidence do you have?" Longfellow said.

"I know you did it," said Matthew.

"Captain Caldwell, please. The Ranger's Prerogative does not apply to such a serious charge as this against a citizen of the highest repute," the President said. "I forbid you to arrest my guest unless you can show me overwhelming evidence why I should allow it."

"The little girl at his house knows he came through Austin the night Cullasaja's body was dumped here," Matthew said. "The stable man knows he changed coach horses."

"Liza and Old Root have been sold," said Longfellow. "They are gone from Texas."

"A fellow named Watson was with him in his coach," Matthew said. "He's the client who owns part of the land where Bowl's Town was. Watson will talk to me."

"Alas, poor Joshua fell overboard and drowned in the Gulf of Mexico," said Longfellow.

"Who drove your coach away from Bowl's Town?"

"Two boys I sold in New Orleans."

"Captain Caldwell, Mr. Longfellow says he was not in Austin the night the Indian woman was murdered," Lamar said. "You have no evidence to prove otherwise."

"Did anybody here see this man that night?" Matthew asked the crowd.

When no one spoke up, Henry Longfellow smiled and licked his lips, his eyes pulled toward the Jew's white skin and and bulging breasts, always a lure for the devil.

"It is an outrage that I should be accused of a crime," said Longfellow.

Matthew slapped Longfellow across the left cheek and then struck the right cheek with a backhand, not as hard as the Ranger's rage was wanting, but smartly enough to make two fast popping sounds and bring tears to the lawyer's eyes.

"I'm calling you out, Longfellow. Name your weapon."

"I forbid this. I will not have it. Captain, you do not have the evidence to arrest Longfellow as an officer of the law, and killing him in a duel will not be allowed to happen," the President said.

"I am not afraid of this blustering bully, Mr. President," Longfellow said. "He has unjustifiably formed some sort of personal hatred for me, and I will be glad to get him out of my life. I accept your challenge, Captain. I choose shotguns at five feet."

"Matthew, don't do this, it's insane," said Hannah.

"Dueling is against the law, Mr. Longfellow. Matthew, in congress you voted against dueling," the President said.

"Legally or not, I am happy to fight you, Captain," said Longfellow. "However, I have several duels pledged to fight before I reach you. So it may be a while, but reach you I will."

"Come outside with me right now," Matthew said.

"Captain Caldwell, as your president I beseech you, for the good of the Republic, to depart my house in peace and be at your seat for our historical Fourth Congress in the morning. If you ever should find evidence that Mr.

Longfellow was involved in the crime you accuse him of, go to court and get a warrant for his arrest. Otherwise, I beg you to remember that you are an elected representative to a republic of people who count on you for strength and wisdom and courage and obedience to the law."

Henry Longfellow held back a laugh as he saw the President's words take effect on the patriot. Henry tried to keep satisfaction from showing on his lips. He knew how dangerous was the game he was playing with the Ranger. This bushy captain was a beast that might strike at any moment. Henry would see to it that Caldwell came to a violent end. If Henry couldn't think of how to do it himself, he would hire it done by killers he knew in New Orleans.

"Please, Matthew, let's go home," Henry heard the Jew bitch say. Stinking seductress, flaunting her flesh, grabbing the captain's right arm, refusing to look at Henry for fear she would betray her desire for him.

Servants brought Hannah her shawl and Matthew his brown beaver hat.

"It is a pleasure to know you, Mrs. Caldwell. You are an asset to our republic. Please come again to visit and talk poetry," the President said. He turned to Matthew. "Thank you, Captain Caldwell. I trust you will be brilliant in session in the morning."

Matthew adjusted his hat above his eyebrows and looked at Henry Longfellow, who had a drop of moisture on the end of his nose.

"Our account will be settled," Matthew said.

"Indeed it will, sir," said Longfellow.

As Hannah and her husband stepped onto the south porch, the wind was roaring and bending trees on either side of the White House.

# 68

"Some say if you talk out loud to yourself, it's a sign of being a loony person," Big Foot Wallace said. "But as long as I am with Old Higgins and some good dogs, I ain't ever talking just to myself. Anybody who is lonesome is in bad company."

Red Beans, the Lipan scout, tugged his blanket tighter over his head and shoulders and huddled down on his mustang. The night wind moaned from the north. Red Beans hated cold weather. His fingers turned blue in cold weather, and his nose burned. He looked at Big Foot, a wide-shouldered figure in buck-skins astride a tall bay horse, riding along talking as if it were a pleasant afternoon instead of a black night that was becoming bitter. Around Big Foot trotted five of his dogs—Spot, Bats, Ring, Spec and Bear.

"I mean, if you wasn't here, Red Beans, and I was the only human being within hearing, I could still talk out loud, because these animals are smarter and understand me better than ordinary people do. I talk to these animals about anything that comes to mind, and they soak it up. I never have to explain myself twice to them. When there's a crowd of people around, there is too many conflicting voices and too little comprehension, but in the company of animals, and with you, too, Red Beans, I feel comfortable to speak my mind."

Red Beans was wishing he hadn't volunteered to go ranging with Big Foot this night. He liked Big Foot and enjoyed his stories, but the cold wind made Red Beans want to be back at Boca Chica Station, where there would be logs burning in the cabins' fireplaces.

"Most think being a Ranger is the act of a loony person, anyhow. Why, I could earn fifty to a hundred dollars a month digging water wells in Austin. I could put a nest egg aside instead of spending my life out here in the wilderness with my animals, and with comrades like you or Old Paint or the boys at the station. I can see the point to the argument that I'm wasting the best years of my life in a carefree fashion instead of saving for my future. I don't want to get old and sick and out of money all at the same time. But that's something a Ranger doesn't have to concern himself about. Rangers don't get old, hee-hee. Old Paint is the oldest Ranger there is, and he ain't so old when you think about Methuselah living nine hundred years. In my honest opinion, Methuselah wouldn't have made it past thirty if he was a Ranger."

Big Foot and Red Beans were northeast of San Antonio, ranging down the west bank of the Warloop. Clouds that had covered the moon blew away, and a pale light fell across the countryside.

"Look over yonder, Red Beans. What do you make of that?" asked Big Foot.

"Buffalo track?"

"Let's have a see."

The two men nudged their horses into a cautious trot, the animals feeling for footing in the dark on the uneven ground. The five dogs ran ahead. Big Foot trained his dogs never to bark when they were attacking or trailing, but to bark only to warn their master of danger.

They came to the track, a black, trampled path in the night earth. Far larger than an animal path, it was a road, a boulevard, grander than any city avenue Big Foot could imagine.

"This wasn't buffalos," Big Foot said.

They kept riding across the track until they reached the other side. The track was half a mile wide. Red Beans slid down off his mustang, ducked under his blanket, examining the torn earth, looking at bits of bone and stone among the marks of unshod hooves and the scattered mounds of horse turds.

"Comanches," said Red Beans.

"Can't be Comanches. Why, it must of took three or four thousand riders to leave a track of this size."

"Comanches went through here two days ago," Red Beans said, crumbling a dry horse apple in his fingers.

# 69

Representative Theodore Gautier, the honorable gentleman whose district covered the west end of Galveston Island, was recognized by the speaker and strode in his high-heeled leather shoes to the podium, whence he began to address the twenty-eight other members of the House of Representatives at the Fourth Congress of the Republic of Texas. Gautier spoke in university-educated English with a French accent.

Matthew Caldwell stretched and straightened his back. The wooden chairs with cowhide seats that had been furnished for the representatives were too small for Matthew and gave him an ache at the bottom of his spine. Matthew had gone into the Senate's meeting room next door and found the fourteen senators had been presented with chairs of the same size as the one he had intended to trade.

"This salubrious climate, this beautiful valley," Representative Gautier was saying.

Matthew listened to Gautier with suspicion. It was true that the climate today was ideal. The norther had passed through and left a sunny, invigorating

October morning. But Gautier wasn't at the podium to brag about the weather. This was Gautier's first Congress. He was new to Texas and recently elected in a district where one powerful landowner had the only vote that mattered. Matthew had met Gautier at Lamar's party at the White House and had disliked the man's mannerisms, the touching and tugging of his clothing, the preening. Gautier was a different kind of man than the old breed, the fighters in the revolution. Only twelve members of the House—they called themselves the Devil's Dozen—had been in Texas three and a half years ago when the battles were fought and the revolution was won.

Each session a few more of the old breed were replaced by newcomers. Matthew found it rare to meet a newcomer in the Congress who had ideas or ideals that went beyond the struggle to own the land and the riches it would bring. Matthew had become a Texas patriot and had entered the terrible war against Mexico nearly four years ago out of the demand for freedom as much as his desire to be a landowner as the Caldwells were born to become. He had no thought for money. Matthew felt he had earned his land grant. These new-comers had been given freedom from Mexican governance without fighting for it, and now they wanted land without paying for it.

There were no political parties as such, but the Republic was becoming divided more or less into the Planters Party—the cotton growers of the south-eastern part of the Republic, who wanted peace and commerce and low taxes—and the War Party, men who moved to the western frontier and demanded expansion at any price, no matter if the expense of killing savages caused high taxes. Sam Houston was in the camp of the Planters Party. Mirabeau Lamar was the political leader of the War Party. Matthew's heart lay somewhere be-tween. He was a faithful follower of the Old Chief and wanted peace and commerce and few taxes, but also he wanted the ten thousand acres he had earned in Comancheria for Hannah and himself.

The temporary capitol building—Fort Austin—was at the southwest corner of Colorado and Hickory streets, six city blocks east of the home Matthew shared with Hannah on West Avenue. The voice of Gautier floating around the edge of his attention, Matthew began daydreaming about Hannah. This was wash day. Hannah had hired Evangeline, an immigrant woman from Louisiana, to help with the household chores and the gardening. Evangeline's Cajun hus-band, Marvelito, worked for the Caldwells as a handyman, mucking the stables and the chicken house and doing the chopping and digging required to grow vegetables. Matthew pictured Hannah bent over the scrub board with lye soap up to her elbows and flecks of it in her hair. Thinking of her, he smiled, and a shot of pain struck his left jawbone, a reminder of Doctor Swift. Matthew wondered if the Comanches had killed Doctor Swift. It was hard to imagine how the clever half-breed doctor could have talked or fought his way out of the situation Matthew had left him in. Matthew felt twinges of regret about abandoning Doctor Swift, but he was far from remorseful. Matthew was not devious or soft-hearted. He told the truth as he saw it. Doctor Swift had desired Hannah, so he had written his own fate, in the eyes of Matthew Caldwell. Doctor Swift should have taken his sister, Cullasaja, and gone back to New York. Now it was too late for Cullasaja, but was Doctor Swift still alive out there in the wilderness? The pain in his jaw reminded Matthew never again to underestimate an enemy.

Matthew glanced out the windows looking south across Hickory Street. He could see above the stockade fence to more new rooftops being erected on the slope. There was a twelve-pound cannon in the yard near the front porch. Fort Austin would be safe from any Comanche raid, Matthew thought. A determined assault by a Mexican army with artillery would breech these walls, but Comanches would never take orders from a chief who told them to charge against a fort with a moat around it. Despite the fort and the cannon, the houses within a few blocks were in nightly danger from raiders. Matthew heard unease growing among the Indian Joes, who sensed trouble. He wondered why General Felix Huston had not arrived with his four hundred regulars and militia. The Rangers at Boca Chica had told Matthew that Huston was moving his army— one hundred cavalry and the rest foot soldiers—less than ten miles a day. Matthew figured Huston was showing Lamar and Johnston that the general who controlled the army was as powerful as the President. Huston had tried that approach with Sam Houston and had lost his army. But Lamar needed Huston and his soldiers to protect the new capital and its expanded frontier.

Gautier removed the eyeglasses from his nose and said, "Yes, we are a proud empire with a future that knows no limits. But think, gentlemen. What do you see around you in our empire? Our financial transactions are in chaos. We are printing redback dollars as fast as our presses will churn, but we have no banking system. No banks! No system of distributing or accounting for our money! We are reduced to collecting our taxes in kind, a chicken here and a mule there. How do you think this impresses European governments from whom we need recognition and financial support?"

Matthew's chair creaked as he shifted to look at Gautier.

"Furthermore, in what condition was the road that brought you here to our capital for this session of Congress? The road from your home to this city? Was it a hog wallow? Was it a strip of dusty, rutted hardpan? Or was there no road? Did you find your way here on trails through the forest? Did you pick a path across the prairie? I say to you, gentlemen, that to be a great empire, we must have great roads. We must have wide roads connecting all our towns, so our people may travel in ease and safety," Gautier said.

Matthew recognized the point the honorable gentleman from Galveston was striving to reach with this speech. The Ranger loudly cleared his throat.

Gautier said, "Our waterways are clogged with debris. We need to open up our rivers for commerce, to ship our goods on the Gulf of Mexico. Shipping is vital to the prosperity of our empire. Consider it, gentlemen, for the public good. We need a banking and treasury system, we need roads, we need waterways. In the past three years our political process has made not one bit of headway with these three major problems. I tell you, gentlemen, these problems are too complicated for us politicians to deal with. We have our own problems at our own homes. We deal with these major government issues only when we convene. Our public servants, bless them, the secretaries and minor officials, are in many cases working without pay. So I cannot find it in myself to blame them for this failure to progress. No, the fault lies in the reality that none of these major problems is a proper function of government."

Gautier tugged at his cuffs and peered over his spectacles, pausing for emphasis as he looked out at the representatives in their chairs. He avoided the gray-eyed gaze of the big man with the mottled beard.

"In the interest of progress, and as a matter of common sense," said Gautier, "I am reintroducing and I pray that we once again pass the Texas Railroad, Navigation and Banking Company act."

Matthew stood up. "Would the gentleman yield?"

"Sir, I am not yet finished."

The speaker said, "The House recognizes Matthew Caldwell."

"Very well, I yield for three minutes," said Gautier.

"It won't take that long, Mr. Speaker," Matthew said, walking to the podium.

Gautier retreated to a space against the north wall, out of reach of the Ranger he had heard bizarre tales about.

"First," Matthew said to the men who were now sitting forward in their uncomfortable cowhide chairs to listen, "this is a republic, not an empire. In a republic the power lies in the heart of every citizen who is entitled to vote, and in us fellows here, who represent the voters. An empire is run by an emperor. That's not us. I don't see an emperor anywhere, do you? We whipped the Emperor Santa Anna and chased him across the Rio Grande!"

The old breed cheered, and the newcomers applauded.

"What this man from Galveston is proposing is that we turn all of our banking, our transportation, our shipping and our millions upon millions of acres of public lands over to the management of a small, private group of greedy men. Gautier works for those men and was sent here to make them richer. Well, boys, this ain't what we fought for. Our public lands belong to the Republic of Texas, not to a few pigs in Galveston, and I intend to keep it that way."

Matthew paused to allow another cheer from the old breed and from newcomers who suddenly saw their business opportunities squeezed by the same sort of legislation that many of them had come to Texas to escape. These men wanted no interference from the government in their plans, but far more they wanted to prevent the Republic's wealth from being controlled by a financial elite that did not include them.

"Three years ago at our First Congress in Columbus, I voted against the Texas Railroad, Navigation and Banking Company act, but it passed the Congress anyhow and would have wrecked our republic if President Houston hadn't cut its guts out," Matthew said. "Now this act comes back again, and President Houston ain't here, so it's up to us to kill it for our own good, to save our land for all our people who qualify. I made one vote in that First Congress that I very much regret today. I voted in favor of selling Galveston Island to a syndicate of land speculators on credit. My reason was our republic was in desperate need of money. I didn't suspect the pig bastards would talk us into giving them the island on credit at a bottom price, and then would not pay for it even yet! Instead of paying what they owe us for Galveston, they spend their money to send slick foreign bankers like Gautier to our House to try to steal everything we have bled for."

Gautier considered himself a cultivated, influential gentleman, not a lackey. He spoke angrily from his position against the wall:

"I have read the records of the First Congress, Captain. You voted yes in favor of giving vast holdings of land to the speculators who built Houston City. It will profit you to learn that President Sam Houston is now a shareholder in the Texas Railroad, Navigation and Banking Company. President Houston is one of this so-called group of pig bastards that you are accusing of plotting to steal the public lands."

"You're a liar," Matthew said. "You can speak any kind of lie within the sanctuary of these walls, but I warn you not to repeat those words in public."

"I will show you the books of the company," said Gautier.

"I don't need to see your books. Your bill is dead in this House," Matthew said.

"Need I remind you this is a republic, not an empire?" said Gautier. "Twenty-eight gentlemen elected to this House will vote on my bill."

The speaker hammered his gavel on the wooden table he sat behind.

"Sorry, Matthew, but your time is up," the speaker said.

"Remember what I say, Gautier," Matthew said. "If I hear of you insulting President Houston outside these walls, you are fair game."

Gautier wisely decided to shut his mouth. Even though he believed what he said was true—that Sam Houston had been given one-sixteenth of the shares of the company in anticipation of his becoming president again—Gautier realized he had best leave this information for history, rather than get himself shot for arguing the point now. Caldwell was only one vote. Gautier had already counted fifteen who had promised to be on his side if their conditions were met.

As Matthew left the podium to walk back to his little cowhide chair, he heard a voice at the rear of the room say, "You can't come in here," and he heard the scraping and rustling and murmuring as the honorable gentlemen of the House turned to look at the disturbance caused by Red Beans, the Lipan scout, entering the doorway.

# 70

They moved in a crescent like the blade of a scythe. More than two thousand Comanche prime men mounted on horses and painted for war. Turk had created and turned loose a force he could not control. Rather than striking a sudden blow against Austin, as Turk had planned, the most powerful of all councils ever held in the history of the families had debated for two days before deciding to follow the desire of Cornstalks, a mighty chief from the snowy mountains. Cornstalks vigorously agreed that the men with hats should shed a river of blood in revenge for their betrayal of the families at the Council House. He believed the town where the chief of Texas lived should be attacked and burned and Old Paint should be killed. But Cornstalks had a vision that the massed warriors of the families should raid first to the Gulf of Mexico and kill many invaders and capture much plunder before they turned around and headed north to pass around San Antonio—Cornstalks had uncomfortable, ghosty feelings about San Antonio and its adobe walls, but he'd long yearned to see the Gulf for the first time—and launch a dreadful assault on Austin from the south, crashing over the invaders like a thunderstorm blowing up from the big water.

Cornstalks's vision met a popular reception. His plan included not only the slaughter of the invaders but also the allure of loot, for it was known among the families that many of the prized goods of the whites—the bags of silver, pots and pans, barrel hoops, bolts of colored cloth—arrived by boat at the towns on the Gulf Coast. The swaying vote at the supreme council belonged to Turk, who held the magic of the creature's head. Turk's dual roles as war chief and civil chief had sharpened his political acumen. Turk read the mood of the chiefs and warriors. They wanted revenge, but they also wanted reward. For a raid of this unheard-of size to succeed, Turk felt there must be unanimity and good spirit among the fighters. Turk proposed that no women or children be taken on this raid, for there would be no pitching of tepees or other labors. He asked the warriors to approach this biggest of raids as if they were a marauding party hitting a Mexican *rancheria*, quickly in and out. Each man would be mounted on his best horse with his finest weapons, a stomach bag full of water and a pouch of dried corn to eat. They would ride at night and move fast. They would reach the Gulf and steal mules to carry their booty, and then they would strike for the Texas town where Old Paint would die. Unencumbered by women and children, the warriors would raid the Gulf and then fall upon Austin before the Texans could realize what they were facing. Turk would lead the two thousand warriors smashing across the river and through the streets of Austin, killing the invaders and burning their houses, and then the warriors of the families would climb the white cliffs and be gone into Comancheria while the Texans lay in death and ruin.

Turk's position and his prowess and his standing confidently beside the black rod that held the white painted skull of the creature—the ultimate in magic—led the council to elect Turk as war chief of the raid against Texas, with Cornstalks approving loudly.

Under cover of night and a north wind that whistled sleet, they slipped down from Comancheria and flowed toward the Gulf, each man other than Romulus wearing a medicine bag of personal magic beside his scrotum. Though Romulus had given his word not to escape, he noted half a dozen warriors stayed near him. He was a prisoner. Turk had never trusted a white man's promise.

The warrior horde was like a flood of lava, Romulus thought. They destroyed everything in front of them and left smoldering track for many miles behind. Isolated cabins and farmhouses flared up in flames, their occupants murdered or captured. Unlucky travelers who crossed the route were mutilated. Romulus saw Comanches slice off the soles of a man's feet as neatly as any surgeon in Edinburgh could have done it, and then tie a rope around the man's neck and force him to run behind a pony. The healer in Romulus cried out to help these people, but the Comanches kept him moving.

Romulus had his rosewood rifle in its scabbard and his pistol in its holster and his Cherokee knife on his hip as he felt his mustang, Gaucha, between his knees, and they both remembered their primal run with wild horses. Romulus tried to make himself feel cold at the sight of slaughter of frontier families, as impartial as a surgeon would be in an open-sided operating tent in the middle of battle. These victims could be looked upon as soldiers in the army of the desperate and the land lunatics. He saw a baby jerked from its mother's arms and tossed into the air and caught on the tip of a lance that pierced its breast and changed its squalling to a gasp. The mother, weathered and gaunt as the poor whites Romulus had known in the North Carolina mountains, caught sight of him and screamed, "A white man! Mister, please, save my baby!" Romulus felt pity for her. "Mister, please, I am the granddaughter of Daniel Boone. Please save me!" Romulus rode on past. Daniel Boone? Could it be? Behind, he heard her screams as she was being raped, but he was a prisoner.

The advancing horde rolled across an expanse of cotton fields and killed thirty Negro slaves with arrows and lances. Arms and legs were hacked off, and woolly scalps waved, dripping blood. The Comanches came like demons, fierce and without mercy, guided by their own logic. Romulus rode on Gaucha beside the Dark Man, who carried the white-painted skull of the creature on his black rod. They were in the middle of the crescent, not far behind Turk and Cornstalks. Romulus saw gulls flying over the carnage and smelled the soft, salty odor of the sea.

A sign painted on a barn identified the town as Victoria. The Comanches swept in like Mongols and lanced several citizens surprised on the outskirts. But rather than whooping through the streets and staging a massacre of the entire population, Cornstalks ordered the warriors to ride a magic ring around the town, a wizard's circle such as could be placed around a buffalo herd to invoke the spirits to make the animals unable to leave the circle. The Comanches speared and hacked apart most of the cattle in Victoria and stole an unexpectedly rich supply of good horses and mules as the warriors circled the cluster of buildings in which the citizens had taken cover. Romulus watched the herd of stolen horses being assembled. He estimated there to be more than two thousand horses, five hundred from one corral alone, and about a hundred mules.

Then Cornstalks, following his vision, burned a few houses on the edges of Victoria and led the warriors away. The Comanches crossed to the east side of the Warloop and followed the vast river bottom on to a bayside town, arriving as an astounding surprise in the early morning while the men at the port were helping sailors unloading a shipment of mercantile goods. Turk ripped open the door of the customs office at Linnville and smashed in the tax collector's skull with his stone axe. Several warriors tore off the clothes of the collector's wife, intending to rape and kill the screaming woman, but they were frustrated by the whalebone corset she wore. They tied the woman onto the back of a mule, so that later they might solve the complexities of her costume.

The residents of the town ran to their boats and rowed out into the choppy water of the bay, as did the sailors who had been unloading goods at the dock. Three hundred warriors galloped their horses in the sand at the edge of the water, splashing themselves and laughing, launching arrows haphazardly toward the boats. The Comanches ripped open the trunks on the dock and screamed with delight at the bolts of colored cloth they found. In the warehouse nearby, Romulus saw a package addressed to Sam Maverick awaiting shipment to San Antonio. He saw a large wooden box marked fragile and addressed to Mrs. Lawrence Kerr in Austin. He had forgotten Dora and Lawrence. He had liked them, and he hoped they didn't get caught in the coming fight. Searching in the warehouse, the Comanches discovered shipments of stovepipe hats, women's undergarments, yards of red cloth, umbrellas, pots and pans, sacks of coffee, bags of tobacco, barrels of salt, kegs of sugar.

The warriors were howling with laughter, wild painted faces with red-veined eyeballs peering through the legs of pink pantaloons. Many warriors fit stovepipe hats atop their native hairdressing, so that scalp locks that were braided and beaded and strung with shells hung down from the brims. Two thousand warriors paraded through the town, on horse and on foot, and in a flush of high humor. Life was mysterious and unpredictable. Life could be as wretchedly barren as a winter on the high plains, but life could be as sweet as now, smelling the fish and the salt water, garbed in magnificent style in silks and satins, mules being loaded with plunder, a horse herd that stretched to the horizon, plenty of sugar in their coffee, beef and vegetables from the kitchens—and look at the invaders, bobbing in their boats out on the water, too far out to shoot with arrows but stuck out there nonetheless, like humans that had been forced to live like water birds. How funny that was. The families from Comancheria owned this Texas town, and the invaders watched from afar, as help-less as herons.

Young Owl Hatching wore a red-and-white-checked cotton bonnet over his topknot, and wrapped a green silk shawl across his chest. As the Thinking Man, Young Owl Hatching was thinking he had ridden along with the emotion of the crowd, but further reflection told him it might be wise to go home now. He sidled over toward the Dark Man, who sat on his pony and held the black rod and magic skull beside the dismounted white healer. Pulling the scraggly hairs on his chin, Young Owl Hatching studied the blackened, charred cheeks of the Dark Man and asked in the language of the families, so the white man would not understand: "Your *portento* . . ."

"Yes?"

"Your *portento* that you and me and Turk would throw away our bodies in a big fight. It is all changed now, isn't it?"

"Why do you say so?" said the Dark Man.

"You carry the creature's skull. I think this is magic that replaces your *portento*, because this is a new event that was unforeseen when you dreamed into the future."

Young Owl Hatching looked at the grinning mouth of the skull, at the rows of yellow teeth. He had seen the creature alive, when it roared into their camp and hauled away the German that the Talking Man had been beating on. Young Owl Hatching had spent solitary nights pondering and fearing the power of the creature. To have the creature's skull here made the Thinking Man tremble with excitement. Certainly this was the biggest magic. If he stayed near the skull, Young Owl Hatching would pass through battle behind an invisible shield.

The Dark Man licked his lips and kept silent. True, the skull of the creature had not been seen in the *portento*. Maybe the Thinking Man was correct about something important at last. The Dark Man rubbed the black rod and felt spats of electricity. This was terribly strong magic, this skull.

Romulus was looking at the citizens in their boats on the gray water. The sailors had rowed out to their merchant sloop and were climbing rope ladders up the side while sails were breaking out. The sight of two thousand Comanche warriors convinced the sloop captain to pull anchor. Romulus could hear a voice calling from the sloop, offering to take the Linnville citizens away. But the people were unwilling to abandon their town.

There was a scuffle on a Boston whaler a hundred yards offshore, just inside the darkening that meant deep water. Romulus saw a gray-haired man in shirt-sleeves, waving a shotgun as he yanked himself loose from two women and another man. The gray-haired man stepped off the whaler as if to wade to shore.

He disappeared underwater, and the women began screaming. In a moment the man reappeared and then swam and splashed toward shore until he could get a grip for his feet. He stood up, water pouring down his body, and began wading toward the town.

The gray-haired man shouted, "I am Judge Hays! I am the law in Linnville! You savage, heathen sons of bitches get out of my town!" He brandished his shotgun, and water was slung from the barrel. "I'm not going to tell you bastards twice! Get the hell out of my town before I start whipping your naked brown butts! I have the full force of the law behind me! I can have the whole pile of you hanged!"

The judge sloshed onto the shore and glared fiercely at the Comanches, who pretended they didn't see him. They walked or rode past him, ignoring his threats and curses as if he did not exist. Clearly the white man was either a crazy person, or he was incredibly brave. In either case, the warriors respected and accepted him and directed their attentions to the looting of Linnville.

Judge Hays's eyebrows flew up in shock when he saw Romulus leaning against the wall of the livery stable while Gaucha drank from the trough. Stomping through the middle of the Comanches, who were busy dressing in costumes and loading trunks and bags of booty onto their mules, the judge marched over to Romulus. The Dark Man sat on his pony nearby with the skull on the pole in his hands. Young Owl Hatching shaded his vision with the brim of the bonnet.

"I am Judge Hays," the gray-haired man said.

Romulus saw the man's soaked shirt breast heaving as he fought for breath. The judge's face was red and purple. Were the circumstances different, Romulus would have advised the judge to lie in the shade and bathe his face and chest with ice, for he appeared on the edge of a stroke or heart failure.

"Are you a white man?" asked the judge. "Are you a foreigner? Spikky French? What the hell is all this?"

"I am not a white man," Romulus said.

"Well, I'm glad to hear that, because you'd make me ashamed for our whole race," said the judge. "Tell your savages to get the hell out of my town! This land belongs to us! You son of a bitches clear out now!"

"Judge Hays," Romulus said, "listen to me. Turn around and walk confidently back across the beach into the water. Keep shouting and cavorting like the lunatic that you are. If you do this, you might reach your boat and survive the day."

"You think I'm fooling with you? You think I am not serious?" said the judge.

"You are an amusement. If you become an annoyance, you will be butchered," Romulus said.

The judge looked up at the white-painted skull and at the ferociously impassive face of the Dark Man. The judge's lips moved, but no words came out for a few seconds as his senses finally began to overcome his rage and register his predicament.

Turk walked over to see what the judge was doing. The war chief had put on no costumery from the Linnville stores. Turk wore his war paint and shells in his hair, and he had a dead woman's gold necklace that fell into his chest hair. With his medicine bag swinging beside his scrotum, the war chief, wearing a loincloth made of soft leather, felt invincible. Turk believed he owed much of his success to the magic of the creature. The Dark Man carrying the creature's head, as it ripened into the creature's skull, had been the authority that had swung opinion Turk's way in many debates in councils all over Comancheria.

"What is this?" Turk asked in frontier Mexican.

The judge, his shirttail out, his shotgun dragging in the sand, was cursing at the top of his voice as he walked back through gatherings of warriors who let him go by as if he was a ghost. "He is a crazy person," said the Dark Man. "Do not touch him." The judge waded into the water. Romulus saw hands haul the judge back into the whaler.

Turk glanced up at the skull and looked at Romulus.

"We are going to finish killing all their cows and pigs and all but the best horses. Then we are going to burn this Texas place down to ashes in the dirt."

"And then we start for Austin?" Romulus said.

"We have killed many Texans, taken many scalps, taken prisoners, stolen a great many fine horses and mules and loaded them with our prizes," said Turk. "I hear that some believe this is revenge enough. They say we should take our prizes and go into our high country and be safe from the men with hats."

"Is this how you feel?" asked Romulus.

"No. I understand what we must do. We must kill the invaders, as we should have done long ago. We must kill Old Paint. We will not enjoy blood revenge for the Council House betrayal until Old Paint's hair hangs from my shield," Turk said.

"Old Paint's hair is mine," said Romulus.

"No. I will kill him, chief against chief," Turk said. "His hair belongs to me."

Turk called a council. More than a thousand warriors gathered to hear the debates. The other thousand were stabbing Linnville's livestock to death, and stacking up dry tinder to burn the buildings, and loading mules with booty, while the residents of Linnville crouched in open boats and burned their skin in the sun. The sloop had long since sailed away. Cornstalks stood beside Turk and listened to speeches from those who wished to abandon the raid and go back to Comancheria with their plunder. Turk replied that the families were great and ruled over all this land; to suggest they feared the Texans and must retreat up the white cliffs was to demean the courage of Turk and all the rest who would fight. "This was all our land before the invaders came," Turk told the crowd. "It will be our land again. A few Mexicans will be spared to raise horses and prisoners for us, but our families will rule this land. The nameless one says we will continue to rule this land like we always have."

The warriors' eyes shifted up toward the grin on the white-painted skull. They began to whoop and cheer. Cornstalks pitched in with his war cry, distinguished by its yodeling quality. Once again Turk's formidable self had won the day with the aid of the creature's magic.

The black and gray smoke of Linnville burning could be seen from forty miles away across the coastal prairie. Advancing ahead of the black smoke was a ground cloud across the horizon, the dust raised by the ponies of two thousand warriors and their herds of stolen horses and their strings of pack mules, a dozen carrying prisoners.

From a mile and a half north of the dust cloud, Matthew Caldwell was watching the advance through a six-power telescope. Matthew stood upright on the seat of his saddle on his Arabian stallion, his moccasins balancing his hips and torso as he peered through the telescope. It was hard to make out individuals at this distance, but Matthew closed his ring around a man in a black hat with a black coat. The man appeared to have white skin and was riding a mustang near a presence that Matthew had recognized was the chief, Turk. Matthew couldn't see the features of the man's face, but he knew that it was Dr. Swift.

Matthew hopped down from his horse and handed the telescope to Big Foot Wallace.

"I'll be damned," Matthew said.

"Me, too."

Big Foot's five dogs lay near their master, tongues lolling, sniffing the wind. Red Beans squatted in the shade of his pony and smoked a cornhusk cigarette. The Lipan Apache scout could feel in his bones the menace of the approach of his ancient enemies.

"You figure fifteen hundred, two thousand of them?" asked Matthew.

"Could be more."

"It will take them three days to reach Austin the way they're weighed down with stolen horses and loot," Matthew said. "We've got to plan a place to cut them off and have it out once and for good."

"We don't know yet but what they might be headed for San Antonio."

"Doctor Swift is riding up front with those savages," Matthew said. "He is coming to Austin."

# 71

Matthew Caldwell had not shared Red Beans's message with anyone in Austin the morning the Lipan scout abruptly interrupted the Fourth Congress. The Ranger went with Red Beans to see for himself how serious the threat was. Matthew wanted to prevent the panic and chaos that had been the death of Nancy and their sons and her mother in the Runaway Scrape early in the revolution. After Matthew rode toward the Gulf with Red Beans and met Big Foot and saw the rank of Comanches stretching across the plain, moving through the dry grass inexorably north toward Austin, he realized the government of Texas had never been in worse peril in the three and a half years since the Republic won its independence from Mexico in battle on Peggy McCormick's farm at San Jacinto. Except for the two hundred soldiers in blue jackets who had marched to Austin with the archives caravan, and the Rangers from Boca Chica Station, there was no armed force to oppose the two thousand Comanches. Even if Felix Huston and his four hundred men trudging up from Houston City arrived in time, the Comanches would have them outnumbered more than three to one, and all the Comanches had the truly bloodthirsty desire to fight and to kill, Matthew knew, unlike most of the Texas regulars, who had wangled scarce openings in the military because a grant of public land was offered in payment for service, and they believed the wars with the Indians were over and a future invasion of Mexico would bring plunder and glory.

From the prairie north of Linnville, Matthew sent Big Foot and his dogs back to Boca Chica Station to alarm the Rangers and spread the news that whatever citizens who were willing to fight should gather at Plum Creek, south of Austin. Matthew decided to place the first line of defense at Plum Creek and prepare to fall back north of the Colorado River for a final stand on the banks of Austin itself. He assigned Red Beans to stay close to the approaching Comanche storm to keep informed of its pace and course. Unless they should change direction for some inexplicable aboriginal reason, the Comanches were taking a route that would bring them directly up Big Prairie beside Plum Creek by the morning of day after tomorrow, in Matthew's estimate.

When he returned to Austin, he rode up to the bridge that crossed the moat and led to the gate in the ten-foot-high stockade fence around the temporary capitol building, but then he decided he would go home first and inform Hannah. Those fellows discussing politics could wait a while longer to hear they might be wasting their wind. Matthew wanted Hannah to know what was coming. At his stable, Matthew dismounted and told the Cajun, Marvelito, to remove the saddle and use the brush but keep Pacer ready. The Ranger was drawn toward the door of the kitchen house by the odor of baked apples. As he entered, Hannah was removing a pan of strudel from the oven. Evangeline was on her knees in front of the fireplace, setting a kettle to boil.

The Ranger embraced his wife and kissed her, and her body felt warm and damp.

"Matthew," she said, pulling back at last. "Let me get a breath."

"Would you leave us alone, please?" Matthew said to Evangeline.

She grinned and hurried out the door.

"We can go to the bedroom," Hannah said.

Matthew had not come there with the intention of making love with his wife, but the sight of her aroused him, and the realization crossed his mind that this might be the last time. They lay together on the kitchen floor.

As they straightened their clothing, Hannah smiled and said, "You stay hungry for me."

"More than anything."

"I love knowing you feel that way," she said.

Matthew pulled up his suspenders, the pair of pistols dangling, and put on his doeskin jacket—not his best jacket but a workaday jacket which was, like his other jackets, well fringed and decorated with beads.

"An hour from now this town is going to be a madhouse," he said. "People will be rushing around like loonies. I haven't thought this all through yet, Hannah, but I need your help. You could escape, there's plenty of time, but I want you to stay here and see this thing through."

"What are you talking about?" she asked. Her husband looked more wrinkled around the eyes—all night in the saddle— but he was generating an animal ardor that excited her.

"Two thousand Comanches are on their way here from the south. We're going to fight them. I don't know exactly where or when, but pretty soon."

"I will fight."

"You're a better shot and braver than most of our fellows, but I need you to stay here in town and open a hospital. I believe we're going to whip these Comanches, Hannah, but a lot of people are going to get hurt. I need you to round up the doctors in town and get many beds ready. Don't let the pharmacists escape with their supplies. Especially keep the opium and the laudanum, all they've got."

"Opium?"

"Every last bottle of it. Rustle up some women to help you. Grab the barber. He's done nursing before."

"I'll go to Dora."

Matthew placed his hands on her shoulders and fixed her with his gray eyes.

"If the savages should break through and come across the river, I want you to go to the capitol building. The guard there will let you in. No matter what happens in Austin, the capitol building will not fall."

"But I can't run to the capitol if there are wounded."

"Hannah, I don't know when I will see you again," Matthew said. "But I will see you again. We will be stronger than ever when this is done."

"I love you, Matthew."

"I love you," he said, and they kissed. She spread his beard aside with her fingers so she could taste his lips.

He was adjusting the tilt of his brown beaver hat when he said, "I'm going to tell you a secret. It's very important you not repeat it."

"I promise," she said. "What is it?"

"Doctor Swift is riding with the savages."

"Romulus is alive?" Her heart leapt and she realized she had used his first name. "What is Doctor Swift doing with the savages?"

"I don't know what he is doing. But we can't forget that Doctor Swift is half savage himself."

"I wonder if he knows his sister was murdered?" Hannah said.

"Well, he's bringing two thousand Comanches with him, whatever he wants. Listen, Hannah, don't tell anyone that Doctor Swift is out there. He is a hero to a lot of people in this town. Let's not confuse them."

Matthew kissed her again, tenderly. He kissed her eyes. He had begun looking forward to the battle against the savages. He pulsed with the blood of his Cold Well ancestors who had been invaders and had fought invaders to protect their women and their land.

When Matthew knocked on the door of the White House, he was admitted by a uniformed Negro who showed him into the parlor, where President Lamar was having tea and cookies with Dora and Lawrence Kerr.

After a round of greetings, Matthew accepted a cup of tea and sat on the velvet sofa beside Dora, who smelled of perfume and managed to touch his hand as she reached for the sugar bowl. Conversationally, Matthew said, "Two thousand Comanches will be here day after tomorrow."

"Yehyehyehyeh," Lamar laughed politely, brushing cookie crumbs off his lap.

"You mean it, don't you, Matthew?" said Dora.

"I mean it. Sure do."

"But how can that be? We destroyed the Comanches at the Council House," Lamar said.

"You made them mad enough to kill you," said Matthew. "You better call Albert Johnston and his soldier boys and spread the word that we've got a hell of a battle in front of us."

"I'll fight beside you, by God," Lawrence said.

"Appreciate it, Lawrence, but I'm going to pick our first fight out on the prairie. You can do best by—"

"No! You keep telling me to stay back and guard the women! I'm a blooded fighter now, Matthew. I'll kill any savage son of a bitch that thinks he can take Texas away from me," Lawrence said.

"Where is Hannah?" asked Dora.

"Putting together a hospital."

"I'll help her. We can use my house," Dora said.

"I'll go pack up my war bag," said Lawrence.

When the Kerrs were gone and General Johnston had been sent for, Lamar sat deep in thought, pulling his nose, twisting his curls above his ears.

"In the eyes of the world, I cannot afford to be driven out of the capital city of the Republic of Texas by savages," the President said. "Our government will collapse in international ridicule. Sam Houston's Planter pack will pick up the pieces and sell us out to their friends in the United States. Our Republic of Texas will be finished."

"I agree," said Matthew.

"How do you propose to stop these savages?"

"I'm going to meet them south of town with my Rangers and the Lipans and Tonks, who hate the Comanches worse than they hate us. I hope there's a few settlers will show up to fight. I believe we might strike a blow that makes the Comanches turn away and head for home. But if I'm wrong and they come through my line, I want your two hundred regular infantry and every man, woman and child in town who can shoot a gun to be behind trees on the north bank of the Colorado."

"What if the savages don't stop at the river?"

"Even if they sack the town, they'll never overrun Fort Austin. You'll be safe in the capitol building," Matthew said.

"You know I'm not a coward. I fought beside you at San Jacinto. I would prefer to be fighting beside you in the front line against the savages, but it is not wise to expose the president in such a way," said Lamar. "I must preserve myself as a symbol of our Republic."

"I understand," Matthew said.

Johnston had been eating sausages and sauerkraut at lunch and was wiping mustard off his chin with a handkerchief when the Negro servant showed him into Lamar's parlor. The President explained what he knew of the situation to his secretary of war.

"I will take command at once," General Johnston said.

"And do what?" asked Lamar.

"I don't know what, except I will send for Felix Huston to hurry the hell up and get here," Johnston said.

"Captain Caldwell suggests we draw up a line of battle on the city bank of the river. The captain will go forward on the south bank with his Rangers and other mounted men to try to turn away the Comanches at Plum Creek," said the President.

"This was decided without me?" Johnston said.

"Captain Caldwell has been fighting savages for years. I trust his judgment. He understands their ways. You are certainly in command, Albert, but I will need you with me to supervise the deployment of our city defense and oversee the battle," said the President.

Matthew set his teacup on the table and was careful not to knock it over when he rose. He put on his new brown beaver hat.

"One of the boys from the Boca Chica Station has already gone to find Huston and build a fire under him," Matthew said. "I'll be down on Big Prairie at Plum Creek if you have anything to tell me."

"Godspeed," said Lamar.

On the porch of the White House waited Wapner, the poet from *The Sentinel*, and Bigelow from the new newspaper, *The Gazette*. Matthew heard a roaring hubbub as word of the approaching Comanches washed over the town like a wave. People were running back and forth from building to building. Wagons were being loaded.

"Captain Caldwell, is it true that twenty-five thousand Comanches are going to attack our city?" Wapner said.

"Nowhere near that many," said Matthew.

"Are they coming to take revenge because you double-crossed them at the Council House?" Bigelow asked.

"The first one we catch, I'll ask him," said Matthew coldly, bristling at the question. The Ranger shouldered between the reporters and mounted Pacer. Congress Avenue was crowded as usual, but there was a sense of urgency without purpose, as though everyone was trying to do something but no one knew what to do, other than those who were packing to flee. He saw a senator cracking a whip at his buggy horse and heading east at a fast trot. Representative Gautier from Galveston emerged from Bullock's Inn with his suitcase in hand. On Legation Hill, Alphonse Dubois de Saligny was departing in a carriage for New Orleans. There was a gathering on the porch of the Kerr mansion. Matthew recognized Hannah among them. He waved as he rode past, but Hannah didn't see him. Matthew was about to rein up and go back when he saw Lawrence come down the steps of the Kerr mansion with a rifle and two canvas bags. Matthew put the heels to his Arabian stallion and galloped toward the river before Lawrence could call to accompany him.

From his second-floor study, Henry Longfellow leaned on his ebony sword cane and looked out his window and saw the Ranger leaving on his white horse. This was good. The savages would do what Henry had not yet figured out how to do—kill Matthew Caldwell. The thought of his enemy stuck through by a Comanche lance filled Henry with joy and made him forget the ache in his leg. Henry turned to the young Negro slave boy who had brought him the news and was twisting from one foot to the other in curiosity. Henry could see wagons going from the land office to the capitol loaded with precious documents pertaining to ownership of the Republic of Texas's primary asset, its land. No heathen savages were going to chase Henry Longfellow out of the house he had worked hard to build and away from the earth of which he already owned a large amount and intended to own much more. He had defeated these savages in Georgia and in east Texas. Let it not be said that Henry Longfellow feared aborigines. "Bring me my shotgun," Henry said to the slave boy. Henry would defend his home.

Throughout the following night and day, fighters drifted in to the spartan camp Matthew helped the men make in the oaks and pecan trees and brush along Plum Creek. Red Beans brought in twenty-three Lipans. Chief Placido of the Tonkawas arrived with fourteen painted warriors. Matthew told the Lipans and Tonks to tie a white cloth around one arm so they would not be shot by white men once the fight started. Lawrence Kerr galloped into camp two hours behind Matthew. He was armed with two pistols and a rifle, and he wore his big hat. Lawrence greeted his Ranger friends from the Boca Chica Station. He was proud to be accepted into their company on the eve of a battle against the savages. Lawrence passed the time with the Rangers, swapping tales, pretending not to be nervous. During the second night, a lone figure dressed all in white appeared in the moonlight. He was a strange, pale apparition, wearing a white wool suit and a large hat that came down to his ears. It was the reclusive lawyer Ridgewood Bone, Matthew's old hospital roommate at Bullock's Inn, where Cullasaja had nursed them. Matthew spoke to the lawyer in welcome. Bone replied, "I didn't come here to visit with you, Captain. I came to kill as many Comanches as I can."

The Devil's Dozen of the old breed from the House were sturdily mounted and armed. Three senators arrived prepared for the fight. These were hard-eyed men who had known battles against the Mexicans. Half a dozen newcomers to the Congress joined them. Farmers were coming in from the east with their guns. Every man and boy in this area of Texas—not including the slaves—owned a firearm and was practiced at using it. Twenty-eight men from the Bastrop militia rode into camp the second night. Ranger Captain Jack Hays and his six men arrived and took their positions on the right flank. An hour before dawn a farmer cheered from the sunrise side of the line. Big Foot confronted the man and warned him to keep his voice down. Then they saw what the farmer had been cheering about—the chesty, curly-haired General Felix Huston was coming out of the dawn into camp with a hundred cavalry.

"What's the situation here, Captain?" said Huston, accepting a mug of coffee from one of the farmers.

"Two thousand Comanches will be here in a few hours," Matthew said.

"Why in God's name are we meeting them out on this prairie instead of using the river as our line of defense?" said Huston.

"Where's your infantry?" Matthew asked.

"Ten miles behind."

"I want your infantry to set up on the town side of the river. We need your cavalry over here on this side," Matthew said.

"Who the hell do you think you are talking to? This is my army. I give the commands."

"Outnumbered as we are, striking a blow against the Comanches out on this prairie will surprise them," Matthew said. "They don't like the unexpected. There's a chance we can hit them hard enough to make them turn away from Austin and veer off back to Comancheria."

"A good enough chance for me to risk a hundred dead cavalry?"

"The rest of us are going to meet the Comanches and fight them," said Matthew. "Turn around your soldiers and run if you don't have the heart for what is about to happen here."

Huston flushed at the insult, but he took a swallow of bitter, tepid coffee before he answered. "Very well, I will meet the savages with my cavalry. But I must insist, Captain, that I am in command here."

"Give all the orders you want to your soldiers, Felix, but take your lead from what me and the Rangers do," said Matthew.

General Huston dashed the coffee from his cup onto the ground.

"This tastes like pig shit," he said.

"You'd be the one to know," said Big Foot Wallace.

The Rangers laughed as General Huston mounted his horse and moved his men to the eastern flank of the line of trees. Lawrence Kerr had never enjoyed a scene so much in his life, not even the melee in San Antonio. He felt good and strong being shoulder to shoulder, knee to knee, with Matthew Caldwell and Saginaw Boswell and Big Foot and Fiddle Man and Cyrus and his other friends from Boca Chica Station. They were treating Lawrence like a peer.

At mid-morning, Red Beans came out of the brush to the west, along the San Gabriel River, from which Plum Creek flowed. The Lipan scout rode across the prairie in front of the Lipans and Tonkawas and Texans concealed in the trees that lined the creek. Red Beans ignored a shouted summons from General Huston in the east. The scout rode to Matthew Caldwell in the center of the line and leaped off his lathered horse. Red Beans lifted his right arm and pointed at the sun and indicated the sun moving three feet until it was directly overhead.

"When this happens, they will be here," Red Beans said.

# 72

*It was a spectacle never to be forgotten, the wild, fantastic band as they stood in battle array. Horses and riders were decorated most profusely, with all the beauty and horror of their wild taste combined. Red ribbons streamed out from their horses' tails. . . . There was a huge warrior who wore a stovepipe hat, and another who wore a fine pigeon-tailed cloth coat, buttoned up behind. Some wore on their heads immense buck and buffalo horns. They bounded over the space between the hostile lines, exhibiting feats of horsemanship and daring none but a Comanche could perform.*

*—written by John Holland Jenkins, who was a Ranger during the fight at Plum Creek.*

Caldwell's men stood beside their horses in the shelter of the trees. The Rangers had passed among the newcomers, being sure each was properly loaded and prepared, and each saddle girth was tightened. Looking out at the line of Comanches approaching at a walk across Big Prairie, Matthew saw a chief wearing an eagle-feather bonnet with a tail that dragged on the ground. The chief dashed forward on his pony and shook his lance and screamed insults. Matthew patted his white stallion's neck and rubbed the horse's ears. The stallion sniggered, thrilled with what was in the air.

The chief in the eagle feathers darted back into the advancing line, now five hundred yards away from the Texans who waited beneath the trees. Matthew looked for Dr. Swift, but in the dust it was hard to pick him out.

"All right, boys, mount up," Matthew said.

There were rattles and clanks and snortings and curses all down the line.

From the eastern flank, they heard General Huston say, "Mount up," and the shuffling, thumping sounds of a hundred cavalrymen climbing onto their saddles.

"At a walk now, let's go see what they're made of," Matthew told his men. "Forward at a walk," Huston cried.

The line of about three hundred Texans and and another forty Tonka-was and Lipans moved out of the trees and advanced toward the oncoming Comanches.

Slowly the two lines rode closer toward conflict. On the flanks, Comanches were whooping and screaming and showing off on their ponies, but Matthew paid no attention to them. He was concentrating on the center of the dust cloud, where the power would be. That the savages had not rushed upon the Texans at once and overwhelmed them with numbers increased Matthew's hopes. Maybe they were waiting to see if there was a surprise force hiding in the trees, or they assumed they could take their leisure in slaughtering this small number of Texans, or perhaps they were surprised at this tactic and were looking for leadership. Matthew saw through the dust that many warriors were staying in the rear, guiding their stolen horse herds and their mules packed with prisoners and plunder, which was slowing the advance of the whole party.

"Keep it at a walk, boys," Matthew said.

He was riding in the middle of the Texan line, and now he gigged his white stallion forward, prancing into a trot, separating himself from the rest, putting himself and his big white horse on display.

Two hundred yards away, Turk saw the hated Old Paint arrogantly showing himself on the white stallion that Turk longed to add to his remuda. A passionate delight pounded in Turk's breast beneath his magical amulets, and his medicine pouch squeezed between his scrotum and the satiny back of his best war horse, whose head was painted black like the face of the Dark Man. Turk was armed with his lance and his stone axe and a knife. Most of the warriors also carried bows and arrows. There were no guns among the warriors of the families except for a few they had grabbed during this raid, but hardly any warriors knew how to load and shoot a gun.

Turk galloped forward of the Comanche line and shouted in frontier Mexican, "Old Paint, you are a coward! Come and fight me man to man, Old Paint! You are without honor! You are a breaker of faith!"

The Dark Man held the black rod with the white skull of the creature and kneed his mustang forward beside Turk, while the rest of the Comanche line slowed to a stop, watching this event.

Turk raised his lance and shook it and screamed, "Old Paint you are old and weak! You are afraid! I will burn your town and take your woman!"

"Hold your line right here, boys," Matthew said.

The Rangers halted their horses in the prairie grass, and the cavalry stopped without waiting for an order from Huston. The Comanche line had ceased advancing, though in the background warriors still drove their herds of stolen horses and plunder and prisoners, veering off to the west now, away from the confrontation.

Matthew trotted forward on Pacer.

"Hey, there, Turk!" Matthew yelled in frontier Mexican.

"Old Paint, your hair will hang in my tepee!" shouted Turk, now only thirty yards from the Ranger. "I will take your woman and make her my slave!"

Smoothly Matthew slid down out of the saddle and slipped Sweet Lips from its sheath in the same motion.

The first boom from Sweet Lips blasted the white-painted creature's skull into dust. Almost simultaneously came a second boom that blew Turk nearly in half and flung his grotesque fragments, showering blood, backward off his war horse and onto the dirt and grass of Big Prairie.

The Comanches stared in astonishment.

Matthew leaped onto his stallion. He hadn't known what the skull was, but it was easy for him to guess it represented powerful magic. The magic was shattered. The Comanches were stunned. A great moan went up, a sigh of mourning and disappointment.

"All right, boys, let's go get 'em!" Matthew shouted.

The first Texan volley knocked down twenty warriors and thirty horses.

"Come on, Huston! Now is the time!" Matthew shouted.

"Charge!" yelled Huston.

Lawrence Kerr aimed his rifle at the odd-looking savage—not that they weren't all odd-looking—with the dark face, the one who had been holding the pole with the skull on it. Lawrence squeezed his trigger and the rifle jumped against his shoulder, and he saw the Dark Man's horse fall, shot in the neck. Saginaw Boswell fired a rifle ball that struck the Dark Man in the mouth. The Magician's horse fell on top of him, and the black rod broke in half. Young Owl Hatching caught a rifle ball in the stomach. He toppled off his horse and sat in the grass, looking at his blood pouring onto the ground, until a charging Ranger called Fiddle Man ripped open Young Owl Hatching's skull with a butcher knife. Young Owl Hatching felt the knife scraping his bone and knew his scalp was being taken. His body had been thrown away. The *portento* was correct. He could not have evaded it. He waited for his spirit to rise up.

Cornstalks's horse was killed in the first volley. As the mighty chief from the snowy mountains struggled to his feet, he was decapitated by the saber of Felix Huston. Big Prairie had become a stage for ghostly riders whirling in the dust, a place that smelled of blood of and gunpowder, that shrilled with the cries of the victors and the dying.

Matthew fought his way into the center of the Comanche line, swinging Sweet Lips like a club, firing his pistols, slashing with his butcher knife, ramming his white stallion into a smaller mustang that fell and broke the leg of its warrior rider. Matthew urged his stallion deeper into the swirling mass. He was looking for Dr. Swift.

Romulus struggled forward on Gaucha, through the clashing of beasts and bodies, until in the dust and noise he saw Matthew Caldwell, mounted on his stallion, firing his pistol into the breast of a grappling warrior.

Romulus lifted the rosewood rifle to his shoulder and took careful aim at the center of the Ranger's brawny torso, a target impossible for Romulus to miss.

He saw Caldwell's gray eyes flick toward the rosewood rifle as if sensing it. Romulus saw his betrayer, his enemy, the husband of the woman he loved, helpless in his rifle sights.

Matthew recognized the figure of Dr. Swift frozen for an instant in the turmoil. He saw that he was dead in the doctor's sights, and the bullet would come before he could duck or dodge away. Matthew could only hope to survive the first shot and then close the distance between them and use his butcher knife.

But Romulus could not pull the trigger. Some force kept his forefinger from squeezing. The moment lay before him, the moment he could kill his enemy. But he could not do it. His eyes fastened for an instant with Caldwell's eyes, and it was acknowledged between them—*Your life is in my hands.*

Big Foot Wallace and Red Beans saw the doctor aiming at Caldwell. Expecting to hear the rifle shot instantly—the shot that would stand out above all others, the shot that would kill Old Paint—Big Foot and the scout galloped through the brawling bodies toward the doctor as the white stallion stood on his hind legs and Caldwell looked down the muzzle of the rosewood rifle and shouted, "Go ahead!"

And still Romulus did not pull the trigger.

Then the Comanche known as The Ram charged Caldwell with a lance. Romulus swung his rifle toward The Ram. But again he could not pull the trigger. Romulus saw Caldwell evade the stabbing point of the lance and wrestle with The Ram. Big Foot's horse, Old Higgins, stumbled and rolled in the dirt. A curtain of dust closed over them. The brown hands of Red Beans reached out of the dust and grabbed for the rosewood rifle. Romulus threw the rifle to him.

# 73

**B**ecause every man and boy who could shoot a gun and hadn't already run away was rounded up by soldiers in blue jackets and taken to positions in the trees along Water Street, near the north bank of the Colorado, Googleye was operating the *Waterloo Queen* ferry by himself.

Googleye was thinking this was a peculiar situation. People had said there was anywheres up to fifty thousand Comanches coming from the south to attack Austin. Googleye didn't believe it. Most people were fools. There wasn't fifty thousand Comanches in the whole world, and having lived his life on the frontier, Googleye knew barbarians seldom came from the south. Mexicans came from the south. But the river-crossing business for today had gone to hell, and just in case this ridiculous story about Comanches could be even a little bit true, Googleye was on the south bank of the Colorado, which could turn out to be dangerous. It would be more prudent for him to wait on the north side of the river, in the event the first customers who showed up weren't Old Paint and his Rangers but feathered savages instead.

As Googleye prepared to pole away from the dock, he heard a familiar voice call his name, and he stared down the road, trying to make out the fuzzy vision of the rider coming toward him. He knew the man's posture and his riding style and his mannerisms and the black coat. Yes, indeed, Googleye told himself. He knew this rider.

"Hidy, Doc!" Googleye called.

"Take me to the other side, Captain?" asked Romulus.

"Anything for you, Doc. You get right on board the *Queen*. I'm about to stow her in the shed for a while. Folks are saying there is somewhere near a million Comanches headed toward us. You believe it?"

"No," Romulus said, leading Gaucha onto the planks of the *Waterloo Queen*. Googleye shoved off from the bank and began poling across the smoothly flowing river.

"First time I brung you across this river, she was a flood," Googleye said.

"I remember," Romulus said, watching the city coming toward him, recalling the tumble-down fence and the few houses that had awaited on his first visit nine months ago, a period that had changed his life entirely.

"Doc, I sure am sorry about your nurse getting killed. I wish I knew who did it, I'd drown him in shit."

"Thank you, Captain," Romulus said. "Has everybody has gone out to fight these mysterious Comanches?"

"Some is out on the prairie, and the rest is hiding along the bank or holed up someplace or running for Louisiana. You could shoot a cannon down Congress Avenue and not hit nothing but Bullock's pigs."

"Where does Henry Longfellow live?" asked Romulus.

Googleye shoved hard on the pole, and the *Queen* caught the current.

"You gonna kill him?" Googeleye said.

"Why would you ask?"

"Doc, I can see inside people. I sail all kinds on the *Queen*. There are lots who need killing, and lots who want to kill 'em. Longellow lives in that ugly peach house on the hill, and I believe he has not left town."

# 74

Henry Longfellow soaked in an enamel tub of warm water, the knees of his long, bony legs sticking up, suds floating around his beak, looking more than ever like a malevolent bird. His eyes were shut in blissful repose. He felt the cool enamel against the back of his neck and the tingly stroking touch of the Negro slave boy's fingers down under the water, massaging Henry's toes and then rising to rub gently the purple scar that marked Henry's right shin from knee to ankle, the souvenir of his first encounter with that Cherokee thug and his whore. What did they call the devil bitch? Cullasaja?

Across his mind floated images of the wicked young Cherokee whore. She had loved wallowing in sex with him. She had cried with pleasure when Henry urged his fool of a client to pull off his trousers and use the bitch. The images of the Cherokee whore began to merge into pictures of the devil slut Jew who

was so often in his thoughts now. As he bathed, he remembered looking through
the slit in the canvas tent at the Fincus Hotel and seeing the Jew standing naked,
posing for him and for the other nude women, displaying her desire, showing
off her round white breasts and her black bush, her eyes sleekly sweeping up
to lock upon Henry's eyes through the slit in the canvas as they recognized
each other as the devil's own. Hannah was close to him in his reverie, rubbing
her bosoms against his face, her armpits stinking of sex. He heard her female
sighs of yearning for satisfaction that could come only through copulating with
the devil. Henry became so aroused that he trembled and slapped the Negro
boy's hand away from the purple knob that poked out of the water. Ordinarily,
Henry would encourage the boy to fondle him. But today Henry had a different
desire. The head of Henry's pecker was the same color as the scar in his right
shin. His souvenir of the Cherokee. Well, Henry had another Cherokee souvenir
that was pulling him toward it at this moment.

Henry ordered the boy to help him out of the tub but waved away the offer
to towel him dry. This was urgent. Dripping and trailing water, like a crane
emerging from the swamp, Henry walked into his bedroom, to the oil painting
of a field of bluebonnet wildflowers that hung above his bureau. Henry slid the
painting aside and spun the knob on the wall safe. Shaking with excitement,
his hand clawed through the money and documents and found a thick brown
envelope. Henry removed the envelope and sliced open the wax seal with a
pointed thumbnail. From the envelope Henry removed a piece of cotton that
was torn and spotted with blood and crusted from fluids. This was Henry's
secret souvenir—Cullasaja's underwear. He stroked his straining, aching groin
with the whore's underwear, but it wasn't enough for him this time. The excitement of devil lust with the Cherokee was growing weaker. This souvenir
was fading in its bewitchment. He needed a new souvenir.

Henry knew Hannah was at the Kerr house, that a hospital was being organized. He called in the slave boy and had himself dressed in a white shirt
and gray wool suit. Henry ordered his buggy brought around and drove it alone.
The streets of Austin were empty, as Henry knew they would be. Many people
had gone to the river with their weapons to fight the approaching Comanches.
Two dozen women were at the Kerr house with the Ranger's bitch. Drunks
were singing in Dutch John's. Henry avoided the capitol building, where figures
issued in and out of the gate in the stockade fence, carrying orders and bringing
information across the bridge over the moat. He cursed and steered around a
herd of Bullock's pigs, who were blocking his turn off Congress onto Ash.

He drove up and down beside the Caldwell house and saw nothing move
except the chickens and the pigeons. Henry had heard while drinking in the

Quorum Saloon, where more politicians and speculators gathered these days than at Dutch John's, that a fleeing senator's carriage had run over Captain Caldwell's mastiff and the driver had climbed down with a pistol and put the animal out of its misery. So there was no vicious dog to deter Henry from what he sought. Henry saw the Ranger's white stallion and the woman's Kentucky thoroughbred were gone from the corral. He hid his buggy inside the Caldwell barn, and, with his pistol hanging heavy in his coat pocket and his penis wetting his trousers, Henry limped on his ebony sword cane swiftly to the bedoom door. Henry called out, "Hello," but there was no answer. He pushed open the door.

Henry entered the bedroom. He saw an armoire in one corner, next to a bureau and a table with a mirror beside it. The Ranger's clothes hung on hooks along a portion of one wall. Henry limped around the bed. He would have hoped the sheet would be crumpled with the impression of her body, but the bed was neatly made. Henry opened the top drawer of the bureau, expecting to find the souvenir he needed—the bitch's underwear. Women put their underwear in the top drawer because they wanted it to be easy for men to find. But this drawer contained three of the Ranger's shirts, and long johns and three pairs of stockings.

Pausing to listen, Henry then quietly closed the top drawer and opened the middle drawer. No underwear here, just blouses. He pictured the bitch's nipples and rubbed his fingers on the breasts of the blouses until he thought he might explode. But a blouse would not satisfy him.

Henry closed the middle drawer and opened the bottom drawer.

At first he was disapppointed to see gloves, stockings and scarves. But then he touched a pile of her underwear in the back right of the drawer. Henry grabbed out a handful of underwear and smelled the clean virginal bloody scent and caressed the garments against his mouth. He tongued both silk and cotton against his lips. Henry rubbed the underwear against his straining bulge. He didn't want to do it here, though. He wanted to snatch a souvenir and be gone and back to his house, where he could savor his pleasure at leisure. What he must do now is pick the correct garment, the one that felt befitting to his desires.

Henry reached his claw back into the drawer and scratched around to see if there was a special garment he had missed, maybe some secret sexual black frilly thing she had brought from Europe.

His nails detected a thickness beneath the linoleum that lined the bottom of the drawer. This was it! Her sex secret! Henry scratched away the linoleum and removed a blue envelope and what appeared to be crushed rose petals wrapped in wax paper.

Henry opened the envelope and read the message written on a piece of blue paper: *I love you. Wait for me, Romulus.*

He pressed a hand against his mouth to keep from shrieking with joy. The devil bitch had been cuckolding the mighty Ranger! Now Henry was the only one who truly understood that Jew slut that everyone else in town glorified. He knew she was depraved, a devil lover, that she stank of sex and sulphur.

Henry was so thrilled with his discovery and the vindication of his senses that he didn't hear the hoofbeats until it was too late. He yanked the pistol out of his pocket and cocked it. He peeked through the netting that covered the windows. Hannah was dismounting from Blue, her Kentucky horse, in front of the house, swinging down in a rush, her skirt catching on the butt of the rifle in her saddle holster and flashing her white thighs. Henry felt she did this to arouse him, as if he needed more arousal. There was no time for him to close the bottom bureau drawer. He looked through the netting and saw Hannah start toward the parlor door. She had left her rifle in the holster on the saddle. Then she turned and walked toward the bedroom door. She was playing with him, Henry thought, delighted. He shuffled over to be standing behind the door when she opened it.

Though it was October and considered a brisk and pleasant month for the climate, Hannah, of the frozen Hannover winters, had sweated through the dress she wore while moving beds and organizing the hospital. She caught a whiff of herself and told Dora she was going home to change. There had been no patients in the hospital as yet other than three drunks who were injured in a street brawl. No word from Matthew and his men on the prairie at Plum Creek. General Johnston had toured the hospital, limping heavily, and had praised the women and two male doctors for their preparation. Hannah's Cajun household workers had gone to the riverbank with all servants who were not slaves. Soldiers and citizens could be heard digging along Water Street with picks and shovels. As Hannah was leaving the hospital, a soldier was carried in, not from a Comanche wound but from a pickaxe buried in his foot.

Hannah was peeling off her damp blouse as she opened the door and entered her bedroom. She tossed her blouse onto the bed and stepped out of her skirt and walked in her chemise toward the bureau for a clean blouse and skirt. She saw the bottom drawer was open.

"Matthew?" she said, feeling a presence behind her.

Hannah turned and saw the tall, crooked form of Henry Longfellow, the hellish squint in his eyes, the wild and sharp streak of his mouth. She looked into the muzzle of his pistol. He held the gun in his right hand, and his ebony walking stick was beneath his right armpit. In his left hand he clutched a piece of blue paper. In a horrified glance, she saw the crushed roses scattered on the floor, and the blue envelope lying open at his feet.

"Get out of my house!" Hannah said.

"You want me, bitch," Henry said.

"I'll call for help."

"Nobody will hear."

Henry was aroused by looking at the black hair that fell onto her shoulders, the bumps of her nipples under the chemise. She smelled like sweat and musk, like the devil's sex perfume.

"My husband will kill you," Hannah said.

"I ain't afraid of your husband. He ain't going to know anything about you and me. Look here, I got the evidence on you," Henry said.

"Give me that note."

"Oh, you're a dirty whore, ain't you? Such a dirty, dirty, lying bitch. You sexed that Cherokee thug behind your husband's back, and I got the evidence right here. Flower petals. A love letter. You dirty whore, you're going to love me right now and every time I want you from now on."

Henry made a long step toward her, unsure if he needed to keep aiming the pistol or if the devil that looked out of her eyes was teasing him and in a moment she would fall on the bed and spread her legs and beg for him.

"Don't be tricking me, you slut. If you make me mad, I will expose you to the whole republic as the whore who gives herself to savages behind her husband's back. How would the famous Captain Caldwell feel about you if he knew you are a whore who put the horns on his head with a Cherokee brute? How would Caldwell feel about his wife then, huh? Come here, bitch. I want you to open my trousers."

Hannah saw no item that could be used for a weapon as the gawky figure loomed above her, thrusting her precious letter into her face. She kicked the shin of his bad leg, hoping it would topple him, but Henry propped on his ebony cane and howled with desire. He dropped the letter and ripped the front of her chemise down to her waist, baring her breasts. She tried to bash her fist into his swollen crotch, but he deflected her move with his cane, and then he whacked her hard beside her left eye with the barrel of his pistol. Lights flashed behind her eyes, and she wobbled. Henry grabbed her and dragged her toward the bed.

# 75

R omulus inquired at the peach-colored house and was told by a boy slave that Master Longfellow had driven off in a buggy. Next the healer went looking for Hannah. He remembered the location of the lot Caldwell had bought from Gruber.

Romulus approached the Caldwell house with care. He pulled his hat low to shield his face and kept to the emptiest roads and came down on Ash Street from the north. He saw a buggy in the Caldwell barn with the horse still in traces, and he wondered at it. He knew Caldwell was well occupied out on the prairie and might be dead by now. Googleye had told Romulus about the hospital at the Kerr mansion. "That's where they need you at, Doc," Googleye had said. But Romulus was not here to heal these people this time.

He had reckoned that his best chance to be alone with Hannah, without being seen by others in town, would be to wait for her at her house under the giant oak trees near Shoal Creek. She was bound to return home for something, he reasoned. When he saw her Kentucky horse, its reins in the dirt, outside the front of the house near the open bedroom door, his spirit soared. She was here. Romulus dismounted from his mustang and crept toward the door. Then he heard a splat, and he heard Hannah's voice moaning.

Romulus leaped through the door and saw Hannah, blood on her face, wrestling on the bed with Henry Longfellow, who had buried one claw into a breast until his fingernails penetrated her skin.

In a bound Romulus crossed the room and clutched the collar of the startled Henry Longfellow. Romulus cuffed Longfellow on the left ear with force enough to burst an eardrum. Then he spun the tall man around, and with a shock of strength Romulus slammed Longfellow against the wall so hard that the house shook and shingles fell and decorative plates crashed off their shelf in the parlor. Longfellow slid down the wall into a sitting position, his head twisted oddly, his tongue hanging out below his beak, his eyes shut.

Romulus started to kick Longfellow in the throat, a blow that would ensure death, but something stopped him before he raised his foot. He turned toward Hannah.

"Romulus!" she said. She pulled up her torn chemise to cover her breasts. "Thank heaven you're alive. Where have you been?"

"Hannah, let me look at your eye," Romulus said.

He sat beside her on the bed and with the sheet wiped the blood from her left eye, which was lumping and turning blue. The cut at the corner of her eye was not deep, and her blood was coagulating already.

"I see my note. You have been thinking of me."

"I shouldn't have," she said.

"I love you, Hannah," he said.

"Don't do this," she moaned.

"Please listen to me," he said.

"No. I won't."

"You don't know what I want to say," Romulus said.

Engrossed in each other, they were not aware that Matthew Caldwell had appeared in the doorway, moving stealthily in his moccasins. Matthew's eyes took in the scene. Hannah's face was bleeding and she sat on the bed touching Dr. Swift. The awkward form of Henry Longfellow was rubbing his jawbone with long fingers of his left hand and struggling to rise by leaning on an ebony cane with his right.

"I don't want to hear it," Hannah said.

"I'd like to hear it, Doctor Swift," said Matthew.

Romulus and Hannah started up from the bed in surprise.

"That man Longfellow tried to rape me!" Hannah cried. "Romulus saved me."

Caldwell grabbed Longfellow by the neck and lifted him to his feet.

"It's a lie. This thug was beating your wife. I tried to stop him," said Longfellow.

"Everybody outside," Matthew said.

He shoved Longfellow, who stumbled out the door. Matthew stood aside, unsmiling, holding Sweet Lips, as the others passed him.

"Doctor Swift, you promised you would one day confront Henry Longfellow in my presence and seek justice," Matthew said under the great oak tree. "Here he is. He murdered your sister. Choose your justice."

Romulus looked at the hideous creature who stood before him, hobbling on a crooked leg, blood dotting his shirt, snot on his upper lip, his jaw hanging slack, gasping for breath. Romulus saw in his own mind another creature he had faced, and he saw the man-ape's statement—*Love must replace fear or you are all lost, as I am.* Romulus realized he felt none of the rage that had been his nemesis. The familiar bursting, the primal anger overflowing, was as gone as yesterday. Now he understood what power had stopped him from pulling the trigger on Caldwell, and had persuaded him to give away his rosewood rifle. He looked at Longfellow and felt sadness and pity, but not a need for revenge. This was the Third Wisdom.

"It is an outrageous abuse of my rights to put me in the hands of a half-breed who hates me," Longfellow said. "When the President hears about this, you will be thrown in prison."

"Doctor Swift, do what you will," said Matthew.

"I don't want him. Turn him over to the court," Romulus said.

Romulus was surprised how simply the words came out and what a swelling of his spirit, a rush of ease and freedom and peace, he felt as he surrendered his desire to punish.

Longfellow hopped on his good leg, supporting himself with his ebony cane.

"Take me to court, that's right," Longfellow shouted. "Because I got the evidence! I got the proof. The bitch has been sexing this savage behind your back, Captain. The half-breed was trying to shut her up, but I came along and saved her. Now she's lying about me because I got this evidence on them. Their love letter is on the floor. The dried flowers. What more does it take to prove to the whole town that you're a cuckold? You pitiful fools don't understand the first thing about human nature. Am I the only one who sees the truth? The guilty parties here are the Jew slut and this damned Cherokee who broke my leg and hurt me!"

Henry pressed the release button on his ebony sword cane. With a fierce squawk he flung the case off his blade and plunged his sword at Romulus, who dodged and felt the blade rip a ribbon of flesh as it scraped his torso.

The butt of Sweet Lips whacked below the back of Longfellow's right ear with a terrible force that made him bob up and down again, like a ball attached to a rubber band. He staggered and grasped his throat as blood bubbled from his lips. Then Longfellow wheezed, squinted his eyes as if peering into darkness and settled to the ground, coming down in sections. He reached out a long claw and dug into the dirt. He gurgled and lay still.

Romulus knelt beside Longfellow.

"You broke his neck," Romulus said.

"I expect so."

Romulus stood up.

"Now it is you and me, Doctor Swift. Our turn to settle accounts," Matthew said.

Hannah stepped between them.

"Matthew, please. Longfellow was lying," she said.

Romulus stared into Caldwell's eyes, seeing death. But Romulus felt composure and harmony, not fear.

"I came to say I love Hannah, but she is your wife, so I am going away," Romulus said.

"How far?" said Matthew.

"North Carolina. New York. Then back to find my people, the Cherokees. I am going among them as a healer and a teacher. This is my calling."

"Your sister's grave is in the cemetery on East Avenue. We'll keep it well," Matthew said.

"Good-bye, Hannah," said Romulus.

"Good-bye."

Romulus mounted his mustang.

"Don't worry, Matthew," he said. "I'm through with Texas."

Hannah watched Romulus ride up Ash Hill. He didn't look back. She turned away and felt Matthew's thick fingers on her face. He was examining the cut on her eye.

"I want you to read the note Longfellow was talking about," she said.

"No."

"I want you to be sure."

"The letter is between you and Doctor Swift. You are my wife. He is gone. The memory is for you."

"Thank you, Matthew."

"You go to the hospital and get your eye treated. There should be some wounded coming in from Plum Creek. I better go back down there."

Hannah came out of the house wearing a skirt and blouse and holding a towel to her swollen, discolored eye. She let her husband lift her left foot into the stirrup of her Kentucky horse and then lift the rest of her body into the saddle. It seemed to her that it took him no effort, he was so strong. He gazed up at his wife with his gray eyes, wind-burned and deep. She leaned down close and kissed his nose with the thin white line on it. She gigged her Kentucky horse and rode up the Ash Street hill toward the Kerr mansion, where early wounded were arriving with news of the great victory at Plum Creek. With their leaders dead and their magic devastated, the Comanches had turned west to break off the fight and save what they could of their plunder. The more recently wounded Texans arriving at the hospital were reporting it had become a running fight against the Comanches, and the Texan rifles were picking off the fleeing warriors like hunters shooting deer.

Romulus found his sister's grave at the eastern edge of the little cemetery, near a lone madrone tree. The grass around the grave was neatly clipped. A raccoon sat on the grave, eating the big red berries, almost the size of apples, that fell from the madrone in October. The raccoon ambled away as Romulus approached. He looked at the two-foot-high granite headstone that had a marble angel with wings unfolded. Below the angel was carved:

CULLASAJA SWIFT

OUR BELOVED NURSE

DIED 1839

Using his Cherokee knife from Bowl's Town, Romulus cut into the pinkish cream sapwood of the madrone until he reached the deep red heart. He dug out a small piece of the heart, not enough to harm the tree. Romulus pressed the heart to his lips and then sliced it into two pieces. One he placed in the earth at the head of the grave. The other he put into his breast pocket.

He knelt beside the grave and bowed his head. His mind was flooded with memories of Cullasaja, the music of her voice, the sweet smell of her skin. His grief would have been unbearable except for his belief that her death had set him on the true path at last, and he would meet her again along the way.

# 76

At lunch in the restaurant in Bullock's Inn, Matthew and Hannah Caldwell said good-bye to Dora and Lawrence Kerr, who were returning to New York City, where Lawrence would raise more capital for his scheme to ship beef from Texas to the cities of the East. President Lamar was to join the Kerrs in New York and be feted by Lawrence in the right clubs and restaurants and boardrooms. Dora planned to hire a lyricist and a scenario writer to help her put together a musical melodrama to be called *Texas*. Lawrence was lean and hard and tanned and was growing muttonchop sideburns and long hair. Lawrence had always been skilled in conversation and dancing and riding, but now he was able to do a squint which implied danger, like the squint of Saginaw Boswell, and there was a new authority in Lawrence's bearing. In a few weeks Lawrence would be telling the fellows in the bar at the Metropolitan Club how he and his Rangers had chased the Comanches fifteen miles during the victory at Plum Creek. Dora said Lawrence was having a taxidermist stuff and mount a Comanche for the trophy room at the Metropolitan Club, which until now was making do with mere grizzly and polar bears and the head of an elephant. Lawrence joined the laughter and expected he would be hearing this joke frequently. The Kerrs would be the most sought-after dinner guests in New York City. They promised to return to Austin in six months and take up residence in their mansion, and Lawrence hoped to go with surveying crews climbing the white cliffs into Comancheria to plat the boundaries of the Kerr Land & Cattle Company.

After lunch, Matthew and Hannah walked hand in hand down the Ash Street hill to their home on West Avenue. Matthew carried his rosewood chair around to the west porch and settled in the seat until he felt the power from the creation of it. He unrolled his house plans and spread the sheets on a table. He heard Hannah being greeted by Evangeline, and then his wife ran around to the porch, her cheeks flushed, waving an envelope and three sheets of paper.

"A letter from my family, Matthew!" she cried. She climbed onto the porch and hugged her husband in happiness. "They are safe. My father was in prison, but he was released, and my oldest brother has gone into exile in France, but Mother is still holding the family together in Hannover!"

"Write and tell them to come to Texas," Matthew said, placing rocks on the four corners of his house plans to keep the papers from blowing.

"Do you mean it?"

"Our children will need grandparents and schooling," said Matthew. "Your momma and daddy will find plenty to do here. He could start a school."

"And my brothers?"

"Bring them all."

Hannah clasped her arms halfway around her husband, which was almost as far as they would go, and buried herself in the wool of his beard until she located his lips and kissed him.

She hurried into the parlor to find her pen and inkwell and writing paper. Matthew smiled and shifted around in his rosewood chair until the comfort was perfect, and he lit a cigar and looked across his house plans and across Shoal Creek and across the river to the white cliffs in the distance where the Caldwell dominion lay waiting for him and his growing family.

Three miles away across the river, among the rocks and brush on top of the white cliffs, hidden and too far to be seen by Caldwell, though they could see his house and his barn, squatted four Comanches who were observing the creeping advance of the invaders. The four were young warriors who had ridden on the raid to Linnville and had escaped the bad turn of fortune when the magic failed at Plum Creek. They had retreated safely into Comancheria with enough stolen horses and booty and prisoners to have made the raid an overall success. Women were mourning their dead husbands and sons in the camps of the families, but the word was passing from family to family all the way out to the snowy mountains that the great war against the men with hats had finally begun.